I0818192

GLASS CHAINS

VAST COLLECTIVE BOOK V

Nicole Hayes

Iona Print

Library of Congress Control Number: 2021911424

ISBN 978-1-7356713-3-8 (Hardcover Edition)
ISBN 979-8-9894105-8-3 (Softcover Edition)
ISBN 978-1-7356713-5-2 (Ebook Edition)

Printed in the USA

Iona Print

nicolehayesauthor@gmail.com

nicolehayeswriter.com

THE VAST COLLECTIVE SERIES

Last of Daylight
By the Pale Moonlight
Asylum in Firelight
Nox's Verse
Glass Chains
Pyrite Prison
Restraining Silver
Korac's Verse
Thirst
Levee
Flood
Featured Verse
Cascading Light

Here's to those of us who have a hard time saying, "No."

TRIGGER WARNINGS

Please consider my entire series 'Rated R.' These books are meant for readers sixteen years and older. Read with the following triggers in mind:

- Graphic Violence
- Graphic Language
- Graphic Sex Scenes
- Psychological Warfare
- Bondage/Domination Sadomasochism
- Mentions of Sexual Assault
- Vague Memories of Childhood Abuse
- Torture
- Gaslighting

CONTENTS

ACKNOWLEDGMENTS

Wow. Book five in the Vast Collective. Big kudos to so many people but I will always start with my husband.

Batman, thanks again for tolerating my crazed midnight bursts of inspiration and my immediate breaking away from the snuggling to type something out. Supportive, patient, and encouraging. You make me better, and I thank you for it. For all ten years of it.

Firefly, our conversations continue to improve not only my books, but myself as a person. I've grown more sensitive and inclusive since meeting you. With that in mind, it will burn you to no end that your resistance to certain storylines drives my insistence on perfecting them. That's right. You make those stories happen. Muahaha. It's only fair since you kept a certain white-haired character from dying in the first book. Looking forward to the next eight books with you.

Jasmine, Write-In Sundays motivated my writing every week throughout the pandemic. I enjoyed our exchange of ideas and critique of each other's work. Your perspectives informed tweaks and changes to my recent work and provided marketing insight into my published material. I can't wait to read your finished work.

And to my fan club, I love the letters. They are an unexpected but welcome surprise. This one's for you.

ZERO

A PROLOGUE TO CONFINEMENT

{Enki | August 2006}

"THREE BILLION COUNTS OF MURDER SUMMARY TO GENOCIDE?"

Pehton's orange feathers rustled when she shook her head. "Recommended sentence reduced to fifty years on Gait as requested by King Rayne of Earth and Cinder. Thirteen counts of tectonic manipulation? Reduced to ten years—Wow. You murdered your way across their planet and they're reducing your sentences to something minuscule for your lifespan. You must be good in bed."

The attractive white-haired man on his knees beside her shrugged casually. Korac, former General of the Icarean race, possessed the ability to aggravate her with only the pleasant cadence of his voice often heard from smirking lips. "King Rayne hasn't had the pleasure, but you can interrogate General Sagan Sterling for her extensive evaluation."

Pehton glanced at the device implanted in her pitch-black palm. Two more convictions completely expunged. "Looks like I don't need to ask her. Come on, Pretty Boy."

He chuffed and spoke in a voice dripping with disdain, "Pretty Boy? Clever. I'm curious to see what nickname you'll coin next." Those nacre glass cuffs—unbreakable—didn't dampen his mood one bit. Even as he waited in the long line to face Enki's Grand Tribunal.

She blinked red eyes at him. "You're very optimistic for an Icarus about to spend several million years in the second-most secure cell on Gait."

The Icarus rose to his full height, towering over her. His pale eyes twinkled with delight. "All you need is the love of a good woman or the favor of a King to keep your spirits high. Fortunately, I have both."

The sheer audacity of this man. The ocean surrounding them couldn't match the vastness of his ego. Pehton scoffed, "You really think you'll break out and race across the galaxy into her bed?"

Korac's rough-chopped, chin-length hair swayed with the shaking of his head. "No. I'm serving my sentence. On my honor, alone."

"Hah! You'll be in a cell."

After stepping another pace in line, he went back to his knees on the shiny stone. As was proper. It should look ridiculous in a kilt, but alas...

A chuckle returned Pehton's attention back to his watchful gaze. She blushed at that arrogant, infuriating, cocky smirk. Caught ogling her ward, Pehton almost groaned.

Obviously accustomed to the admiration, Korac didn't comment on it. Instead, he proclaimed, "A cell which could not hold me unless I wanted it to."

She threw her head back and laughed. Of all the egotistical, bombastic, ludicrous boasts her prisoners claimed over the years, this was a first.

In a flurry so fast Pehton barely tracked his movements, Korac jumped his cuffed hands to the front of him and used them to knock his Monarch 3 drone escort unconscious. Before Pehton reacted, he swept her legs out from under her.

His face appeared above hers with no sign of exertion. "When you find me outside of my cell, don't add more charges. Remember this conversation. No. Additional. Charges."

And so Pehton took a recess. Leaving Korac in Eminent Lance's custody, she stepped through the conduit connecting Enki to Gait. The din enveloped her like a comforting embrace. Advertisements for food, sex, and pain blared from the billboards projected in the surrounding air. Her boots splashed in puddles of neon green pollution and waste. The aroma of synthetic food reached her from the street vendors lining Mercy's Row. Beneath that, the familiar scent of sweat and desperation clawed at her nose.

Pehton smiled. Gait was her home. The derelict space-scrapers. The purple Overseers with their silent engines patrolling from above. The bustle of the Prisonborne as they struggled to make a living on a planet of inmates with overdue expiration dates. Three million—no—four million years ago now, she was born here. And this was where she expected to die.

She headed down the misty Row, willing her azure Lyriki armor to recede. A revealing halter top and short-shorts should satisfy. It left plenty of Pehton's toned pitch-black curves exposed for her current errand. The orange feathers from her wrist to her elbows flared momentarily in anger as she considered the task.

It never got easier.

Pehton paused outside the door and lowered her red eyes. Remember what matters. *What counts.*

A loud utility vehicle passed overhead, interrupting her mantra. She sighed before collecting herself. Biting her black lips to ensure they swelled into an enticing pout, she opened the door to Razor's Emporium of Exotic Experiences.

"Welcome home, Peh Peh," Razor called from somewhere within the twilight warehouse. Renovated, of course. Antiqued mirrors lined the walls and reflected the whiskey lighting from the tarnished chandelier.

Like rows of teeth, the Divine Booths stood as eerie sentinels. Their charcoal alcoves hungrily awaited clients to siphon off their pleasure and pain. Consume their minds. Consume their souls.

Pehton, Executive Warden of Gait, closed her eyes to fight the shudder threatening to expose her weakness.

A tawny finger placed under her chin brought her around to face her jailer. Deep brown eyes, filled with pity, gazed down at her from a significant height advantage. "I can ease your troubles."

Infinite promises swirled in Razor's stare.

They were all bullshit. "I brought something for your Emporium."

He measured her response a little longer than she liked before breaking into a delighted grin. Releasing her, he held out his palm. "You bring me the best wares."

Pehton retrieved the capsule from her armor. She paused before handing it over. Did she want to do this? It felt dirty this time. Rayne's ferocious expression came back to her. Deep within that girl's electric-blue eyes was the strain of trauma Pehton recognized from the mirror.

Razor's warm voice derailed her train of thought. "I've upgraded the booth for perspective realignment. You can see from outside yourself now."

Pehton dropped the capsule in his hand.

He peered at it between his fingers. "Is this who I hope it is?"

"King Rayne of Earth and Cinder."

The illumination from his smile almost blinded her. "Most perfect. I can't wait." He turned away. "Tell me about our latest resident, first."

Pehton scoffed, "Can you believe it'll take two years to process this guy? Two years! That's how extensive his crimes and sentences are! He's done things to people I can't even pronounce. But I'll never forget the look on those girls' faces when we cut his hair. Total. Devastation. Tameka—the redhead, of course—is the only one with any sense."

As Razor climbed the wrought-iron, spiral staircase to the mezzanine, he offered, "Korac is quite famous for his mystery and charm."

Pehton's heart skipped a beat as the dark-haired man moved through the glass stacks of wares toward the vault. *What counts . . .*

Continuing the friendly venting, she added, "That's been understated. He's gorgeous to look at and his voice... It's the most grating, sexy, deceitful—"

"You're making me jealous, Peh Peh." Razor appeared at the banister with an alluring smirk and her vice in his hand.

Pehton swallowed and licked her parched lips like an addict. "No one is as charismatic and seductive as you, Razor."

"You owe me seventeen thousand."

Her wrist gliders flared as she snapped, "I just handed you the entire honey pot."

He nodded, solemnly. "I'm most impressed. And if you'd managed to acquire Nox's death as agreed, you'd be clear. Revisiting your own memories is very delicate work. Precision costs more."

What counts. "What. Do you. Want." Defeat.

Razor hopped the second story banister, landing hard enough to disrupt the parquet flooring. He applied his best solicitous smile as he crossed the room with a casual air of a man accustomed to getting his way. "Well, me and the others want to know who's locked in the big cell. Out of harmless curiosity, of course." He waved her sin in her face.

It passed Pehton's eyes twice before she tried to snatch it. He let her capture one end and held the other in an iron grip.

She licked her black lips, confessing, "I don't know."

Razor jerked her close using her own depravity and gazed into her eyes. The infinite promises swirling in those brown depths hardened into infinite punishments.

"I swear I don't. I haven't even seen the block since they told me of the new arrival." Pehton tugged on the device as he curved an arm around the small of her back.

Closer was bad.

Her voice strained with panic, "They only told me the new inmate was the most dangerous warrior in the galaxy."

With the ghost of a kiss on her lips, Razor released Pehton's corruption. "Go on." He gazed at the capsule she delivered once again. "I'll acquaint myself with our King Progeny."

In three quick strides, Pehton crossed the warehouse and locked herself in a booth. Inserting her vice, she ignored the port point. Although she relied on this recall technology, only junkies resorted to nacre porting. Poor souls. She caught her reflection in the frosted glass as the immersive simulation loaded. Chest heaved, hands shook, pupils dilated. Poor her.

"Activate."

Maybe an hour later, Pehton exited, drained and lost. Would it ever get easier? No. It shouldn't. This mattered.

Razor whistled behind her. She turned and hid her initial dread. His brown skin pulsed a rhythmic glow under the chandelier. His lips swollen from biting as he finished. Pupils swallowed the irises of his eyes. He got off and high on Rayne's pain.

The wicked Curator beamed at her. "Truly exquisite. The fear. The vulnerability. A treasure trove of bones broken and boundaries crossed. I'd dare say it's better than Korac whipping Celindria."

Pehton shook her head to hide her disgust, but he provided a great excuse to change the subject. "I can't believe they made her a fucking Eminent. I've dedicated beyond millennia to doing good in this place, and they reward that bitch with my prize." Rubbing the back of her neck, she growled, "She looked so smug taking the First Wave Progeny back to Enki where she can do Elden knows what to them—"

Razor watched her with a predatory intensity that let her know she spilled more than she intended.

With as much warmth and sincerity as she could muster, Pehton acknowledged, "Thank you, Razor. I know without you, this wouldn't be possible."

His gaze lingered on her. His eyes bounced from the pulse in her neck to the fists she'd yet to unclench. The silence stretched into the uncomfortable reminder that she remained, as always, at his mercy. All of Razor's teeth gleamed when he smiled. "Anytime, Peh Peh. After sampling the girl's suffering, I want to knock a few thousand credits off your debt."

Pehton's eyes widened. "Thank—"

He pressed a slender finger to her lips. "Admittedly, I owe you thanks for the exclusive rights without asking for a partnership. I'll build an empire on her exceptional agony. I can afford to cut you some slack."

Pehton shivered.

Razor tilted his head, inquiring.

"There was something odd about the way she carried it. That girl isn't unpacking like a normal person. I can almost see the leashed devastation beneath that placid surface, and there's only a breath holding it back."

His brown eyes sparkled as he smirked. "As long as she doesn't hold back, I should keep in good business."

Pehton's voice was grave as she warned, "Let's pray she holds it. Nox ruled like a hurricane, but Rayne holds the death of everything in her eyes."

ONE

ESCAPE ISN'T YOUR ONLY OPTION

{ENKI | TWO YEARS LATER}

SAGAN LEARNED TO SEAMSWALK OUTSIDE EXTERIOR DOORS AND KNOCK. People often freaked if she popped in unannounced. And there was that one time when she walked in on Lynn and Pablo experimenting with—

Tameka answered while muttering, "John, how do you keep locking yourself out? The door responds to your face—" She gaped once she finally looked up from the kid with hair as red as her own attached to her leg. "Sagan… Where the hell have you been?!"

Sagan winced and brushed a strand of barely long enough blond hair behind her ear. The two axes holstered on her hips shifted with her movements. Her best friend—sister, really—had the most beautiful green eyes that hardened to glass when riled. Properly scolded, Sagan mustered an explanation for her absence, "Sorry for the long wait. It's hard to keep time when Seamswalking. I know three months—"

"Try six."

Shit. "I'm sorry."

"Mommy? Who's dat?" Pax searched Sagan with eyes identical to Xelan's. Black with a midnight blue ring on the outside.

A twinge of grief twisted her heart and took her breath away.

Tameka caught it and offered her a sympathetic look before answering, "This is your auntie who forgets to visit from her travels."

He took his fingers out of his mouth and peered up at Sagan. "Will you eat dinner, Auntie?"

Melted on the spot, Sagan glanced at Tameka for permission.

The redheaded mommy clicked her tongue. "No matter how long you're gone, you're always welcome home." She breezed away in her wrapped skirt and crop top, leaving the door open.

Pax held on for the ride with his topaz complexion blending with hers. He called out, "When you twavel again, can I go with you?"

Sagan pulled the hood back on her mauve duster and unzipped the corset-tight bodice. She liked the way the long material flared around her. Honestly, she commissioned it from the Lyriks because the color matched her eyes and she thought a certain former Icarean General might find it sexy.

The longer she waited to answer the little boy, the glassier Pax's eyes became. "Cross my heart and hope to die. I'll take you to see new worlds when you're old enough."

Tameka scoffed as she crossed a bridge over the pool of water in the middle of her house to the kitchen.

Pax peered up at his mother.

She beamed down at her son. "You'll never be old enough to go without me."

Cutest. Pout. Ever. The kid abandoned his crutch and played with fish in the water.

Sagan leaned on the counter and watched her bestie navigate the cabinets and heating units. Tameka glowed. Her red three-c curls foamed in all their glory to her waist. The white beachy clothes complimented the ocean bungalow surroundings and contrasted beautifully against her brown skin. Dark freckles popped high on her cheeks.

"These six months were good to you and Pax."

Tameka shrugged and fiddled with a chain around her neck. "For the first time in my life, I don't want for anything. Nacres are a marvel. Sometimes I wonder about our lives before and after the invasion. I can't always make sense of it." She nodded at Pax. "But I'll tell you one thing. I love that little boy to death."

Enki's equivalent of a catfish clomped onto his arm, prompting him to cry out. Tameka laughed and rushed to him with a mother's practiced patience.

Sagan admired them. "So precious and so cute."

"Takes after his mother," a gravelly voice called from a plank above her. The Icarus dropped to the first floor and snatched the nearest green apple with a satisfying crunch.

"Caedes, it's good to see you." Sagan smiled with genuine warmth.

Dressed in all black—as if he wore anything else—one of their best soldiers ducked his gaze at her fondness. Changing the subject, he muttered, "That's the second time this week he let a fish get the better of him."

He wasn't looking at Pax. He was looking at Tameka. Sagan leaned in, dying to know. "So have you two . . . you know?"

Caedes startled and dropped his apple, choking.

Tameka called out without looking back at them, "Everything okay?"

Sagan snickered. "Fine! How's the fish?"

"I think Pax caught dinner."

A little red in the face, Caedes looked Sagan over before answering, "No. But I can wait. And if she never . . . Well, that's fine too. She's worth it."

"Damn straight she is." Sagan turned back and glimpsed the loss and longing in her friend's gaze as Tameka kissed her son on the head. Sadly, she added for Caedes, "But you may be waiting for a while." The axes dug in when she shifted as a reminder of her own longing.

After dinner, Tameka set Pax to work on a Tritan puzzle box. She laid out on a chaise with the ocean serving as her backdrop. "So all this traveling... you know it's not healthy, right?"

The blond Progeny tried to shrug the focus off of her. "I know. I just had to keep busy."

Caedes fiddled with a comms device beside Sagan on the couch. His shaved head shone in the light of the star powering the Dyson's Sphere. Obviously a deep-thinker, he stuck out his tongue to help him concentrate.

Tameka nodded as her hands idly traced the seam of the furniture. "Trying to keep your mind off of him in prison?"

Damn. Right for the throat. Trademark Tameka.

Sagan fell back against the couch and stared up at the sky with a groan. "Prison isn't the problem. It's Enki. They've been processing him for the last two years." She sat forward and folded her hands together. "But it's finally his arrival day. I'll go show my support. You wanna come?"

The redhead recoiled. "And take my child to see the man who did nothing to stop his father's murder? No thanks."

Sagan winced. "Oh, c'mon, Tameka. It wasn't like that and you know it. You read Nox's Verse."

"Don't mention that name in front of me again." Tameka folded her arms and looked away.

Caedes spoke up from his task, "I can watch Pax. You can go support Sagan. It doesn't need to be about Korac."

Sagan jumped up and kissed his cheek. "I always said you were a prince."

The Icarus chuffed with his pretend-grumpy self.

Tameka's voice came out soft, "I'm not ready yet. But I wish you safe travels."

Sagan nodded her understanding. "I want to be there for him."

Tameka and Caedes shared a look. "I don't think they allow visitors on Gait."

"They don't have a policy on Seamswalking."

{GAIT}

Korac ruminated his gratitude for the advanced healing. The glass chains chafed his wrists the entire two years he wore them without reprieve. His knees ached raw on the stone and bled on several accounts.

But he didn't care.

"...And so we sentence you to one million years on Gait. Two hundred alone for your atrocities on Earth..."

Two hundred years until he was free to hold Sagan. That's all he cared about.

Eminent Lance bowed. Eminent Abresson sneered. And Eminent Celindria's absence was "excused due to her indisposition of her laboratory." Where she no doubt tortured her fellow First Wave Progeny, exploiting their abilities.

Was his life ever simple? Reasonable?

Images of violet eyes flashed. Blond lashes fluttered closed. His pale gray hands on her tanned, freckled—

Who wanted sense? He only wanted her. Two hundred years from now.

"Let's go, Pretty Boy. Your cell awaits."

When Korac stood, Pehton barely came to his elbow. But he knew better. Even though he bested her on the first day, the Icarus still considered the Lyriki warden a threat. With a deadly beautiful voice, the siren race could shatter the nacres in their victims' chests. Not that he needed to worry about that. Instead, their song left him with a debilitating migraine.

The tiny badass beside him mused as they transported him to the conduit, "Excited to change out of that kilt?"

Korac smirked down at her. "You gonna miss it?"

She cursed and looked away.

They traversed the rest of the way to Gait in silence.

Home.

When they crossed through the conduit, Korac needed time to adjust to the noise, lights, and activity that assaulted them upon entry. Two and a half million years...He never knew his actual age when Umbra rescued him from this hellhole.

It…matured. The pain industry transformed the formerly barren wasteland into a compacted colon of wicked abandon. With flying transportation and soaring structures. And blinding lights.

The prison lived in the center as a vigilant ziggurat, awaiting his return. Pehton wasted no time rushing him and his parading Monarch 3 drone escort inside.

Once they reached their third Tritan-tech lift some hundreds of stories underground, she turned to the drones. "Monarch 3's escort stops here. Only wardens can access this floor."

The Mon3 soldiers narrowed their gazes, but ultimately acquiesced.

The last lift dropped the General and the Executive Warden a significant distance below ground. When it finally eased to a stop, she smiled up at him. "Welcome home."

Korac shot her a bitter grin. The woman was clueless how close she came to the truth.

They stepped forward with the sound of his boots echoing down the sterile-smelling hall. Black metal. Abyssal. They passed twelve empty cells before reaching the largest on this corridor.

Pehton sang into the lock, and the nacre barrier fell, permitting his entry. "This is Infernus block. Reserved for the worst war criminals in the Vast Collective. You'll never leave this cell. We will serve your meals here, including synthetic Vittle supplements. If you press your hand to that panel, the floor treads for your exercise. You can request books from the approved reading list. No visitors under any circumstances. Questions?"

Korac turned and stretched his cuffed hands behind his back to Pehton.

She unlocked them with a heavy sigh. "You won't even beg for your freedom? I'm honestly impressed. I've never met an Infernus prisoner who didn't bargain during their incarceration."

He almost purred with the relief of losing his restraints. "They obviously never served under Umbra." One million years in this cell is nothing compared to what he endured in service of Nox's father.

"Clothes are on the cot."

Korac suppressed a chuckle. A mauve jumpsuit. The color of Sagan's eyes. The bottom would hit his knees. The sleeves couldn't make it beyond his elbows. And that's if he could fit it over his chest. Who had shoulders this narrow?

Holding it up to display the measurements, he cocked a skeptical brow at Pehton.

Her giggle was a pleasant sound. Unprofessional in every way, but he suspected Pehton wasn't Executive Warden because of her professionalism.

"I might submit a special request for a tailor."

So she *was* trainable. Splendid. "Much obliged, Executive Warden."

"We take care of our prisoners here."

He remembered full well.

After Pehton sang the barrier closed, she confessed, "I can't believe you're so cavalier, Korac. I admit your sentence is startlingly short for your crimes, but you won't see daylight for one million years."

"For two and a half million years, the only light I saw was a star exploding over our heads. Besides," he shrugged casually, "you'll find me out of this cell soon enough."

Pehton shook her head and walked to the lift. She called over her shoulder, "I'll get that tailor in tomorrow."

The lift whispered as it returned his warden to the surface. All alone. Korac rotated his wrists and stretched. Room enough to stretch his wings, too.

In one corner of his cell, water sprayed from the ceiling when he stood on a designated tile. He showered away the crusted blood, dust, and battle ink. He wrapped a sheet around his waist to protect the Executive Warden's modesty. He certainly didn't have any.

After that, he searched anywhere for something that might pass for a mirror. Korac wanted to check the hack job on his hair. He kept recalling Sagan's tears when it fell to the floor after Rayne's Tribunal. The heartache—

Sagan stepped into his cell from thin air.

He blinked.

She wasn't a dream this time. Axes gleamed at her hips. Her blond hair cropped close to her ears with spiky layers. Heavy makeup around her violet eyes. The sexy coat only accentuated her gorgeous curves—

"Elden, you're a sight for this Icarus' sore eyes."

Without breaking her stride, Sagan demanded, "Put your hands on me."

Korac met her half-way and wrapped his arms around her. Her lips trembled under his with yearning. Two years was a long time to someone raised with the expectation of a human lifespan. As the scent of watermelon filled the cell, he growled. Two years was too long. Lifespan be damned.

With rough pulls, he jerked the coat off of her. When Korac's hands found his favorite General warm and bare beneath, he broke their kiss to consume her with his gaze.

"Always like this?"

Sagan blushed under her freckles. "In case . . ." Suddenly shy, she licked her swollen lips.

Korac purred in his chest and dropped the sheet. He couldn't get enough of her skin. She confessed she couldn't get enough of his hands. He found himself. In her. In love with her.

They christened his cell. Every. Surface. For hours.

"We can't go that long again." Sagan curled into him on the cot and tended a chain around her neck. They both gazed at the bruises and bite marks fading with her nacre healing. The burn from her lighter would take deliciously longer.

Korac pecked his lips on her freckled shoulder. "It's charming how two years is long to you when I wasn't expecting to see you for two hundred years."

She turned in his arms, searching his eyes. "I wouldn't let that happen. Nothing could keep me from you."

He kissed a fingertip. "Your timing is impeccable. How did you know where to find me?"

"With the war, I never had time to tell you. I can feel you when you think of me across the Seam."

That got a chuckle out of him. "Your radar must work sporadically, or you—"

"I Seamswalked into Enki over three dozen times to find you on your knees waiting for the Tribunal. Anytime you thought of me, I came for you."

Korac did nothing to prevent his grin at her choice of words.

She blushed and swatted him. "So, try controlling it a little until you want to see me."

"I always want you to come for me."

Sagan ignored him and brushed a finger through his hair. "It's taking so long to grow back."

Korac kissed her neck. "They keep cutting it."

"Then I'll kill them all."

He growled possessively against her throat. Her protectiveness aroused him. Korac could count on one hand the number of people willing to champion on his behalf.

He clutched her tiny wrist. She was certainly the smallest. When he gazed into her eyes with the promise of pain, Sagan returned with trust and love. Certainly the strongest.

Unfortunately, Korac expected Pehton to return any minute and ruin his time with the General. "Sagan—"

"I can walk you out of here. Come with me. Please." Tears spilled down her cheeks.

Damn. Korac released her and gently kissed her adorable bangs. "I promised Rayne. I serve my sentence for Earth, and she grants me asylum on Earth and Cinder."

"I know." She lowered her head with a sniffle. Something about the thick lashes around her eyes. Or the flush of her button nose. Or the wobble of her delicate chin. Sagan always looked beautiful in her tears. She disarmed Korac. Utterly.

He averted his eyes. "I won't ask you to wait for me—"

"I will. All two hundred years."

Mercy for his mind. "Thank Elden because I can only stand the thought of sharing you with Rayne. No one else." Korac grinned. "Actually, I quite enjoy the thought of you with her—"

She punched him. He caught her fist before it landed. They both stared at the connection, panting with the acceleration of their pulse.

Korac pinned her hand to the cot. He matched the other. "Safety word?"

Sagan swallowed hard, tantalizing him with her throat. "Butterfly. All of it to you."

He closed his eyes, basking in her faith. When she giggled unexpectedly, his eyes snapped open with a cocked eyebrow.

"Where are the guards?" Sagan squirmed playfully in his grip. "Are they too scared of the notorious Icarean—"

"In a twenty-eight hour day, they patrol on seven-hour rotations." The male voice that answered sounded as deep as a chasm and spoke in a lascivious tone.

Sagan cried out as Korac blocked the view of her from the barrier. "What the fuck?!"

The voice continued, "One hour and ten minutes from now, they'll make their way down here. Be sure to smile for the cameras. In the meantime, please continue as if I'm not two cells down."

Korac turned to find Sagan dressing with her face flushed and her pulse beating at her throat. "I'm sorry, Sagan. I assumed I was alone on this hall."

Her eyes darted wildly toward the source of the interruption. "It's fine. I'll get used to an audience with time." She smiled reassuringly at him, spinning the axes before holstering them.

His mouth dropped open. How was he this fortunate? How was she this perfect?

Sagan snickered and bumped his chin to shut his mouth. "We'll work a schedule out. Now, that you're not in Enki,

I can bring you clothes. Do you mind if you're my anchor again? I only need to recharge every three months. But regular contact with you would steady me."

Korac kissed the pulse point on her wrist. "Take from me what you need. I won't complain."

"Neither will I." Their voyeur was relentless.

Sagan shuddered, and Korac planned to restructure his blockmate's face. Then a notion occurred to him. "How are you able to withstand so long without contact?"

She beamed, and he committed every centimeter of her face to memory. In a futile attempt at privacy, she whispered, "I got help from Legir on Yu." At Korac's wince, her face warmed with compassion. "I know. Some of the story, anyway. I understand why it's a difficult subject for you."

He frowned. "How?" They never found the time to exchange histories.

Sagan glanced beyond him to the barrier. "I can't say. But..." She retrieved a bound book from her knapsack. The same book Korac delivered to Xelan's stronghold two years ago. "It's not fair that I know these things without you sharing them. But it's been invaluable to me. Understanding Rayne. Investigating leads. You."

The Icarus accepted the book and peered back at her.

"Korac, do you know where I can find Razor—"

He cursed and turned away. Not that. Never that.

"—Or any intel I can use to engage him?"

His voice cracked as he explained, "You don't know what you're asking me."

"Tell me."

He did. Mostly. Once finished, he cupped her soft cheek. "I consider you an equal, so I won't ask you to stay away from him. Instead, I'll ask you to be cautious. Xelan never spoke of him for a reason. He's dangerous. And you're the perfect mark for his predation."

She frowned prettily. "Because I like pain?"

"No. That's not the only reason." Brushing a strand of hair behind her ear, he shook his head. "In your eyes, I can see a heart open to anything. Not to mention that curiosity attached to your intellect. I'd feel better if someone were watching your back."

Sagan smiled. "We both know I'm a badass and can take care of myself." Her soft fingers brushed his cheek. "I promise to be careful and check in with you often. So, how do I find this ultra predator?"

"When you're ready, he'll come to you."

His favorite General left a few minutes later after their sweet goodbyes. Korac rubbed the back of his head where his heart ached. She's strong. Worry for her later. Deal with the most pressing issue now.

He approached the barrier and called out, "Hey, thanks, wingman. Your intrusion on my good time was most appreciated. From hereon, you keep your mouth shut if you want to keep your tongue."

The blockmate chuckled loudly. "Does she taste as sweet as she smells?"

Korac thundered, "Don't get any ideas about her. Not only will you have to contend with me, but she can summon hell to do her bidding. Trust me. You don't want that. Mouth. Shut. And be grateful to experience her existence, even cursory."

He heard the mock-salute. "Understood, General."

Celebrity-status. Great. "You're not qualified to speak to me." Korac turned his bare ass to the hallway and addressed the conspicuous state of his cell. Hurricane Sagan. He smiled.

"I much prefer the cursory admiration of your woman to the company below us."

Korac turned with a frown. "There is no lower floor on Gait." Infernus was the most secure block. For war criminals only. Which certainly didn't recommend his blockmate for conversation. Korac was the most dangerous prisoner in the facility. The Tribunal said so.

The disembodied chuckle came again. "Aren't you knowledgeable? But no one knows everything on Gait."

"Who is it?"

"So deadly, he isn't allowed space. So clever, he isn't permitted interaction. So evil, he isn't granted light. The bottom floor of Gait houses the most dangerous warrior in the galaxy."

No. How could they...? She killed him. What had they done to him for the last two years? More importantly. How could he be saved?

Korac gripped the book in his hands and ground out, "Nox."

{ENKI}

Tameka wandered the glass corridors. They circled and interlaced the oceanside bungalows into a colony. A colossal white stone and glass city surrounded by the biggest moat in the galaxy. With surveillance everywhere.

It was empty.

Only her little family occupied a single apartment. She ran into an unfamiliar Tritan once. He said he needed to perform some maintenance in the colony, but he didn't carry any tools. He also ducked his head through the corridors. Tritans, even the plain ones, stood at least four feet taller than her. So, why did they build a city with ceilings low enough for a human or an Icarus?

Questions abound.

The Eminents swore up and down that they welcomed Tameka anywhere on the planet but the Pantheon. For religious reasons. Yet, every time the Progeny girl wanted to access the archives, they insisted on a chaperon.

Oh, and actually getting there sucked. She walked into a conduit in the center of the empty city. This conduit branched to three. Then twelve. And finally she resorted to throwing herself into portals until she reached her destination. Or somewhere more interesting. Innocently, of course. She mastered the art of unintentional travel.

At least this time, Tameka intended to pop into the lecture hall. A giant bone-white amphitheater surrounded by—once again—a vast ocean. John's voice reached her at the conduit. Today, he lectured the Tritans on Jesuits.

She chuffed. Espionage and corruption. Enki's comfort zone.

"Sovereign Ambassador."

Tameka whirled to find Wiw, the most aged Tritan she'd ever met, standing behind her.

He bowed to her.

"Eminent." She smiled. No bowing. Ever. "It's good running into you."

He inclined his head. "But you didn't—Oh, another idiom." He chuckled gently, warming her through.

Wiw disarmed her the most. The wizened alien stood twice her height with his blue skin paled from age. Ancient black blood vessels dimmed to gray. Wrinkles surrounded his eyes, more almond-shaped than the others. A million smile lines decorated his lip-less mouth. He came across as so genuine, but she deemed the entire Tritan race untrustworthy. Safer that way. For Pax's sake.

Tameka tossed a thumb behind her. "Were you attending the lecture?"

He shook his head. "I'm expected at Celindria's residence."

Jackpot. "Can I join you for the walk?"

He kept his hands locked behind his back as he stepped by with swaying robes. The lines around his eyes tightened. "I'm afraid I can't extend the invitation without her permission. I'd pay you the same courtesy."

Damn. "I understand." Tameka fought to keep the disappointment off her face. "Have a good evening, then."

"You as well, child."

She took careful note of which conduit he took to start. Enki, the eternal labyrinth. Identical oceans, halls, colonies, and terraces. White stone and seamless glass. If she'd never saw the land masses for herself from above, she'd doubt their existence. No one in her household had set foot on a continent, yet.

"Ready to go?"

Tameka smiled as she turned to John. He kept his dark brown hair short, leaving his deep brown eyes clear. The Osage in him tanned his complexion since moving oceanside. It suited him. "Always happy to explore the stacks."

John held out the bend of his arm, and she crooked hers through. They got lost twice. Took one rest for John's bad leg. An hour later they arrived.

He muttered, "Another day. Another route mapped."

"Good. I was starting think this place shifted around."

The "archives" made Tameka laugh. No way this tiny structure contained the entire wealth of Enki's knowledge. No. She suspected the Pantheon was the true accumulation. That explained why Xelan—

Tameka gasped.

John frowned at her, but he didn't ask. They lived together for the last two years. Her household recognized the signs of her grief. It never got easier. Never felt lesser. Any thought of Xelan twisted a knife in her heart that only holding Pax could cure.

"We can go home right now."

She squeezed her eyes shut and swallowed hard. Tameka, the dragon slayer, would not let this paralyze her. "I got this." With her shoulders straight and her chin high, Tameka glided into the archives. John followed.

Both Earthborne visitors ignored the Tritan, who materialized like a shadow behind them. This was standard operating procedure by now.

They spent hours in the glass stacks. John siphoned the Tritan's public history for educating their people on Earth. Tameka scoured for knowledge of the Primaries, Eminents, the Vast Collective races, and any scrap of information on a certain Icarus her heart wouldn't allow her to name.

But today, she researched Gait. The levels of the prison. The history of commerce. Technology. But one thing stuck out to her. Gait, itself, had no history. No account of the prison's establishment. She expected to find a story similar to the British prison colonies. But nothing?

John turned the corner. With his lips set in a grim line, he shook his head. Would they ever learn any specifics about the Primary mentioned in that asshole's Verse?

Defeated, Tameka sighed. "Let's go home, John."

During the silent trip back, she reflected on her findings. She needed to contact Karter and Sagan. The Icarean Valkyrie because she lived through most of the history described in those books. And the Seamswalking Progeny because she intended to investigate leads on Gait. That thought left Tameka cold.

The nacre-resistant barrier dissolved for the pair as they returned to the house, always filled with an ocean breeze. As soon as they entered, the redheaded Progeny knew something was wrong.

"Tameka," Caedes called from the kitchen. Calm, but alert.

She and John exchanged a glance before Pax called out, "Uncle Tu came to visit, mommy."

Through the fire feature in the great room, she watched Tumu, Tritan Officer of the Third, stand to his significant height. He turned the corner, and her heart sank at his somber expression.

"Hello, Peaches."

If Tumu showed up at her door, it meant the Eminents denied her request to return home.

In a voice layered in three pitches, Tameka demanded, "Take me to the Primary."

{Earth}

Blue. Earth's sky was blue. White fluffiness patterned the clean atmosphere. Ozone and sandy grit filled each inhale. And food. Delicious food grilled off to the side by a collection of friendly-seeming humans. Short and fuzzy people.

"Welcome to Earth, E7.3 through E7.5. Please continue to the final Progeny screening station and wait for your number to be called. In the meantime, help yourself to a meal and some water. Even nacre-bearing Icari are prone to dehydration in the deserts of Egypt."

The young Icarean woman woke only four days ago. She couldn't find anyone to tell her how long she'd slept. But the sight of Umbra's Spire in ruins both startled and delighted her. The Night Prince's reign already came and went. How old was she now?

"Care for a kebab?"

She spun to find a short man holding seared meat on a stick. The aroma enticed and disgusted her all at once. Her stomach growled and turned. She slept too long this time. The man's jugular throbbed in his dark neck. Food wasn't enough.

He noticed. The kebab shook, and his voice wavered, "We have volunteers in the tents." One long finger pointed at a row of shelters.

She didn't mean to move faster than he could see. She was just so thirsty. He yelped when she gripped his shirt front. Those beautiful black eyes widened in fear and searched her face. "Please!"

"Feed . . ." The word rasped from her unused throat. Parched. Thirsty—

Powerful hands gripped her wrists. A firm male voice reasoned with her from behind. "Let him go. We'll get you fed after your long nap."

This close to her, the man at her back smelled funny. Like herbs and cologne. The one in front of her smelled of adrenaline. She found both equally enticing. "Feed." Satisfy all her appetites.

"We got another one." The firm voice assured.

The human in her grasp licked his lips and glanced behind her. "Copy that."

"One. Two. Three—"

She lunged at the first man's throat right as the newcomer shoved his forearm in the way. Fangs sinking in, she moaned at the taste of his blood. He pulled her against him and let her feed with a grunt through his clenched teeth. The other human ran back to the tents.

They were alone.

Sweet nectar flooded her stomach, regenerated cognitive cells, and stimulated her stunted metabolism. Leaning back against him, she purred into the bite.

"That's right. Take what you need."

His throat convulsed against the top of her head, and a strange smoke surrounded them. A sweet herbal smell. It left her dizzy. His blood . . . Dizzy.

"Shh . . . Easy. Progeny blood is wild on the lower castes. Just breathe through it."

Progeny? Why did humans speak such nonsensical words? The Icarean female lost her grip. The desert dunes swirled to the top of her vision. The sky dripped into her eyes. The sand ground into her bare knees. Who was she?

"I've got you."

Indeed, strong arms gripped her. Voices called out. One belonged to the first male. "Sir, do you want us to detain her?"

The firm reasonable voice replied, "No. Have her taken . . ."

Their conversation swirled into the spinning scenery. The course of his blood inside her. The sensation of the sand against her skin. The smell of herbal smoke. It all assailed her senses and overstimulated her addled mind.

So long she slept. No memory of before. Who was she? Why was she?

Wait . . . the confusing words stopped. Her distracting hunger abated. Her unnecessary thoughts ceased.

That's who she was.

Silence.

TWO

WAS THIS LIFE EVERYTHING YOU WANTED IT TO BE?

{EARTH}

"NO MEMORY AT ALL?"

Pablo nervously chafed the chain on his neck as Kyle explained a most interesting case to him over the Icarean comms device.

The Progeny screener sighed. "The only memory I gleaned from her is that she didn't wake up. She was awoken. Her memory's choice of words. Not mine."

A chill shot down Pablo's spine, making him shiver.

"Look, man, I know you're busy saving our races, but I'll need you to make this a priority." The telltale pause followed by a long exhale meant Kyle took a hit on his joint.

Pablo absently wondered how he kept in rolling papers, post apocalypse. "I'll find someway to access nacre memory banks." A thought struck him so hard that he frowned. "... Or push through encryptions."

"Thanks, Doc. Over and Out."

Nacres stored memories perfectly. Without all the interference from emotions and unreliable recollection.

Three years into their reconstruction work and this was the first instance of Kyle failing to download a person's history.

King Rayne of Earth and Cinder declared all Icari required examination upon entry into Earth. The Progeny males, nicknamed Story Taker and Conscience, screened the evacuating population of Cinder. Once cleared, they supplied the refugees with provisions before relocating to integrated communities dedicated to establishing a united world. Jobs, responsibilities, and education came with the package and all their needs fulfilled—as proclaimed by Rayne's brother, King Regent of Earth, Jack Callahan.

For an Icarus to pass through the conduit without initial introduction to the system and supply no memories to screen certainly raised some red flags—

"Dr. Suarez. You're needed in Med Lab 2."

Pablo pushed up the sleeves on his lab coat. The medical calls never ceased. He crossed the suspended walkway connecting the cliff-face entrance into the Tritan-made facility, hanging off the mountainside. The seamless glass floor gave him an unobstructed view of the surf crashing miles below.

The sight of the water colliding with the rock reminded Pablo of the reason he hit up the comms device in the first place. Nothing—not even a weird nacre mystery and an inconveniently timed page—could ruin Pablo's good mood. He hopped down a precariously mounted staircase and danced his way into Med Lab 2.

"Oh, not this again." One of the technicians groaned the moment she laid eyes on him.

The second one held up his hands to stave Pablo off. "No. No. This is a professional facility. I won't permit it."

The newest technician stared at Pablo as he crossed the room with a dance slide to the glass panel. "What's going on? Dr. Suarez? Is something wrong?"

Pablo Suarez grinned until all his teeth showed. "Not. At. All."

"He only gets this way when *she* comes to visit. How long do we have to batten down the hatches?" The first technician made the sign of the cross.

Pablo chuckled without answering as he entered the lab.

Before the door closed behind him, the male technician remarked, "We may as well take off for the week. He won't get any work done with Chief Lynn here."

He was so very right. The Chief Medical Officer of the Two Worlds rubbed the gold-laced tattoo on his sternum. No work at all.

"Good morning, Dr. Suarez," the Icarus called from his cell.

Pablo smiled. "Hello, Twenty-One. I apologize for interrupting your sleep rhythm."

The tall alien shrugged in his scrubs. "I'm unbothered. Your presence is always welcome. What's the occasion for the visit?"

In the dim lighting of the detainment pods, Twenty-One affected Pablo as a polite, retired soldier. His carriage always that of a man prepared to fight, but not encouraging one. In the scrubs, he almost came across as unintimidating.

But then Pablo remembered when Kyle told him the man's memories included the lone massacre of a Colombian village during the initial 2006 invasion. How the Icarus laughed at the human children on fire crying for their parents. He belonged in this facility, and now Lynn wanted him transferred to hers.

"Twenty-One, you'll see the night sky soon," Pablo assured.

"Transferring me to weapons, are they?" The man approached the nacre-resistant barrier separating them.

"Well, you volunteered for this over Gait."

The three-hundred and twenty pound mountainous warrior shuddered. "Anything is better than that hell."

Pablo popped his brows and sighed. "Good to hear. I'll get you set up—"

"You didn't intend for it, Dr. Suarez, but your treatment of me here was better than anywhere else in my entire life. I thank you."

Pablo shoved his hands in his lab coat pockets and tilted his head to the side as he considered the Icarus' words. Nox's Verse. It prepared him for moments like this. The decision to allow a man to find reformation under the care of better treatment. To consider this an opportunity for rehabilitation. To forgive.

"You're right, Twenty-One. I didn't intend for it. I treat you like a person ought to be treated, so maybe you'd learn how to treat others." He scanned the Icarus' eyes, a brown darker than his own. "We'll find out during your transfer if I was wrong."

The Icarus put his fist to his nacre, the salute of the Progeny's asylum efforts. "I won't disappoint you, Doc."

Pablo smiled on his way out the door. He offered over his shoulder, "Good. You don't want to upset Lynn."

He let the door close on the Icarus' shiver.

The three lab technicians—two lifers and one newbie—set about their preparations for the next experiment. Trademark design of the Tritans, the entire facility consisted of white stone and glass. But the original crew made it their own. A black, white, and gray color palette with the occasional pop of blue and red.

For Xelan.

Gray tile flooring and black walls for this lab. Dim perimeter lighting appeased the residents. The nicer word for the detainees.

"Did the volunteers sign all the consent forms?" He picked up a clipboard with the answers to his question. All six prisoners agreed to the latest Vittle supplement trial. "Good. Make sure we patch the results over to Conscience. He'll want to adjust the growth formula based on this."

This and the weapons facility existed to research nacre interaction on human and Icarean kind. The Brethren—the body governing the Two Worlds—hoped to improve performance, famine-tolerance, and intellect. While Enki sentenced most of the war criminals to Gait, many prisoners volunteered as specimens for the betterment of their people.

He approached the technician standing at the Enki projection of an advanced alien computer. "Can you pull up all the files for me on the nacre memory banks? It's a direct request from Story Taker. If you could, I'd appreciate getting it by this evening. Please."

"We'll see to it, Dr. Suarez." The newbie chirped up at Kyle's codename.

Pablo didn't mean to stare at the young woman for so long. In this life, they learned not to trust people. People with an abundance of enthusiasm were often spies. Imminent spies. Enki spies. Hell, human spies.

The original apocalypse crew, or the Shadow, looked after each other. Their mutual dependency mattered. They loved and lost together. They saved the Two Worlds together.

"I need some air." He wasted no time to order a second, more extensive background check on the new technician. No chance of someone accusing him of paranoia. They lost so much to treachery and misplaced faith already.

As Pablo left the lab, he paid special attention to the expansive slate sign bearing the facility's name.

IONA MEDICAL ECOLOGY

Take no chances.

{EARTH}

"And we know from this anonymous Verse that there existed planets in the Vast Collective that lived in peaceful communal harmony. We can follow that example. In three days, I plan to visit a few refuges. I'm sorry I can't say which ones in advance, but I'm sure those listening can understand why. I'll take account of any grievances in our current system and prepare measures to address them. Please, have patience. This world we're building is new. But it's first and foremost yours. Thank you."

Chris gripped Jack's slumped shoulder as the young man disengaged from the comms device. "Great announcement, kid." Iron Hope, the Iona network's train, rocked and pitched the tall black man until he gripped a handle. He whistled, signaling a change of subject, "Tracks through Mexico are kind of rough."

"I don't like that we can't tell them in advance." The seventeen-year-old planetary monarch looked up at Chris with earnest, hazel eyes. "Every time we visit a community, they're upset they weren't prepared. No matter how much I explain that we don't care about provisions or the state of lodgings, the people still feel inadequate." He angrily shoved a tan, white hand through his short dark hair, as he sighed and leaned back in the booth. The scenery outside the cafe car took his attention, then.

This argument got harder with every visit. "After Imminent's last attempt on your life, we can't be too careful. And you need to give people more credit. They look forward to your visits. Lack of preparedness only disrupts things initially. After the first day, everything comes together." Chris patted the back of the boy's booth. "Have faith, your royal pain-in-the-ass."

"Hey! It's our two favorite boys," Karter called through the noise of the train as the door closed behind her.

The sight of her sent Chris' blood traveling to so many places. Tall, strong, fierce. Her gray skin darker than most Icari. Her voice a deep, sinful melody. She braided back her rainbow-colored hair recently. He loved it now, and he loved it when she styled it as a mohawk. He mostly just loved her.

There was a goofy grin stuck on his face. Slapping it off, he greeted both her and the young human lady in her company. "Hey girls, how was the mission?"

Judging by the forlorn look on Ross' face, he hesitated to guess. The Story Taker's own sister spent the last two years following Cult of Night leads to locate the youngest sister, Bethany. Karter accompanied Ross on every mission at Jack's request.

The teenage boy sure perked up in the brunette girl's presence. "I can send more assets with you next time. I'm sure we'll find her soon."

Chris almost blew the air out of his cheeks. He glanced up at Karter. Over Ross' head, the Icarean female's eyes went tight. This was a mess.

"Fuck it. Let's retrace our steps again, starting with square one." Chris hunkered down and drew circles and squares on a nearby notebook like a playbook. "We know the Icarus that attacked your residence took her to the local CON compound—"

"The same one Lucy and Matt worked in," Karter pointed out with renewed optimism.

"She's gone."

The entire car turned to Ross.

"I'll never find her. I—" She hiccuped and tears fell from her soft hazel eyes. She hung her head and sobbed. "She was only twelve."

Jack knelt and put his face in hers. "We will find her. I will never stop looking for her." He brushed thick wavy hair back from her face. "Can you hold out a little longer for me?"

This qualified as the closest thing to a romantic act from him so far. Jack ruled an entire planet from a train. And he did it pretty well. But with his crush on Ross, the boy seized up. Floundered like a fish out of water. With this, there might be hope for him, yet.

The girl nodded with a sniffle that broke Chris' heart.

"Okay. So, let's do this. Please, continue, Batman." Jack nodded to the diagrams.

"Like Karter—" Chris didn't bother to control the wink in her direction. It got a giggle out of Ross, so job well done. "...explained, Matt and Lucy were at the same compound but saw no one matching Bethany's description."

Karter picked it up from there, "So we know they transferred out. Two Enforcers we interrogated told us the underage girls went to the Utah compound."

"We went there and found nothing but a burnt city," Jack began and rubbed the back of his neck. Both women stared at the boy—codenamed Robin—captivated by his speech. Freaking twenty on charisma. "There was a trail of girls taken, but not by Icari. It led us here." He gestured to the area. "Hey, I'll get in touch with Matt. I think I have an idea."

The eighteen-year-old girl shook her head. "I don't know. He's nice and all but—"

"He and Lucy incinerated eighty CON compounds in the last two years. Alone." Chris raised his eyebrows. "That's not just efficiency. That's fucking savage."

Karter grinned. "I like 'em just fine." Her Valkyrie muscles bunched as she fiddled with the chain on her neck.

Damn.

Jack licked his lips. "I'll admit they're two crazy characters that standout in an already hard-to-believe story. But my sister and the Progeny trust them. So do I."

Ross took a harrowing breath that shuddered. The room turned to her. "I need to see my brother soon."

"We can absolutely arrange that," Jack offered.

She smiled warmly at him. "Thank you." Her gaze swept over each of them. "Thank you, all."

Karter pulled her in for a side hug. "This is what it means to be one of us. We take care of each other."

Chris chuckled and threw them all in a group hug. Emphasis on getting Jack close to Ross. The kid needed a healthy distraction from post apocalyptic clean up. Ross needed a healthy distraction from her worries. A little dating couldn't hurt.

Karter whispered in a sultry voice against Chris' ear, "Para's coming to visit this week."

Nope. Couldn't hurt a thing.

{EARTH}

"It's time to wake up, Conscience."

Andrew groaned. "Ugh, you know I hate when you call me that."

The Icarus in bed beside him chuckled. "There's no way to make it sound appetizing, is there?" He pecked a kiss on Andrew's mid-length brown hair. The gray sheets whispered when he climbed out of bed.

"Stay," they said.

And when Andrew opened his heavy eyelids, he had to agree. He'd never tire of that man sleeping in the nude. "Can't we take the day off? Just this once?"

Lucas stretched, and the Progeny almost fainted. His golden-eyed partner glanced over his shoulder to catch Andrew watching—of course, he was watching.

The rosewood wainscoting complimented the man's tastes. Elegance. The plush oriental beneath his feet almost left him tall enough to touch the cabin ceiling, despite him being the shortest Icarus they'd met so far.

Running a hand through his short sandy-blond hair, Lucas threatened, "If you don't get up, I'll get dressed rather than join you for your morning shower."

That did it. After a shower and their morning exercise, they prepared to face the day. Only two hours late, too. A record for them. Andrew rinsed their plates in the black sink surrounded by Carrara marble countertops and took a moment to evaluate the current state of his life. Uniting the Two Worlds. Day and night improving a race's chance to survive. Spending every waking second with—

"Let me help with that." Lucas hugged Andrew from behind and dried the dishes with a towel. Calm. Patient. Always. He asked quietly against the Progeny's ear, "What's on your mind, philosopher?" The man's soothing tenor tortured Andrew in the lower registers.

He actually wanted to talk about his thoughts. "I'm happy."

Lucas squeezed tightly. "Is that not a good thing?"

"It is, but...I think I've been living with survivor's remorse for a while now."

The Icarus purred—a truly comforting talent—against his back in response.

"I know. I know. I'm lucky. We're here now, but even Rayne isn't *here*. Is it okay to be the happiest I've ever been after everything and everyone we lost?" Andrew closed his eyes and swallowed hard. Finally. He told someone.

Lucas stepped back and turned the Progeny around to face him. "I've survived many wars and witnessed substantial loss over my life. I'm sorry that it never gets easier. Not truly. But those people we lost wouldn't want you to feel this way. They'd be proud of you, Andrew. As am I."

Andrew buried his face in Lucas' chest and breathed. In. Out. Spicy goodness. "Thank you."

Someone rapped on the metal door.

"That'll be Boklo. We're much, much later than usual."

Andrew nodded and took one last breath. He gripped the pendant on his chain for good luck. "Let's get to work."

Lucas opened the door, "Good afternoon, Boklo. Apologies for our tardiness. We—"

The Icarus shook his head full of dark braids. "Save it. I came to deliver a message to Conscience."

The Progeny grumbled at the name.

The man's voice spoke in depths similar to Tumu's, "Story Taker needs you to relieve Colton and Six of watch duty late this evening. Something about a special screen."

Lucas frowned. Correction. Pouted. How cute.

Andrew kissed the man's cheek. "Don't worry. When Sagan gets back, I'll make her pull a triple shift." The regular rotations to watch Rayne strained the two male Progeny while Tameka and Sagan remained off-world. Para, Bones, and Colton volunteered to lighten the load.

He followed Lucas out of the zeppelin. Yes, a zeppelin. The Icarus acquired it during World War II and hid it away in a European bunker. He kitted it out with more luxury than toys, but Xelan would still approve.

They anchored it in the outback of Western Australia. Boklo assured them the environment best matched

Celindria's Vittle plantation on Cinder. As her main agriculturist, they took his word for it and planted crops when the war ended.

Two years later, Andrew stared out at the vast rows of Vittle vines. He grinned. They'd be proud, all right. He sure was.

Lucas blew him a kiss. "I'll see you after my meeting with Lynn." That gorgeous man flew off in a navy Gucci suit on majestic black wings. Damn.

Andrew threw on some hiking boots to go with his dirt-stained cargo shorts. Grabbing a berry-picking rake, he set to a hard day's work. This wasn't enough to support the Icarean population. But it allowed Doc Pablo to create supplements until The Brethren worked with humanity to expand the farm. Tempest and Dolor looked pleased with the progress at their last visit. And given they represented two votes each for The Brethren, the future looked bright.

About three hours into picking, a warm and all too infrequent sight caught Andrew's gaze. "Sagan!"

The blond girl stopped knocking on the zeppelin—something they were all glad she learned to do after the Pablo and Lynn incident. She Seamswalked over. "Hey! Still living up to your old nickname, eh?"

He snickered at the "Golden God" reference. "You don't do social calls anymore. What're you doing here?"

Sagan looked caught. "Sorry. I mean to visit . . . I lose time s'all."

He staved her with a hand. "I know. It's okay. We're all adjusting still." Her intentions were muddled. She wanted something, but she also wanted to talk about something. "Out with it, girl."

"Do you think any of Lucas' clothes would fit Korac?"

Andrew roared with laughter. Slapped his thigh, held his stomach, and everything.

"Oh, c'mon! The prison clothes don't fit him. Or suit him. And if anyone would get that, it'd be the golden-eyed hottie."

Absurd. Absolutely absurd. He cleared his throat a bit and wiped the tears from his eyes. "Unless Korac shrank almost two entire feet in height and grew one foot in the crotch, they won't fit."

She pouted.

Damn.

"Okay. Okay. Let's see what he's got." He shoved a finger in her face. "But you're staying for dinner, and you'll ask Lucas, himself. He'll have a better idea of what's in that extravagant closet of his."

Her violet eyes went wide. "I heard a quarter of the airship is just closet space. Is it true?"

Andrew nodded gravely. "It is."

Sagan helped cook. In the past, this led to several infamous memories. When they learned to make funnel cakes, she managed to explode the baking powder into the ceiling fan of Rayne's weird-ass kitchen. When Andrew first taught her how to make spicy fried chicken, she worried the melted Crisco got too hot and dropped a few ice cubes in the pot to cool it off.

But tonight, the blond surprised him. She assisted him with the precision and rapt attention of a surgical nurse. "This is garlic powder, right? No, this is onion. I found it. Here ya go."

After thirty minutes, he set the table with a simple chicken and pasta recipe. As if the Icarus installed a special food radar, Lucas suddenly appeared. Andrew rolled his eyes. Boys.

"Smells delicious in here." He kissed the top of the Seamswalker's head. "Sagan, you look beautiful. I love the bangs."

The young woman beamed at him. "Thanks. I love your place."

They sat down for dinner as Lucas carried on the conversation, "Well, we invited you to the housewarming, but I suppose Lacceirus-Capra is a rather captivating planet. Or so I've read."

The Progeny and a handful of the Shadow read Nox's Verse. What Rayne let them have of it, anyway. Some pages were missing and passages marked out. And when she gave it to Karter for Jack to use during Story Circle, she asked the Valkyrie not to let him see it or know who wrote it. Andrew worried that might bite her in the ass one day.

In the meantime, Sagan explored every planet Nox mentioned to find leads on Imminent. Specifically, on Razor. One of the more elusive figures in the organization.

"...And so you want to raid my wardrobe?" Lucas peered at Sagan with his eyebrows raised. Bewildered.

Andrew looked between them, fighting the urge to giggle at the situation.

"I'm sorry. It didn't sound so ridiculous when I thought of it. Please, forget I said anything—"

Lucas set his fork down and sat back in his seat with his hands folded on his lap. "I will find and tailor clothes for your...suitor. But on one condition."

She perked straight up in her chair, eager. "Name it."

"You create a regular visitation schedule with the Shadow. One member. Once a week. You are detaching and with your current assignment, I'm concerned for your safety."

This was very Xelan, and Andrew approved.

Sagan lowered her eyes and nodded. "I can do that." She let out a shaky exhale. "Yea. I know. I need to pitch in and help where I can now that I'm better with the Seamswalking." The next smile beamed. "I got this."

"Good. And I must say, there's something appealing to dressing up the former General like a doll."

Andrew drowned in his drink and spit it back in the glass. When he finally drew air, he choked on his own laughter.

Sagan patted the Progeny on the back while asking, "What measurements do you need?"

Andrew swung a knowing glance at Lucas.

"Oh, I don't need any. I'll see to everything."

{Gait}

Loaded down with her care package for Korac, Sagan stepped onto the streets of Gait. It snowed since she last left. Cold enough to accumulate in piles shoveled along the curbs. She thanked the Lyriks for her coat before scouring street vendors for food. Prison food sucked, right? Surely Korac would appreciate something from out here more.

The pack bounced on her back like a stuffed turtle shell. She recalled Lucas' warning, *"Don't leave these in here too long or they'll wrinkle."*

Sagan snickered in the middle of a prison planet. Korac faced two hundred years in a cell. He'd learn how to de-wrinkle his clothes.

The Seamswalker relied on her hood to hide her expression. She learned from her travels that smiles and "resting nice face" often led to sexual harassment by locals. No need to knock a Prisonborne's face in the dirt unnecessarily.

Following the enticing scent of grilled mushrooms, Sagan turned the next corner. And stopped. Atramentous flashed in her blinding fury.

The street ended at a rectangular glass building with gilded accents, boasting a sign, Martyr Complex Bar & Lounge.

When she finished with it, the sign would read future site of construction.

It was warm inside. Plushy booths, an expansive glass-top bar, and strange twinkling lights made up the interior. No one called her out on the double axes at her hips. The place looked dead. Only one random at the bar and the tender behind it. Good. Fewer people to evacuate before she demolished it.

A flash caught her eye. Four projection screens in the corners of the room played an advertisement on loop. Sagan stepped closer to the nearest image, staring. Something about it was wrong. In a ten second loop, a giant of a man threw a woman against a rock chair.

Enormous. A throne? As he took her clothes off, the girls' face flashed for one terrifying second.

Rayne.

"One Million Credits" blinked over the looping footage.

Sagan clutched her stomach and cried out, but no sound came. She heaved and fought her buckling knees. It repeated, and tears squeezed from her eyes as she turned away.

"Yo, barkeep, can you turn this shit off? I think it drives the clientele away."

The man at the bar stomped his glass on the counter and repeated his request. Sagan caught his gaze in the mirror behind the bar. Unusual eyes split vertically with orange on the inside and green on the outside. Bright red hair cut short.

He nodded to her as he continued chewing out the bartender, "King Rayne is a gracious and powerful woman. She must be lonely, as well."

Sagan caught her breath.

The bartender looked up at the closest projection. "What makes you think she's lonesome?"

The man scoffed in his glass. "Cause she can't go anywhere without this tacky shit playing. Now, turn it off." He threw back the rest of his drink. And his eyes sparkled as the bartender switched it off.

Unsure what else to say or do, Sagan mouthed to his reflection, "Thank. You." For ending the disgusting loop of Rayne's torment.

"And get me two more of these." When he received the drinks, the tan stranger held them up for Sagan and nodded toward a booth.

She didn't know this man, and this place didn't exactly reek of class. But if she let him talk a while, maybe she'd glean some information from the local scene. Besides, she was always armed. With that reassurance in mind, she sat across from him.

The man touched the pulse point on Sagan's wrist with two fingers. Then pressed those two fingers to his own nacre. A greeting? Where were his fingernails?

After that, he wasted no time. "I know you're not her. You're the Seamswalker, right?"

"How did you know?"

Chuckling, he scratched his five o'clock shadow. The burgundy leather of his long coat protested with his movements. "Five young people from Earth take down the most badass race of elite warriors known to the galaxy—You're a bunch of celebrities. Also, purple eyes are uncommon in the Vast Collective."

Sagan stared into the warm blue liquid. "If only it ended there. It left us all...broken, you know?" She spared him a glance. The intensity in his gaze made her duck her own.

"You can tell me about it." Such a soothing voice. And his eyes. Limitless.

Shaking her head, Sagan forced herself to stop staring at the handsome stranger. She bit her lip before answering, "The Tribunal sentenced my boyfriend here."

He nodded, listening kindly. "Must be hard."

The Progeny girl set the hood back and fluffed her hair idly. He absorbed every move she made, but not sexually. More predatory than that.

"It is. I've never felt so alone." She chafed her arms as if chilled. "I don't know what to do with myself."

"I can ease your troubles."

There was a weight in those five words, as if they held their own gravitational pull. They sought something from her.

Softly, Sagan confessed, "I miss our time together." She looked anywhere but at him.

He leaned on the tabletop, smelling of vanilla and darker things. "I'm sure with someone like the Icarean General you can appreciate the desire for pain and other exotic experiences. Can you tell me what it was like with him—"

"How much were you planning on selling mine for, Razor?" Sagan turned back to him with ice in her veins. "Half a million?"

Those bizarre eyes flashed. It was his turn to ask, "How did you know?"

That greeting. Nox's encounter described in his Verse helped her identify the Pain Curator, but the Icarus' description varied from the man in front of her. Even so, she refused to give her source away.

The bastard held out his hands to placate her. "I'm not a bad guy. This is simply how I make a living on this hollow rock."

"What about those ads for Rayne?"

"Rayne is a special case." He leaned into the booth and spanned his arms along the back. "Her experience is the highest and fastest growing market. Ever. And while I was aiming for Nox's death at her hands, I'd gladly settle for your near death experience at his."

Sagan pressed her fingers to her temples. "I cannot believe I'm hearing this."

"The people made the legend. I just built a franchise with it."

She let her hands fall to the table and frowned incredulously. "What legend?"

Razor signaled with his hand, and the bartender ran the advertisement again. The "One Million Credit" sign barely censored the brief glimpses of the atrocity. "The epic love story. Tragedy, lust, revenge. Nox claiming Rayne to prevent the Tritans stealing her away as a broodmare. Rayne sparing Nox in their lone battle, so he can return for her once the Icari are migrated safely to Earth."

"And people... believe this?" Sagan grimaced and swallowed the bile back down. She felt the chain around her neck as if heavier than before.

"How else would you describe the way he looked at her? The way they fought. There are songs and films. Written fiction. It's beautiful really how their love united the Twelve Worlds."

She glared at him, too shocked and too angry to speak.

"Come by the Emporium sometime." Razor slid out of the booth and stood over Sagan. "We can discuss why you're looking for me. And maybe you can satisfy your curiosity with Rayne's experience."

This monster held answers she needed to shut down Imminent. To understand the pain markets and the public's obsession with it. But how could she withstand another second in his foul but oddly pleasant company?

Razor chuckled at Sagan's silent censure. He waved to the bartender on his way out. "Have a good one, Puk!"

"G'night, boss."

It was time for her to seek professional help.

THREE

BEGINNING IN YOU

{???}

RAYNE DARED NOT LOOK AWAY. UNBLINKING, SHE WITNESSED THE ENTIRETY OF NOX'S LIFE. Experienced his thoughts and feelings. As the mental reel approached that fateful day in Umbra's Spire, tears finally speared her bright blue eyes.

"Enough."

The exchange stopped. No lies. Only candid emotions. Well, what he called emotions. Although she felt everything he felt, the experience through his eyes left her hollow. Shallow. Only his feelings toward Xelan and Korac felt proportionately appropriate. Everything else...detached. Rayne lacked the education in psychology to know if the difference was because of his species, gender, or individual experience.

In her mindscape, she sat on a couch similar to the plush ones in the Iona rumpus rooms. She wore calf-length leggings and a purple flowy tunic. Hiding her bare shoulders and back, her black hair grew to her waist over these last two years. She didn't feel the need to tie it back in his presence. Here, she was safe.

Beyond her haven, *Hellsing* played for the fiftieth time on the television. Andrew liked to repeat episodes of anime they used to watch together. She loved him for it. During the exsanguination cycles, he increased the volume. As if he couldn't stand the sound.

Rayne knew the feeling.

Focusing on these tiny details allowed her to process the life she witnessed. So very long. So very unhappy. None of it excused Nox's actions against her and the people she loved.

Therein lie her rage.

But without a healthy moral compass. Without ever experiencing love—wholesome, romantic, platonic, etc.—what chance did he have for rational decisions? Healthy choices?

Therein lay her compassion.

This internal conflict shit sucked.

Rayne stood and kept her eyes dipped low. No doubt the emotional boxing match showed in them. Not to mention, the man in question watched her from the other side of the room. Intently.

Colossal barely covered it. Tall and broad with long black hair, the mountainous Icarus stood out among his own people for his size and features. Handsome, with sharp angles and full lips. He preferred going without a shirt. Always in black. Here, she dressed him in white jeans and a t-shirt. Because she thought it would be hilarious. It only emphasized his dark smolder.

Rayne killed him once, and she'd do it again. Only...

She crossed the space to him. His combats boots looked shiny from this angle. Did she do that? Or did he polish them—

Get on with it, Rayne.

For the first time in the two years since she executed Nox, Rayne looked into his eyes. The weight of six million dark years stared down at her. Patient. Unassuming.

"I know you, now."

After her proclamation, Nox searched her gaze. Uncertainty flickered in those obsidian eyes.

He would find no judgment here. No outrage. That was not her place. Rayne killed him and delivered justice. Protected the world from his destructive disposition.

Here, she could safely access his council and strategy. Memories full of much needed information. No risk to the others. No risk to herself. Safe.

The King of Earth and Cinder leveled her gaze to her predecessor's chest and stepped around him to walk away.

"Rayne."

With her back to him, she closed her eyes. No one ever said her name like that. She once likened it to the man waiting his entire life to say it. But as it turned out, he waited roughly two thousand years.

A plain of green grass and a scattering of tall oaks replaced the abyssal mindscape. While busy roads and two hospitals surrounded the area, this small park granted a much needed natural respite to the concrete desert that was Little Rock, Arkansas.

"You look so peaceful here." Nox walked over to the tree Rayne occupied.

Sat on a branch with her back to the trunk, she idly tied knots in a rope with the sun setting behind her. "I am. The Weapon is sated. And no one here expects me to look them in the eye and tell them about the worst day of my life. Because we were both there for it. Weren't we, Nox?"

As she turned her gaze on him, he looked away. "Is it already time?"

She returned to her chore of tying the rope. Softly, she answered, "Not yet. I'm not ready. Are you?"

He swallowed hard. "No."

They both required more time before broaching that topic.

Nox pivoted and took in the expanse. "There's not this much vegetation on all of Cinder. My brother would love this place."

Rayne clenched her fists and—

He held up a hand to stop her. "I know you don't appreciate when I speak of him."

"It's not that. It's how casually you talk about a sibling you murdered."

"Executed."

"Nox, that hardly—"

"It matters." He turned back to her and explained, "Before he ever met you, he knew his fate. He chose it the day he betrayed us. It's something you'll come to understand better as a ruler."

Rayne gripped the rope in her hand and glared at him. "No. He wasn't like that. I won't be either. And I'll have you know, he loved this park."

"You took him here?"

"Where do you think I learned to dance like an Icarus?" Rayne hopped out of the tree and crested a slope. In faint images of themselves, the Progeny sat on the hill and watched as Xelan took turns teaching them to dance. For "undercover operations."

"Tameka, you're doing great." Xelan beamed at the young woman in his arms.

"Thanks. You're okay." She giggled, but the light blush on her freckled cheeks belied her youthful crush. With a final twirl, she hesitatingly stepped aside.

Kyle grumbled, "This is kind of stupid."

Sagan sighed from the grass and grabbed her bag. "Sorry, I need to duck out. It's eight."

Andrew's eyes widened as he intentionally looked away. No one liked to acknowledge why Sagan disappeared this time every night.

Rayne watched her younger self frown and spare Xelan a beseeching glance.

The Icarus shook his head. How could he help with Justin? He could kill the teenager. And some part of Rayne knew he considered it, as did she. But...

"Do you want me to take you there, Sagan?" he offered uncertainly.

The blond girl's smile was reserved, sad. "No, thanks, coach. See you tomorrow for training." She waved and headed for the bus stop.

Younger Rayne watched her go with a pounding heart.

"Rayne, it's your turn."

She turned to find Xelan's warm and kind presence standing over her. Hand outstretched, he offered a wholesome distraction from her darker thoughts.

Rayne took it. And they danced.

Current Rayne paused the memory. She stared up at Xelan as he gazed down at her younger self with love and respect. A little fear. Why was he afraid—

"You look at him now, the same as you did then. I've never seen so much naked adoration." Nox observed quietly as the scene played.

Rayne wondered what the fallen King took from it. This loss was unprocessed. "Xelan was genuinely the most amazing person I ever knew. He loved us all so much. I only hope..." She let the words die as she stared into the eyes of her fallen guardian.

"He was proud of you."

The lights went out. The scene melted. Back to the empty mindscape.

Nox sought her in the darkness. "Are you shutting down? He wouldn't want you to do that."

"Well, he's not here, and it's your fault..." She stared down at her bare feet. Rayne's emotions threatened to swallow her. How could she reconcile this? "My fault."

"By Elden, how in the worlds can you blame yourself for his death?" Incredulous, he frowned at her.

Her voice grew smaller as she confessed her darkest truth, "I should have sensed you. Maybe if I didn't drink Celindria's blood—disabling myself—he could have jumped with us..."

"You're right."

Rayne gasped. "What did you say?"

Nox stepped close enough to tower over her. His icy voice arrested her, "You should have done something."

Jabbing her finger at him, she cried out, "You executed him! How was I supposed to stop that? My nacre wasn't activated. I could barely stand from—" She went silent and considered her words.

In the void left from her outburst, Nox quietly assured, "I'm not one of your friends, Rayne. I won't coddle you and entertain yourmartyr complex. My brother engaged a self-destruct code he placed in his nacre to die protecting the people he loved. There was nothing you could do. Don't betray his memory with misplaced guilt."

Rayne looked up at him as he finished, less conflicted than before.

"Let it go," Nox instructed.

No cruelty. Pure understanding. Acceptance. His version of love. Nox believed he loved her.

Rayne walked away, preparing to shut the scape down.

Nox called after her, "What about you?"

She stopped with her back to him. "What about me?"

"In my life, I've known no one like you. The same parents that raised me raised Xelan. Korac's younger life was so much worse than my own that he never shared it. And I never forced him. But I wonder what makes you the way you are. I want to understand you. I suppose it starts with loving parents."

Nox asked to live her life. Wanted to experience her upbringing. Rayne frowned with her back to him and tried to keep her voice steady, "What do you hope to gain from this?"

She heard his boot hit the floor as he took a hesitant step closer. She absorbed his every emotion. He felt unsure how to explain himself. There were no ulterior motives in his thoughts. "I want to know where I went wrong. Why I am wrong." He struggled to say the next, "I know I am wrong."

Rayne's eyes closed. So much of her wanted to hurt him. To scream at him until she was hoarse and beat him until it appeased the anger in her. But a part of her wondered how exposing him to her life might affect his cognition.

"You'll feel everything as I felt it. I won't shield you from anything." She licked her lips and turned to him. "I'm not sure you're prepared to feel unconditional love and family."

"What else would you have me do?"

Good question. Beating him came back to mind. But served no constructive purpose. Maybe Nox would prove a better asset if she went through with this.

The couch appeared behind him. Behind her, the story of her life played on a screen. She opened herself to share her thoughts and emotions with him.

Nox sat down, and Rayne walked behind the couch to introduce the show. "I was the last Progeny born. The youngest. Ray and Michelle Callahan were my parents. Dad was a night-shift nurse and mom . . . was a dreamer. She always wanted a bookstore—"

Their images came on the screen.

The loss of her parents punched the air out of Rayne. She clutched at the pain in her chest, trying to breathe before the tears fell. She never processed their loss properly, and that was part of the reason she elected to sleep in the Martyr Complex. To hide from it.

A gasp tore her focus back to Nox. He clutched at his head with his eyes shut tight. When he looked at her, he opened them. Sheer. Panic. "Do all humans experience emotions this . . . enormous?"

Rayne licked her lips, uncertain how to answer. "We can stop."

Brusquely, Nox shook his head and set his jaw tight with resolve. "Continue when you're ready."

FOUR

THE LIES WE'RE TOLD THROUGH SHARP TEETH

{GAIT}

KORAC FOUGHT HIS THOUGHTS OF SAGAN THROUGHOUT THE DAY. He didn't wish to disrupt her concentration from her errand. Come evening, he held back no longer. The guards made their rounds an hour ago, leaving only six hours for him and Sagan unhindered.

"Sorry, I'm late."

Speak of the gorgeous devil.

Sagan stepped into his cell, hauling a trunk on her back. "I brought you—"

Korac swallowed her words with a kiss. She returned it with no regard for her burden. When he pulled away to let her breathe, her eyes opened lazily with a serene smile.

"Hi." He smirked down at her.

"Hey."

He almost expected their audience to interrupt them, but the bastard blockmate kept quiet all day.

She gently cleared her throat, redirecting the subject. "I brought you . . ." She peered over her shoulder at her pack. ". . . A few things." Those purple eyes sparkled with mischief.

Korac helped Sagan slip out of the gear. On his knees, he opened the trunk and took it in. A gift. This was a gift. He smiled at her. "You went shopping?"

"I had some help." She giggled at his arched brow. "I have no idea what's in there."

He took her hand and kissed her palm. "Anything is better than that." Glaring at the ill-fitting jumpsuit on the floor, he willed it to incinerate.

Sagan's precious giggle bubbled into laughter before sobering completely. "I wish we could stay this way."

Six hours. Prolong her happiness—

The aroma of grilled mushrooms elicited a growl from his stomach as she opened a second, smaller pack. "Who made you so perfect? The food here barely passes for oatmeal." He grabbed the first clothes off the top and hoped they sufficed for their dinner date.

"I'll let Pehton know I won't stand for her feeding my badass warrior oatmeal." Light danced in her eyes as she watched him select clothes.

"I love the way you look at me, but you'll get your show when I'm ready." Korac grabbed an axe and headed to the frosted glass divider, constituting a bathroom.

As he dressed and tried to work with his shorter hair in the blade's reflection, Sagan called to him, "I could bring you stuff to cozy the place up."

The Icarus paused. The offer was genuine, but her tone implied deflection. Something happened.

Dinner first.

Korac rounded the corner, feeling like himself for the first time in two years. "Lucas helped with the clothes, didn't he?"

Those purple eyes doubled in size. "How'd you know?"

"Devil's in the details."

They shared mushrooms. He purred his gratitude and smirked at her stories. But a light tension pulled at his shoulders the longer she avoided the situation.

"Sagan."

She sucked a noodle through her lips and ducked her eyes.

He crooked a finger under her chin and raised her gaze to meet his. "You can tell me."

Swallowing, she confessed, "I met Razor. And you were right. He found me. Not the other way around."

Korac nodded and left her the space to continue. He resented the incarceration, preventing him from helping her. Razor wasn't some cult minion or simpering Tritan diplomat. He was something . . . other.

When Sagan finished recounting the story, he blew the air out of his cheeks. "It's a good strategy. Setting him up to comfort you in order to break down his barriers."

She snuggled her back against Korac's front, sitting between his legs. "Yea. Too bad it didn't work." She turned to catch his gaze. "Korac?"

He brushed his knuckles down her arm. "Hmm?"

Shivering, she soldiered on through his attempt to distract her. "Tell me about the pain."

"The pain *and* the control. I know Razor recognized it in you immediately and will work to coax it out. I know because it was done to me, and I did it to you. But I was careful and kept it within our trust. Trust makes a difference. He's reckless and won't care for your fragile mind. He'll seek to break it. To break you."

Now she trembled. Korac held her tight and kissed the top of her head while Sagan absorbed his words. "I want you to understand the risks I believe you're considering. And understand the one to me if he does."

Sagan turned around in his arms to face him with a question in her eyes. "Risk to you?"

"This prison will not hold me if he harms you."

The only person who mattered to him straddled Korac for a kiss. Her warm hands ran under his shirt. Nails played at his skin. He purred and repaid in kind when she suddenly cried out, "Hey! I didn't know Lucas saw you that night at Mercy's compound in Phoenix."

"Pardon?"

"This." She bunched her hands in his shirt. "This is the exact outfit you wore that night."

He grinned. "You remember my clothes in that much detail?"

"This girl likes her devil very much," Sagan said with a cute blush. Then she frowned. "How did he know?"

The black shredded t-shirt and white jeans hardly seemed worth the fuss, but he admitted, "I only saw you and Kyle that night."

Anger flashed in her eyes momentarily at the mention of the reformed Progeny's treachery. Korac took both her hands in his and kissed her knuckles. "How many times did you read Nox's Verse, Sagan?"

Her eyes refocused on him with warmth. "A few...dozen." She smiled shyly.

"Then you know everyone's personal story is complicated." Was he defending Kyle? No. Was he trying to ease Sagan's mind by lessening her anger at the Progeny male? Yes.

Worth the smile, too. "You're right. I learned so much from it. I hope you don't mind I read all those things about you."

Learning that Nox knew of Korac's relationship with Xelan after all that time almost killed the Icarean General. He liked his privacy, but feeling his King's acceptance meant the worlds to him.

Korac smirked. "Spared me the trouble of telling you the stories myself." A thought occurred to him. "But you need to take that book with you and hide it somewhere. Xelan's stronghold would do."

"Oh, why?"

"In the Vast Collective, it's illegal to write of your own history. The Tritans funnel all history and education through the Reipon Lamias. For . . . conditioning. Nox's Verse and Elden's Verse are criminal offenses, and if you're caught with them, you'll be arrested for counter-indoctrination."

Sagan's eyes flashed. "Rayne's back..."

He nodded. "Illegal when exposed."

"Korac, at that awful bar...the promotion of Rayne's pain—"

The Icarus gently cupped her cheek. "No, she's fine. That's not her selling it. Fame and infamy aren't illegal. Self-promotion is."

She pressed her face to his chest. "What do you think Rayne blacked out and tore out of his Verse?"

The book solved a few mysteries, but the black markings hid the rest. It surprised him to see how much of it protected Korac and his secret. He appreciated the sprite's caution.

"Do you want to know what I'd tear out?"

Sagan nodded against him.

"Ammunition. Anything and everything which might be used against me. King Rayne has a lot of enemies now. She's smart to keep certain things out of their hands. But Sagan?"

"Yes?"

"Have you thought about asking her, yourself?"

His woman's body seized up, and her breath caught.

It was as he thought. "When was the last time you saw her?"

Sagan sniffed. "It's hard . . . to see her like that. The mechanism . . ."

Korac rubbed a circle on her back. "Nothing I'd offer you would ease this grief. I only wish I could help."

She straightened in his lap to stare in his eyes. "You do."

He kissed her, and they worked off the mushrooms. With no interruptions from the blockmate.

After four hours, Sagan lamented, "I need to go. Lucas is making me meet with the Shadow once a week."

"Stay connected. A schedule is good to maintain when working a dangerous mission." So she was always expected.

She dressed. He watched, languid as a cat. She made a show of it for him. Prison wasn't so bad.

"Can I get some of that food?"

Well, at least the blockmate waited six hours before intruding.

With a forgiving smile Korac did nothing to deserve, she kissed him goodbye.

"Wait, Sagan. You mentioned professional help. Who?"

"Remember the CON compound in Little Rock. The whole razing it to the ground?"

Korac dipped his head to the side with a smirk that said, "Go on."

Sagan beamed. "I'm good friends with the ones who did the razing."

From down the hall, "I like the way she talks about arson. Girl's got potential for marriage. You hear me? Hold on to her and don't let go."

{EARTH}

Kyle sat at the massive desk, filling out paperwork for The Brethren. The desert fortress' observatory served as his base of operations for screenings over the last two years. The eastern and western walls boasted millions of years of Icarean history in books lining wooden shelves. An enormous telescope took up a third of the room. Glass comprised the northern wall and ceiling for an unhindered view of the stars and dunes. Wood and leather furniture scattered across the rest of the space.

It wasn't really Story Taker's style. But the Progeny male liked the idea of claiming Nox's desk after Rayne sent that fucker to Hell or Eternity or whatever they called it.

Fuck. Him.

He glanced at the copy of the bastard's Verse that Andrew left him to read. Covered in dust, untouched.

No, Kyle settled for taking pleasure in cleaning up that waste of space's mess. Speaking of. He reviewed the preliminary findings Pablo sent him on the device Tumu left them for secure document transfers.

NO INSTANCES OF NACRE MEMORY MALFUNCTION IN CURRENT KNOWN HISTORY.

Shit.

Kyle would have to reach out to Tameka for access to the Tritan archives on Enki. And he really hated the idea. She kept her kid a secret from him until a year after Pax came into the worlds. Not that he blamed her. It just hurt.

Standing, he stretched and tried to keep the groaning to a minimum. Peeking over at his puzzle, Kyle took another cursory examination of their feral refugee.

Feral. Naked. Refugee.

They covered her with a sheet. He kept reminding himself she was old. Ancient. She looked barely a day over twenty. Athletic, for a heavy sleeper. Strong, too. However, those weren't uncommon traits for an Icarean female.

But her hair…black with a bright blue stripe down the right half of her bangs. It draped down to her feet after sleeping for so long. And those gunmetal gray eyes of hers also raised some red flags. Supposedly they looked like King Umbra's. Sire of the previous Mr. King of Cinder.

Kyle tilted his head to the side as he wondered what her Atramentous looked like. Ultimately, that was dark mode for Icari. Her eyes should change, and her voice should layer in three pitches.

A good voice, too. Deep. Soft.

The twenty-year-old man crossed the room before he realized it. The thick midnight-blue carpet suppressed his steps. He stared down at the sleeping woman in nacre cuffs, not as if she were a threat. But as if she were a pleasant distraction from his daily headaches and constant reminders of him betraying his friends.

Kyle lit a joint to relieve the migraine he currently nursed. He let the herbal aroma soothe him—

The sleeping woman groaned and stirred.

Take a step back? Or get closer to subdue her?

The woman's eyes fluttered open and examined her nacre cuffs. When she sat up, she didn't try to cover herself as the sheet fell to her lap. But what did he expect from a woman who walked naked across one planet onto another? Her head tilted this way and that as she puzzled over her restraints. She made no other reactions to indicate panic or aggravation.

And, no. He didn't have a problem keeping his eyes on her face. Beautiful, yes. But Kyle dealt with beautiful Icarean females all day every day. He still conducted his work professionally and prided himself on it.

Might as well get this out of the way. "Sorry for the cuffs. At first, we mistook you for a starved servant borne. We get a lot of those. But we checked, and you have warrior blood. We're running an analysis now to see how many upgrades you're behind. It will help us age you and estimate when you went into hibernation."

The woman stood, and the sheet fell to her feet. The only hair on her entire body cascaded from her head like a curtain to shield her nudity. On long legs, she walked over to him and held the cuffs up between them.

Kyle tensed, uncertain what approach to take. Naked women gliding up to him seemed like a great thing. But nothing made sense to him since April 2006. So, he took a hit on his joint and fiddled with the pendant on his neck.

She smiled. Like a Julia Roberts *Pretty Woman* bright lights beam. Perfect teeth. Perfect lips. Sparkle in her gray eyes. Just beautiful.

And then she broke the cuffs.

"Fuck! Cypher!"

The woman kicked Kyle square in the chest, sending him a few steps back. His wingman and crew busted through the double doors just in time to catch the female open her glorious wings.

Blue.

Every Icarus he ever met possessed black wings. Some, like Tameka, had colored accents. But nothing like solid blue.

The warrior woman narrowed her eyes at him before rocketing through the glass ceiling. Shards rained down on him and Cypher's men. They covered their heads and looked away.

Once settled, Kyle stepped into the middle of the room and took in the mess he made.

Naked. Blue wings. Awoken.

"Son of a bitch."

{Enki}

"Do you think I'll ever get to meet one?"

"John, why in the worlds would you ever want to meet a Primary?" Caedes kept his eyes on the projected screens.

He worked in "the room" day in and day out. What passed for Tritan computers and tablets consumed the surfaces of a weird pocket closet in Tameka's bungalow. The gruff Icarus always debriefed John in this regularly scanned room. No spy tech here. Tumu's detectors made sure of that.

"Well, you know? The honor and all. Meeting a god." John found the stratification of Tritan society fascinating. But the Primaries interested him the most. Only four of them remained since one died in 2006, around the same time the Progeny visited Enki.

While anyone of any race could perform enough good deeds to earn Eminent stature, similar to a Saint, only Gargantuan Tritans held the title of Primary. They represented the last vestiges of the oldest evolution of Tritan. Very rare. Very protected.

Which also made John extremely curious about Tumu because technically—

"Uncle Caeda?" Pax called from the other side of the closed door.

Caedes hopped up and headed over. No sigh of irritation. No grump or grumble over the interruption. Nope. That man's prickly exterior was all show.

"Hey, kiddo, do you need anything?"

"Can I play?" The boy pointed under the largest desk.

No hesitation. "Of course. Your mom will be home soon, and then you can help us cook dinner tonight."

Pax beamed up at the bald Icarus with teeth that shined like the man's head. Then he burrowed under the desk and played caveman. Caedes even let him color cave paintings on the wall.

John pointed to one with hieroglyphs. "Hey, that's really amazing, Pax." Like really amazing. How could he know the story of Seshat? And accurately depict the Egyptian god's life? Is this what educated children looked like when raised in a Dyson's sphere?

Caedes caught John's eye as they both observed the two-year-old. He shook his head. Agendas currently too full. Don't look too hard at the super smart toddler.

Got it.

Glancing back at the screen, John pointed to a new message. "It's from Kyle."

The Icarus stared at it a moment, and then the grumbling started. "It's an update on that woman he found yesterday. He lost her."

"Caedes, she broke her cuffs—"

"I know. I know. No one is capable of that. He also wants some help to research nacre memory loss. Can you and Tameka hit that up in the archives?"

"I'll add it to my to do list." John rubbed the thigh of his bad leg, agitated.

Caedes harrumphed and added, "The sh—stuff keeps piling up, doesn't it?" The soldier glanced briefly at Pax. "So there's no history of the lock's making?"

Code. They spoke in code even around Pax to prevent exposing him to a stressful childhood. No cussing allowed either. Lock meant Gait. "No. Missing or doesn't exist. The temple is the best bet." Temple meant Pantheon.

"We've gone two years without accidentally stumbling onto the route there. This maze will swallow us."

They ran across so many oceans and halls and colonies like this one. A vast emptiness. They kept a dossier of every Tritan they met. So far, they only accounted for fifteen. Not counting the Primaries, which required a special audience request to see them. Why was this colossal sphere so empty and so hard to traverse?

John peered at Pax. "Do you think he'll let her go home?"

"Not a chance. She's only going as a formality. To exhaust all the avenues before she..." Burned everything down.

John knew few certainties in this life. Intelligent life existed outside humans of Earth. Miracles came in the guise of your loved ones.

And there was no way in the Vast Collective that Tameka Phillips would stay a prisoner for long.

{ENKI}

"Permitted."

"Agreed."

"Denied."

Could Abresson look anymore smug as he disagreed with Eminent Lance and Eminent Wiw to grant Tameka an audience with the Primaries? With only four of their deities left in the galaxy, the other Tritans guarded them jealously.

Tumu, a demoted Primary, stood at Tameka's side. She smiled sweetly into the smug Eminent's dark blue face. "I understand the Primaries sequester themselves to preserve the foundation of the species, but Rem vowed to the Progeny that he would help us if we sought it. I am seeking it now."

Eminent Lance nodded solemnly. "I witnessed his promise to you." He glared up at Abresson as he continued, "And I thereby grant you audience with—"

"Primary Rem is unavailable." Abresson cut off Lance with a wave of his scarred hand. "As are Lon and Xhi. Bol is the only available Primary." He shot Tameka a nasty smile.

Wiw winced at the name and shook his head. "You'll find no help with him, Sovereign Ambassador."

The stagnant ocean stretched to the horizon in all directions, surrounding them on the platform. The gray sky reflected Tameka's mood. Not quite a storm, but one building beyond the soft exterior. After living the last two years in Enki, she grew accustomed to the smell of brine and seaweed. But something varied here on this marble platform. Less fish, more... rock. Not sedimentary. No, something... igneous. Fire.

Tumu gently pressed his hand to her bare back, returning her from her senses.

Abresson zeroed in on the gesture with a narrowed gaze. "Oh, I say we let her see Bol. Tameka can clearly tame any Tritan. Even the Primaries." He used "tame" as if it were another four-letter word.

Tameka cut Tumu off to say, "I humbly accept your offer to meet Primary Bol."

The smug Tritan's mouth fell open, and Tumu turned aside. A familiar gesture intended to hide his humor at the expense of the snotty Eminent.

Eminent Lance beamed with pride and tapped his staff once.

Eminent Wiw stood. "Very well, brave Progeny. But heed my advice. Primary Bol's only concern is the preservation of the Tritan species. You face a mighty challenge to draw his attention onto any other matter."

Tumu indicated for Tameka to follow the wizened Tritan to one edge of the platform where a conduit crackled with electricity. The Officer of the Third assured, "I'll wait here for your return."

Abresson rolled his eyes with a humph.

Tameka beamed at the three Eminents. "I look forward to meeting Bol. I hope to meet all the Primaries before I return to Earth with my son."

Tumu stiffened.

Wiw missed the point, or he ignored it graciously because he gestured for her to follow him through the conduit. "They look forward to meeting you, I've no doubt. You are a fine representative to your planet."

Tameka never got used to the Seam between conduits. A grayscale world of a bone-white hall with cathedral ceilings stretching on forever into an ashen snow fall. Sagan said it smelled like Cinder. As the only person able to step foot in it, the blond Progeny would know by now if it was populated. So sad and so empty. Lost and lonely.

Tameka couldn't relate. Never lonely. Even mourning Xelan, she knew a wealth of love and kindness only afforded to the fortunate. Friends. Family. Pax. And never lost. She remembered why they fought. The people they freed. More people waited beyond that. Every step she took brought them closer to saving others, and nothing could stop her.

Not even a potentially unpleasant Primary.

"All right, Sovereign Ambassador. I welcome you to meet Primary Bol. Please proceed." Wiw pointed at the structure beyond the conduit.

Same set up as Primary Rem. White columns climbed high but not as high as the Gargantuan Tritan in the center. Tameka climbed the steps to the glass lift and paused.

In Rem's temple, the black flames of Cascading Light fell from a waterfall into a fountain base. Here, the light splashed around her in dividing channels. It fell from the edge of the platform, and that's when she realized the marble slab hovered in the atmosphere over a continent.

The flitting flames pooled around the marble rather than succumb to the fall. It stretched like the infinite cosmos and danced in its most beautiful abandon. A sea of burning stardust in the sky.

"It's breathtaking."

Wiw smiled kindly down at her. "It's the reason I asked for his assignment. It's the most beautiful view in all of Enki."

He confirmed one of Tameka's suspicions. They assigned Eminents to the Primaries. She figured Lance guarded Rem, and now she knew Wiw looked after Bol. Only Lon and Xhi remained. In his Verse, that bastard who murdered Xelan wrote of a Primary that haunted their family. Abresson must guard him.

Lon or Xhi?

"Thank you, Eminent Wiw." Tameka smiled at him over her shoulder and proceeded to the lift.

The Gargantuan Tritan's mass writhed in the center of his temple. A deep blue, almost purple, his skin concealed black blood vessels. The striations of his muscles faded in color to a pale silver. Almond-shaped eyes blinked, spanning the size of her.

Tumu compressed and decompressed enough around her that she learned Gargantuans look different in either form. Not for the first time, she wished for a lineup to point the evil one out and have it over with.

"You request my audience?" The depth and volume of his voice popped her ears and resonated in her chest.

"Yes, sir. I am the Progeny, Tameka. Sovereign Ambassador of Earth." She smoothed down her white skirt.

"The mother."

Tameka hid her wince. "Yes, sir."

"You do our race a great service raising your son here." He blinked again. "He has much to learn and will benefit from his education in Enki."

Diplomacy. Bureaucracy. Xelan taught them how to fight for the planet, but not how to run it or represent it. Would the father of her son risk a war to remove Pax from this environment? If not yet, then when? As a fighter, she wanted to drain them all dry and evacuate her little family back to Earth. But Elden only knew how many Tritans would rise from the ashes and eliminate her home.

A thought occurred to her. "Primary Bol, Officer of the Third requested my guardianship of Rayne for one week on Cinder. My son has never seen the worlds that bore him. I'd like to take Pax with me and help Tumu. For one week."

The Primary cocked his head to the side. "How does guarding the Weapon serve Enki?"

Tameka bit back her initial response and tried hard to answer this question respectfully. "It is an educational opportunity for my son, which you implied serves Enki. Guarding Rayne is a favor I do the Tritans."

They wanted Pax as the son of a Progeny and an Icarus. Not just any Icarus. Xelan's inventions and capabilities interested Enki. He also spent some time rummaging through some of their most sacred locations for knowledge. Knowledge they feared in his possession, or so Tameka suspected. No doubt they expected Pax to obtain her ability to drain nacre energy. And perhaps, for that reason, they wanted her just as badly.

Tameka found herself, once again, wondering what Rayne redacted in Nox's Verse regarding the Primary and Xelan. She worried they performed experiments on the Icarean Prince that might affect Pax. But Tameka withheld her pregnancy from Rayne before the Progeny King returned to sleep in the Martyr Complex.

What a clusterfuck—

"You may fulfill your duties to the Officer of the Third for one week. Allow one of your men to watch the son."

Drain his nacre. Experience power unknown. Destroy everyone in the way—

"My son stays with me."

The Primary shook his massive head. "Those two worlds are unstable. It is unwise for residents of Enki to travel there. When the son is matured and has completed his education, he is free to travel where his adult heart desires. We agree and insist."

"All the Primaries?"

"Sovereign Ambassador, each Primary will give you the same answer." He blinked.

For a second, her own reflection in his eyes matched the icy resolve inside her. Take a deep breath. Let it out. Think of Xelan. What would he do? Tameka almost smirked at the thought of what Rayne would do in this situation. Not one structure would remain. She'd level the place.

Tameka missed them both.

"I accept and will plan accordingly."

The Primary nodded. "Your wisdom will afford you great opportunity. Peace and givings, the Progeny, Tameka."

The lift took Tameka down where Wiw waited for her. As she stepped off, she stared into the fire that sourced the Probability Matrix. Struck with the sudden urge, she reached out to touch it.

"Tameka."

She stopped and turned. The Eminent never once called her by her name until now.

Grave. His face was so grave. "Please. Don't touch it."

Straightening, Tameka stared at him. She wanted to ask so badly why not, but something in his expression told her the answer wasn't with him. Wasn't his to give. He didn't know. He only knew that she shouldn't.

"Thank you, Eminent Wiw."

The old Tritan's body let out a sigh of relief she couldn't relate. They made quick work of the conduit paths. She memorized them on the second round. Forty-seven conduits separated her apartments from this Primary's temple. But the good news was she didn't notice any guards.

Tumu waited for them alone on the oceanic platform. "How'd it go?"

"I believe Primary Bol liked our Sovereign Ambassador," Wiw smiled between them before nodding to Tameka. "Good luck." Then he disappeared through a conduit on the far side of the platform.

Tameka relaxed her shoulders, but the tension lingered in her jaw and temples. "I can guard Rayne for a week, but they want Caedes or John to watch Pax in Enki."

Tumu smiled sadly at her. "I think Caedes enjoys babysitting duty, at least." He swept an arm to the conduit, asking her to go first. To test how well she memorized the path.

They walked silently back to the ocean colony as she considered her options. They won the war. Why were there still prices to pay for their peace—

Tameka shook her head. Melancholy wasn't her thing. It was okay to take a moment and let things process here and there. But a force motivated her to soldier on. To continue fighting until the foundation finally settled, and the rocking stopped for a time. Heal the cracks. Clear the debris.

Yes, the time for that was coming.

But first the Tritans would soon find out that Tameka was their earthquake. And if they stood in her way to freedom, she would bury them.

FIVE

THESE GLASS HOUSES ARE MADE OF NACRE

{GAIT}

FOUR LYRIKI GUARDS FLANKED PEHTON AS SHE STEPPED FROM THE LIFT INTO INFERNUS. The pound of their uniformed boots shook the floor and echoed off the walls. The lithe females with their pitch-black skin and feathers in varying shades of fire brandished nacre rifles with permission to fire on command. The carbon walls drank the perimeter lights, leaving them in near darkness.

Pehton smirked. Good thing Lyriks upgraded to night vision two million years ago. Fire alarms blared as they searched the first hall. The flashing white and red lights alerted the prisoners of their fate. The nacre shields to their cells remained intact. As the name of the floor implied, they could burn.

This block contained twelve cells. Three on each hall. Six inmates. Once triggered, the floors of their cells opened up and swallowed them into pits. Twelve feet deep.

"Check them," Pehton ordered as she walked over to Korac's cell. She peered in, expecting to find their tallest prisoner mildly irritated in his metal grave.

Nothing. Empty.

"Wait!" She held up a fist with her orange glider flared.

They stopped before rounding the corner, alert.

Pehton refused to panic. She was the Executive Warden. Slick tricks from one prisoner who promised she'd find him out of his cell couldn't intimidate her.

"I'll go first."

"Remember this conversation. No. Additional. Charges."

So earnest. So confident. So god damned irritating.

Pehton turned the corner with a fierceness riding in her wake.

There he was. The Icarean General leaned against a wall beneath a smoke detector in the ceiling. The flare of the cigarette as he took a drag illuminated silver eyes set in a distractingly handsome face. He didn't inhale before blowing a smoke ring at the censor.

The white jeans and black t-shirt complimented the casual hand in one pocket and the flick of the ashes onto the paneled floor. When Korac dared to meet Pehton's eyes, he smirked.

"A cell which could not hold me unless I wanted it to."

Oh, she seethed.

"Now, now, Executive Warden." He dropped the cigarette and smashed it under a pair of black sneakers. "We had an arrangement."

Pehton tossed her head at the guards. "Check the other cells. I'll handle him."

Korac shook a finger. "I'm sure Sagan won't appreciate your choice of words."

She pinched the bridge of her nose and fought not to groan. "I don't know how you got out, or where the hell you got those clothes, but I'm warning you. Don't get on my bad side."

"You're absolutely right. No disrespect meant, Executive Warden." He snatched the cigarette butt from under his shoe and shoved it in the pack. Then he held out his fist, squeezed at the wrists. "I'll be good. For now."

A genuine smile this time. Not a smirk. It suited him.

Right. The cigarette smoke smelled nasty, and Pehton wrinkled her nose as she gripped his bicep. "Let's get you back to your cell."

Korac *let* her take him back. He knew it. She knew it. How did he get out?

As the question clawed at her, Pehton noted the state of his room. Sheets and blanket strewn across the floor. Pillows tossed aside. With raised brows, she turned to him, "I figured you more for the neat type." As soon as Pehton lowered the nacre-resistant shield, Korac glided gracefully inside.

He sat on the bed and shrugged. "You caught me on an off day." The General looked up then, waiting.

The Icarus expected Pehton to ask about his magic trick. But she knew he'd gain satisfaction from withholding the answer from her. No sense in playing a game she couldn't win.

She shook her head at him.

And. He. Pouted.

Rolling her eyes, Pehton turned to the stomping of the wardens' boots. The Lyriki guards assembled down the hall and marched for the lift. "Executive Warden, Infernus block is clear. All six prisoners accounted for."

"Good job, ladies. Let's head out." When she glanced back at Korac's cell, the man sat utterly dejected on the edge of his bed. The faker. "Korac, stay put if you want your breakfast in the morning."

"Executive Warden."

She turned back to him and inclined her head.

"Are you honoring our arrangement?" He looked serious with eyes like snowfall on a winter's eve. Was he developing trust in her?

This situation confused and infuriated her. Under Celindria's command, Pehton neutralized and delivered the First Wave Progeny to hands far worse than the man in that cell. A girl barely in her breath of existence lay in a glass box with her blood siphoned from her every hour on the hour. Meanwhile, Razor made a fortune off Rayne's pain.

Two and a half million years ago, when Pehton fought her way through the ranks before earning Executive Warden status, this wouldn't phase her. Pehton, herself, committed unspeakable acts worthy of the big cell. But after Inanis—

Pehton turned away. "Good night, General Korac."

"See you, tomorrow, Executive Warden."

The Lyrik paused at the lift and wondered what it meant that she actually looked forward to it.

{???}

Number 324 still cried at the crack of the whip. Tears fell before the strike cut deep where it landed. Feet dangled. Arms stretched high in the restraints. Blood cooled where it dripped down their back. Teeth wore grooves into the bit.

Only twelve more to go until they were allowed to rest and the next person took their place. Their screams meant 324's relief. Their pain, 324's peace.

The next strike tore a shriek from 324's throat. Their fingers tingled. Their mind numbed.

Only eleven more to go.

{EARTH}

Underground. No windows in sight. After surviving J.A. Fair High School, Lynn Renee felt right at home. Iona's Arsenal was a proper bunker at least.

The Brethren requested its unique construction from Tumu, invoking Tritan aid. Thirty-two stories underground, the bunker stored all physical and chemical nacre weapons testing on both human and Icarean subjects. Meaning weapons and defenses designed from and targeting nacre technology.

As Chief Engineer, Lynn oversaw the entire arsenal. So, naturally, she started with redecorating in black, gray, and white. The occasional pop of orange, red, and blue appealed to their Icarean guests.

But to her? This interior choice represented home. She lived in Xelan's Iona installations for a year after the Invasion. He'd approve of her choices. And that made her smile.

"You ready?" Smith rounded the corner to the cylindrical lift where she waited. He took one look at her and stopped dead in his tracks. "Chief, I think you're overdoing it this time."

Lynn batted her lashes, heavy with mascara. "Whatever do you mean?" The red leather pants suit was a gift from Lucas. He gave the best gifts. She paired it with a black blouse, letting her matching red lingerie peek through the sheer fabric. Nude lipgloss and modest stilettos completed the ensemble.

"I'll send my condolences to his madre. One look at you, and the sudden shift in blood flow will knock him dead." Smith smiled with his bright white teeth beaming against his tanned skin.

Since the war ended, he stopped rocking the nondescript, covert-ops look. Brown hair slicked back with a nice fade on the sides. He lined his brown eyes with kohl each day. It worked for him. The female Icarean inspectors certainly thought so. Talk about unprofessional…

On that note, Lynn straightened her blazer and smiled. "Thanks, Smith. And you? Looking to hit it off with any of the lab techs?"

He chuckled. "I don't kiss and tell."

"Shocker."

The lift took them above the surface of the surging waters. The Atlantic Ocean roared in a storm. Cape Hope off of Africa produced waves as high as one hundred feet. The clear nacre glass chute traveled two hundred feet above sea level. Frothing waves climbed high, so very high, only to crash beneath them.

"I never grow tired of that." Lynn gazed at the awe-inspiring sight.

When Tempest first suggested building the arsenal under an ocean, Lynn thought the Icarean woman was being facetious. But, naw. She meant it. Impossible to reach. Truly secure. Something Xelan would envision.

Security checks on personnel ran twice a week. Only two hundred people currently operated the arsenal with mandatory on-sight residence. Vacation requests, involving leaving the facility, garnered extensive paperwork and thorough research. Advanced notice didn't cover it. Lynn did everything short of selling her first born for this leave.

Living separately from Pablo killed her. Was this what they fought for? Didn't they deserve a break—

"Chief?"

She turned to find Smith waiting for her at the conduit. Primary Rem made a special visit to Earth to "allow one to open" for them. Suspicious wording. The cylindrical chute leading from the conduit in the sky to the arsenal underground scanned nacres for identity confirmation. If someone entered the lift without a cleared nacre? Incinerated. Dolor, the other Brethren member on their side, did not fuck around.

Lynn rubbed the gold-laced tattoo over her nacre and smiled. "Ready."

They stepped through together and onto a cliff overlooking the Mediterranean Sea. The wind carried salt, spraying it in her mass of black locs.

"Lynn."

She closed her eyes. So much warmth. So much love. Lynn turned to face Pablo. How did a white labcoat and black scrubs look so sexy? She watched too many medical dramas to escape from her parent's survivalist lifestyle. That had to be the cause.

She took in the sight of him for so long that he crooked those utterly full lips into a smirk. Folding her arms, she decided to get the man's ego in check before his head couldn't fit through a conduit.

Rich brown eyes drank her in, repaying the compliment. When they returned to her gaze, the intensity there unfolded her arms involuntarily.

Okay, maybe Lynn could forgive the ego if Pablo kept looking at her like that—

"Ahem."

They both turned to Smith and blinked.

How could she completely forget his existence?

The man laughed in a burst of good humor. "The techs are right. We won't get work done for a week with you two running things. Nobody can pull you apart..." His words faded as he disappeared into Iona Medical's entry, leaving them alone.

Pablo walked to Lynn and reached to twist a loc. Deep and warm, he asked softly, "Do you think we'll make it to the bed this time?"

Lynn grinned and snatched that bottom lip with her own.

They wouldn't make it inside.

Pablo peeled her blazer off as she tore his labcoat from his shoulders. He filled out so much since their first kiss years ago. As he finished the last button on her blouse, he stepped back and gaped appreciatively.

They both grew up since then.

Lynn peeled her belt from her pants and dropped them altogether. Like a gentleman, he held out a hand for her to step out of them.

Pablo had a smile meant only for her. Pure adoration and joy. She pressed her forehead to his and basked in it. He cradled her nape and kissed her, soft and slow. The way she liked.

Meanwhile, the sly doctor used his feet to spread out his labcoat. He even folded Lynn's blazer to use as a pillow. They went to their knees and reconnected to the sound of the surf surging with them.

After the second time, Pablo leaned in and kissed their vows tattooed in a ring over her nacre.

NEVER ENDANGER THIS. NEVER RISK YOURSELF WITHOUT ME. NEVER LEAVE WITHOUT COMING BACK.

Lynn flattened her palm against his matching tattoo as they kissed deeply in their bliss.

As the last Renee, she kept her maiden name. And Dr. Suarez was perfectly fine with that. Her work, of all things, turned out to be their biggest hindrance.

"Too long." He groaned against the chain around her neck. Pablo enjoyed engaging her in conversation while kissing her there.

She hated it. Lynn's eyes rolled back as he teased the sensitive bend. Yup, just hated it.

He chuckled as if he read her mind and knew better. That ego grew the most since high school. "You know we monitor the conduit with visual recordings."

She twined her fingers in his thick black curls. He liked his hair short but kept it a certain length just for this reason. Lynn purred with another kiss on her throat. "Smith is the best wingman ever. I'm sure he temporarily interrupted the monitoring. Or..."

Pablo sat up and smiled at her, waiting with a raised brow.

"He's recording it with every intention of blackmail. We are technically on the clock, Chief Medical Officer."

He repositioned his hips between her parted thighs and purred with carnal intent, "Chief benefits are the best kind."

Mr. Pablo and Mrs. Lynn would find their way inside. Eventually.

{Earth}

The woman's skull caved with a satisfying crack under the pressure of Matt's thumbs. He clenched his jaw tight as he met his target's bright green eyes.

Bleeding. Terrified. Filled with the certainty that death came to claim her. Her feet dangled off the metal in an uncontrollable fit. Reflexes responded to the negative stimulus of pain. The body twitched with the instinct to live.

Matt's jaw clenched tighter as he squeezed the bones harder. Slowly. Countless bodies littered the site, surrounding them. Each killed by his bare hands, give or take a two-by-four. He singlehandedly dismantled the last Cult of Night compound. The bastards even posed as a group dedicated to the reconstruction of post-apocalyptic Columbus, Ohio.

Trash.

Justice Wendy ordered her Collectors to recruit boys aged five to eight. Any older than that and they wouldn't meet her particular tastes.

Matt squeezed harder. The woman's eyes rolled wildly. She choked on the bloody gasps in her throat. They—he. Just him. He always saved the leaders for last. Made them witness the fall of their empire built on a foundation of lies. Witness as he released their victims to safety. Set fire to it all.

But mostly, he wanted them to look into his eyes. See into his soul. See that there was nothing there to pity them.

Blood pooled from Wendy's brunette hairline. Her eyes fluttered shut. Her body fell still.

Still, Matt crushed until his thumbs found gray matter. He threw her body from the tower of the hammerhead crane. Several stories high, the wind threatened to beat him down. It smelled of smoke. What little sun filtered through Earth's Sphere promised to further freckle his otherwise fair skin not covered by his shorts and t-shirt.

His auburn fringe kept blowing in his face. He cut it this way for Lucy. She liked running her fingers through it. She also suggested it made him appear less threatening. Good for infiltration work. Like this job.

The wind captured the fire below, spread it across the site. Matt missed the way it reflected in her dark blue eyes. So empty. So beautiful. More than that, he missed their post-mission ritual. He smirked. She'd love sex on a crane. She'd make him hold her up and take her standing—

The comms device in his back pocket went off. Been a while.

"This is Ginger. Over." Matt didn't mind the appointed codename. Truthfully. He liked the crew running the planet and trusted them to keep the world on the straight and narrow. "Trust" and "like" felt foreign to him. But the Shadow earned it. With that thought, he gripped the pendant on his chain.

Batman's voice came on the line, "Hey, how fast can you join us on the train?"

"I'm in Ohio."

The man's warm, incredulous laughter filled the line. "Why?"

Matt chuckled and shook his head. "Celebrating. CoN is no more."

"Congrats to you and the lady! Hell, congrats to all of us!"

He let the comment about Lucy go. No need to correct the guy. "Yup. That's how we do it. Where's the train?"

"Mexico."

"Fuck." Matt spied his white Chevrolet Malibu parked three blocks away. Little worse for wear given he drove it through the apocalypse. But he wouldn't dream of dumping it—

"Sorry, but I need you right now." Sagan Sterling grabbed his arm. Then peered around and absorbed the destruction. "Somebody had a party. Where's Lucy?" She turned to him with those violet eyes open and full of respect.

"Long story, but she's not here." He glanced at her grip on his arm. "You need me for something?"

Sagan stepped off the crane and onto the train, dragging Matt with her. Xelan paneled the library car in rosewood, polished to a high shine. Books from Earth and Cinder filled every shelf. Cozy and warm.

He fixed a hard stare on the superpowered girl. "Hey, if you don't mind, I'll need my car."

The short, blond woman beamed at him. "I wouldn't part the two of you if it wasn't important." She pat him once on the back hard enough his eyes almost popped out. "Don't worry. I'll get you back to your precious baby."

Chris reached out with a dark hand. "Hey, man."

Matt clasped it and pulled the older veteran in for a quick hug. "What's this all about?"

Batman glanced at the Seamswalker, and she nodded to him. "You go first."

"Okay. We're looking for Ross' sister. Do you remember giving us some info on her before?"

Matt nodded.

"Okay, she's still missing. I was wondering if you got any more information during your run-ins with the other compounds."

"Yea, actually." Both listeners perked up. "I know I told you they moved the girls to Utah. But after I razed that dump to the ground, we learned they evacuated them to Pennsylvania when Nox threatened to detonate the tantamount in that area. But here's the thing ..."

He gripped his chin and paced the car. "There were no females at the Pennsylvania compounds. None. We asked. Some zealot said their masters took them."

"Icari?" Sagan frowned. "Why would they?"

Batman added, "Yea, and where would they take them?"

"We thought maybe those compounds ran a ring of sorts. Humans for alien pets."

Sagan's hand covered her parted lips. "Oh, no. No, they took her off-world."

The Dark Knight put a hand on her shoulder. "Do not give up hope. We can still find her."

She shook her head, looking forlorn. "Do you have any idea how big the Collective is? They don't just call it 'Vast' to compensate."

Chris folded his arms. "I'm not giving up."

Matt stopped pacing. "They gave her a nacre first. That's why they were sent to Utah. It enabled them to ... endure more. Maybe Tumu can help find her."

Sagan nodded, suddenly perked with positivity. "He's coming back soon to change out Rayne's guard. I can ask him to speak to you, Chris."

"He usually visits Jack when he comes to the Two Worlds, so I'll catch him then. Thanks, you two. You've been a big help."

"Glad to hear it." Matt smiled because he knew he should. But the look on Sagan's face brought it down some. "What is it?"

"I need your particular expertise for a mission. It'll be dangerous. And it'll take you off-world—"

"I'll do it." He didn't care what it entailed or where it took him. This was the opportunity he needed.

Finally. Matt could find Lucy.

SIX

MOVE FORWARD; DON'T YOU DARE LOOK BACK

{EARTH}

LUCAS FINISHED THE CALL ON THE COMMS DEVICE. "I'm relieved Sagan lived up to her end of the deal." His rich voice reached through the dark and comforted Andrew.

"Well, you did provide her bad boy toy with six months' worth of clothes." Andrew rolled onto his side, putting his back to the Icarus. He worked all day and into the night without a single ache or pulled muscle. Nacres. "If they gave Bethany a nacre, what does that say about..."

With his back to Lucas, Andrew felt the man shake his head. "Best not to worry until we know for certain."

Of course. Calm. Reasonable. But what other reason would an alien want a human for a pet?

"Are you cold?" Lucas chafed Andrew's arm.

"I first met Bethany when she was seven. She wanted to follow me and Kyle to a Progeny meeting down the street." Andrew choked out the next. "She'd lost a tooth the day before and said that made her big enough to join our secret club."

The Icarus kept up with the comforting touches, but Andrew needed some air. He sat up on the edge of the bed.

"Think about it, Lucas. CoN is gone. Kyle lost a potentially dangerous asset. There's an entire fucking trafficking ring we knew nothing about. We need to call a meeting."

"Progeny or Brethren?"

"Both."

Lucas sucked air through his teeth. Yes, this was a big deal. "We can check with everyone and try. But I don't have to tell you, this poses a major risk."

Andrew nodded. "I know, but…There are too many balls in the air, and we've dropped a few. We need to regroup and consider how to proceed."

"Let's meet with the groups separately, so we don't risk overexposure. Will that work for you?"

The Progeny shrugged. "I guess it'll have to."

"It'll be good for you to get out. I think you're missing our Shadow." The Icarus kissed his shoulder. "That's reasonable."

"No. Lucas." He turned to meet the man's golden gaze. "I think something is coming. Again."

A keening howl pierced the night.

Andrew groaned as Lucas chuckled and said, "It's your turn." As the Progeny dressed, the Icarus added, "Shame that."

It was Andrew's turn to chuckle. "Don't worry. You'll get your remedy when I get back." Running a hand through his brown hair, he left his partner happy and excited for his return.

As he should be.

Blue lights glowed softly along the zeppelin. They illuminated the surrounding area enough that he didn't need to rely on his Icarean-inherited eyesight. He picked his way across the stubby grass to the shack behind their home.

Pisces howled again, announcing his arrival. The massive hellkite climbed to her twelve-foot height. Six limbs, tipped with claws, opened. Andrew spread his arms wide and fell onto the monster. The beast rolled onto her back as if the Progeny's weight was too much for her. She nuzzled Andrew with a crocodile's snout.

Andrew repaid the affection by running his hands across the deep red scales. "What's bothering you? You've been talkative lately."

The hellkite snuffed and garbled a response only pet lovers would understand. The war left the sabers, drakes, and hellkites orphaned and purposeless. But Kyle and Andrew saw potential. No. Not freakish experiments. Just good ol' fashion guardians. Each facility employed one or several for their own protection. Perfectly trained, they obeyed every command.

Except for Pisces. Recently, she wanted to howl through the night. Last night, Lucas said she went into a fit until the Icarus stepped into the light. Then the hellkite was fine.

"You getting lonely, girl?" They used "girl" loosely with an asexual/a-reproductive animal. "You need a friend?"

Hellkite tongue was extra textured to sloth skin off their victims. Rough and wet, like a soggy industrial file. The affectionate licking gave Andrew an excellent view of the creature's forearm-length fangs.

He patted the super ripped belly and stood. "Gonna need a shower after this. You be good. Don't wake the town. They work hard and deserve their sleep." He kissed a horn. "And so do you."

Like a good girl, Pisces stayed in her shack. There was no tether to hold her. The beastie just liked it here. She flew off occasionally, but always returned by nightfall.

Andrew walked back into their home. Through the living space, the kitchen, the library, and into the master suite. Light shone into their room from the bathroom. Steam filled the space as the sound of water reached him. He sniffed. Lavender and chamomile. And beneath that, the overwhelming spice of ginger.

The Progeny stripped in three quick seconds and marched right into that marble bathroom. He stopped dead in the doorway.

Lucas waited for him in the sunken bathtub. And he got started without Andrew. His hand disappeared and reappeared in the water with his efforts. Peering up at the

Progeny with molten gold eyes, he smiled softly. A little breathless, he instructed, "Close the door and get inside."

Andrew happily did as he was told.

{Cinder}

Bones stepped out of the scorched forest and into the modest village. Several servant caste Icari waited outside their rock dwellings. They loaded up packs and carts with all their possessions. So few compared to the humans of Earth. They peered at him with wide, hopeful eyes. A little confused. A little concerned.

But that would change. He asked, confident in their answer, "Everyone ready to go?"

With one firm nod from their local leader, they followed Bones onto the road. He never noticed how much his homeworld smelled of soot and death. The air on Earth was so much fresher. Even in the desert. Life waited for them, there.

Mute. Silenced. The people behind him were so far behind on nacre upgrades that they couldn't even speak.

He shook his head. It was criminal. But even though they were several thousand in number, they probably ate less than one human. This level of nacre subdued their needs. Prevented starvation. But also prevented intellectual progression and reproduction. That double-edged sword was sharp.

They would fix it. The Progeny would make it right.

After hours of trekking the dusty road, they made it to the main thoroughfare where his team waited. He turned back to the villagers, "Follow them to the conduit. You'll be safe."

The leader, a wizened Icarus, gripped Bones' shoulder. His eyes filled with the words he couldn't speak.

Returning the gratitude with a gentle pat, Bones encouraged him to take his people to paradise.

His comms device chirped, prompting him to fly to a nearby mountaintop for privacy. Into it, he said, "Go ahead."

Story Taker ran a tight ship overseeing the migration. The news about the amnesia victim hit the crew pretty hard. Breaking nacre glass? Unheard of. The Progeny memory reader prioritized this blunder with some urgency. Possibly because of rumors of his earlier transgressions against the Shadow.

Kyle asked every hour now, "Any sign of her?"

Bones sighed. "No. I don't believe she'd return to Cinder."

After a long exhale, the other man agreed, "She came to Earth for a reason. I'm just not sure what."

The Icarus gazed across the horizon toward Nox's castle. "Does the King sleep peacefully?"

"Yea, I'm watching her with Para."

Bones opened his wings. "I'll be there within an hour. We can think tank a solution together."

"Thanks, man."

Not only did the Progeny trust Bones, they made him an official member of the Shadow. A family of sorts. After losing his brother-in-arms during the war, belonging somewhere mattered to Bones. And these people overwhelmed him with how much they cared for each other. For him.

That's why they wore these chains around their necks. Bound by family.

The uneventful flight to the castle ended sooner than expected as Bones plummeted into the perfectly square rock tower. Inside the black castle, their King slept in a pit. Surrounded by a lake. In a glass coffin filled with her own blood.

"Hey, thanks for stopping by." Story Taker approached with a clasp of their hands and a tap of their shoulders.

Bones avoided the Martyr Complex. He regarded the King's temperament, "The weather's been nice lately."

Kyle looked over at Rayne and took a hit on his blunt before nodding his agreement. "She's smiling a lot, too. She's happy."

"Hi, Bones." Para smiled from the ramp with an arm full of snacks. She recently colored her short hair a bright blue. The shortest Valkyrie at five foot nine inches, she could easily wipe the floor with him. "Come to join us for guard duty?"

The male Icarus rushed to help her carry the goods.

With her load relieved, she smiled. "Cold. Thanks."

Kyle's rich laughter snapped them both around. "It's 'cool.' Just when I think you've got the slang thing down, you slip up. And it. Is. Amazing." He snatched a snack sized bag of Cheetos as she walked by and offered, "It's part of your charm."

Bones unloaded and organized the food as Para dumped them on the counter that lined one corner of the pit. It was a small kitchen. There were couches and palettes. A major stereo system. A huge Enki projector screen along one wall. These amenities provided some comfort for the grim task.

Shaking her head, Para shared, "I've got more than plenty charm. You want some, Bones? I can't keep the Earth boys off of me." She finished the statement with her hands on full hips, barely covered in a worn leather skirt.

Bones barked out a laugh. How could this woman hope to avoid male attention? "No, thank you. My hands are full."

"What do you mean 'Earth boys?' I never did anything to you," Kyle scoffed.

Para gestured at the Progeny. "Exactly. That's why I'm here. I'm completely safe with you. You are as harmless as they come."

Kyle frowned as if he calculated how much Para meant for that compliment to backhand him.

Bones chuckled into his work of sorting the snacks into the fridge and pantry. The two went at it for another fifteen minutes. When the space suddenly fell quiet, he turned.

Both Para and Story Taker stared at the Martyr Complex as if startled by it. Bones hated his own cowardice for not wanting to investigate. Some part of him couldn't stand that Rayne—the woman that ended Nox's tyranny—spent her days submerged in her own blood. Aware.

"Is everything all right?" His voice cut through the silence, startling both the Valkyrie and the Progeny.

They heaved a terrified gulp of air, and Para gave a little laugh. "Sometimes it's spooky down here."

Kyle didn't laugh. Green eyes hard, jaw set, and shoulders straight, he confessed, "Every mistake I make hurts Rayne. I have to find that woman. I can't let someone strong enough to break nacre cuffs go untracked without learning her intentions."

Bones nodded. "We'll find her." He turned to Para. "Were any of the Valkyrie strong enough to do that?"

Para shook her head and shoved a hand in her hair. Her "thinking" gesture. "She doesn't sound like any Icarus I've ever met. Or even heard about."

"Is there a trap we can set? Guys, I don't know enough about Icari for baiting them out." Kyle went over to the counter and rolled another one. He never stopped. Everyone acclimated to the habit after Volcano Day.

"Warrior Icari need blood, sex, and food," Bones started.

Using the joint, Kyle toasted to him approvingly.

Para continued, "Lots of it. You gave her blood. The kind that would satisfy her for a few weeks at least. Sex and food is next."

"She will *not* have a problem finding the former. The woman's stacked and not wearing any clothes."

Para glared at Kyle with her arms folded and an eyebrow raised.

He spread his hands, defensively. "What?! I was a gentleman. But it was kinda hard not to notice." He lowered his hands and grew serious. Frowning and shaking his head, he explained, "I kept getting this trace off of her memory, but it made no sense. It was the only word I picked up clearly."

Bones glanced at Para, and they exchanged a look before simultaneously asking, "What was it?"

"Silence."

{Earth}

A massive crowd gathered in El Paso, Texas to air their concerns during post-war reconstruction. People of all ethnicities and ages rushed the train. Karter grinned. Jack beamed. And Chris tried not to panic.

This was tight. He didn't like it. Too many opportunities to rush in and take Jack. That's right. Take. The Brethren was concerned the King Regent made a target for abduction and control. To lure Rayne out.

These visits unnerved Chris. He went to the door and looked at Karter. She nodded to him from behind Jack and Ross. He trusted the Valkyrie at his six. He spoke into his earpiece, "Ready, Colton?"

"Ready, Batman."

The door opened, and people shouted. So many things. Some of them nice. Thanking Jack as he rushed out with his entourage surrounding him to the local leadership's facility. In secrecy, they informed only the "mayor" or whatever he called himself of their arrival. But apparently he took it upon himself to share. He might have a beat down coming to him.

Some shouts weren't so nice and doubly unnerved Chris. "King Jack! Sir? What will you do about the criminals consuming nacres?"

Chris' head snapped around, searching for the source.

"The Tritans will kill us for idiots eating them, right?"

Batman shook his head and shouted, "Don't answer that," at the same time Karter did.

She winked at him amid this mess. Beyond her beautiful face, he spotted the culprits. About four people with signs. They varied in verbiage but ultimately they pitted "Nacre Humans v Natural Humans." Whatever the fuck that meant.

As three humans imbued with nacres, Chris gripped Jack and Ross, accelerating the "get the fuck out of here-ness" of the situation. Karter caught on and before long they arrived at a courthouse with its columns blown to bits. The roof begged to cave in. And all the windows lost their glass.

Nope. Didn't like it. Too exposed.

Colton, another nacre imbued, melanin-endowed human, appeared at his side. The vehicular-genius knew how to move through a crowd. He nodded to the shitty building and said, "We'll do what we can to provide cover, but the team doesn't like it."

Karter led Jack and Ross inside, shouting over her shoulder, "What's to like?"

Local security finally wrangled the public back from the entrance, allowing Chris and Colton to pop inside and sweep the place. Ugly green carpet like billiard cloth. Chartreuse cushions lined the benches like pews. To add insult to design injury, someone approved paneling the entire room in a pale oak that clashed with the dark walnut furniture.

Oh, and there wasn't any electricity.

"Welcome King Jack!" The "mayor" stood at the judge's bench in the back. He sounded appropriately jovial for the occasion. "El Paso is eager to speak with you."

Flanked by Karter and Chris, the teenage world leader approached the stranger. Jack smiled generously and spoke with an eloquence beyond his years, "Thank you for the warm welcome. I appreciate the preliminary introduction to El Paso's concerns regarding reconstruction and Tritan compliance. Even if we weren't expecting an audience immediately."

Smart kid. His hazel eyes even scanned the room for vantage points and exits. Survival instincts switched to "on." Almost like he fought in an interplanetary war or something.

Karter whispered in Batman's ear, "You're grumbling."

Oops.

Ross covered her snicker with a cough.

"The people are fortunate to meet their King." The "mayor" stepped down and stood as close to Jack as the Shadow guard allowed. Even Ross stepped closer, gripping the chain around her neck. Hopefully, now wasn't the time for that.

Short, the man had to look up at the teenage boy. "We listen every Tuesday and Saturday for Story Circle. Brilliant strategy to include entries and contributions from all over the globe. It seems we are well on our way to re-establishing society."

Jack beamed at him. "What can we do for you here? We may not meet every demand, but we will work to the best of our resources. Nothing will stop us from integrating the Icari and humans. From forming a stronger Earth. To obtain the future we fought for."

The leader—Denton, that was his name—searched Jack's face with sharp brown eyes. What was he looking for? Sincerity? The kid had that in spades. Capability? He was growing into it. Whatever he wanted, he found because the man suddenly broke into a thousand watt grin that popped off his brown skin.

He reached out a hand. Jack took it. And with a shake they opened a friendly dialog that gradually assuaged the tension in the ruined space. Ross visibly dropped her shoulders. Karter never truly relaxed, but her jaw unclenched. Glancing up at the busted rafters, Colton's sniper gave a thumbs up. The man's boss muttered discretely into his earpiece.

Good. This was good.

Several hours passed during which selected representatives entered and shared their concerns. Food, supplies, technology, communication, etc. The Tritans promised a printing tech that would address most of these issues.

The Brethren currently worked with the Dwarves of Pil to solve the worldwide communication drought. Those amazing engineers constructed a quantum communication facility powered by the Hoover Dam. They expected to go online within the year.

The final issue chilled Chris to his bones. A tall woman approached. He recognized her as one of those sign holders. She swept her ass-length mousy brown hair over one shoulder before speaking, "King Jack. First, I'd like to thank you . . ."

Chris tuned out the repetitive platitudes—and there were many—until she reached the point.

" . . . And that's why we're concerned with the overwhelming amount of people who illegally harvest and ingest nacres. Will the Tritans not see this as a violation of our treatise and retaliate?"

When she blinked, one blue eye closed and then the other. It made the hackles raise on the back of Chris' neck with immediate distrust. Nope. Not good.

He whispered into Jack's ear, "This is not an issue we were prepared to discuss."

Jack nodded and leaned to Karter. "Is there any threat?"

Karter glanced from the possibly inbred woman back to the King regent. "I wish I had a solid answer. The Tritans are unpredictable, as you read in the anonymous Verse."

Again, Jack nodded as if he could shake his brain hard enough for the right thing to say. He turned back to the woman, who smiled crookedly. He answered with more confidence than Chris expected, "I meet with The Tritan Officer monitoring our planet within a few days. I can pass your concerns along and communicate an answer during an address in one week."

The speaker's eyes didn't reflect any light, but somehow conveyed glee. "So, the law stands, and we can begin arrests—"

"—Until then," Jack interrupted her just in time, "We will not take action against those humans in possession of a nacre. We have every reason to believe the Tritans will grant us that technology soon. At least this way, we have volunteers to study the effects on human biology."

He glanced back at Chris, who cut at his throat with one hand. Time to wrap this shit up.

"That will be the last question for this visit. I hope to return before too long. Your community here is thriving.

You're doing monumental work, and I'm proud to count myself among survivors such as yourselves."

Mayor Denton stood and addressed the locals.

Jack stepped back, looking exhausted, almost as gray as an Icarus. Despite that, he did outstanding work.

Karter clasped the kid's slumped shoulder and muttered reassurances. Ross drifted into space as one does when missing part of their world.

"The best time would be now," Colton announced over their earpieces.

Right. They slipped out the back, attracting one or two stragglers. Chris called into the mic, "We need a better method for the surprise drop-ins. They haven't been much of a 'surprise' lately."

Colton responded, "Agreed."

"We'll nap first, then get to it." Karter sounded genuinely concerned. "I'm two seconds from picking Jack up and carrying him back."

Codename Robin groaned, "I'm fine." And he almost made it to the train without fumbling. "Why am I so tired?"

Colton, badass train conductor, launched without hesitation.

Ross took Jack's hand, making him duck his eyes. The girl sat him in a booth in the dining car. "If I didn't know any better, I'd say you were sick." She pressed the back of her hand to his forehead and recoiled. "I think…I think he's running a fever."

"With a nacre?" Karter looked aghast as she checked. She whirled to Chris with a confirmation of horror.

Well, shit.

{Enki}

John waited in the shrine leading to Earth. The seamless glass encasing the conduit granted visitors an unhindered view to admire. And he did. He only wished for Progeny or Icarean eyesight to grasp the full scale of the Dyson's Sphere.

Enki. A world of mysteries.

"...one week, Tumu. You think that's fair? And without my son. I haven't been without him a single night since he was born." Tameka glowered at the thirteen-foot tall Tritan.

Tumu absorbed her fury with boundless patience. Almost as if he understood completely. Before the man responded, one of John's bags slipped from his hand. Papers spilled and scattered at their feet.

"Shit. Sorry." He scrambled to retrieve them and reorganize the chaos.

Tumu and Tameka almost bumped heads trying to help. In that ridiculous moment, they looked up at each other. The Tritan's large voids blinked at her almond-shaped green eyes. And for the first time in two years, they smiled at each other.

The Progeny woman went through a lot since the war. The Shadow grieved with her. Losing Xelan hurt them all, but it wrecked Tameka's entire world. She never let it show. No, not that warrior. But everyone saw it when she looked at Pax a certain way. Heart-wrenching. And even Tritans had hearts... Somewhere, anyway. They never found a record of their anatomy.

They stepped through the conduit and into the freezing Siberian tundra. No need to shiver. Nacres regulated body temperature. Even in this extreme frost, they only felt a slight chill.

Tameka pointed southwest. "The airstrip's a quarter mile that way."

"I received an urgent message from Karter," Tumu said as he frowned at his comms device. "I need to see them as soon as we reach Egypt. Are you good on Cinder?"

"Is everything all right?" Tameka asked automatically before startling. "You can leave me unchaperoned?"

The Tritan smiled down at her. "Everything will be fine. And not officially. But we're on my planet now. The only authority higher here than myself is Primary Rem. And he's 'unavailable.'"

There's the beam. Her freckles even sparkled as she rallied, "Well, all right. Let's get this show on the road."

John spent the flight to Egypt organizing his presentation for The Brethren and the honest-to-goodness truth he prepped for the Shadow's briefing. The Brethren meant well, but the Shadow defended the planet. Their intel took priority.

Tameka turned in her seat and rested her chin on the back. "Are you ready for this?"

John blew the air out of his cheeks and answered honestly, "Not really. And I wish I could stay on Earth."

Her eyebrows shot up.

"I can't stand being in that place, but I know it's important. I just don't know why I'm being held captive—"

"Honorary resident," Tumu corrected.

"—there, too. I'm nobody." John patted his bum leg for emphasis. "I'm not even a complete human."

Tameka's eyes softened along with her voice, "John, why didn't you take up the Tritans on their offer to restore your leg?"

He glanced away sharply. "They made me sound like a waste without it. But I fought a war with my leg like this. With a nacre, I don't even feel the pain or fatigue most of the time. I..." Shaking his head, he looked down. "I am capable." When he looked back up, his eyes stung with determination, "And I'll show them."

The Progeny girl's eyes glittered. The smile that spread across her lips illuminated the fuselage. "Yea, you will. And I think they suspect that. Hence, the shared prisoner status." She wagged a finger between the two of them.

"Heh."

They both turned to Tumu, who stared out his window. Tameka asked, "You got something to add?"

The Tritan twisted all the way around in his chair. He looked uncomfortable compressed to only seven feet of his colossal height. John saw it in little winces, as the brown compression suit twisted with him.

"Enki historically underestimates its opponents. Those they manipulate and try to control. The Eminents learned their lesson, and now they want to lock down your little tribe." The Tritan reclined his seat to lay flat. He spread across it, languidly.

Tameka and John shared a glance. Both looked down at the chains around their necks.

Casually, Tumu added, "Still, I've never met a group quite like yours. You pose a threat with your love for one another. And Enki has never seen the likes of that before." He sighed heavily. "I don't wish ill on my world. Or yours. But only one will survive the impending confrontation. I've no doubt."

John swallowed hard against the foreboding knot in his throat.

Tameka stood and stared the Tritan down. "They invite confrontation on themselves. Imprisoning innocent people. Micromanaging this galaxy. Harboring someone like Celindria." With each offense, she took a step closer to the ancient alien. "Tumu, tell me you understand?"

The blue man sat up in his seat and considered her.

The jet formerly belonged to the Icarean army. Korac decorated it in black everything. It sucked the light into an abyssal void. In the vacant darkness, the silence that stretched between the Tritan and the Progeny opened a gulfing breach. The vacuum waited to see which one would jump in first.

The Tritan's impossibly deep voice erupted so suddenly that it popped John's ears, "I understand, Sovereign Ambassador." The simple response hid some deeper emotion Tumu chose not to convey. He turned his back on them and righted his seat.

Tameka slumped back in her chair with frustration obvious in her folded arms and clenched jaw. She stared hard out the window.

John wanted for one aspect of his life to be uncomplicated. Just one. No confusion. No worries. Was that asking too much? As he turned back to the duplicitous presentations, and spied the topic he didn't want to cover, he supposed that it was in fact asking too much.

SEVEN

TELL ME AGAIN OF THE STARS

{CINDER}

TAMEKA DID NOT MISS THIS PLACE. The bloated star in the sky. The black rock of the castle. And the lonely girl trapped in the lake's center at the bottom of a desolate pit.

Elden, she couldn't bear to look at the Martyr Complex.

Two years. She lived in Enki for two years following the end of the war. And although the clinical smell of the interiors and the salty scent of the exterior offered little of home, the smell of Cinder took her straight to Hell.

The stink of ash only a reminder of the days following that hopeless encounter in Umbra's Spire. The days Tameka waited to hear the news that Xelan died, and Nox captured Rayne.

The Progeny woman opened the eyes she shut the moment she stepped into the pit. Kyle stood at the bottom, accompanied by Para and Bones. He looked happy, but always a sadness lingered. As it should for fifty years.

The brown-haired man looked at her then and smiled hesitantly. He waved a hand holding a joint and called out, "Hey, thanks for doing this."

"I'm doing this for Rayne." Tameka walked down the ramp. She kept her gaze from the center of the room. "You need to find that woman you lost."

Bones and Para shifted uncomfortably, averting their eyes.

Kyle winced. "I know. Okay. I know I fucked up again. I'll find her."

Tameka looked him over. The faint dark circles under his eyes implied he wasn't resting enough. Even for the nacre. Worry drew his brows tighter than usual. Softening, she offered, "I know you will. I trust you to do that much."

"I'll keep you informed." He headed out. "Bones. Para. I'll see you on Earth."

Tameka bit the inside of her cheek. She wasn't too hard on him, but... applying constant pressure on someone couldn't be good for their morale. If morale went bad, so did the job. And Kyle's job was important.

"He'll be fine," Bones offered, snapping Tameka out of it. She reached out and pulled him into a hug as he asked, "How is the glass prison?"

Tameka shook her head and drew Para into the hug. "Beautiful. And terrifying."

Para pulled back with a resolute expression. "We're ready when you need us."

"Thanks, guys," she muttered. Something about the Complex drew her gaze. She stared, transfixed, as if expecting Rayne to get out.

"Tameka."

She startled and turned toward the two Icari. Shaky, she said, "I'm so sorry. I—"

"That's the second time she's done it, today," Para confessed, meaning Rayne.

Bones opened his wings, looking grateful to leave the space. "Go see the King. I think she misses you, as do we all." He smiled once more before flying out.

Para blew a kiss before following him.

Alone, Tameka walked over to the stereo. She selected a mix tape with plenty of Missy Elliot before heading to the lake. There, a glass skid appeared. Like in Enki. She allowed it to take her to the center where the Complex waited.

A mighty monument of solitude.

Stupid fucking martyrs.

"Why did you go?" Quiet. Soft. Sad.

No response.

"I know some choices were taken from you. I know, Rayne. The Weapon. The Tribunal. But...I know you."

She paced around the glass coffin, gazing into the blood. Her friend's serene face lay unresponsive in the glowing red.

"You needed to leave. To avoid everything and everyone. Without...without..."

The knife twisted in Tameka's heart.

Tiny, small, she said, "He loved you so much. He wouldn't want you to hide, Rayne. To volunteer yourself for this—"

Tameka scrubbed away the tears with the heels of her palms. She swallowed once, twice, before confessing, "I know you wanted this. To hide. So, I didn't tell you then, but I'm telling you now...I have a son with Xelan. His name is Pax." In a tearful half-laugh, she added, "You're an auntie."

For a long while, Tameka sat on the island in the lake and told her best friend everything about her son. His intelligence, his inquisitiveness, his kindness. His unluckiness with fish. All of it.

And Rayne listened to every word. Tameka wasn't sure at first. But only moments into the talk, she peered into the casket and found the woman glowing. Not just smiling. No, Rayne glowed with a warm light.

"He's our peace. We'll make it out of this mess, and his future will be waiting. And this is how..."

{CINDER}

Silence knew little. Little of herself and little of the world. She only knew this was not the world she expected. When she went to sleep so long ago, the world she knew surged in war.

This world poised on the brink, but not the same as Cinder of old. No. These people were organized. They worked together. Funny, they rarely bothered to look up.

Silence hovered in the sky for days, observing the churning parade of Icari migrating from Cinder to Earth. To paradise, they called it. The remnants of Umbra's tyranny rained grief the color of sin down on her people. Even his son fell to corruption in the end.

The forgotten woman struggled with sorrows of her own. She stared at her gray arms. The muscle deeply striated as if she maintained her form, even in her sleep. A cobalt streak pulsed under her skin.

And such power.

What was Silence made for? Why was she awoken? And by whom?

Among the cacophony, the fortress stood sentinel to the bridge between worlds. It bore the testimony of millennia in asylum like a silent witness. They since repaired the damage she caused during her exit. The male with the intoxicating blood occasionally traveled from it through the conduit. Never without an entourage.

Curly brunette hair cut short. Athletic build. Average human height. His eyes...A perfect green. They held more warmth than Silence remembered in her entire—

She shook her head.

He wore ridiculous clothes. Bright, colorful patterns. Often oversized, swallowing him. Hiding him. And in the pants' many pockets, she imagined he stowed dozens of those hand-rolled, sweet herbal inhalants. In his appearances on the balustrade and in his journeys to Cinder, he always walked with one in his hands. At his lips.

She liked his smile.

Silence clenched her fists until blood dripped from her palms. Work awaited her. She wasn't sure what work exactly, but an assignment of some import.

An azure pulse surged across her entire body.

Yes, important work. She needed her mission made clear. The male mentioned they used her blood to investigate her lineage. Perhaps his resources held the key to unlocking her memory. Then she could rediscover her mission.

Music erupted from the thoroughfare. Flags and signs erected in Icarean, Egyptian, and English. They demarcated game stands, entertaining contraptions called "rides," and food stations. Metal cylinders opened and even all the way up here, she smelled smoked meats and grilled vegetables.

Silence's many appetites hungered. The male fulfilled the most immediate one most sufficiently. But the others—

Her empty well of a stomach blared like the horns of Umbra's Spire. It twisted and cramped. Her acute focus on the male's features belonged to the remaining appetite. If she didn't see herself serviced soon, she would desire to the point of distraction.

Silence shuddered, ruffling her feathers. No one wanted that.

The lone woman lingered in the air another hour until sunset, and the dizzying display of lights tempted her into joining. Only one problem. She required clothes to blend into the crowd. And her hair...it was far too long. The blue might attract unwanted attention.

So, Silence acquired camouflage to blend in.

Before long, she walked amid the strobing lights, sounds, and smells. Sweat, food, grease, and sand. People worked the stands and offered wares for free. The meat tasted salty, and spices lingered on her tongue. A frozen cream on a sweetened chalice shivered and delighted her. The games involved throwing many things on targets through irritating obstacles. The rides, although intriguing, confined their participants. She refused them.

At every stand Silence attended, the men and women stationed at them observed her with lingering gazes and pleasant smiles. Their fingers brushed hers during exchanges. One volunteered the time of his evening retirement from his duties.

Yes, she would fulfill all her cravings this night.

All finished at the last stand, she turned to take in the thoroughfare and stopped smiling. Empty. Everyone disappeared.

Well, not exactly everyone.

The male stood at the other end. Alone.

Silence knew better. He never went unattended. He was important.

She wondered what gave her away. The clothes she took off the human covered her. Sure, the top was too short, stopping at her ribs. The pants at her knees. Maybe the hair? She cut it with the guard's knife without a mirror. Then wrapped it in a flag.

"Melissa has worked for me since the war ended. She's one of the nicest people I've ever met. You choked her unconscious and left her naked in the dunes." His voice grew colder the longer he spoke.

A gust blew through the festival, stealing the flag from her hair. The dark strands fell jagged and uneven past her shoulders, exposing the blue stripe.

He looked away then. Harshly, he cursed. "We don't mean you any harm. We're here to help." The male raised his eyes to hers with an arresting sincerity. "Please, stop giving us reasons to treat you like a threat. I saw your memory. You're aimless and alone. Let us help."

Silence sensed his garrison hidden in the stands. Twelve. Not her memory, but instinct declared that they underestimated her. The azure pulse traveled across her skin, drawing a gasp from him.

His green eyes searched her, fascinated, but harmless. The male's offer felt genuine. She saw it in his loose, empty hands and the tightness of his features. Unarmed. Almost desperate.

When she escaped the fortress, Silence wronged him. He suffered from her exit. She needed him. And the Icarean woman thought of only one way to make it right.

Silence stripped out of her clothes, ignoring his shock and averted gaze. Humans were so modest. With the articles folded, she glided over to him. She tried to present as non-threatening.

He watched her come to him, perplexed, but a little intrigued. When Silence held the clothes out to him, the male brushed her hands as he took them.

"I apologize for the wrong I committed against your guard." Her speech required some practice. The words took time to form, and her voice came out hoarse. She almost didn't recognize it.

"Thank you." He tucked the clothes under his arm and signaled for his garrison. The male focused with some difficulty on her gaze. In a pleasant tenor, he asked, "Will you come with us? I want to help you. My name is Kyle, by the way. But everyone calls me Story Taker. You don't have to. Obviously. But—" He cut himself off as if he realized he was rambling.

She smiled, drawing his gaze to her lips. "Kyle."

He glanced momentarily to the side and gave a single chuckle. "Yea, that's me. Do you remember your name?"

Around them, people dismantled the festival. The armed soldiers maintained what they considered a decent proximity. Amateurs. Her body knew better.

With that in mind, she gave him the only information she knew for certain, "I am Silence."

Kyle's eyes widened, and he caught the gazes of a hazel-eyed man and an Icarean warrior nearby. The three communicated without words before Story Taker returned his attention to her.

Awkwardly stretching his arm behind his head and clearing his throat, Kyle asked, "So, Silence... do you go everywhere naked?"

{EARTH}

"I've seen nothing like this," Karter repeated.

With every recitation, Chris' concern for Jack amplified. Exponentially. "You okay, kid?"

Jack lay in a pool of his own sweat, wearing only gym shorts and his chain. They took him to the infirmary, the last car before the freights holding gold and iron for the foundry. The young man swallowed hard before shaking his head.

"Okay, fresh ones." Ross set down rags and a bowl filled with cool water.

"Thanks." Batman soaked one and patted the kids' feverish noggin. "What's the thermometer say this time?"

Karter retrieved it from his ear. "I'm not sure. Is 104.5 high for a human?"

Ross dropped the discarded bowl with her eyes wider than saucers.

Jack's teeth nattered together, as if he were freezing.

Chris cursed. "How much longer for Tumu?"

"Before he reaches us? An hour, at least." Karter gazed down at Jack's flushed body and winced. "Too long, I think."

"Okay. This is what we'll do. Gather everything we need and take it to car fourteen."

Karter and Ross exchanged an uncomfortable look.

It wasn't like the Icarus' ghost haunted the place or anything. Chris assured, "I know. I know. But it's the only one with a bathtub big enough. Now go."

An hour later, Batman carried Robin into what the Shadow formerly called the "Love Nest." Xelan and Tameka's old cabin. The black tile with white grout climbed a half-wall and sank into a substantial tub. The girls filled it with ice water.

Karter stood at the end, twisting her chain. Ready for her part. "Ross, can you please grab us some more towels? For a few minutes."

Ross hesitated before nodding and following her orders.

"Robin." Chris tried to get the kid to focus on him. "This won't feel pleasant, but trust me. You need it."

He lowered Jack into the tub. The young man screamed a ragged shriek. Karter took his legs, and Chris got his arms.

She called over the sound of his cries, "It's almost as if his nacre stopped working. He's not strong enough."

Batman grit his teeth, but not because Jack fought too hard. But because somehow they were in this situation at all. That Jack was in this situation and in pain. Chris also suspected—

"Oh, my god. Will he be okay?" Ross returned and dropped the towels on the counter. "Can I help?" She put her face in Jack's line of sight. "Jack, it's okay. They're helping you."

The kid immediately relaxed. Hazel eyes fixed on her face, and his body settled into the ice. Sure, his lips were blue, but he didn't fight anymore.

Chris damned near let go and walked out of the room. Seriously? Years of watching him. Almost taking bullets for him. Building a friendship. Earning trust. Did any of that calm him down? No. But one look at this girl, and the boy melted into a puddle.

Even Karter rolled her eyes at the end of the tub. That's right, kid. Everyone knew. Oh, and he should fear when Ross wasn't in the room. Because Chris would never let him hear the end of it—

Colton applied the train's brakes. On the walkie, he confirmed, "Batman, this is Colton. Tumu is at the rendezvous, as promised. Over and Out."

Chris started, "Ross, will you—"

"No, I got him. Let her stay." Karter shot him a wink before heading out.

Ross continued whispering soothing phrases to Jack, who continued lying in a freezing tub. Chris rubbed the tension out of his neck and grazed the chain there. Was it time?

"Been a while since I was in this cabin," Tumu confessed as he ducked to enter. He compressed down to seven feet of his normal height. It made for an uncomfortable fit, judging by the tightness around Tumu's eyes and mouth.

"Thanks for coming. He's in here." Chris looked back to the kid and tried for reassuring, "Hey. Tumu's here. Let him look at ya."

Jack faintly nodded, but when Ross made to move, terror filled his eyes.

"Don't go, Ross," Chris encouraged. "You're good company."

The young woman smiled weakly and turned back to Jack. She scooted to make room for Tumu, but kept her face in frame for the kid.

The blue alien searched Jack with almond-shaped voids. A film blinked over those black disks. "He's only been like this a few hours? Since the El Paso visit?"

"That's right." Karter leaned her side against the wall and folded her arms. "Have you seen anything like it, Tritan?"

He smiled gently at her. "I've seen many things." In his ancient voice, the words sounded wrong and old. He pointed at Jack's sternum. "The nacre he shouldn't have is deactivated. Afterward, something or someone introduced him to a pretty nasty infection."

Karter's eyes widened at Tumu's revelation.

Chris figuratively cut at his neck with both hands. "Wait a minute. No one touched his nacre. How could—"

"There are a handful of ways to disable a nacre," Tumu explained. "This was terribly deliberate."

Batman cursed like a Bat-sailor.

Ross winced slightly as he carried on, spurning him to rein it in. She asked, "Is there anything we can do to help him?"

"Lay the towels out, 'other human with a nacre that shouldn't have one,'" Tumu observed.

Ross ducked her eyes, but did as he asked. Once she left his field of vision, Jack squirmed in the ice bath. Tumu lifted him out of it and onto the towel pallet.

The young woman sat on the floor over his face, smiling. Jack calmed with the mild trace of a shiver. Karter also connected her butt to the tiles close by. Chris stood over Tumu, who knelt over the kid.

"So, what's the treatment, Officer?" Batman fought to keep the stress out of his voice.

"It's always the blood."

Karter nodded.

But Ross had the right idea with, "Huh?"

Tumu nodded to Chris' thigh sheath. "Do you mind?"

Once he handed the knife to the Tritan, the man cut his wrist and put the black blood to Jack's lips. As soon as he opened the vein, the smell of coconuts and pineapples filled the room. Like Juicy Fruit gum.

Jack shook his head a bit.

To which Tumu assured, "It will jump-start your nacre like a car battery and heal the infection. It's only good for a few minutes."

"Wait, would any of our blood work?" Chris would feel pretty fucking stupid if that were the case.

Fortunately, Tumu shook his head. "No. Gargantuan Tritan nacres exist on their own circuit of upgrades, kept separate from other nacres."

"Oh, so his nacre won't be able to retain your nanites because the OS can't apply it the same," Chris observed.

The Tritan turned all the way around to look up at him. "Are you sure your relationship isn't open?"

Karter laughed as Jack's eyes widened with a little snicker from Ross.

Unoffended, Batman patted the Officer on the back. "Only if you were Wesley Snipes. And only if you dressed as *Blade*."

The Tritan's sudden burst of laughter was warm and genuine. It sounded underutilized. He pulled his wrist from Jack's mouth.

The young man already looked better. His coloring went from scalding red to pasty white kid. Those eyes of his focused properly, even if they only focused on Ross.

She announced, "His fever feels gone."

Karter fell back on the tiles in relief. "Thank. Elden."

"I certainly wasn't looking forward to Rayne skinning me alive."

At Chris' confession, the Tritan flinched. He pressed, "We need to find who did it. And how. For the unforeseen future, Jack cannot interact with people outside of Story Circle. Understood?"

Ross muttered, "No. I don't think you should move—"

Jack sat up and frowned heavily.

Chris prepared for a fight by pinching the bridge of his nose. "Please, kid—"

"It had to be those nacre human/natural human assholes." Oh, thank god. That wasn't what Chris expected him to say. Certainly nothing as rational as what came out.

What Tumu had for eyebrows were raised high as he asked, "Pardon?"

Karter explained, "At El Paso. Some people accused us of not controlling nacre integration. That those people who ingested nacres risked everyone at the mercy of your kind."

Tumu blinked at her. "You come across as kinda racist."

"I hate the Tritan governing body, not necessarily the individual." Karter stared up at him from the floor. And he stared down at her from his great height.

An accord passed between them as the Tritan returned to the topic at hand. "I am authority on this planet, but I am not the enforcer of our restrictions. Eventually, they will come here pending my investigation into human compatibility with our technology. My recommendation only goes so far. Try to keep the ingestions to a minimum. And in the meantime, deal with the radicals. They shouldn't have the technology to disable an alien nano-computer."

Ross draped a towel over Jack's shoulder and stood, offering her hand to him.

Chris put his hand on Karter's shoulder. "We can go back."

"No. Whatever you do, never take Jack back there. I'll send a strikeforce. You dissuade the organization during your sermons." He turned to the upright King Regent. "Can you do that?"

"Yes."

"Good. I like you, kid. But I also don't wanna find out what Rayne would do if anything ever happened to you."

{Earth}

"Twenty-One, do you understand the terms as I've recited them?" Lynn stared hard into the slaughter-happy Icarus' dark eyes.

The prisoner of war ducked his buzzed-cut head and acknowledged, "I understand."

The perimeter lights in the gray cell illuminated from the ceiling and the floor. A bunk sat into the wall. Same as her facility. The Icarean resident stood in the center, wearing the standard-issued maroon uniform. A cross between scrubs and a prison jumpsuit. He was a big guy with a slightly unassuming presence. It was dangerously disarming.

So, keeping his gaze lowered in deference affected Lynn. Of course it did. She read the same Verses as the rest of the Shadow. But she spent her days learning how to destroy nacre-bearers. The work kept her aware of the threat a man like Twenty-One posed. Not everyone deserved redemption.

Lynn looked down at the paperwork. "Do you have any reason to contest this transfer?"

"No. I won't let you and Dr. Suarez down." It was hard to look small at his size, but he managed. Reduced by shame.

"Good. I hope you like your new home."

Lynn left the lab and took the suspended stairs in the glass atrium. She stopped on a landing to appreciate the ocean made clear below her feet. The Brethren certainly enjoyed their impossible architecture.

Before encircling his arms around her, Pablo gave the warning. He learned after many hilarious incidents of violence not to sneak up behind her. Lynn covered his hands with her own, and he settled his chin on her shoulder.

"Stressful, isn't it?" His voice was so comforting this close.

Lynn nodded. They did good things. The Shadow all performed well at their task of reconstructing the world. But...

"Does it feel like things are getting hard again?" She moved so she could look in his eyes. "The amnesiac.

Andrew's meetings. Jack. Hell, the Tritans letting Tameka come here must be a fucking portent."

Pablo squeezed and assured, "Tumu took good care of Jack. Andrew's being cautious. And we can handle an occasional anomaly from an alien planet." He paused and searched her eyes. "You're not just feeling uneasy, are you?"

She shook her head.

"Then trust your instincts. Bring up your concerns at the meeting. We all respect each other. No one will shrug off what you have to say." He kissed her forehead tenderly.

"My god, you two never work."

They uncoupled and turned.

Smith leaned on the banister with a shit-eating-grin, and his hands raised in defense. "I know. I know. The time away is hard and all that." He tossed a nod over his shoulder. "You're needed at the comms, Mr. and Mrs. Boss. It's Story Taker and Fury."

Lynn always suspected Tameka nicknamed herself. "We'd better head up."

Pablo put his forehead to hers. "If it ever overwhelms you, I can whisk you away from here and all our responsibilities. Just say the word."

"Banana."

He laughed, sudden and hard. One of Lynn's favorite sounds. She only heard him make it for her. Shaking his head, he led them up the stairs.

"Hey, you two. Thanks for joining the call," Tameka started over the comms. "Kyle's on King duty with me. Andrew is on the call. Lucas isn't available. Batman is here. Sagan is...somewhere. We'll catch her. This phone call is to plan the best meeting place for the Shadow. Andrew, I'll let you take over."

"Wait...wait," Kyle jumped in.

Andrew gave the go ahead.

"Conscience, if we have the meeting there, can you hook me up with some of that Australian stuff?"

Pablo snickered, and Lynn gently elbowed his ribs.

"Ow. Ow. Fuck, I get it, Tameka. Stop!"

Oh, now they both snickered.

"Please, Andrew. Start." Tameka's voice dripped with the glare she no doubt paid Kyle.

Conscience cleared his throat before beginning, "Right. So. There's been a lot happening. We can chalk it up to coincidence. Or we can be smart and try to be proactive. Does anyone disagree?"

Batman called on the comms, "I came this close to waking Rayne up so she could kill me for the near-miss with Jack. Hell, I wouldn't blame her if she executed me. I'm all for preventing a tragedy here."

"You handled the situation well. But you're right. We don't want to see anymore of these situations, do we?"

Lynn practically heard Andrew push his fingers through his hair in frustration. She agreed with his points completely, but stress hurt their jobs. Their jobs were important.

"Pablo and Lynn. That transfer you're planning. Is there any way I can get you to postpone it?"

They looked at each other before Pablo responded, "Do you mind if we ask why?"

Lynn turned to make sure the door to the soundproof room was closed and caught Pablo's appreciative nod as Tameka explained, "We're worried about the timing of it paired with the emergence of this nacre hating-group and—What was her name?"

Kyle answered on an exhale, "Silence."

"Silence's arrival," Tameka finished. Off to the side, they heard her ask him, "Where is she?"

"Cypher's watching her at the fortress."

Chris sighed into the comms. "The trouble with all of us working such strategic roles is that we're indispensable. When would be convenient for all of us? And where is a safe enough place for the entire Shadow to convene?"

"The nacre chamber," Andrew offered.

Chris muttered, "Wow."

Pablo's brows shot up, and Lynn gripped her pendant. They heard about it. Where Rayne ended the war, but they never saw it in person.

Tameka and Kyle answered simultaneously, "Agreed."

Lynn whistled, impressed. "Well, how will we get the Seamswalker to keep still long enough to transport us all?" She paced around the device with Pablo's eyes on her.

If the others sensed what she did, then were her concerns validated? Were they unsafe? Was it starting again?

A warm hand slipped into hers. She looked up into rich brown eyes and a warm smile on perfect lips. He squeezed, and she smiled for her husband.

Tameka explained the technical details. With her confidence, she made one hell of a leader. "Does anyone have questions?"

"So, Sagan will bring Silence to Iona Medical after?" Pablo confirmed.

Kyle took the mic, "Yes. She volunteered. Is that good with you, Doc?"

Pablo nodded until Lynn nudged him. He smiled bashfully as he remembered they couldn't see him. "Yes. Thanks, Story Taker."

"I'm coming with her, if you don't mind. Tameka will have King duty for a few more days."

Lynn and Pablo exchanged a look. While the rest of the shadow went laxer on Kyle, she still resented what happened to their entire unit because of his betrayal. He tried. He did. She knew that. Which was why she nodded after chewing on her lip.

"The light is green. Looking forward to seeing you. Anyone else want to drop in?" Pablo checked.

Chris started, "Well, now that you mention it—Ow." The rest he muttered, "I'm just messing with him. He knows..."

Andrew's voice came on the line, "Can I say one last thing?"

Everyone assented.

"I miss you all very much. And I'm so proud of every single one of you—"

"What the fuck did I just call into?"

"Hey, Matt! I don't know, man. Andrew got all mushy on us out of nowhere," Kyle answered.

Lynn hopped on the mic, "Where have you been, Ginger?"

"More importantly, where are you?" Andrew asked.

"On my way to rendezvous with Iron Hope, then I guess I'm heading to this super important meeting you called."

Batman asked, "How is Lucy?"

It got quiet. Like dead air.

Matt's voice sounded stony when he finally replied, "Working."

Well, that certainly didn't invite any prodding questions. Pablo and Lynn exchanged a glance before shaking their heads.

"See you soon, Matt. Lynn, Pablo, Andrew, Chris. Thanks everyone for joining the call." Tameka killed the line.

Lynn bit her lip some more.

"Tell me what's on your mind." Pablo rubbed the back of his neck.

Should she share this? "What should I do? I can't just stop that transfer. My schedule isn't the only one affected. We're testing a new weapon, and we need..."

Pablo crooked his neck to either side, yielding a satisfying pop. He and Lynn rarely fought, but he struggled with the ethics of her mission. And she struggled to explain to him what he couldn't see.

After a long stretch, he finally came out and said it, "You need someone you'll care less for hurting. Is that right?"

Lynn looked away and mumbled with less conviction, "They volunteer."

"They volunteer to avoid Gait. Imagine the hell that place must be? But are we better? Are we sure?"

"I don't want to fight." Near tears. Not good. She reached out to him. "Please?"

He crossed the room and chafed her arms. "This isn't a fight. You asked me what I thought of going through with the transfer. To appease those schedules you spoke of. But, Lynn..." He lifted her chin until she met his gaze. "... Ask yourself what the hell is so important down there that those people would consider ignoring an order from Fury?"

"The future, Pablo. It's our future."

EIGHT

LET THE PAIN TAKE YOU, BUT DON'T LET IT HAVE YOU

{Gait}

All through the war, Korac wanted one thing. Sagan all to himself. Now that she was naked in his arms, he could hold her forever. There was only one problem.

"Are you sure the Shadow doesn't need you somewhere?" After he asked, he squeezed the tops of her thighs for two reasons. One, he was a sadist and enjoyed teasing her to distraction. And two, he wanted to reassure how much he loved that she came to him. "You have worlds to save. People to liberate. Or whatever heroes do."

Sagan gasped for him and writhed in his lap. She turned and gazed at him. So much knowledge stared back in those young eyes. His woman understood the universal truths and then some.

"Korac, I waited two years for you while the only other person I love served an undeserved sentence. I can't touch her. But I can touch you. And I'll stop touching you when I'm damned well ready."

He stoked the fire in her with a kiss.

Released for air, she brushed fingers through his hair. A goofy grin blossomed on her face. Truly adorable with those freckles. She confessed, "Now that I've said that, I technically have to leave for Earth. We have a big meeting, and I need to transport everyone."

He kissed the dip of her collarbone and traveled left from there. "Criminally underutilized," he whispered against her throat.

Sagan let her head fall back, giving him access. Her sweet scent coaxed him. Her voice was breathy, desperate, "Please."

There were few things in these worlds that satisfied Korac. A lover begging him in that manner counted among them. She trusted him completely, and he would destroy the Vast Collective to keep her safe.

"Get the rope."

"Yes, Master."

He did a double-take and, when he caught her smirking deviously at him, he almost shivered. Only she enticed him that way.

Sagan collected quite a hoard of pleasantries for his cell. A mattress pad for the hard plank Gait called a bed. Sheets. A suede duvet. All white, of course. A Pil weight set. An actual wardrobe including a drawer for her things. An assortment of rare hygiene products from exotic planets. And . . . supplies.

Cheap polypropylene rope among them. Reflecting on her answer when Korac questioned the reason made him actually shiver. Who made her so perfect?

She returned with the frayed rope and an excited smile. Ready. Always.

Korac backed her into the center of the cell. "No sound." She stretched her clasped hands high. "Eyes on me." He tied the rope into a handcuff knot. "I'll grant you a special treat if you can manage without tears." And waited.

As Sagan grew more comfortable with their encounters, she became firmer in her negotiations. "I consent with one caveat."

He nodded for her to go on.

"Because I have another engagement, I request that after one orgasm you release me."

A wicked, lascivious grin spread across his lips, and he did nothing to stop it. "Granted." The girl underestimated his talents, but she would never forget it after this lesson.

Korac loved to hear Sagan beg.

They installed a crude hook in the ceiling for suspension. He looped the rope onto it, careful to avoid the rope's shedding splinters. He glanced to make certain, and, sure enough, Sagan watched him. She obeyed instruction like no one else.

Stretched naked for him—Damn, what a picture she made.

Korac cursed, "Wait, one second—Shit."

Without a word, she asked the question with her curious eyes.

"I wanted to sketch you, but I lack supplies." At her insistent movements, he chuckled and relented, "Talk."

Sagan offered, "I can get some for you."

A precocious impulse hit him. "No. Thank you. I think I have a more fun idea in mind—"

Korac stopped talking when Sagan, dismissing an errant hair from her face, shook her entire body with a hands-free gesture. Every muscle. Every curve. Her soft, supple skin waited for him. Worthy of a painting, but that would come later.

She beamed at him. Sweet lips. Beautiful teeth. Sparkling eyes. Open. Honest.

There was a more immediate coming that concerned him. Without wasting more time, Korac kissed her thighs. He looked up and caught her wondrous gaze. Even as he lifted her legs onto his shoulders, Sagan stared at him. Silent.

Her weakness at the inner thighs amused him. How well would she fare? He kissed over the femoral artery, expecting a gasp or a flutter of her lashes. He watched her intently. Eyebrows slightly drawn, and her teeth sank into her lip.

That was his weakness and always tempted him to break before her.

Korac licked her. She swallowed hard and strained silently in the ropes. At her obedience, he continued. Pride suffused him as Sagan maintained her control for longer than any other session. He almost broke her with the sucking. He filed biting away for another encounter.

Refusing her silent pleas for release hurt him almost as much as it hurt her. But he deemed the pain necessary.

These moments were for learning each other and themselves. Testing their limits. With every cut, Korac promised Sagan fire beyond burning. But with every open smile, she melted more of the ice he hid behind. They loved each other.

Progeny blood dripped from the hook where she writhed herself into a tangle. The plastic rope's splinters shivved into her delicate skin. The nacre healed it, of course. But the splinters stayed inside her, healed over. She didn't exactly advertise it, but he caught her chafing her wrists together. Further agitating the nerves. Korac found it curious.

Edged to oblivion. Flushed so deeply, her skin almost matched her eyes. Blistered with tears. Strained from thrashing while suspended. And her wrists...a mess.

Sagan never looked away from him. Never made a sound. The entire block smelled of watermelon.

"Who made you so perfect?"

She shivered almost pitifully, and that broke him. Gently, he gripped her sides and pulled her off the hook. All the while, soothing, "Shh. Shh. You did beautifully. Shh. Amos, you're wonderful. We're almost finished."

Korac carried her to the bed and laid her across the black suede, leaving her arms stretched above her. He kissed away the burning salt of her tears. Softly, he observed, "There's so many. Sagan, are you crying because you ruined your prize?"

Sagan kept her gaze on him as she nodded with a wince. Her legs scissored beneath him as she tried to smother the fire in her. He settled his weight on her to pin them down.

The war criminal stole a kiss as he assured, "You've more than earned it." Korac spread her thighs wide. "Make all the sound you want." And then he gave her what she needed.

His name from her lips shocked the quiet cell and scattered in echos throughout the block. He kept to their arrangement. One orgasm, and then he'd release Sagan for her engagement. After this four-hour lesson, he suspected she'd specify duration from hereon.

They held each other as before. Her sitting in his lap. This time, he performed the aftercare she enjoyed with these ropes. Sagan appreciated when Korac delicately removed the plastic splinters from her wrists and hands. She watched intently and shivered as he slipped another out. He kissed the top of her head to show how much he loved exploring her mind with her.

With the last one removed, Sagan kissed him. Despite her attempt to distract him, he still caught the sadness in her eyes.

"I'll be back in a few days. I promise." She finished buckling her coat closed. Always naked beneath.

He slipped his long legs into a pair of faded denim jeans and appreciated how well they fit. Lucas could tailor his wardrobe anytime. When Korac's eyes met Sagan's again, he released an involuntary growl. "General. Control yourself."

She looked close to drooling. "I can't help it." With a hopeless shrug and a wink, Sagan walked through the Seam. Both axes on her hips.

Elden, he loved her. And that's how Korac found himself slumped against one wall with his ass on the floor. Worried about her.

It sounded messy out there with the Progeny. Were The Brethren prepared to claim and retain the planet? From their own populace? From their Tritan benefactors? Because it would come down to both, eventually. It always did.

And Razor.

Korac let his head fall back against the wall with a thud, filing his fingernails. Thinking about which length Sagan preferred them suited the Icarus far better than thinking about the Pain Curator sinking his nail-less claws into her. An infinite malice lived in those hard red eyes.

Korac trusted his girl to hold her own. She could summon a portal to Hell, for Elden's sake. But... If she weren't careful, Razor would chew her up with nothing left to spit out.

And then Korac would divide the world apart to claim the bastard's spine.

There was one other item on the retired General's mind. He blew on his nails and idly glanced at the lift's direction. How far could he get around? How long before he searched for Nox? Should he even...

Again with the thud. He clenched his jaw to draw out the tension in his neck. In his fucking conscience. Maybe Pehton—

"Hey, son?"

Korac stopped paying his blockmate any consideration during Sagan's visits. He spared no time or thought for anything but her. So when the man's deep voice thundered through the hall, Korac sighed angrily. "What?!"

"Do you mind telling me what *the* fuck I just listened to?"

{Gait}

"Peh Peh, Inanis cannot be explained. And the dozens of thousands of credits negative in your account proves that."

The Executive Warden of Gait pushed her hands through her orange feathers when Razor turned his back on her. He leaned on the wrought-iron banister overlooking the Emporium. She considered simply killing him, but they weren't alone. Shapes scurried in the dusky lighting as employees scattered to prepare for the grand reopening.

After procuring the adjacent warehouse space, the Pain Curator doubled the venue's floor plan. An upscale restaurant, high-rent space for auctions, and a museum of ancient wares.

Oh, and six more charcoal Divine Booths. Like headstones, they lined the parquet floors, marking the death of another innocent. Those were the updated nacre port experiences. Two new booths occupied a dais on display. Massive, they were set apart from the others. They shone with a pearlescent light on white enamel.

Fully. Immersive.

An entirely new experience. And they exhibited only one person's history. Only one person's misery and pain.

Rayne.

Razor easily made several hundred million a night off that girl's life. In the regular booths. Now, he stood to make a billion in profit. In a single night. Off Pehton's soul.

And there he was, hassling her over a few hundred thousand in credits. "So, whose pain will suffice my debt this time?"

Yes. It always came to this. How could she sink so low over and over again?

What counts.

Right. Once again, Gait's Executive Warden straightened her shoulders and held her chin high as Razor turned to assess her.

"Maybe this time, I'm not asking for someone's pain, Peh Peh." Brown fire danced in his eyes.

She wondered many times if it'd ever come to this. And long ago, Pehton decided she wouldn't fight him. Instead, she fought to keep her red gaze level with his.

Reduced. To this.

The man with skin the color of her nacre pushed away from the banister and stepped into her personal space. Razor searched her eyes as Pehton kept her ground. He inhaled and shook his head.

So close that when he spoke, their lips brushed, "I want many things from you, love. But that will never be one of them."

That brokered no relief. Instead, her gliders flared. Not in anger, but in fear. And the twitch at his lips told Pehton that he knew.

"What do you want, Razor?" The steadiness of her voice surprised her. The tightness did not.

Razor went ahead and let that twitch stretch into a smirk. "Preoccupy our charming Icarus for me. And provide me with any updates on the big cell."

Pehton frowned so hard that it hurt her head. "Korac? Why?"

He chuckled as he stepped around her in the vault's direction. "Need I explain myself to you?"

When she turned around, he held Pehton's vice in his blood-stained palms. Damn it. The Executive Warden redirected her tactics for more wiggle room. "I've given you everything else you've asked for, but risking my station on Gait is asking more than usual. The rate is higher, and the fee is information. Why Korac?"

The Pain Curator tilted his head as if considering her terms. After a shrug, he casually offered, "The others are interested in him. And I want the Seamswalker as my own personal project. If he's preoccupied, she's available to me."

Red flags. Big ones. Pehton fought not to wince. It hurt to admit it, but she liked Sagan. Ugh. And maybe, begrudgingly, a little, sorta, kinda was coming to tolerate the fallen General. Then it hit her, "What do you mean preoccupy him from her? He's in Infernus block. No visitors."

The man's smile upped in the wattage as if he knew a secret.

Korac's breakout. The stuff in the cell.

"Motherfucker!"

Razor's rich laughter irritated her further.

Wow, she gave that guy a chance. And he abused her hospitality like that? Risked her station? If the Tribunal learned of this disgrace—

"This arrangement benefits us mutually, does it not?" He held out the device.

Blackmail. This was blackmail. A small part of her wanted to barter on behalf of Sagan. She was so much younger than all of them. Inexperienced. But if Pehton asked Razor to go easy on her, then he'd exploit the Executive Warden's soft spot for his new fixation. No. Best keep it close to her chest. As always.

"I want a booth every time I perform a task." She held up a pitch-black finger before he could argue. "If I lose Executive Warden rank, we both know what happens to me. I will not risk it for anything less than Every. Single. Task."

"I can live with that, Peh Peh. But can you?"

As she snatched the device from his hand and headed for the booth, Pehton was confident that she could live with a lot worse.

Because she already did.

{GAIT}

Technically, Sagan didn't lie to Korac. A big meeting awaited her particular skill-set on Earth. But first, a quick drop in on the primary mission.

Razor's Emporium of Exotic Experiences. The sign projected against the starless purple sky. Sagan questioned all her contacts throughout the Vast Collective about this place and its Curator. Less than forthcoming put it mildly. No one spoke over two words on the subject. And those two words were always the same.

"Don't. Go."

The line in front of the glass revolving door garnered a bouncer and a velvet rope. Classy. When they rolled out an actual red carpet, Sagan rolled her eyes and folded her arms. Leaning against a wall across the street, she caught a rare glimpse of an anti-grav car. Sleek lines, chrome paint, and it hovered a foot off the road. Maybe two or three of those babies existed on the entire planet.

The Tritan, who stepped out with an usher's help, took the arm of a Reipon Lamia in a magnificent little black dress. No compression orb in sight. But there was something slimy about colluding with their archivists.

A glimmer caught Sagan's eye beyond the Tritan entering the Emporium. Through the revolving door. On the mezzanine.

Razor watched the Seamswalker. Not his line. Or his fancy guests. He stared right at her. The bastard even smirked when she cussed at his observation.

The guy gave her the serious creeps.

But since he spotted her, it was time to properly introduce herself. Last time, he caught her off guard. It wouldn't happen again.

Sagan stepped away from the wall. Wearing thigh-high boots, she smiled at how much Korac appreciated the stilettos. She glided across the street in her violet armored coat. Axes on her hips. Her man's kiss on her lips. Armed. Ready.

Skipping the line, she Seamswalked right through the bouncer. The Pain Curator watched every step. When she Seamswalked onto the mezzanine, he shook his head with an arrogant smile. The stuffy crowd gasped and gaped. The corrugated metal flooring connected with her heels on a satisfying "clunk." It added weight to her entrance. An entrance she knew Korac would've applauded. It was for him, after all.

The creep in question, like many creeps, looked quite attractive. Especially in a three-piece white tux that contrasted with his tan skin and red hair. Those eyes, though. They gave his true nature away. In the green half, a light swirled, but the orange half? Flat. Dead.

Sagan looked at the people still murmuring about her. Dollar amounts for her pain were among the chatter. The building? She could see the elegance, but it smelled of gluttony and avarice.

"Did I come at a bad time?"

Razor's grin pulled at the rugged angles of his face. "Damn, Seamswalker. You're making my guests envious. Who could top that entrance?" He raked his eyes down her body. "Are all the Progeny this arresting?"

She ignored the glance and the question. Resigning herself to tolerate the testing of her boundaries, she remarked, "Quite the gala."

The grin narrowed into a smirk. A secret one that said, "I will wear you down, eventually."

His words said, "In honor of my new expansion. Would you care to join me?" With his cane, he indicated to the addition below.

Sagan peered down at the crooked arm he offered. When she looked back up to his eyes, she gave her own secret smile. And Seamswalked to the addition.

Again the crowd gawked. Amateurs. The creepy Tritan with the anti-grav car nearly salivated at her.

Do. Not. Shudder.

The Pain Curator glided down his spiral staircase and swept across the expanse to her side. He nodded for the quartet to resume the music. Whispering to a caterer, he glanced at Sagan.

Finally, Razor reached her, "What would you like to see first?"

She turned her back on him and wandered into the shop. The people still stared at her, but with more subtlety. Maybe even a little jealousy, what with her private tour from the owner and all. Some aggression in Sagan repeated, "That's right, motherfuckers. I can summon monsters you can't imagine and certainly can't fight—"

"You're lost."

Sagan closed her eyes to his words. She trailed her fingers across the nacre glass items on the crystal shelves. The pretty track lighting made them glow like amber. "What makes you say that?" The everyday goods—dishes, game boards, figurines—cost hundreds of thousands of credits. All made of nacre glass.

"Because I see that expression on many people that patron my wares." Razor watched her with that half-dead, half-alive gaze as he continued, "Have you ever considered—"

A drunk couple stumbled into the room with many giggles. After one glance from the Pain Curator, they sobered the hell up and left.

She Seamswalked behind him. "Considered what?"

Languidly, he turned and locked eyes with her. His voice almost sounded sad as he asked, "Why you love the pain?"

Before she covered her reaction, Sagan's eyes widened.

The bright white space pulsed once. "One moment." He left her there with the question she wondered many times herself. Korac made her feel good. She trusted him. But was there anything wrong with her—

"Hungry?" Razor silently laughed at his own double-entendres and offered her a small plate of hor d'oeuvres.

It smelled amazing. And all the Seamswalking left her famished. Although something warned her not to eat it, she ignored it. If shit went sideways, she could simply walk out. Besides, why travel if one wasn't willing to try the local cuisine?

Sagan plucked one and popped it in her mouth. And then moaned. Spicy, smoky, sweet. So good.

One glance at Razor made her regret the sound. He looked so pleased with himself. "Yun Gecko."

She immediately spat it out on the nearest item for sale. No fucks given. "They don't allow harvesting, hunting, or eating of animals on Yu. It's punishable by death." Life was sacred to them.

The Pain Curator's smirk condescended on her apparent naivety. "It's quite the delicacy."

Eyes closed. Deep breath. Count to ten. Do not. Fuck up. His store. Hell, his entire Emporium teetered on the brink of destruction. What a messed up tactic to unnerve her.

She opened her eyes.

Razor looked sad. Genuinely, unhappy with himself. "I apologize. I thought you'd enjoy it. I mean, you seemed to."

"Stop serving it."

He inclined his head as if he misheard her.

"Now. Stop serving it. If you want me as a customer… Hell, if you ever want customers from Earth or Cinder… Serve no meat from Yu again."

The Pain Curator didn't hesitate. He left the room and when he returned, he asked, "Would you like to verify for yourself?"

After Seamswalking around the place and the extremely well-stocked kitchen, she returned to the shop. He waited for her with the same forlorn look on his face.

Quietly, she confirmed, "Gone."

"I want to establish a trust with you, Sagan. With Earth and Cinder. I imagine an assorted human and Icarean clientele would appreciate my experiences. I see it in your own curiosity. So, perhaps, you can pilot this flagship for trade? I could cultivate your experiences, myself."

Razor crossed the shop to stand over her. "And in time, we can get to know each other. I've been around a while. I can answer your questions about the Vast Collective. And perhaps use some of my connections to make your Icarean General's stay more comfortable."

That lifted Sagan's gaze. The green in his eyes glowed with sincerity. The red reflected her like a glossy glare. The promise and the threat. She internalized her seething rage.

Every time the Pain Curator moved, she expected him to touch her. But he never crossed that line. No. He managed well enough with words alone. "With a sample of your pain, I can tailor every nuance to suit your…needs. Explore your relationship with pain. Understand yourself."

The coat Sagan wore as a dress covered her nudity, but Razor still made her feel naked. She ducked her gaze as she considered the mission.

A weakness lingered in her. A need she couldn't fathom. With so many wonderful things in her life, how could she remain so conflicted? Superpowered. Super awesome friends. Super awesome, superpowered friends.

But…an emptiness required filling. If she accepted this exchange, was she at risk of falling into Razor's infinity?

His voice startled her when he whispered, "Take some time to think on it. A few days—"

"I want to bring a friend with me."

Razor smiled and bowed with his head. "Of course. The Progeny are always welcome—"

"He's human. But trust me. He's not like any human on Earth."

The man looked more delighted with each surprise. "I look forward to seeing you both in a few days. Now, would you like me to walk you to do the door—"

Sagan walked into the Seam.

But in her wake, she heard Razor say, "Of course not."

{Earth}

Kyle trusted Cypher with Silence. Since returning to the fortress, the group formed a quiet rapport. They spent the day exploring the observatory, reading books on Cinder's history to learn exactly when she fell out of it. The exotic Icarus devoured the volumes with rapt fervor in silence. Pun intended.

She spoke three words since surrendering at the festival. "Yes," "No," and, "Stop." The last she said when Cypher started singing "Constant Sorrow" from *O' Brother Where Art Thou*. Guess she wasn't a fan of the man's Clooney impersonation.

Sagan Seamswalked right into the observatory while Kyle watched the amnesiac finish her three hundredth tome. The book crashed to the floor when Silence bolted out of the chair. Not frightened. More excited.

For Elden's sake! Didn't the Seamswalker learn to knock after that one time with Pablo and Lynn? Sure, the observatory was more public, but sometimes Kyle locked the doors and went shorts-free.

"Oh, please don't tell me this is all you have for her to wear?" Sagan scoffed, taking a gander at the refugee's ensemble.

Silence repaid in kind while dressed in one of Kyle's oversized Hawaiian shirts, and Cypher's tactical pants fit her like capris. The Seamswalker ditched her trademark coat for a fluffy double-knit cowl neck sweater and jeans. The cream color of the top brought out the amethyst in her eyes. The skin-tight jeans brought out one of her better assets.

In an awkward turn of events, Silence's gaze snapped to Kyle right as he was assessing the particular asset in question. On a reflex, of course.

But something in the Icarus' gunmetal gaze told him that excuse wouldn't fly.

Kyle cleared his throat and stood from the desk he leaned against. "Okay. So, you two." He waved his joint between Cypher and Silence. "Play nice while I'm gone. Sagan and I will be back for you both once the meeting is over. I want you in one piece. Got it?" He glanced at Cypher, who gave him a salute.

Silence was scanning Sagan with intensity, ignoring Kyle. Instead, her eyes glittered, and her chest heaved when she inhaled deeply. The flare in her gaze implied she liked what she smelled.

Sagan broke into a mischievous grin, which Silence returned with that movie star smile of hers. Oh, Kyle was not sleeping tonight. The idea of those two together would keep him up for a month.

Cypher ruined the moment by speaking, "Don't keep Fury waiting. The last time that happened, I had to carry your ass around for a week while you recovered."

Sagan broke the spell with a little shake of her head. She finally drew her gaze away from Silence and nodded to Kyle. "Right. Let's go."

He fought not to pout as the Seamswalker took them to the nacre chamber. Grumbling the entire way about murdering Cypher for ruining his fantasies, Kyle took his first step into a phenomenon. The nacre chamber capped the entire north pole of Elden's Sphere on Cinder. Encased in the amber glass, it enshrined the nacres of its makers. The Coalition and Elden. They sacrificed themselves to encase the planet in the unbreakable material when Li imploded into a red giant. But…

Silence could break it. She shattered those cuffs.

A hand on his shoulder startled Kyle. He pivoted to find Andrew smiling at him. As far as smiles go, Conscience's warm beam reminded Story Taker of family. Of home.

Forget the hand clasp and shoulder tap. They stretched and grappled each other into a bear hug.

Muffled against the other Progeny's shoulder, Andrew asked, "How long has it been?"

Although they kept to a revolving King duty schedule, they rarely bumped into each other anymore. "Nine months, I think. Where's Lucas?"

Andrew separated first with a heavy sigh. "Finishing up with The Brethren. I'll be honest, some of their findings were less than reassuring."

Kyle raised his brow in question.

The other Progeny shook his head. "I'll explain to everyone when they get here."

Sagan Seamswalked back into the chamber by the central pedestal with Tameka and Pablo. Pablo looked like he just went through wringer. And judging by the look on Tameka's face, she helped put him through it. Fury was her name for a reason.

Andrew hugged the fuming woman, anyway. "What's wrong? Where's Lynn?"

She spared a fervent glance in Pablo's direction before saying, "You won't believe what's happening." After spearing her fingers into her curly hair, she stressed, "It's Lynn. The Brethren insisted on the transfer. And it's going down."

"When?"

"Right now."

NINE

KEEP IT STEADY

{EARTH}

LUCAS TALKED WITH DOLOR—ANOTHER BRETHREN MEMBER—LOOKING THOROUGHLY TRAPPED. He waved for John to leave for the Shadow meeting without him. Sagan waited for him in the chateau's kitchens after already sneaking off with Andrew. She preferred hiding in there rather than interacting with the governing body of the Two Worlds. As Tempest stepped up to John, he envied Sagan's decision.

"John, you gave a wonderful presentation. When do you think we could get together to establish the global education system you proposed?" The female Icarus responsible for constructing the Arsenal and the Ecology swept one errant strand into her sleek, short-cut hair.

The Brethren always made him feel under-dressed in their formal business suits and chic hairstyles. John thought he looked positively well-traveled in his Enki-issued jumpsuit. Until he walked inside The Brethren's fancy headquarters. Now he felt like a janitor.

He cleared his parched throat before answering, "Thank you for the kudos. Eminent Wiw is working directly with me on the distribution of Icarean communication units for global virtual classrooms. But as you're aware, it, like all the comms, depends heavily on the Pil quantum machine in Nevada."

One hand on her hip, she tapped her pointed shoe while biting her lip. Deep thinking. "Right. Okay. I'll see if I can get a better estimation from the Dwarves on that project. Let me know the next chance you get to take another break from Enki. I'll try to have it ready by then."

John hid his wince as he quietly nodded and headed toward the kitchen.

"John."

He stopped and Tempest closed the distance between them once more. With his back to her, she put a friendly hand on his shoulder. Gently, she assured, "They won't keep you two in Enki forever. But I'll try to keep you both in official reasons for returning." She squeezed before taking off.

Good people surrounded them. Mostly good, anyway. Or maybe John was becoming an optimist. He pushed into the kitchens, where he caught Sagan stuffing her face with a tray of veggies and dip.

She smiled at him, pointed to the food, and called out, "Hey! This is pretty good. Have you had any? And do you think anyone would miss it? Cause, you know? We have mouths to feed."

John grinned and shook his head.

Her defensive "what" came out more like "wot" with the food stuffed inside her mouth. Hidden behind her hand, of course. Manners.

"What the hell? Let's take it. I'm sure the ancient nacres of the coalition members won't mind if we chew in their presence."

"Hell yea!" She pumped her fist in the air and transported both him and the nibbles into the most mind-blowing setting. And he lived in a Dyson's Sphere.

John openly gawked. This was his first time on Cinder. The star…It really swallowed them. He gripped his fingers in his hair, trying to fathom it.

A hand patted him on the shoulder. "Yup. Sure is something, ain't it?" Kyle took another hit on his joint and offered it to John.

Another voice muttered from behind, also in awe, "I'll take some of that, Kyle."

John turned to see King Jack gaping at Li. His face reflected John's wonder. Except the educator was Osage Native American, and the King Regent's ancestors were from the Caucus mountains.

Kyle inhaled before croaking out, "No way, man." He coughed and continued, "Your sister will kill me in her sleep. Hit me up when you're eighteen." Indicating to Andrew across the chamber, he added, "He'll even get you some of that Aussie shit."

Jack, the King Regent of Earth, grumbled as he sulked away with his tail between his legs. Until Sagan Seamswalked in with Ross. Rayne's teenage brother kept his peripheral on Kyle's teenage sister as she ran into her brother's embrace.

John siphoned the secondhand family love. The reminder of his parents' deaths hurt like a fresh wound. And it might never stop hurting. But seeing Ross and Kyle together soothed some of the ache.

Sagan grinned and snipped a glance at Jack, who looked away quickly. "Sorry for the late arrival. She begged me for more time to get ready." She tossed a wink at John.

He chuckled and returned it. Everyone was a matchmaker.

Ross smiled unabashedly. "It's been a while since we've all been together. I wanted to look nice."

"Elden, you took two hours to get ready for school each day. *Before* you started wearing makeup..." Kyle reminisced until Ross thumped him in the arm. "Ow. Nacres hurt—"

"Look at us."

The crowd stopped and turned to the top dais. Tameka stood there looking over them. It was a good turnout. Matt and Chris both stuffed some celery in their mouths next to the tray in front row. Pablo leaned against the sphere, looking bereft. Andrew glanced around, waiting for Lucas. Bones and Para flanked Kyle and Ross. Jack, Sagan, and John stood in the center.

The Shadow.

Minus some faces. Lucy took on some mission. Karter took on a strikeforce for Tumu. Said Tritan watched over Rayne. Colton stayed with Iron Hope. Six traveled North America with her husband in Molly. Caedes had to babysit Pax. Cypher had to babysit Silence. And Smith and Lynn apparently went through with their transfer. Thus explained the bereft Pablo.

At the sight of everyone together, John's chest swelled. He may have lost his parents, but his family got so much bigger. Minus one important face.

"Rayne would be so proud to see us here. All of us doing such important work." Tameka smiled brightly. "I know I am."

Well, that warmed John's heart and pulled his mouth into a smile to match hers. A cursory glance at all the smiles in the crowd said the feeling was mutual.

"But I know we carry our burdens. Things became complicated recently. We called this meeting so we could invent proactive measures to handle any resulting surprises." She nodded to John in the back. "We'll start with what we've learned from Enki so far. And then Andrew and Kyle will report. Chris next. And anyone else who wants a turn. We'll be here as long as it takes."

John headed to the front, limping a little as his prosthetic despised Cinder's gravity. The entire walk, he received nudges, pats on the back, and shoulder squeezes. It made him miss Earth and lament the return to Enki's clinical, icy formalities.

Once at the front, John stood on the tallest dais, and Tameka stepped down. Their lives came into a bizarre, surreal perspective. He stood in a crazy bubble blister made of unbreakable glass under a red giant on an alien planet. It was all so fucked up. The room listed a bit.

"You got this, John!" Was that Jack?

A few other people whistled. Some hollered encouraging words. And the room stopped spinning. John patted his brow and took a few deep breaths.

That's when one voice bellowed across the entire crowd, "Just remember to imagine all of us naked! I'll even strip if it makes you feel better!"

Thanks, Kyle. Now, John had this.

{EARTH}

"The future, Pablo. It's our future."

"My only future is with you."

Lynn felt like dog shit. Her man loved and supported her. And this was how she repaid him? Placing her job first and putting his ass on the line with Fury? She'd never forget the look on his face as the Seamswalker took him to the meeting. Alone. Oh, Lynn was going to Hell—

"It'll work out, boss," Smith muttered beside her. He seemed right at home in the covert operations gear. All black.

They waited in the lab for The Brethren's guards to cuff Twenty-One. The Icarus' body made for an impressive medical chart of every experiment performed on him at the Ecology. If he fell into the wrong hands, so would Pablo's research. Everything about this swap was so clandestine and shady. It gnawed at Lynn's nerves. And her heart.

"How can you be so sure?" She traced her fingers over the tattoo and pulled the necklace's chain in a one-two nervous tic.

Smith pulled his own chain out of his collar as proof. "Because we're the Shadow, and we will always remain."

"Right."

The Brethren's guards escorted the gigantic Icarus through the lab. Seriously. The guy was almost as massive as Nox. Lynn called out to the giant, "How ya doin, Twenty-One?"

The prisoner looked over his shoulder at her as they climbed the stairs. "Just fine, Chief Renee." The sincerity in his brown eyes arrested her. Were all Icari so repentant? He even smiled warmly in reassurance once they reached the front exit.

The glass walls afforded them an uninterrupted view of quite the lightning storm outside. The night sky flashed and split apart. Not a trace of thunder. Eerie.

Once outside, the light breeze teased Lynn's dark locs. Ozone carried on the wind with the fresh ocean salt from below. Something in the night bothered her. A whisper. A touch. Something.

"Do you feel that?" Smith muttered to her.

Oh, Hell no. When the Anthrax Guy got a case of the nerves, something was up. She signaled, and they rushed to either side of Twenty-One. Lynn ordered, "We need to go back. Now."

One guard shook his head. "We're only thirty feet from the conduit. Why would we stop?"

"Because there's something—"

A whistle pierced the night. Strange and lonesome. Tuneless.

"What the fuck?" The second guard gripped his sword. "Come on. Let's go back."

"Sounds like a plan," Smith scoffed with a side glance at the guards.

As they turned back, the whistle dropped pitch. Low. The hair rose on the back of Lynn's neck.

"Steady," Smith commanded. "Almost there."

The whistle stopped.

"Chief. No matter what happens. I promise I won't let you and the Doc down." The timing of Twenty-One's assurance frightened her.

Every muscle in Lynn's body seized. Only her logic and her bones kept her going. "Let's hope it doesn't come to that—"

White light—bright and vast—blinded her. By their cries, it sounded as if it blinded everyone in the night. She shielded her eyes because even with them closed it seared her retinas to the point of tears. Lynn never thought she'd wish for the nacre glasses from Volcano Day.

"God damn!" Smith shouted.

Twenty-One growled, "Will it ever—"

The light vanished as suddenly as it came.

"—stop?"

"What the hell just happened?" Guard one asked.

"We did."

They whirled to find a team of humans dressed in embarrassingly similar covert gear. Lynn blinked through tears. Her eyes hurt like a bruise.

"What was the point of that entrance, if you planned to let us know you were here?" Lynn couldn't make out any of their features. Maybe if she tried bigger blinks. "Who are you with?"

"Someone interested in your research." That was a man. White by the sound of his voice. But she couldn't make anything else out.

Smith muttered to the guards, "Get him through the door and activate the emergency locks."

"Sir." They headed for the entrance.

Lynn stepped up. "Whose first?" She hoped to come across as intimidating despite the excessive blinking and tears. Unsheathing her weapons, she found it terribly disconcerting that they just stood there.

From the Ecology's entrance, someone cried, "What the fuck just happened?"

The lightning freaked Lynn out. The whistle definitely raised her hackles. But the sound of her own voice from behind almost made her piss herself.

Turning, she wiped her eyes. Twice. Through the blur, a woman stood between Twenty-One and the Ecology.

And it was Lynn.

{Cinder}

Andrew shook his head as John finished his presentation. Fucking Tritans. A murmur of side conversations washed over the Shadow. Reassure them, they survived the war for more than this.

"We'll get through this like we always do. Together."

The crowd stopped whispering and turned to him.

Andrew headed for the front and continued, "I know it looks murky. Again. But we got this. Thanks for sharing with us John." He pulled the guy in for a quick hug.

The human shook on his steady prosthetic. "Thanks, Conscience."

"The crops are doing great. The evacuation is going well. The medical and weapon research keeps us healthy and well-defended. Let's focus on the good we've accomplished."

The murmuring returned. Tameka approached Pablo and patted his arm. "I don't like the transfer taking place right now, but I understand. You guys work hard with tight deadlines. I'm sorry I—"

He squeezed her hand. "Don't worry about it."

Chris leaned into Jack and whispered, "Maybe it's time we hit up Six and travel on Molly. Let Iron Hope rest a bit. Or maybe we could settle down somewhere. What do you think?"

"Yea. I think Karter would like that." Jack smiled especially brightly for a kid that almost died a few hours ago.

Ross sighed heavily. "Dunno about the semi. That's a lot of boy smell cramped into one tiny space. She may not appreciate it as much as you'd think. I'm doubtful myself."

Jack flushed a bit, and Chris belted out a hearty laugh.

Andrew cut into the peace. "Let's recount our concerns." He nodded over to Story Taker.

Kyle headed up to the dais. "So, we learned Imminent is a conglomeration. Not necessarily a Tritan-only club. We also suspect they're behind the attempt on our King Regent. I know this nacre human vs natural human group might be legit, but they stink of Imminent. Does anyone disagree?"

Many thumbs down and shaken heads.

Conscience took the floor again. "External activities should slow down for now. Don't expose yourself without serious cause and without discussing it with the Shadow."

Tameka said, "I'm concerned about the timing of these events. Within the same week of learning I'm a permanent resident in Enki, Jack was almost assassinated, the Ecology and the Arsenal have a risky inmate transfer, an Icarus with no memory who can break nacre glass appears, and all while Sagan's working a dangerous mission on Gait. We're stretched thin."

"And Imminent knows it." Kyle frowned as he announced it.

Para added, "And we're all here . . ."

A weight settled in the room. An icy chill followed. Andrew shivered. Everyone stood. The anxious chatter that erupted included an uneasy urge to head back to their respective stations.

"Watch out for each other. Check in once a week, except for me obviously. I'll be fine." Tameka rushed over to hug Jack.

"I'll find out what I can about the history of Gait from my source," Sagan offered. "If the Tritans hide it, it might be significant to them."

Kyle let go of his sister and called, "Pablo, we're heading back to get Silence now."

"Be right there." He turned back to John. "Yea, I'd love to check out this limb sometime. Enki tech is so fascinating."

"Next time I'm Earthside, I'll drop in," John promised as they hugged goodbye.

Sagan counted heads on her passengers. "Let me take Jack and them to the train first. Then . . ."

Matt wandered from her side, peering at the Coalition nacres.

Andrew licked his lips, nervously. "Do you mind taking me back to the chateau? I want to find Lucas."

She smiled and held out her hand. "You first."

He took it and already felt better as they stepped through the Seam. The Brethren's grand auditorium echoed their footsteps. So empty and lonely with its expensive wainscoting and polished wooden floors.

"Maybe he's gone home already," Sagan offered.

Andrew hugged her tightly. "Go. I'll fly home. It's not far, and it'll help me clear my head."

Sagan patted him and squeezed out, "I love you, Conscience."

"I hate that name."

"I know." She grinned mischievously at him and vanished.

Alone, Andrew rubbed his eyes with the fingers on one hand. He trusted his family to take care of themselves, but that never stopped him from worrying. One more loss, of any kind, might send him over the edge he refused to acknowledge.

And with those happy thoughts, he flew back to Neverland. Lucas loaned The Brethren the gorgeous chateau as their headquarters. But mostly because he kept the zeppelin close by, the cheeky Icarus. The rest commuted from remote locations around the world.

The night suited Andrew's mood. The fresh air healed some of his anxiety. But he really needed a hug—

Far out on the horizon, in the farm's direction, an ominous light glowed against the night. Andrew's heart stopped in his chest. No.

No, no, no, no—

Andrew couldn't think it hard enough, so he started muttering it. Then screaming it until his lungs went hoarse while his wings struggled to keep his hopeless soul aloft.

"NO!"

Every square foot of the Vittle crop blazed in black flames.

{EARTH}

Anxiety riddled Pablo. Something felt terribly wrong since the foreboding mention of Imminent. As if they could summon the ghostly entity from the ether to wreak havoc on their sanctums. But as a physician, he couldn't help but notice Sagan's growing fatigue with each transport. He kept quiet and let her go at her own pace.

Meanwhile, he hugged everyone. It helped. He even took a sample from Jack. Sure, the gargantuan blood diluted in his system if not completely neutralized, but it made for interesting research. The symptoms and effects reminded Pablo of a project Lynn mentioned, and it bothered him.

A pang hit him in the chest. Just an anxiety attack, surely. They weren't uncommon since the invasion.

"Ready to go?" Sagan made her way over to him while rubbing her temples.

Pablo wanted nothing more but…"Do you need to rest? Let me look at your vitals."

Her pretty smile reminded him of their younger days. "Doc, I got this. Let's get you to your girl."

"Don't forget the pit stop," Kyle called from behind.

"How could I? I've got a thing for shackled Icari." Sagan's grin held a secret.

Pablo and Kyle exchanged a look before they transitioned through the Seam.

The observatory looked the same since the last time Pablo visited. Cypher stood from one of the many leather chairs and nodded to the arrivals. "Hassle free, Story Taker."

"Thanks for the report. At ease." Kyle took another hit before turning around as if he needed it.

A woman waited behind them with crazy features and what a smile. Her unusual attributes agitated Pablo's hereditary studies brain. "Wow. I'm Dr. Suarez, and I'm very pleased to meet you, Silence." He held out his hand and waited.

The woman with a blue stripe in her hair looked at it before holding up both her hands, cupped. She bowed over them.

Pablo smiled and bowed at the neck.

Sagan trailed her fingers over Kyle's desk. Softly, she commented, "You haven't read it."

"And I won't." Couldn't miss the "end of discussion" finality of his tone.

Her eyes flashed before she skipped back over. "Right. Everybody ready?"

"See ya after a bit, Cypher." Kyle toasted him with his joint as they transported once more.

Into a war zone.

And Pablo fought on a proper battlefield. He knew what one looked like. The small stretch of grassy cliff between the Ecology's entrance and the Arsenal's conduit lit up with bizarre weaponry and screams.

"Get down!" Sagan shouted as she Seamswalked them out of danger.

Pablo immediately hauled up and took off. They called after him, but he couldn't hear anything. Only his heart beat wildly in his chest.

Never endanger this. Never risk yourself without me. Never leave without coming back.

"Lynn!" He broke the line and dropped for cover. "Lynn!"

Someone fired a bizarre cannon over his head. It dispersed an electrical discharge into the pre-dawn night.

"God damn it, Doc!" Kyle slid through the dirt and stopped beside him. "Don't take off like that again."

Across the way, Sagan cried out Lynn's name. Her voice changed location occasionally as she Seamswalked around.

Silence glided, gracefully, into the fray. Slow. Sure. An assailant attacked the Icarean female. She wrenched the rifle from his grip and smashed his face in with it. Teeth fell from his gums, soaked in blood. In a blur, she pounced on another opponent. He screamed until he fell...silent.

"Do you think that's how she came by the name?" Pablo asked Kyle.

Surprisingly, he found the normally laid back Progeny straining to monitor her. "I don't know. The way she moves...it's familiar—"

"Dr. Suarez!"

Twenty-One.

He bolted toward the Icarus. This time he was smarter about keeping close to the ground.

Sagan appeared at the cliff, waving him over. "I found them!" Before he took another step, the Seamswalker popped him to the scene. They both hit the dirt.

"It's been a hell of a night, Dr. Suarez." Twenty-One lay on the rocky edge of the cliff beside his warden. He wielded another strange rifle, prepared to aim at trouble. The Icarus was protecting Lynn.

In the light of the rising sun, her normally dark skin paled to Pablo's shade of medium brown. The pupils of those beautiful brown eyes blown wide open. She was breathing too fast as she searched his face uncertainly.

"Baby, let me check your vitals." Clammy skin. Rapid pulse. She couldn't focus. "Lynn, I don't know how, but you're in shock."

"Here." Sagan pulled her sweater over her head, revealing a white a bra he tried not to notice. "Will this help?"

"Yes. Thanks." Such was Lynn's state, that Pablo pulled the sweater over her head, and her hands through the sleeves with no reaction from her. He kissed her hair. "Don't worry. We'll figure this out—"

"It was me. It was me..." Lynn muttered.

He exchanged a worried glance with Sagan, who shrugged, shirtless.

Twenty-One explained, "The enemy played some kind of mind trick. It left us all quite disturbed." He even shuddered.

Pablo lay next to his wife, curling against her for added warmth. "I've got you, baby."

Sagan stared in the Ecology's direction. "Do you see Silence? She's moves like..."

The fierce warrior decimated her opponents in a fight of agility and raw strength. The woman had both in spades. And she knew what do with them.

"Like a Valkyrie." Kyle nonchalantly walked over to them. "She reminds me of Para, Karter, and the rest."

Three assailants tried to retreat across the plain. Silence tied them together, linking them with their broken arms. With a single blow to their throats, they fell unconscious to the ground.

Kyle announced, "I think it's safe to head over."

"Where's Smith?" Pablo asked while coaxing Lynn to stand.

Twenty-One kept the weapon at the ready. "He went for reinforcements."

Sagan hopped up. "I'll go find him—" She screamed.

They all screamed. A bright white light, not unlike Rayne's ability, blanketed the cliff. Lynn's shrieks broke, and she trembled against Pablo in terror.

"No, no, no, no! Not again!" She cried into the void.

His Lynn. Terrified.

Silence stood beside them. Sagan apparently Seamswalked them to the Ecology entrance. Before they ran inside, the light dissipated.

In the quiet of its wake, Silence whispered with steely eyes lit in reverence, "Inanis."

"What the fuck is Inanis?" Kyle asked, scanning their surroundings.

Sagan rubbed tears from her eyes. "What the hell just happened?"

"We need to get inside," Smith called from the conduit to the arsenal. He approached Twenty-One cautiously. "Hand it over."

Twenty-One handed the gun to the human slowly. Once finished, he clasped the back of his head with both hands. Unarmed. Harmless. Honestly, kind of a hero.

Once inside the Ecology entryway, everyone's body released an enormous sigh of relief. Home. Safe under the sign of Iona.

Pablo chafed Lynn's arms. She quit muttering repetitively. But her silence concerned him. He whispered against her hair, "I'm here for you. I won't go anywhere." To Smith, he asked, "What happened?"

Smith looked Silence once over and almost did the same to Sagan, but stopped himself. Clearing his throat, he explained, "It's hard to answer that question. Everything went sideways. Fast. But weird shit happened like the light. And..."

"Me," Lynn muttered.

"There's no body, Lynn. I already checked," Smith announced.

"She didn't imagine it," Twenty-One reassured. "She was here."

Kyle pressed his palms out. "Whoa. Whoa. Somebody please explain. I've had way too much pot for this guessing game shit."

Lynn finally focused on Pablo. And even though he smiled for her, she still looked terrified. "A woman that was me...another Lynn...came. And I killed her."

"Inanis."

Everyone turned and looked at Silence, who smiled beautifully as if she said something helpful.

Kyle actually snuffed his joint out on the palm of his hand. "Okay. I'll take the bait. What's Inanis?"

"In the void, you will know yourself. Within Inanis is us."

TEN

PROTECT THAT HEART OF FLAME AND LIGHT

{EARTH}

SAGAN'S DEAD.

No. That wasn't right.

Kyle died. No.

Tameka?

Oh, god. Where was Rayne? They took her. They hurt her.

Why? Why?

How could Andrew save them all? So many times. So many ways.

He never met Rayne. They were married. Kyle was the best man.

No. No.

Andrew punched the ground. He punched it until he hit rock. And then he punched it some more.

The images never stopped. The memories. The lives lived. The lives lost.

The Icari deserved to die. For what they did. For everyone they took.

No. The Icari died. All of them. Eradicated in the tectonic decimation.

No. No. No.

He punctuated each "no" with his fist. Blood wept from his knuckles. From his eyes. Elden, his eyes.

Were they even open?

The burning Vittle produced no smell and still broke his heart.

Why? Starve the Icari. End the enslavement of humanity.

No. No. "NO!" He howled. In his heart, this was all wrong. But—but how—

"Andrew."

Lucas. Thank, Elden. No. Kill him. He cost them the war. No, he didn't. He sacrificed himself to save them all. He betrayed Xelan. Xelan was an evil spy for the Icari—

No. No. No.

Andrew's scalp split open where he banged it against the rock. Blood oozed down his face.

"Help. Me."

His voice. Atramentous wasn't right. It wasn't multiple pitches. It was multiple voices.

"Please. Help. Me."

Fear compounded until his heart stuttered. The pain of it pulsed in his neck, wrist, and inner elbows. He wailed in the loss of it. Of his sanity.

"The fire started an hour ago. By the time, we arrived, it was too late to save it. Conscience... I can't touch him." Boklo. Icarus. Celindria's spy. Imminent trash.

No. No.

Friend. He helped grow the crop.

Their intentions. He swept over Boklo's mind.

How can we salvage this? If we start first thing tonight, maybe we can recover the loss. But we need Conscience and he's—

The intentions of the Icarus' heart made Andrew groan. Love. He loved them.

How could Andrew reconcile this?

"Help. Me."

Lucas took a single step toward him.

Traitor. Liar. Monster.

Andrew looked to the smoky night sky and roared. Both Icari went to their knees as he *suggested* they stay down. All the field hands that came to stop the fire fell to their knees.

Conscience stood. All of him stood.

Which one was he?

"Andrew," Lucas called from his knees. "You touched Cascading Light?"

Did he? Yes. Yes, Andrew tried to stop the fire. Not all of him came to stop the fire. Some came to start it. To starve the Icari. To hurt the invaders. But many of him tried to stop it.

"What…" Millions of his voices layered in his head. He clutched his ears and swayed. Lost his fucking mind.

"No!" A voice cried from the zeppelin. The source appeared behind Lucas. "Elden, no!"

Sagan.

Always the same. Perfect. Kind. Never a traitor. But sometimes dead. Korac killed her. Nox killed her. She died stopping the Tantamount. She disappeared. She married Rayne, too.

The blond girl looked around at all the people on their knees and then gazed back at the fire. The black flames reflected in her eyes, glassy with tears. "Oh, Andrew. I'm so sorry."

He closed his eyes to her love and fell to his knees.

Lucas and Boklo jumped up immediately.

"Don't touch it," Lucas called to Sagan as he ran to Andrew's side. "Andrew. Andrew, look at me? Please."

So desperate. So kind. Andrew obeyed, and Lucas recoiled. Tears sprung to the Icarus' eyes. Must be pretty bad then.

"Don't worry. We'll help you." Lucas kissed his hair.

The smell of him broke through the barrier. Expensive cologne and a hint of ginger. Andrew reached out and clung to him.

With everything and every him swirling in his head, Conscience's heart broke as he wept into his lover's chest. "Help. Me."

"Shh...shh...I have you." Lucas rocked him. "We'll take you to Dr. Suarez. He'll help us."

"Uhm. That's kinda why I'm here," Sagan squeaked out from a respectful distance away. "Something happened at the Ecology. The prisoner transfer introduced a new element of fuckery."

Pablo and Lynn. Alive. No dead. No, one of them alive and one of them dead. One of them killed the other. Andrew groaned and buried his head in Lucas' chest.

"I'm happy to take you, anyway. I'm sure they can help." Sagan took another step toward them, and Andrew swept her intentions.

I hope everyone's all right. This can't be a good sign. How much more could happen in one night? What about Rayne? Is she safe?

There. He remembered.

Rayne. All the way across the conduit, their King slept soundly. Safely. Her intentions always open to him. Love. Kindness. Strength. And a terrible sense of responsibility that left the young woman grave and severe. Resolute in her purpose. But—

"Rayne is safe. She's undisturbed," Andrew assured from where he sagged in Lucas' comforting arms.

Sagan didn't question him. She just sighed heavily in relief. "How do we put the fire out?"

"We don't." Boklo sounded so defeated that it crushed Andrew for doubting him. "Cascading Light never stops. You're looking at acres of unquenchable, untouchable flame. How in the hell did this happen?"

Sagan shoved her fingers into her short hair. "Imminent. It has to be. Somehow, they knew we were preoccupied. I need to check on everyone. But first, let's get you to the Ecology. I came here to find Lucas because you're needed there."

"Can you stand?" Lucas whispered against Andrew's ear.

All of him could. Every single one. He climbed to his feet with Lucas' steady help. The eyes. He looked through so many. His worlds blurred. But he had to try. "Boklo?"

"Conscience." The other man straightened.

Andrew hung his head, heavy with the many inside. His voice carried their numbers, "Rebuild. Please."

The Icarean botanist shouted orders, "You heard the Progeny. Get the tills. We begin anew. Let us build our fields in view of the flames to show we know no end. We will not be intimidated from our course. For Earth and Cinder!"

The people scattered and set to work in the dark.

Sagan hurried over and tucked herself under Andrew's other arm because without her and Lucas, he'd kiss the dirt. His heart swelled. And cracked. And burned.

Every single one of him.

{CINDER}

"Okay. Can you repeat that? Cascading Light?" Tameka fidgeted nervously with the pendant on her chain. "Wait. Wait. Hang on. I got something in from Jack." She read the message and felt her eyes bug out of her head. "I need to call them. They captured someone from Imminent. What was that Pablo?"

"I'm worried, Tameka. Please let me know when you hear from the others."

"I'm worried, too. I'll update you as soon as I have the full picture."

"Thanks. Over and Out."

Tameka took a second to breathe. Holy. Shit. So many attacks perfectly coordinated to take advantage of their secret meeting. Hot damn. How did Imminent know—

She pivoted in the Martyr Complex's direction. Her breath caught as she waited. A vast silence filled the pit. Like a heavy giant, it took up its own kind of space.

Was it time?

"Peaches, what in the name of Caprent acid is going on out there?"

Tameka startled and swung her gaze to the Tritan rushing down the ramp. "Imminent launched its first attack in two years. The transfer went bad, endangering Lynn, Smith, Pablo, Kyle, and Silence. They set Andrew's Vittle crop on fire with—get this—Cascading Light."

The Tritan's almond-shaped voids widened into a full circle.

Rubbing the back of her neck, she deduced, "It's safe to assume they're behind Jack's assassination attempt. What news do you have?"

"Karter reported she captured an agent of Imminent in league with those 'nacre human vs natural human protesters.'" Tumu glanced over at Rayne as he said the next, "I think we need to put Jack and them in the stronghold for a while."

Again, Tameka's eyes flared. But after another second, she nodded. "You're right. Jack needs to be safe, and there's nowhere safer."

"Safe even from me." Tumu said the last with a wince, as if it hurt his feelings.

Tameka changed the subject as she paced the lake's shore, "I need to reach out to the other groups. Where's Matt?"

Tumu followed her with his gaze as she wore a trail into the red dirt. "He and John asked to wait for Sagan at the fortress with Bones and Para. I just came from there. They're fine. No attacks."

As she considered potential targets, Tameka's heart suddenly jumped into her throat. "Pax?! Is he safe? He's safe in Enki, right?"

Tumu gripped her biceps, stopping her fretting. "He's fine. The only place safer than the stronghold is Enki."

She clutched him around the waist and pressed her face to his stomach. "I'm such a horrible mother. How could I not think of him first?"

Tumu gently pressed a hand to her back. "You're doing fine. Xelan would be so proud of how you look after your friends. After your son."

Tameka pulled away from him suddenly, shocked and ashamed of her weakness. Although, what he said hit at the heart of the matter. She often worried if she raised their son how Xelan would want. And in that moment, she believed she failed him.

Turning away, she swiped at the tears. Her voice thick with emotion, she declared, "We get this mess straightened out here, and it's back to Enki. I need to see Pax is safe."

"Of course, Peaches."

A female voice called from the vent, "Can you two believe the crazy shit happening all over Earth?"

Para alighted with Matt awkwardly stepping out of her arms. They were wet.

Bones alighted with John, who announced, "I've never seen black lightning before. I thought we were gonna die, Bones."

"Nah. I'm five million years old. Give me some credit."

"What do you mean crazy shit on Earth?" Tameka stared between the two.

Bones glanced at her and Tumu like he expected them to know. "There're storms reported across the entire planet. Sand storms. Tornadoes. Cyclones. Blizzards. It's even storming on Cinder."

Matt added, "There's lightning striking the sand in Egypt. I took some glass from it."

Tameka looked over at Rayne. "She knows."

"Damn, I'm hungry!"

They whirled to find Sagan with Jack, Chris, Karter, and Ross. The blond Progeny woman stumbled over to Para. "Hold me up for a second, would ya?"

Para smiled with concern in her eyes. "Seamswalker, you've exhausted yourself."

"And we thank you for it." Chris nodded to her.

Tumu stayed on task. "Where's the Imminent prisoner?"

Karter assured, "We dropped him off at the Ecology with the rest of the party. I can't believe how heavy they hit us—"

Jack took a step toward his sister's glass casket. "I guess we're burying me, too."

They all fell silent.

Then Ross elbowed the teenage boy. "This way, you can focus on your Story Circle. Maybe add another night a week."

Karter seconded the idea, "Yup. I'm sure you can feature people nightly if you wanted."

"We know Xelan set up the equipment for it," Chris encouraged.

"Yea." Jack perked up. "I can even put in some bulletins for missing persons. Maybe we can get some leads on Bethany."

Poor Ross. Even while she smiled, Tameka recognized the death of hope in that girl's eyes. The redhead saw it more and more in the mirror each morning. Day one on Enki, she knew she'd find Xelan. Alive. By day seven hundred and fifty-eight, doubt wormed its way into her heart and left a hole.

"Matt and I will find her if she's off world. Try to hang in there." Sagan squeezed Ross' shoulder while the other redhead in the room offered a reassuring smile. It warmed the room, even with those dead eyes of his.

Tumu watched it all. Patient as a sentinel. But with the first break, he announced, "We need to get them squared away in the stronghold. I'll watch Rayne until you return. Then Bones and Para, if you don't mind, you'll have to take over King Duty with Conscience hospitalized and Kyle overseeing Silence. We simply don't have enough Progeny to spare."

Para glanced at the Complex. "Don't worry, Officer of the Third. I consider it an honor."

Bones nodded. "We'll look after her."

Karter laughed hard, and they turned to her. "I'm sorry. Sorry. The pretense is just so funny to me."

When some tilted their heads in confusion, Chris elaborated for her, "That any of us think we're looking after Rayne when it'll always be the other way around."

The room filled with the smell of ocean, sand, sunscreen, and ice cream. They turned to gaze at the Complex. Even Tumu. The Shadow clutched their chains.

"We will always remain."

{CINDER}

Matt awoke from another dream of Lucy. His body reacted to her absence per usual. Every muscle strained and hard. He clenched his teeth almost to chipping.

Mornings like this, Lucy would tease him. First with her hand. Then with her mouth. She loved morning sex. Shit, so did he after a few months of it.

After a knock on the door, Sagan called, "We're heading out."

"Be right there."

He stood in the room made of black rock with only one narrow bed. More like a cell in a monastery than any royal chamber. Nox's Castle redefined minimalist. Spartan was more like it.

Matt headed to the pit where Rayne slept. Glancing at the Martyr Complex, he occasionally wondered about the cylinders drilling into her back. How much did it hurt? Exactly how much blood drained from her per hour? Was she aware of it?

"Love you," Sagan said in a tight voice as she hugged Tameka.

"I love you most." The redhead scratched the other girl's back. "Be safe. Come see me more often."

"You know I will."

They separated with a squeeze of both hands.

Matt understood. He didn't get a goodbye. Just woke up one day to a note and no morning sex. The nod from Tameka passed for a better farewell. He waved to her. "Take care."

Sagan stepped over to him and within a blink, they stood on an entirely new alien planet. Smelled awful. Pollution, garbage, and terror. Massive black vehicles passed between him and the purple sky above. More black metal and glass composed their surroundings, varying between warehouses and skyscrapers which kissed the atmosphere. Lights and sounds assaulted him from every surface.

Gait.

"It isn't what I expected," Matt admitted.

She scanned the area and the sky before crossing the wet street. "It's a prison planet. What exactly were you expecting?"

"More people in cells."

Her laughter hit the right note for a good mood. "One would assume. C'mon. The Emporium is down the block."

Matt followed and placed a smile on his face for her benefit. He liked Sagan and the rest of the Progeny. They kept him working. Working kept him sane.

Now that Gait busted his expectations of the planet, he considered the bizarre Emporium. Sagan stopped at the revolving door to a glass and metal warehouse. Vast, it stretched on and climbed three or four stories high. Elegant and rusted, it promised pain and a pillow to sleep off the nod after.

Matt pushed on the door. "It's locked."

Sagan took his hand and Seamswalked them inside. Onto a mezzanine with glass shelves. Someone whispered below.

"It's okay to cry. But you're old enough now to know it won't do any good except to upset you further. Do you understand?"

In the dim of the dusky chandeliers, a man knelt to meet a girl's eyes. If Matt could even describe that as a man. Tall, with a deep blue complexion and light blue hair.

A heavier man—a Mon3 drone—waited nearby. His wings rustled as he noticed their arrival.

"Are we interrupting?" Sagan's icy voice raised the hair on Matt's arms.

The blue man stood with his back to them. He turned to the drone and said something too low for them to hear. The heavy man took the girl. Blond, but not naturally. Her complexion was mottled from the crying. And then she was gone. The drone took her through a hidden door.

In Matt's work, he saw a lot of crying girls. It set his teeth on edge.

"How old is she, Razor?" Sagan spread her hands across the railing and leaned.

Razor? That's what he looked like? Huh... Matt swore Sagan described him as—

"Everything I trade in is perfectly legal within the Vast Collective, Seamswalker." He turned and trained carbon eyes on them. Razor smiled pleasantly, which felt odd given the conversation. "I don't employ sex workers under the age of legal maturity. Ergo, she is not a sex worker."

Casually, he rolled up the sleeves on his white dress shirt before shoving his hands into the pockets of his white slacks. Razor smiled even as Sagan flitted two steps away from him, leaving Matt to use the spiral stairs like a normie. It made the Pain Curator glance at Matt. And then he did a double-take. He hid it well, but the redhead learned a thing or two about body language in his years of infiltrating Cult of Night.

"I'm still skeptical about the legitimacy of your work. How exactly is this different from dealing drugs on my planet? I want to know before I work with you." Sagan stared up at him. A tiny woman ready to end this guy's career.

It made Matt smile. Dark gray eyes flicked to his. The weight of infinite lives pressed to escape them. Matt stared them down, but every muscle twitched with the urge to look away.

Razor regarded them both, "After the first experience, I'm sure you'll comprehend the difference. It will afford you an insight into yourself that you won't look away from. You'll embrace it. I know you're curious, and that's healthy. Your caution is well-earned. But I promise it's a valuable service your planets will appreciate."

Sagan hugged herself through the big sweater. Razor's eyes tracked her movements. The more nervous she looked, the more harmless he tried to appear. In little gestures, like the softening of his smile and the slouching of his posture.

To break the tension, Matt took a step forward. "I'll go first."

Razor bowed with his head. "With a sample of your pain, I can curate your experience. Or you can choose anything from our diverse catalog."

Matt ignored the request for his pain and walked over to the booth without waiting. "Hit me with your best shot."

Sagan popped over to his side and searched his eyes. She trusted whatever she found there because she backed away. "Be careful."

The Pain Curator explained the booth, "Ignore the nacre port for now. Put these goggles on and grip those when it's time." He pointed to nacre glass bars spiderwebbed from the ceiling to the walls. "Questions?"

"Yea. You know anybody looking to hire around here? I've retired my purpose on Earth, and I need something to do."

Sagan barked out a laugh, and Matt winked at her.

Even Razor's eyes sparkled with humor. Humor and too long a life lived. "We can talk after you're done. I might be looking."

"All right. Load me up."

The booth closed with him in it. Silent. The goggles deprived him of light. At first. A sensation thrummed high on his sternum. His nacre. An image appeared in his head. Asphalt. Rough. It scraped at his bare knees. Agitated his skin. His bottom lip stung. Puffy. Bleeding.

A slim finger with one long nail crooked under his chin. A woman stood over him. A Lyrik. Naked. Yellow feathers. Golden eyes. And that trademark pitch-black skin. Curvy and short.

She kissed him. Hard, and it hurt against his busted lip. Her teeth sank into the soft tissue. Matt groaned, and she sank to her knees. She kissed his bleeding palms. Sucked on his bruised fingernails. She straddled him, sinking his knees into the aggregated pavement.

The sensations confused him. Striking and burning. Arousing and agonizing. Every time he came close to shoving her away, the Lyrik apologized for her punishment with her lips and her tongue. It overwhelmed him.

Grinding against him, he hardly noticed she slipped his belt away. Her fingers trailed across his skin as she stepped behind him.

Finished. What a bizarre experience—

A starburst exploded in his vision. The split of leather on his back bruised his bones and left him breathless. Dopamine and serotonin rushed from his brain. He gripped the bars then. Something glided across the raw damage. Warm and wet. Her tongue. It fucking hurt, but did he—

"Thanks for coming."

The naked Lyrik with the deep purr vanished. Along with the entire simulation.

What. The. Fuck.

Flooded with endorphins, Matt released the bars and removed the goggles. Remotely uncomfortable, he checked his pants and found even that was simulated. Good. It wasn't like he brought spare clothes.

Matt stepped out of the booth. Razor waited for him with a devious smirk. He quirked a brow, asking a question he already knew the answer to.

"It was more than I expected."

Razor's smirk transformed into pure satisfaction.

The redhead cleared his throat and licked his lips. He half-expected to feel the sting of the busted one. Intense. "Where's Sagan?"

He gestured to the addition. "The Seamswalker isn't accustomed to sitting still. She's perusing the museum."

"You talk as if you know her."

"I know much about the Progeny. But not about their associates. Take you, for instance. You're quite the surprise."

Matt shirked off the man's interest and recovered enough from his experience to smile at Sagan, who Seamswalked over. "It's extremely immersive. There's nothing like it on Earth. And it's safe. I'm fine."

"Thanks, Matt." Her smile fell as she turned to the Pain Curator. "All right, Razor. I'll give you my pain. But I want to know more about Gait in exchange."

Razor held out his hand. "As you share your story, so will I. Let me ease your troubles, Seamswalker."

Sagan placed her hand palm down onto his. He quickly pricked her with a small capsule. Matt expected the other man to force the contact. To linger. He came to expect that of men involved in these kinds of dealings.

But Razor released her without hesitation. The man stared into the vial between his fingers as if it were the true prize. "I will begin at once. Give me a day. Return tomorrow, if you will. I promise to have something for you."

Sagan didn't meet his eyes. "Tomorrow." She turned to Matt. "Ready?"

"Actually, do you mind if I interview…Matthew, is it?"

"Matt. And sure. I'm interested in your work here."

Sagan glanced between the two before settling on the redhead. "You're sure about this?"

"Go on. I'll see you tomorrow."

After one look with uncertainty in her gaze, Sagan walked through the Seam.

"How many people have you hurt?" Razor cut right to the chase.

"More than I can count."

The man let the silence stretch between them before he pushed, "You're searching for something."

Matt looked away for a moment and changed the subject, "You got a place I can sleep tonight, boss?"

Razor stepped into his line of sight with eyes like tombstones. "I'd offer to ease your troubles, but you and I both know there is no easing what troubles you."

No. There wasn't. There was only *her*. And now she was gone.

{Gait}

The white void opened up and blanketed the entire city. Pehton learned later it covered the whole of Gait. She stepped around herself, frozen in the memory. Young, sheltered, the Pehton of two and a half million years ago screamed with tears streaming down her face. Blind, she couldn't see. Couldn't watch. Watch them be taken away.

"Peh Peh."

Present Pehton closed her scalding eyes. Never come at Razor from a place of anger. Not until—

"I know the news from Earth is startling. But I'm concerned about your expectations. I'd hate to see you hurt."

Bastard.

Gait's Executive Warden exited the booth, not with the force of her voice or the siren of her Gale. No. She held her chin high and her shoulders back. But damn, she could only think of setting this den ablaze.

The evenness of her own voice impressed her. "Thanks for the session. I'll begin the assignment this—" A flash of short auburn hair on the mezzanine momentarily distracted her. "New employee?"

Brown ice glazed over Razor's eyes as he considered her. Her gaze didn't follow as he captured her black hand in his brown one. "You work too hard." He pressed irritatingly soft lips to her wrist's pulse point.

It wasn't sexual, and it became a frequent occurrence. He measured her vitals this way to judge if the memory diving damaged her. Wouldn't want to harm his favorite prison informant.

Sick of her own bullshit, Pehton withdrew her hand. "I'm late to fulfill our arrangement. Be careful with the human." She nodded to the young man upstairs. "The Progeny look after their people like family."

He looked up at the mezzanine, watching the human inventory the wares. The Pain Curator's voice dropped an octave, "I'll keep that in mind." She hated when he did that shit.

Pehton made it halfway to the door before he called after her. She stopped, refusing to face him lest he see the raw loathing in her eyes.

"I look forward to your report."

The job. *What counts.*

The Executive Warden repeated her mantra as she descended into Infernus. She'd yet to decide how to punish Korac for betraying her kindness. Or even what to do about it. No precedent for Seamswalking existed. In truth, she hardly blamed Sagan for this. The young, impulsive woman missed her lover. But the ancient Icarean General knew better.

Empty cell. Not an Icarus in sight. Though, truly, someone redecorated. New sheets—white, of course. Some even draped from the ceiling, affording them privacy from the security recordings. Weights from Pil. A bench. Books. Clothes. A locked trunk.

But no Korac.

"Remember our arrangement."

She didn't look at the source of that elegant cadence as he walked toward her from opposite end of the hall. Hard not to notice the resonance of well-made boots on the metal floors. "Our arrangement implied you left the cell of your own ability. Not a certain Progeny woman."

"Ah, so you figured it out." He stopped a few feet away. "She's quite... tenacious. I can't begin to describe my prosperity in her."

Prosperity was one word for it, the lucky son of a—

"But she's not the cause. If I left it to her, I'd be liberated from Gait, entirely."

Pehton turned to him then. Korac leaned his side casually against the wall. Skin tight leather pants and a black silk button down. The man fidgeted with his nails. Recently manicured. Were his feet perfect, too?

Elden, damn him. "You're costing me security interest with Infernus block. You're risking my station—"

"Sketchbook."

The Lyrik recoiled. "Pardon?"

"Provide me with a sketchbook and other art supplies, and I will stay in my cell. I'll ask Sagan to practice some discretion. Though, surely you know by now I don't presume control over her." "Outside the bedroom" hung in the air.

Pehton was tired of men asking things from her when she wanted nothing in this life more than—

"Let me back in, Executive Warden."

In her momentary spiral, she didn't notice Korac step up to his cell. He waited patiently and measured her with a weighty gaze.

Pehton let him in and avoided his eyes. "Stay put, General." She stared at the floor, exhausted. It took a sheer force of will to ask, "Has Sagan updated you on the state of Earth and Cinder in the last twenty-four hours?"

"No. I haven't seen her in thirty-four hours and twenty-eight minutes."

Resisting a startled reaction took something out of Pehton. She pinched the bridge of her nose. "I researched your file extensively. You were found on Gait."

He nodded, his eyes searching her as if he calculated how these things corresponded to Earth.

"Are you familiar with a phenomenon that occurred on your last day here?"

Korac narrowed his pale eyes at her. "What happened on Earth, Executive Warden?"

"Inanis."

He bolted away from the nacre shield and shoved a hand in his hair. "How many?"

"What—"

"How many were taken?"

So he remembered.

"None."

He regained his composure with his back to her, but Pehton couldn't wait. "Why were you the only child that wasn't taken that day?"

Korac glanced over his shoulder. "We don't even know they were taken. For all we know, they disappeared or died."

"No!" Her voice rang through the block.

He turned as if finding her insistence interesting.

"All eight million, three hundred thousand children on Gait were taken. Except you." Pehton knew this. She knew so strongly that her body trembled with the certainty.

"Executive Warden, I need to know what happened on Earth." He scanned her with intelligence before offering, "Then I will tell you what I understand of Inanis."

Pehton told him of the coordinated attacks. "Most recovered, but a few were hospitalized. The Seamswalker was unharmed. Reports even placed her at Razor's Emporium."

A flick of his gaze was the only indication of his concern.

Seizing the opportunity to dig at the Pain Curator, Pehton pressed, "She's provided him a sample of her pain and assured him she'd return tomorrow for her first experience."

Korac looked completely away. His jaw clenched. "About Inanis?"

Right. Business. "Can you tell me what you remember of that day?"

"After two and a half million years, would you believe it was hazy?"

Pehton leaned back against the wall opposite his cell. "Try."

"I was with other children. We worked together—"

"This was before the changes to labor legislation?"

"Yes. We worked in the prison."

She frowned at him, but he blazed on, "They took us out to the yard. We didn't know why. Hell, I didn't even recognize the people that led us outside. I remember... It snowed. A blizzard that blanketed the yard. Our blood was so bright..."

Pehton glanced away, unwilling to press for those details.

Korac shook his head. "I can't remember much before the light. It seared our eyes. I think I passed out because I remember waking up to a man standing over me. The other children were gone."

"A man?"

"I couldn't see his face. Everything was blurry." The Icarean General rubbed the back of his neck and stretched. "Anything else?"

"You experienced Inanis one other time in your life—"

"How do you know about that?"

"We executed one survivor here years later. He said you invaded Thailea with King Nox." She glanced at the floor, imagining seeing through the tiles to the big cell. "Can you tell me about it?"

"Sure, Executive Warden. We 'invaded.' The moment we stepped foot on the planet, Inanis blinded us. The others fell unconscious. I was...less affected and harnessed that opportunity to guard my King until he awakened." Korac also glanced at the floor.

Did he know?

Pehton shook her head, losing the distraction. "So, you don't recall that either? You need to get your nacre checked."

"Maybe I do."

It was like talking to stone. Carved, attractive alabaster. "Your encounter on Thailea was the last known emergence of Inanis until yesterday."

Korac shook his head. "No. Rayne. Her eyes... It's a similar effect."

"I agree. But I don't believe the source is the same. I believe the source was present at all three instances. And I think you can help me narrow it down."

"Executive Warden, I'm a war criminal. Remember? Convicted and serving my sentence. Why would you trust me? And, since we're getting so personal here, why is this so important to you?" He narrowed his gaze at her again and stared as if he weighed her heart in his eyes.

"A terrible event blighted my planet."

"Before you were Executive."

"It affects my peace of mind."

Korac's lips twisted into his trademark devilish smirk. "Trust me with anything but your peace of mind."

Pehton pushed off the wall and approached the shield close enough to smell the peppermint on his breath. She searched his eyes beyond the mischievous humor. Beyond the warrior. She wanted to find the lost boy inside.

This was important. More so than he could imagine. She needed to trust someone. "Will you help me?"

Korac considered her question. He scanned her again. What sort of picture did she make? The Executive Warden begging for help from her prisoner. One that hid behind so much ice.

"Inanis endangers Sagan. I'll investigate your unsolved case until she's safe."

Pehton allowed relief to wash over her. She even sighed, looked to the ceiling, and thanked Elden.

He watched every second of it.

"I'll return in two days, and we can start." The Lyrik turned her back on her prisoner and went to the lift.

Before it took her upstairs, Korac called after, "Executive Warden?"

"Yes, Korac?"

"My sketchbook?"

Between the relief and maybe her first break in two and a half million years, laughter burst from Pehton. Bright. Happy. Hopeful.

"Granted, General."

ELEVEN

HOLD ONTO A GOOD SOLDIER; THERE MAY NEVER BE ANOTHER

{EARTH}

"I KILLED HER, THOUGH. I KNOW I DID. LOOK!" Lynn held up her hands, no longer soaked in red blood.

Pablo chafed her freezing fingers, unsure what to say. Yesterday, he scraped blood samples and tested the DNA. At first glance, his hands shook so badly that he dropped the results. Delivering the news to her destroyed him.

Her voice grew more shrill, "I killed her and there wasn't a body! Killed me. She was me."

Lynn, the strongest person he knew was reduced to hysterics. This woman faced an apocalyptic invasion with self-assured composure. Threw a bomb into a renegade vehicle with a broken ankle. Completely calm. But this...

"I'll talk to Lucas. I'll be right back."

She nodded without seeing him. Maybe without hearing him. His wife stared out at the ocean and watched herself die at her own hands repeatedly.

Lucas contended with his own partner's issues. Andrew slammed his head into a cement wall shortly after arriving the day before. Knocked himself out. Pablo pumped him full of experimental sedatives for nacre-bearers. The padded walls of his new room waited patiently for Conscience's mixed accounts of non-lives.

Pablo knocked gently, straightening his lab coat. Then he straightened it again. Brushed the back of his hands. Four times.

Lucas finally came out. "Doctor, can I do anything to help you?"

"Up to an interrogation?"

The Icarus' eyes shifted to teal. His voice layered in three pitches, "Absolutely."

They walked to the lab together in silence. Their quarry waited in the farthest cell, apart from the Icarean residents.

From his old cell, Twenty-One called, "If you need any help, Dr. Suarez, I'm known for this."

Pablo nodded to the surprising Icarus, genuinely considering his offer. He stepped into the private observation room and turned on the lights in the cell.

The plain-looking man sat with his back to the wall. Knees up, wrists resting on them. He stared straight ahead as if disinterested. His voice sounded hollow, "I wondered how long before you'd show up."

Lucas leaned casually against a table and folded his arms. He sounded composed as usual after resurfacing from Atramentous, "You work for Imminent."

The man nodded, staring straight ahead.

"They coordinated attacks against the Progeny in one night."

Another nod.

"Why? Why attack them? What does Imminent gain?" Lucas sounded genuinely confounded.

"We've reached the limits of which I can participate in your investigation." He looked at them with pale brown eyes.

They both recoiled.

Crazed and wild, his expression begged for something. "Time to persuade me."

Pablo was a healer. The idea of torture typically disgusted him. But the thought of his Lynn upstairs, too frightened to leave the room, fractured him into a man with few limits. He accessed the comms device on the wall.

"What's up, Doc?"

Ahh, that joke. "Kyle, I need your expertise. Med Lab 2."

"With pleasure. Can Silence come?"

Pablo nodded before he remembered the Progeny couldn't see him. "We may also require her expertise."

"On our way."

"Yes. Call your superheroes. They do your dirty work and clean up Enki's mess." The Imminent trash huffed and faced forward once more.

"You aren't in league with Enki, at all?" Lucas stood and leaned against the glass.

No response.

Kyle knocked, and Pablo let them in. Silence found some clothes that fit her. A spare suit Lucas brought for the trip. Well, part of it anyway.

His loose-fitting white pants with the suspenders stretched over a white lacy bra she borrowed from Lynn. The bright shade popped off her dark gray skin.

Catching sight of her through the glass divide, the Imminent trash stood. "Who is she?"

Lucas, Pablo, and Kyle exchanged a glance. They wanted to know if Silence shared any involvement with the organization. It was hard to say.

The Icarean female ignored him and peered at the room as if she considered the dimensions.

Kyle, sans joint, waved his hand. "Don't you worry about her for now. You and I are about to get better acquainted."

"I look forward to it, Story Taker." The stranger returned to his favorite position on the floor. "Am I not to meet Conscience as well?"

They ignored his knowing smirk.

Pablo let Kyle into the cell with Lucas for backup. Silence watched from the glass, transfixed as Story Taker knelt beside the man. He closed his green eyes and took the stranger's wrist. The connection began. The man jerked involuntarily, and Lucas gripped him from behind.

Silence crouched in an avian perch and cocked her head to the side. It caught Pablo off guard. He desperately wanted to start the research on her memory, but these attacks took priority. Until then, he kept one eye on her and one on the cell.

Kyle fell back on his ass. "Son of a bitch!"

The man grinned at him from Lucas' grasp. "That's right, Story Taker. Nothing here to take."

Silence straightened her head as Kyle looked sharply at her.

"What is it?" Lucas pushed.

The man barked out a laugh. "Why're you looking at her? Bitch can't help you—"

Lucas gripped the bastard in a sleeper hold. Pablo rushed in with the sedatives.

Silence followed, measuring the Progeny. "Yes?"

"Fuck." Kyle thrust his fingers through his hair, angry. "His memory. It's full of holes."

They all looked at the stranger flooded with tranquilizers. An ugly sneer on his lips and dark laughter in his pale eyes.

Through the hold on his throat, he croaked, "You'll never know why if I don't."

Pablo cursed, "Memory encryption."

"Son of a bitch."

The outburst from Silence took them off guard.

Kyle stared up at her and shook his head. Great. He taught her to swear.

"You can say that again."

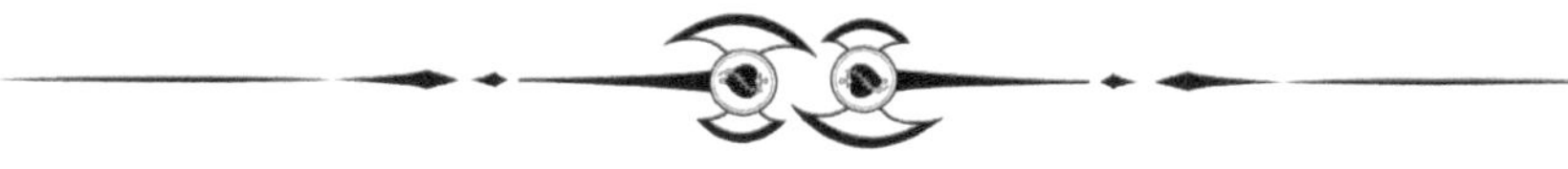

{Gait}

What a fucking week! Sagan never moved so many people around in her life. The upside to all the exhausting activity was the much needed hugs. Nothing beat quality time with the family.

She arrived on Gait after checking in on Jack, Chris, Karter, and Ross. They asked for a few accommodations for entertainment in Xelan's stronghold. Just call her the Confinement Decorator.

With that on her mind, Sagan wanted—no, needed—some time alone with Korac. Not only his physical presence, but his intellect. Things felt scattered and alive, like lightning in a storm. Guidance. Sagan craved his guidance.

But not yet. First, tonight, she visited Razor's Emporium as a patron. Cringe-worthy, really. But Matt assured her of the legitimacy of the experience. The ginger made great backup if shit went sideways, too. She worried over the Pain Curator's motivations for employing her friend, or Matt's motivations for asking. But who had time for psychoanalysis? Matt had her back, and that's all that mattered.

So why were her hands shaking as she stood outside the packed Emporium?

Could it be that Sagan wondered about herself? About her desires. About the way she attracted men like Justin, Korac, and Razor. The three were not the same, but shared similar wants. Her among them. Her pain. Control over her.

The Seamswalker gripped her axes. Her fingerless gloves creaked with the strain. The Lyriki coat made a comeback because fuck feeling vulnerable. This violet warrior could drop Razor off in space. He couldn't hurt her. Couldn't even touch her.

"Let's get this over with." Sagan Seamswalked to the mezzanine where the Pain Curator waited with his eyes already on her. Again.

He gave a little bow of his head. His bright red hair still startling against his brown skin. Tonight, he wore what she assumed passed for casual on Gait. A black carbon fiber jumpsuit that squared off on his broad shoulders.

The handsome bastard caught her looking him over and smiled. "This way."

"Wait." She messed up and touched his arm.

The Pain Curator stared a long time at the contact. When he looked up, the green half of his eyes switched places with the orange half. She dropped her hand.

After swallowing hard, Sagan confessed, "I have some reservations."

"You had a guide on Yu, Monarch 3, Pil, and Lukemore. Let me be your guide on Gait." His words came out patient and genuine.

Sagan still couldn't fathom this. "Razor, what do you want out of this? I don't have any credits. You're not getting sex."

He barked out a laugh. A good one, damn it. "Few people are candid with me. It's refreshing. I told you. I would like to broker a trade with the two planets your organization represents. It's business. You are the most likely candidate to entertain this business. Therefore, you're in charge of negotiations." He searched her eyes a minute before adding, "I also believe I can help you find your answers with no danger to you."

All the right things for him to say.

Matt appeared from a storage area toting glass crates. "Oh, hey, Sagan. Sorry for interrupting."

"You're fine." Razor pointed down and instructed, "Take those to the kitchen. They add some *inspiration* to the drinks." He grinned at the other redhead.

Who grinned back. Everybody got along so well in a pain establishment.

Sagan took a deep breath and nodded. "I'm ready."

"Very good. I'll meet you at the booths—"

Sagan flitted down into the crowd. Legir of Yu warned her about proximity to others on Gait. The usual pickpockets aside, the upper echelon accessed rare technology like the pain capsules. They might snatch her pain or some other experience for themselves. Fucked up.

"Ahh, not those booths," Razor called through the crowd. The white, shiny monoliths loomed in the addition. "They're for more advanced experiences."

She flitted to the smaller ones. "More advanced?"

He nodded almost solemnly. "They require nacre ports. Something I don't think you're ready for yet. But you will be."

Interesting.

Inside the booth, the Pain Curator beamed with excitement. "All right. Like with your friend, goggles and grips. I must admit, I'm quite ecstatic for your reaction to the first experience." Sadness flashed in his eyes. "This kind of anticipation... It's almost foreign at my age."

Sagan didn't want to buy it. "Well, remember our deal regarding information? I need answers to more than myself."

"Of course, what'll it be tonight?"

She considered her questions carefully. Although tempted to blurt out, "What do you do for Imminent," Sagan kept her cool. "How long have you been on Gait? Do you know its genesis? And why the Tritans keep it a secret?"

Creepy. Razor went stone still, but his eyes swirled again. When he spoke next, his voice dropped an octave, "I'll consider your inquiries. Ask again when you've finished."

Once he left the booth, Sagan shivered. Bizarre. The sensory deprivation between the goggles and soundproofing set her teeth on edge. Anxiously, she waited.

"Okay, so you're the princess. And you're waiting for me to rescue you."

Rayne. Eight years old. Braids and a blue dress that matched her eyes. Sagan's bedroom done all in princess pink with a canopy bed.

Sagan swallowed back tears. Why would he show her this? What does this memory have to do with pain—

Rayne tightened the knot around Sagan's wrist. The polypropylene rope splintered and shivved under her skin. The pain hit her. Sharp and immediate. She hissed.

Her best friend noticed, leaned forward, and sucked the splinter out with her teeth. Another in many encounters where Sagan realized her sexuality swung both ways. Always with Rayne.

"Do you still want to play?"

Sagan's visual moved up and down when she nodded. Endorphins rewarded her as she experimented with the pain while she pretended to sleep. Rayne whisked up their imaginary tower—the hallway—and found Sagan waiting for her kiss.

The image switched.

A lighter flicked. Flicked again. The flame lit the room as Sagan lit a candle. One second. Two. She pressed the metal to her wrist and hissed. Not in pain. In satisfaction.

She always enjoyed the pain.

The scenery morphed. Darkness. Not her memory. Her arms were not her own. Male, Icarean, and chafed with heavy metal until they bled raw. The sting of the wounds and the chill of the metal married within her. A hardness filled her mouth. Solid. It tasted of leather. Despite her experience with Justin and Korac, Sagan remained a virgin only in one respect. A self-check came back with soreness in the one place she'd yet to be touched. The full feeling confused and intrigued her. Uncomfortable, but not unpleasant at all.

Until the other man continued surging.

Sagan groaned as the Icarean male groaned. This hurt. And felt good. It also felt wrong. This wasn't discussed—

A blade sliced her shoulder. Sagan bit down and reached for the grips. Sharp, but not too deep. The assailant soothed it with his lips, lapping her blood. Still surging. Faster now. Too much. It hurt.

Fangs bit into her neck, and her knees buckled. The pain converged into the pleasurable fullness. The taking and giving.

A familiar rich voice enticed her, "So close, my Prince."

Sagan ripped the fucking goggles off. She knelt on the floor with her heartbeat thundering in her ears. The fullness lingered, but the memory faded. It wasn't hers, so she couldn't keep it. But...

That voice.

A knock sounded from the door. She hugged herself, not ready to open it. The memory left a hole. Unfinished. Unfulfilled. More. She wanted more. No...Sagan *needed* it.

"The first time is quite intense, but I understand more so for enthusiasts."

Razor entered before she permitted. He draped a carbon fiber jacket across her shoulders. Oversized enough that Sagan burrowed into it as she stared into nowhere. She tried so hard to chase the memory. To hold on and never let it go.

The bastard sat on the parquet floor beside her with his knees tucked in. He didn't touch her. Thank Elden for that. But his presence—the knowing in it—touched her in another way.

Razor owned a piece of Sagan, now. And both people sitting on this floor knew it.

"Gait was born a prison. And we are all its prisoners..."

{CINDER}

"Get Rayne and get out! Now!"

The warm light. His signature grin. His last smile.

Tameka knew without waking that tears spilled from her eyes. She relived this moment many nights in her dreams. Lately, it came less frequently. Did that mean something? Was she moving on? How does one move on from a tall, sexy alien lover with gorgeous hair and a nice ass? Or was his presence fading—

A new development. A change in the narrative. This time Tameka stayed and clung to Xelan. The light kissed her skin with its devotion. Not blinding or painful like Rayne's eyes. No. He fought with his love for them. And Tameka wouldn't let Nox take him this time.

The scenery shifted. A beach replaced the parapet in Umbra's Spire. The sand so white it reflected the sun. The boardwalk stretched into the ocean. A storm formed on the horizon.

With the storm behind him, Nox—the immense, rueful half of the similar sibling pair—stood across from them, no longer maniacal. His expression...neutral, waiting. Not with anticipation, but with unending patience. It made no sense to Tameka.

Until Rayne stepped out from behind him. Nox's face mirrored hers. They both waited.

"Rayne... what's happening?" Tameka reached out to her.

Both Kings of Cinder took a step out of reach and shook their heads. The blue-eyed woman looked into the distant storm and assured, "Not yet."

Nox mirrored her every move. They both watched the lightning strike the water. Serene and somber.

"It's not time." Tameka jumped at Xelan's whisper in her ear.

"Time for what?"

Her fallen lover kissed a tear from her cheek and looked at Rayne. The young woman's face fell, and her eyes brimmed with tears. Nox's mournful expression matched hers.

Rayne's voice layered in six pitches. Three hers and three his. "Time to end it. And then it will be time to say goodbye."

"No. I won't lose you, too." The redhead lunged for the girl. To embrace her despite the no-touching rule. To hold her and share in their grief.

But her form dissipated like shadow in her arms. Nox disappeared with her. Only Xelan remained.

The sun set behind him as he smiled down at her with so much love.

Tameka looked into his midnight eyes from mere inches away. Her voice broke as she begged, "Please, don't go."

"Protect Pax and be ready. Just a little longer, Tameka."

"Xelan!"

"Tameka."

She startled at John's voice. He sat on the sofa looking lost. Couldn't blame him. With each gasping breath, Tameka regained her reality. The pit. Asleep on a pallet of blankets. She and John waited for Para and Bones to relieve them while Tumu arranged their return to Enki.

Thunder cracked and echoed through the vent. The storms raged over the last two days. What did Rayne confront inside her dreams? Or was she worried about them?

The Osage human still peered at her from the leather two-seater. She waved him off with a promise, "I'm fine, John."

"Been a while since—"

"I know." She didn't mean to cut him off so sharply, but the uncontrollable aspects of her grief were private. Softening her tone, she added, "All the stress got to me. It's perfectly natural."

He turned back to the TV as Tameka unfolded and stretched. She heard the voices before they breached the chamber. Tumu and—

"Eminent Abresson, this isn't necessary. Rayne is perfectly safe under Progeny guard."

They entered the pit, and the short, dark Tritan paused at the top of the ramp. Abresson, former Officer of the Fifth, stared down at the Complex. Even at this distance, Tameka watched the possession and greed pass in his round eyes. His voice filled with it as he muttered, "Truly lovely. The Probabilities harmonize into a chorus around her as she sleeps, unaware of the destruction she wrought." Banging his fist once on the banister, he added with a snarl, "Curse Nox."

The source of Abresson's life hummed to Tameka, and the thirsty well inside her beckoned like a siren's fury. Her voice went low, not yet Atramentous, "What the hell do you—"

Behind the Eminent, Tumu shook his head in a flurry. His eyes stern, and his mouth tightened into a thin line. A warning.

What the fuck was happening?

"Eminent, it's so nice to see you." John hopped off the couch and stepped over. He managed the professional facade far better than Tameka wanted to.

The dark blue Tritan smiled at John. As they shook hands, Abresson's robe fell back, revealing scars stark white against his navy skin. "Educator, I'm always pleased to see the only Earthling I've met with manners." He tossed a jeer at the redheaded Progeny.

Her Atramentous flashed. She couldn't stop it. Tumu caught her gaze with a raised brow. He mouthed, "Remain. Calm."

"Fascinating," Eminent Abresson said before dismissing them with his back. He stared out at Rayne. "We're appointing one Tritan guard to accompany her Progeny fan club."

Tumu stepped in. "Don't be ridiculous. It's unnecessary. And only a Primary can order—"

"Primary Bol's orders." The dark Tritan held out his palm and displayed a projected missive in a language Tameka didn't understand.

The friendlier Tritan read aloud, "'Instated once we lift the Progeny embargo.' Embargo?" Even with a nacre, Tameka sometimes found it hard to make out the expressions on a Tritan's face. They didn't have lips or raised noses. No eyebrows either. But as Tumu comprehended the exact meaning of the message, the look of terror in his almond-shaped eyes was unmistakable. He breathed one awful word, "No."

"Yes."

"But, Eminent, if Enki enacted an embargo on the Progeny then . . ." John shared the same horrified expression as the Officer of the Third.

The two good men turned simultaneously and looked at Tameka. Both in panic. Wordlessly, both asked the same thing of her, but she couldn't quite decipher it.

Anxious, she searched for their meaning. "What? What does that mean?"

Abresson answered with his back to her, "It means Enki is closed to hybrids until further notice. King Jack, a Progeny inherent, contracted a deadly virus. We must place your kind under quarantine while we investigate." He turned with his signature smug grin as he announced, "You can't return until I say."

And then there were no more lights on Cinder.

{EARTH}

"But don't lose hope, Sonya. It's hard without our loved ones. I know firsthand. We can make new families, and it only gets better from here. Remember that none of the Progeny are related, but they're closer than family. Hang in there..."

Chris leaned in the archway as Jack carried on his marathon Story Circle. The kid went nonstop for the last ten hours. The announcement to stop ingesting nacres did not go over well. So he ran interference to compensate. At this rate, his soft tissue repair would need a break from the damage to his vocal cords.

Karter looked up from one of Xelan's many journals. Tens of thousands of them lined the hexagonal walls of his three-story study. The black fire flicked and flared within the fireplace. After catching Chris' eye, the Valkyrie shook her head.

Ross traded out her volume for another. Softly, she muttered, "I don't think I could live long enough to read all of this."

Chris smiled sadly as Karter's expression wilted. Xelan's loss would never stop affecting the Shadow and so many more lives he touched.

"We're also looking for someone. Please, if anyone knows where the Cult of Night took Bethany Roberts, we'd appreciate any information. I'll repeat her description. White, no freckles. Fifteen years old. Dark brown curly hair. Golden brown eyes. Birthmark on her right shoulder. We lost her during the invasion. Please..."

Jack kept at it. The poor teenage King slumped his head into his hand, stretched across the desk's surface. Tumu hooked them up with a Tritan comms device. It ranged beyond the many stories beneath the desert.

Xelan's stronghold was part modern spa, part nifty alien museum. Chris imagined the Icarus with an eye patch swashbuckling across the Vast Collective gathering artifacts from precious locations. Tumu confirmed the suspicion, "That sounds right. Except there was this one heist he pulled sans eye patch and in the buff."

Karter stood abruptly and stretched with a yawn. "I loved that Icarus to the end of the worlds and back, but he wrote for some dry material. Like bread crust and no spice. All tech manual, no drama. I'm headed for bed." She turned to Ross. "We'll pick it back up again tomorrow."

"Bed sounds good," Jack mumbled and rubbed his eyes. "How long was I on the air?"

"Forever," Ross answered without looking up. Though she gave a small smile.

Chris put an arm around Karter with a grin in her direction. "Think we can find a bed big enough?"

She laughed, pure and rich. "I already checked. Though we should avoid the Progeny rooms. I think they stay down here sometimes."

"Who could blame them?" Jack stood and stretched with an audible crack. He slumped over to one wall and retrieved a volume. "Where are we up to?" he asked Ross as he sat beside her on the black leather couch.

"You must be exhausted. Go to bed. I'm fine up on my own."

As the two teenagers carried on, Karter shot Chris a look with a nudge of her elbow. Oh, right. "Good night, you two."

"Night."

"See ya in the morning... afternoon... whatever time it'll be." Jack waved with the book before settling back on the sofa.

Chris was headed for the crazy chasm with the step-responsive glass when another elbow to his ribs stopped him. Karter put a finger to her lips and flattened herself against the wall near the study's entrance.

"Eavesdropping?" Chris mouthed with a brow raised in disapproval.

She shrugged with a mischievous grin.

Batman joined her with a quick shuffle closer.

"Thank you, Jack, for trying so hard. And for...you know? Letting me come with you guys. It's been a great way to stay in touch with Kyle and—"

"I like you, Ross. Sorry for interrupting. But I've been waiting for the best time to say it. And, with everything going on, it still doesn't seem like the best time. But I need to get that off my chest. Regardless of if you think about me in the same way or if you just want to be friends, I'm finding your sister. Nothing would make me happier right now than reuniting the two of you. On that, I promise you."

A silence stretched. The tension built until it hurt. Chris and Karter both almost leaned into the study. They exchanged a look with wide eyes. He offered a thumbs up to her, but she shook her head solemnly.

Damn.

Ross finally said, "I like you a lot, but I want to be as honest with you as you were with me. I haven't thought much like that since Invasion Day. I miss my sister. And I can't shake this feeling that we're close to finding out if we can save her or if I lost her long ago. That said, I'm grateful to know you. I hope you understand."

"I understand missing your sister. And I can feel it. We'll find her. Soon. I'm almost certain of it."

"Thanks, Jack."

Chris wanted to pat the kid on the back. Rough shut down, but completely understandable. No more matchmaking until after they found Bethany.

Karter took his hand and led him through the glass maze and down a tunnel some floors above the common space. He asked, "Do you think Kyle got any intel off the Imminent prisoner you caught?"

Several doors lined the quiet corridor. Their voices echoed.

Karter explained, "No. When the strikeforce hit the apartment building, the scumbag was just waiting for us. He expected us to find him."

"What do you think this all means?" Chris took in the concern etched in her high cheekbones and striking brows.

She dragged him into a room as she confessed, "That we may not get much private time in the near future, so I'm taking advantage of it while I can."

The floors, ceiling, and carpet were black. The bed was black. It was an abyss. She lit a candle and another. Twelve candles in the vacuous space.

He'd longed to do this for the past several days. Chris loosened her braids, slowly, appreciating the soft curled rainbow hair that he freed. They met eye-to-eye at her height. She kissed him with a purr. He pulled Karter up by gripping under her thighs, and she wrapped her legs around him. Mercifully, she untied her red shirt and ripped it open.

The saint.

Karter's complexion struck him as unusually dark compared to the rest of the Icari. Charcoal against his deep brown skin. He liked their hands locked together with the contrast. And that's what she did. She laced their hands together, and they both stared.

As if they had all the time in the world.

TWELVE

LIARS RARELY MAKE FOR GOOD COMPANY

{EARTH}

PUSHED.

No.

Dragged in. Thrown in. Jumped in.

"Stop!" Andrew railed against his nacre glass restraints and screamed.

They won and killed all the Icari.

They lost. The Icari enslaved humanity.

No one won. The Tantamount detonated and plunged Earth into volcanic winter—

"Help. Me."

"What do you see?" Lynn asked as she gingerly entered the padded cell. Traitor. Best friend. Wife. Dead.

Andrew twisted until he moaned in his pillow. "Make it stop."

The dead/not-dead woman stepped closer. Her voice sounded distressed and pitying all at once, "I can get you a sedative."

Her intentions blared at him.

Help him. Hold his hand. We both could use a friend.

He nodded as fresh tears poured down his scalding face. By now, the tears blistered the corners of his eyes. How could he stop crying? Every other second he lost a friend that wasn't dead. Then they resurrected before his very eyes. Everyone wanted to help, but looking at them hurt. So many others echoed beyond them in shadows of unlived existence.

This was what madness felt like. Not exactly what Andrew read in the brochure.

The needle filled with experimental tranquilizers punctured his skin and plunged home. Lynn slipped a bandage on it and kissed it almost on reflex. It healed within minutes, but the tenderness soothed hours of the confusing mess in his chest.

"Thank. You."

"Shh...They're busy with the Imminent guy." Lynn pressed a cool cloth to his face, and the relief almost brought more tears to Andrew's eyes. The sedatives kicked in, and he barely followed the rest of her explanation, "They targeted us. Deliberately. Driven crazy to weaken a position we hold. When you wake up next, keep that in mind. Think on it. And then tell me. Why us?"

Andrew stared at her face as his vision blurred and blackness swallowed it away. For a second, a different Lynn sat there. Confused and reluctant. But she was dead now, wasn't she? Or was she?

Analyze the attacks. Find the pattern. And answer the important question.

Why them?

{GAIT}

Korac bolted upright on his cot, fitted with luxurious white sheets made from Luk silk. Adrenaline pumped through his veins and burned like mercury. He sought anything in the cell to distract him from the nightmare. The pillow, damp with his sweat, smelled of the oils from

Monarch 3 that he rinsed through his hair. The ones Sagan picked out for him. Like the sheets.

Breathe. Deep.

Amethyst eyes. Freckled nose. Lavish lips. Brilliant. Sweet. Never satiated of her—

A ghost of his Sagan stepped into the cell a foot from his cot. The blond girl approached him with a hand cupped over her mouth. She stifled a whimper. Salt scented the room.

Korac sprung from the bed with his hands out, weaponless. Scanning her flushed face, he offered, "I want to check you. Will you let me touch you?"

A sob choked from her and broke his heart. Yet still, she gave a small nod. The former General brushed Sagan's hair from her face and searched for external injuries. Tension racked her neck and shoulders as she cried softly into his chest. She trembled in his arms.

Against her hair, he muttered, "Are you willing to tell me about it?"

"What the fuck is wrong with the Tritans?"

The subject took Korac by surprise. He leaned back enough to search her eyes, red with tears. So determined. She meant the question, and she came to him for an answer.

Solemnly, he shook his head. "No one really knows the motivations for their ways." An honest answer.

"No one with that much power should go unchecked." Sagan's eyes burned with violet fire.

Korac led her to the bed and sat them both down. He patted her tears with the sheets. "What fresh travesty brought on this unexpected conversation?"

She looked away from him.

Ah. This was her tell, then. When Sagan visited Razor, she felt the need to hide her eyes from Korac. Shame? Guilt, maybe? He'd have none of it.

The Icarus tucked a finger under her chin and brought her gaze to meet his. "I trust you in all things. I'll never judge you for what you experience while protecting your people. Or anything, for that matter. You can tell me anything, Sagan. I will love you regardless of how wrong you think you've behaved." Korac refused to stop the smirk from spreading across his lips. "Hell, I might love you more for it."

The soft blush amid all those tears meant the world to him. Sagan looked into his eyes and confessed what he already knew, "I came from the Emporium just now. I... I went through with the first experience. And afterward, Razor told me about Gait's formation."

Bewildered, Korac recoiled. "Gait? This prison?"

"No, and yes. The entire planet's establishment. It's monstrous. I know you told me you were found here. Are you familiar with it?" Sagan curled her legs under her and sat cross-legged. Less sad. More determined to share the tale.

He encouraged her, "Go on."

Sagan pushed her short hair back nervously. "Just some insignificant planet the Tritan's experimented with different gas compositions in the atmosphere. Eventually, it terraformed with this purple sky. But they withheld the same bacteria and DNA for life they placed on all the other planets. Preserving it for a darker purpose."

Korac's lips twitched with the urge to smile at her dramatic flare.

"As our planets formed life, the Tritans feuded with the Ancients for technology." The turn of topic made Korac frown, and Sagan drifted further away into the story. "Those people were untouchable. Probably the only force capable to rival the Tritans. But one who benefited from switching sides betrayed the Ancients. The advantage turned the tide in the opposition's favor.

"They chased the Ancients back, eventually to Thailea. In the meantime, the Tritans contended with the Ancient traitor. What reward fitted him best? They exiled him on the planet with a purple sky.

"They did the same with anyone who troubled their tyranny. Until the planet itself became a prison with no regulations."

This was not a history Korac heard in his lifetime. Ancients. Tritans. A traitor. None of this.

Sagan's purple eyes fell, and she bit into her lip. Obviously she withheld some ugly truth.

"You can tell me." Korac pressed his thumb to her carotid and felt the flutter of her pulse.

"Korac, they made children work for that prison. The children born on Gait. I knew of the Prisonborne. But I never considered how few rights they had until recently when the wardens enacted labor laws."

His life's story. Was it time to share it with her—

"Who built the prison?"

Sagan and Korac glanced at one another before the Icarus rolled his eyes. Fucking blockmate. The Icarus growled, "What do you mean?"

"Well, if they dropped people off as prisoners then the entire planet belongs to the inmates, right? So who built this prison facility and why? Why would the Tritans hide this history? It sounds fairly benign on the surface." The man's voice echoed through the hall with reasonable points of contention.

Sagan called out, "What's your name?"

Korac raised his brows at her, and she offered an innocent shrug. Engaging a thug in this cell block seemed ill-advised, but alas…

"Remorse," the blockmate answered in a voice thick with some unidentifiable emotion.

She smiled. The purity in it twisted Korac's heart. Warm and sincere. For a stranger's sake. The concept was foreign to him. Then she shocked him further, "I like your kind of thinking, Remorse. I'll add your questions to my research. Anything else you want to contribute? Like why you're in here?"

After a stretch of silence, Remorse shut down, "That's enough talking for now."

Sagan turned back to face Korac. The pout to her lips at Remorse's rejection affected him. It was a slight at most, but her personal response to it made him want to rip his blockmate's limbs off until he apologized and made friends.

The former General barked out a laugh. Sagan screwed her face up at him, and it warmed his laughter. He kissed her confused, pouty lips, and happiness filled him even while stuck in this cell.

"I think my experience at Razor's involved you somehow."

That sobered Korac instantly. "Why?"

She shook her head slightly as she grasped at the memory. "Your voice. I heard it."

So, the rumors were true. Korac cleared his throat before offering, "After The Vacating, Xelan traveled great distances to track Celindria. I understand at one point he crossed paths with Razor. It's why I sought the Pain Curator out, which ultimately led to Nox's access to Cascading Light."

Her short hair bounced as she nodded. "I think that makes sense. I was unprepared for it. I can barely remember it. Is that because it's not my memory?"

Korac lifted Sagan's hand and kissed her palm. "Yes." Then placed a kiss on her fingertip. "I understand it's an intense experience."

She stared, fixated at his attentions. She forgot to breathe, and when she finally remembered to exhale, it left on a feminine sigh. "At first it was intense, but then I felt empty after."

He sucked the tip of her finger and pricked it with his fang. She inhaled sharply, and her eyes fluttered closed. Between laps of her blood, he explained, "I understand there's only one true remedy for it."

Breathless, she asked, "What's that?"

"Proper administration of real stimulation."

She swallowed hard enough for him to hear. "Yes..." Her eyes rolled back as he nipped at her wrist. "Yes. I already feel better."

Korac chuckled. He loved her utter relinquishment to him. "Then why don't you show me everywhere the nasty simulation touched you. I'll kiss it and make it better."

And lick. And suck. And bite.

{CINDER}

All of them fell to their knees. Tameka couldn't care. She never knew power like this. A glow encompassed her. Not white like Rayne's, but green like Tameka's eyes. Was there a point past Atramentous? Nanite circuitry buzzed inside her like live wire. Electric. Almost on fire.

It burned.

It hurt.

Somehow it needed release. There was too much, and it threatened to consume her. Tears spilled so hot down her cheeks they left scorch marks. Use it or send it somewhere else, her instincts begged.

But the power was so enormous, so monumentally colossal. Where could she send it? How could she use it without killing her friends? Rayne was right. It wasn't time yet. If Tameka killed Abresson now, she'd never see her son again. Even this display of power risked her precarious position.

Tameka sought a vessel vast enough. A nacre called to her. With only one intention. To consume.

It lived in Li.

Tameka fed it. Let Cinder's star take it all before she committed a crime against the Vast Collective and killed her best friends on accident. The red giant pulsed in time to her heartbeat as it drank from her. Purple. Then red. Then purple again. Until all of it drained away.

Tameka. Fury. Sovereign Ambassador of the Two Worlds just fed a star on her power. A star with a nacre at its heart.

"Like Celindria ..." Abresson muttered while gazing at her with a sneer.

Fuck that bitch. Tameka's power was unique, and she refused to let someone compare it to that evil, skanky—

Abresson held up his hand to stave her. "You wouldn't want to hurt your son, now would you?"

Tameka still couldn't talk after serving up a planet's worth of power to a sun, but she didn't need words to beat Abresson's ass.

Tumu barked, "What kind of threat is that—"

"I'm not a monster!" The darker Tritan looked genuinely offended. He even shot a glance at John. Kneeling in the red soil, their human friend looked like shit. The troll helped the one-legged man up. "I thought to warn you before you accidentally harm your own child."

A cry carried from the pit's entrance. Caedes' voice cut through the noise, "Slow down, kiddo."

Pax. On Cinder.

Tameka broke into pieces and flew up the ramp.

"Mommy!" Her son cried as he entered the space with Caedes behind him.

The tiny Xelan lookalike jumped into her arms and clung with the strength of his races. A life she almost snuffed out without realizing her own strength. A warm hand pressed against her back, making her flinch. Caedes, with so much concern on his face, blocked Abresson's view of Tameka's reunion with her son.

"Thank. You," she mouthed, meaning it.

Pax muffled against her a few times before she let go enough for him to talk. "I know this place, mommy. I see it in my dreams."

He jerked until Tameka let him go, and then he ran down the ramp. With a wave to Tumu as Pax ran by, the boy took the skid to the center. Everyone watched as he approached the Martyr Complex. Except Abresson. He stared intently at Tameka.

"Hi, Auntie Ray. I bwought Uncle Caeda like you asked. Safer together, right?"

From the top of the ramp, Tameka gazed down into the glass box. Her heart stopped. Rayne smiled, warm and alive through the illuminated blood. With Abresson present, it wasn't likely she'd send a more obvious message.

"That's right, Pax." Caedes flew down to the boy and muttered to him about the girl named Callahan in the box.

Tameka finally looked Abresson in the voids. He took that as permission to speak, "As I said. I'm not a monster. I wouldn't separate you from your son. I pulled a lot of strings to arrange this against Bol's initial protests. Consider yourself owing me a favor."

John muttered, "Thank you, Eminent."

"Of course, John, you're welcome to return, being human. You and Caedes are not a part of the embargo."

"After a night, we'll return," Caedes answered for the other man. He spared a wink at Tameka.

Was that amazing Icarus onto something in Enki?

Since Pax's arrival, Tumu remained silent. But Tameka caught glimpses of him glaring upside Abresson's head. As if the Tritan imagined his colleague's skull as a statement piece for his office. It was the most naked violence she'd seen from the Officer of the Third.

Eventually, Tumu broke in, "What about the mandatory guard?"

"Ahh." Abresson turned back to Tumu as if he forgot his presence altogether. "You can select the guard as long as Earth remains your jurisdiction."

Definitely a hint of a threat in there.

"Lamassu."

Who?

Abresson recoiled with a full step back and everything. "The Chef?"

Tameka looked at John, who shook his head in confusion. In all her time on Enki, they never heard of anyone referred to by that moniker.

Tumu nodded without backing down. "He's qualified."

The not-brow raised so high on Abresson's face that it bordered on his bald lack of a hairline. "Very well. Now, is there anywhere I can find accommodations and entertainment on Earth without risking poison in my food? I'll stay until John and Caedes leave."

The aforementioned Icarus took the skid back across the lake, to Pax's delight. The boy glided his fingers across the black water with glee, blissfully unaware of the surrounding diplomacy.

"Iona Medical Ecology," Tameka blurted out. In Nox's Verse, Abresson seemed pretty chummy with the unnamed

Primary. Ultimately marking him as an Imminent suspect. Maybe housing him with the current suspect in custody could help with their investigation. Not to mention, Tameka needed to share with the rest of the group that Li contained a nacre, for fuck's sake.

Abresson looked shocked. "Oh, really?"

Tumu shot her an "are you sure about this" look. John gave a thumbs up behind Abresson. Caedes, in his usual tough-guy facade, nodded as if he feared nothing either way.

Tameka stood straighter and held her chin higher. "Yes. We'll ask Bones and Para to guard Rayne, and then we'll all head to the Ecology. Maybe we can demonstrate the measures we're taking with the virus there and assail any fears regarding the embargo."

And keep this creep away from Rayne's unconscious body in the process.

{GAIT}

Matt stared at his reflection in the bar he polished to a pristine shine. His dark brown eyes looked haunted. Seven months. Soft blond hair. Dark blue eyes. Tan skin.

Not for seven months.

A heavy crate filled with bottles of bizarre fluids dropped on the counter beside him. Razor rested an elbow on it as he indicated a projector along the south wall. "That's the competition."

A band played a festival scene with lots of pyrotechnics and mosh pits. The stage reminded him of something offhandedly familiar, but Matt failed to see the connection.

"What, boss?"

Every time he used that word, the Pain Curator smiled extra at him. They established a kind of rapport with their exchange of prodding questions and boundary testing. It kept Matt's mind stimulated enough that he drifted off less over Lucy. It also allowed an avenue to help Sagan out on her mission.

For instance, learning about Razor's business and competitors.

The strange man with dark blue skin elaborated, "Night Rayne. They offer a truly unique experience that even my clientele patronizes. In secret, of course."

At Matt's raised brow, Razor punched his free palm. "Violence."

The redhead perked up then. Sounded all right to the twenty-year-old human.

With a crooked smirk, the Pain Curator continued, "That's right. Everyone appreciates good violence. And while I offer a measure of it here, Night Rayne isn't simulated. That—" He pointed with a nail-less finger. "—Is authentic. Every night ends in death."

"How's that? Aren't there regulations?"

The boss shook his head solemnly. "None. The lead singer there is Rayne. Perfect likeness of her, anyway."

Matt gauged the woman on stage and fought the urge to argue. Rayne was taller, more muscular. Her hair was darker. The girl on the stage made for a close counterfeit. And it was an interesting concept. "So, a rock musical with a singing Rayne?"

"One song." Razor held up a finger. Again, no nail. "They perform only one song a show. In that time, she chooses a lucky member of the audience as her Nox."

Matt widened his eyes for effect.

"That's right. She takes his nacre and kills him. Swallows it and everything. There's nothing like her and nothing can simulate that anticipation and gore. The spectacle of it..." Razor stared off as if seeing something other than the Martyr Complex Bar & Lounge.

Gore. Violence. Romanticized a rape-based tragedy for the credits. Matt clenched his jaw and took the crate. It drew his boss back to reality.

The Pain Curator swept his gaze across the place and nodded appreciatively. "You're doing good here. But I suspect you'll need your fix soon. I don't think the booths will satisfy you."

The redhead kept his eyes on his task and his mouth clamped shut. "I'll manage. Hey, where did you get the idea for them, anyway?"

"It was a collaborative effort. My idea. A contributor's technology." Razor waved goodbye as he headed for the door.

"You mean Celindria?"

At that, the man came to a screeching halt. After a long pause, he turned and met Matt's gaze. Those gray eyes expanded. Still pupil and iris, but no more cornea. "What makes you say her name?"

"She stole memory tech from the First Wave Progeny." Throwing around this level of intel really tested the advantage, but nothing ventured, nothing gained and all that. "Then she weaponized it in capsules like the pain one you carry around. I figured the booths evolved from that."

He nodded so slowly it hurt Matt to watch it. "Although the Divine Booths predate her, I can see how one might reach that conclusion. What has you so curious?"

"Well, I wondered how your business will do now that she swore off the vice trade to join the ranks of Eminent?" Matt glanced over at a projector with a Rayne advertisement before returning his gaze to Razor.

"How loyal are you to the Progeny?" He sounded genuinely uncertain.

The projector behind Razor played its millionth repeat of Nox violating Rayne. Her bright blue eyes steeled for the assault to begin. Matt considered the definition of loyalty before he gave an answer, "Not at all really. They keep me working, and that's all I need."

A smirk spread across the Pain Curator's deep blue lips. "Then you are no more loyal to me."

"As long as you give me work, I'll be as loyal as you need."

"Follow me." Razor walked out the door.

Matt mentally congratulated himself for this breakthrough as he followed the other man to the Emporium. Passed the mezzanine's spiral stairs, around the concrete accent wall, and into the kitchens. The man with periwinkle hair glanced around, checking the pristine conditions as he continued to the back storeroom.

This was it. Matt hoped the Pain Curator would reveal what he secured away in the back half of the addition. He kept it locked with only one employee—the Mon3 drone—allowed entry.

Razor paused and turned to Matt with acuity in his expression. "The Seamswalker wouldn't like what's behind this door. Do you understand me? It's perfectly legal, but not everyone can appreciate the finer intricacies of an enterprise such as mine."

Matt licked his lips and confirmed with a nod. "I won't breathe a word to her. She has enough on her plate, anyway. No need worrying over 'perfectly legal' activities."

Again, the approving smirk. Without another word, Razor opened the door.

To Hell.

THIRTEEN

BREATHE WHILE YOU STILL CAN

{EARTH}

LYNN SAT WITH ANDREW FOR AN HOUR AFTER HIS BREATHING TURNED EVEN. The man always struck her as tender and eager to help anyone. To see him in so much anguish set her teeth on edge.

With renewed purpose, Chief Lynn headed down to the labs. She snuggled deeper into the sweater she forever borrowed from Pablo as she accessed a Tritan-grade terminal. Similar to the tech in the arsenal, she navigated the database until she retrieved the file she wanted.

Twenty-One's image stared back at her. The heavy-set Icarus wore the same patient and, frankly, kind expression in the archived footage of his tenure since Volcano Day. Perfect health. Excellent reflexes. But the most recent round of testing interested Lynn and the arsenal's secret benefactors.

Abresson came to them and requested a weapon. One which targeted and disabled nacre from a fifteen-foot distance. Predicting mutual benefits, The Brethren accepted his request. And Lynn engineered it.

Imagine how many wars they could stop. How many lives saved. How many disabled weaponized nacres like a certain sleeping King.

The arsenal successfully created it. And then they lied to the Tritans. As far as Enki knew, the disabler failed. The Brethren partially withheld the truth because it required more testing and extensive monitoring that the tyrants refused to endorse.

But mostly because The Brethren wanted Rayne's approval.

See, they were good guys after all. But the top secret project might turn stomachs and more than a few heads, so they forbade Lynn to share it with even Pablo.

This was their future.

With that in mind, she believed the Tritans wouldn't dream of creating a weapon like this without a counter. And she found it in Pablo's tests on Twenty-One. Staring at the file, Lynn recognized the chain of releases in nanite functions. But in reverse. A virus, with Dr. Suarez's signature attached to it, prevented tampering with the carrier's nacre. Another signature on the form next to her husband's name chilled Lynn's blood.

Abresson.

One weapon neutralized Rayne for potential assassination. The other shielded her nacre beyond manipulation. Permanently. The virus's antibodies never left the nacre's systemic drive.

Jack Callahan made for a helluva trial subject.

How could Lynn not anticipate this? Pablo tested the virus on Twenty-One. She knew that. It made him the perfect candidate for testing the disabler. But she didn't know Abresson ordered it until now.

Is that why Imminent wanted the prisoner of war? To reverse engineer it and manufacture it? To weaponize it?

Or did they mean to lock Rayne in that Weapon forever?

A knock on the door startled Lynn. She turned to find Pablo leaning in the doorway, hands in his labcoat pockets. Even with a nacre, he had bags under his warm brown eyes.

"I'm glad to see you up and around." He nodded to the terminal. "Does it help with the stress?"

Lynn smiled weakly at him. She wanted so badly to try for him. "It's a distraction. But I think I'm onto something helpful."

He grabbed the nearest office chair, pulled it up, and straddled it. "I'm looking forward to any good news at this point."

She winced with concern. "I'm not sure how good I'd call the news. I think they intended to replace me with that copy. To gain access to the weapons. To this one in particular." She pointed to the screen.

Pablo leaned across her to read it. "The nacre lock?" Stretched forward, he spoke the words close to her ear.

The warmth beckoned goosebumps to freckle her dark skin. Well, at least Lynn's sex drive recovered. Now if her sanity would please follow, she could salvage this vacation with her husband, solve the damned case, and kick Imminent to the curb.

"It pairs with the weapon we wanted to test on Twenty-One. That's why Imminent came for him." She turned to her husband.

He turned to her. Their eyes only an inch apart. Pablo licked his lips. Lynn's heart somersaulted in her chest.

"There you are," he breathed against her lips. Brushing a loc from her face, he leaned into kiss her.

And damn her, Chief Lynn stopped him with a finger against his soft, full, tantalizing—

"No." She shook her head, as much to dissuade him as to stop herself. "We need to focus. Then after, I plan to mark every surface in this lab with you. But not until we solve this."

He smirked and mercifully put some distance between them. "Yes, ma'am."

"Good. Now listen carefully and tell me if you think I'm onto something."

Lynn told him about the nacre disabler and about her theory involving Imminent's intentions.

"Abresson requested these. Why would he put his name to it? Not exactly clandestine," Pablo reasonably pointed out.

She rolled her eyes. The man always pointed things out reasonably. "He's cocky and important. He doesn't think it matters. And maybe if they succeeded, it *wouldn't* matter. I'd be dead and the other Lynn would cover his tracks..." Her words grew breathier until they trailed off.

Dead. Replaced.

A warm hand took hers and brought Lynn back around. "You're doing great. This is the sort of evidence we need for the Progeny. Possibly The Brethren. And you're here, Lynn. You're safe."

Lynn nodded a few too many times and a little too quickly. Pablo pressed his lips to hers. One peck. Two. A deeper kiss. Soft, warm. His scent so familiar. She brushed her fingers into his black hair, coiled soft and thick. The tangible access to him comforted her. Fought back the anxiety and replaced it with something much more preferable.

She hopped off her chair and into his lap, straddling him in the chair. Lynn liked him in scrubs. She always knew how happy Pablo was to have her this close to him. He moaned. She purred.

The sweater disappeared first. Then the bra. He covered every exposed inch of her with his eager hands. When he squeezed her ass, she cried out for him and ground against him.

Pablo was very happy.

"...Do we know when the testing will complete—Oh! I wasn't aware The Brethren included this incentive in your salary."

Lynn yelped and hid herself inside Pablo's labcoat. Lights blinded them. Once her sore eyes adjusted, she groaned. And not the sexy kind.

Abresson stood in the doorway with Tumu in tow. He made no effort to look away from the couple in the room. Pablo glared at him as he swiveled the chair to shield Lynn's nudity. He helped her get dressed with as little exposure as possible.

Meanwhile, she barely registered her surroundings. Too many shocks, too close together. Her head felt airy and fuzzy. "I think I need to lie down."

Abresson huffed. "Yes. Why don't you find a residential cabin to 'rest' in rather than the semi-public laboratory?"

"Eminent." Tumu's voice held a warning.

Tameka bolted around him into the room. Her voice held genuine remorse, "I'm so sorry. I tried to get here first, but there were too many people who needed to talk to me. How are you doing?"

As she searched Lynn's gaze, the darker woman took in so much compassion. "I'm making it. We'll catch up after my nap. Pablo, can you come with me?"

He put a comforting hand on her back and walked her out of the lab. They both expected some snide remark from Abresson. But they passed him without incident.

Instead, Tumu followed them out. He looked sheepish—if that could be said for a Tritan—as he requested, "I need a favor. And you can't tell Tameka."

Pablo and Lynn exchanged a look. Honestly, all this exceeded her capacity for the day. But still she took the bait. "What is it?"

"I need you to take a sample of Pax's blood. And run this list of tests for me."

Take blood from the son of Fury and Wingmaster. Endanger the foundation of their friendship. Fall deeper into the Tritan agenda.

"Sure, why not?"

{???}

324 reached their breaking point. The tears never stopped. The shame never ended. Every lash of the whip, every strike of the belt, every knife in the ribs—

No. More.

They waited in their bunk for the next rotation. Rocking. Crying. Repeatedly weighing the desperate choice. Endure? Or end?

Clean. Never dirty. Fed. Never starved. Healed. Never scarred. In perfect health. But day after day, night after night, they suffered.

No one would find them here. No one would save them. This concluded their story.

No. More.

324 secured their sheets to the bunk and fashioned it around their neck. Their breath shook. Their hands trembled. It was time to take control of their story, if only for the end.

A light burst forth, bright and unyielding. It illuminated the bunk and the lost soul within. Pitched in perpetual darkness, 324's eyes found it hard to adjust. Blurry, a face came into their vision.

No. This person left them the most conflicted out of all the handlers.

"Let's take a break."

A break. Yes. Please. A break.

{Earth}

"Sagan, are you all right?"

Tameka's voice finally cut through the white noise in Sagan's brain. Fury's green eyes filled with enough genuine affectionate that it nearly filled the void inside the Seamswalker.

Nearly.

"Sorry, I drifted off into space. Not literally this time." Sagan winked at her best friend with a half smile.

Said best friend—her Progeny sister—looked concerned. And with the news Lynn and Pablo just delivered, how could she not? Imminent wove enough threads into the Shadow's super-secret, worlds-saving operations that the unraveling of it left them all exposed to raw danger.

Under the Iona umbrella, the Medical Ecology and Arsenal represented a collaborative effort to protect the worlds. The idea of the clandestine organization infiltrating those efforts would normally enrage Sagan.

But she couldn't feel it. A sting. A needle. But no spark, and certainly not a fire.

Kyle caught her eye across the group. He raised an eyebrow at her while withdrawing a baggie partly out of his pocket.

She shook her head at the offer and noticed for the first time in two years that he wasn't actively smoking anything. His eyes, a darker green than Tameka's, glowed with absolute acuity. No general haze. It looked uncomfortable.

"Thanks. Anyway," she mouthed.

He nodded and looked back to the Doc.

"So, we've been keeping him sedated. He's struggling. I'm hoping a visit from you three will ground him." Pablo opened the door to Andrew's padded cell.

They entered, and Tameka immediately went to him. Sagan and Kyle lingered near the door with no sudden movements.

"Andrew. Do you know it's me?"

Their Shadow brother groaned and jerked away. The restraints wouldn't let him fall off the bed. If they were made of anything other than nacre...

Sagan stepped closer and called out to him, "Hey, Golden God. Remember back in Australia? You got along with me just fine."

"Sagan. Tam-Tameka. Help. Me."

Tameka looked sharply away, but Sagan caught the forlorn expression. It proved a more formidable task than they first assumed to reach him. Kyle stopped behind her.

Fuck it. Sagan took Andrew's hand as he clutched the air. "I am Sagan Sterling. General of the Two Armies. The Seamswalker. I'm desperately, hopelessly in love with former Icarean General, Korac. I'm your sister. Together, we saved the worlds, and we watch over Rayne."

Tameka rolled her eyes and clicked her tongue at the romantic confession, and Sagan shot her a mischievous grin with a casual shrug.

Kyle touched Andrew's shoulder. "Kyle Roberts. Story Taker. I guard the conduit between our worlds by searching memories. I have two sisters, Ross and... and Bethany. Ross is with Jack. I'm a traitor, and I'm not proud of it. But if it helps you to calibrate who I am, then I'm glad I said it." He ducked his eyes, but kept his hand on Andrew.

Conscience looked between them with tears spilling from his blue eyes. He set them on Tameka, who started her introduction, "I'm Tameka Phillips. Fury. I can do some really freaky shit with nacre energy. I was stuck on Enki, and I have to say, I wasn't expecting this for my first trip home in two years."

They all sniffle-giggled.

"My son is Pax. You haven't met him, yet. But if you feel up to it, he's here. I know he'd like to see his Uncle Andrew."

While they spoke, Andrew's demeanor shifted. His hands warmed and squeezed back. His eyes focused rather than flitted around. More even breathing calmed the rise and fall of his chest. Even his tears seemed less from pain and more from relief.

He gave Tameka's hand a single shake and roughly said, "I'd love to."

So, why was Sagan—not even an hour later—outside of the Emporium rather than standing witness to the beautiful moment? Curiosity? FOMO? An itch to scratch, maybe?

No.

Sagan stared into the Emporium and calculated the odds of Imminent fucking shit up back home around the same time she met its Pain Curator.

And yea, maybe a peek inside a booth and a stop at Korac's cell wouldn't hurt. She was only twenty. What was life but making a few less than savory decisions while young? Regrets came later.

Convinced, Sagan straightened her coat against the snowy night and sauntered across the street. She stared at her boots connecting with the wet pavement. Some part of her feared looking up. To catch bizarre orange and green eyes on her. Which was stupid. She planned to face Razor anyway, but it bothered her that he sensed her arrival every time.

The Seamswalker raised her gaze. The Pain Curator stood on the mezzanine, but with his back to her. Did it bother her more that he might suspect her discomfort and attempted to assuage it by turning around?

That was too much deep thinking, and Sagan felt too empty to care appropriately.

Skipping the rest of the walk, she stepped in front of him on the mezzanine. The crowd below reacted less interested. The regulars must be used to her by now, and what did that say about the frequency of her visits?

"I'm ill-prepared for you, tonight. You must wait a few more days, if that's all right?" He smiled congenially at her. Those bizarre eyes sparkled. He freshly shaved his red beard. The hair…looked JBF as fuck. Red spikes ruffled everywhere. Black slacks with the suspenders down. White button down with the first two buttons undone and cuffs rolled up on his hairless arms. He tossed back a tumbler filled with a green viscous liquid.

"You look a little rough."

"Hah! That's one way to put it." He toasted her before draining the dregs. After which, Razor pressed the perspiring glass against his temple and winced. He caught her watching the gesture and offered, "Unfortunate encounter with some associates. They were displeased with the outcome of a joint venture."

Interesting. Was there blood in his hairline? Sagan stepped into his personal space, scrutinizing the swelling.

He stiffened but allowed the proximity.

No blood. Disappointment flooded Sagan. Nox's Verse and the war taught her to discern various races by blood color and scent. She hoped for a clue as to Razor's species.

To cover the intimate search, she took his glass from him and positioned it better to reduce the swelling.

Leaned against the banister, the Pain Curator met Sagan's eyes at level. As if his throat hurt, he croaked, "Thank you. Korac's a lucky Icarus."

She shook her head. "I'm only twenty years old, and I know how to triage battle wounds on various galactic species. I don't think he'd call that lucky."

He leaned forward. Too close. How can a man rake his gaze over a woman without ever breaking eye contact? That's what it felt like as Razor admitted, "I'm sure he knows how lucky he is."

"Is creepy your default setting?"

Laughter burst from him. It wavered in depth, but it never sounded unpleasant. "C'mon. I'm sure you're hungry, and I could use a change of scenery tonight." He headed down the stairs and waved over his shoulder. "Bar down the street. You know the one." The crowd parted for him.

Razor stepped outside before Sagan decided if she wanted to join him or not. His presence got to her, but he served his purpose.

Not to mention, she needed something to distract her from the creeping disappointment that the next experience wasn't prepared yet. It hit her harder than expected. And that scared her.

She Seamswalked to the Martyr Complex Bar & Lounge.

The glass restaurant looked unchanged since her last visit. It filled up after dark. All the booths looked occupied, and the place smelled of rich food. Sagan's stomach disrespected her with a conveniently timed growl.

"Whose side are you on?" she whisper-groaned to her belly.

"Don't worry, Seamswalker. There are no forbidden delicacies here." Razor stealth-bombed her from behind in the crowded space. "Our booth is above the bar—"

Sagan booked it upstairs. A server waited near a wet bar in the private space overlooking the lounge. Music videos played on the projectors with the occasional pain experience ad. The lack of Rayne promotions offered some relief, but Sagan refused to let it blind her.

No. Razor wanted her comfortable. Speaking of...

"Is this acceptable?" He gestured to the wide booth with a view of the floor.

Sagan scooted in, careful not to flash him as the coat rode up. He sat opposite her with a respectable distance between them. They looked like friends at a meal rather than foes.

"Do you mind if I play host and select the dishes?"

Sagan's stomach loudly agreed for her. "Sure."

Humor glittered in his bizarre eyes as he called the server over and ordered. Distracted, she took in the restaurant and scanned the crowd. So many aliens below all grinding, eating, possibly fucking if that Pil Dwarf and Lyrik were any indication.

"Are all of them Prisonborne?" Even she thought her voice sounded lost.

Razor watched her. Not the people. "Mostly. Some are Tritan guests permitted to visit Gait for establishments such as mine. But the Lyriks are wardens."

She turned to him, frowning. "All of them?"

"Lyriks are without a homeworld." He paused as the server approached with a million small plates. "The Tritans breed them for protection. That's why they're all females."

That's definitely noteworthy. And also... Sagan practically salivated. Food of all colors, textures, and smells scattered across the table in servings petite enough to sample everything. Delighted, she looked up at him, unable to hide the grateful smile.

He chuckled and waved. "Go ahead. Don't let manners—Wow, you can really eat. I never thought I'd consider that an attractive quality. But it works for you."

Sagan's place setting collected a slew of empty plates like a graveyard of fallen foodgasms. She swallowed the flambéd canapé in her mouth before responding, "Needed to refuel. Everything is so delicious. Oh, my—Can you pass me that?"

She ate. He watched. Admittedly, it wasn't the strangest interaction she had with a "guide" from an alien planet. With calories restored, she jumped right to it, "How are you involved with Imminent?"

Why did the men in Sagan's life smirk so much? Korac's signature smirk defied appropriate timing with pure sex in a promise. Razor's smirk pronounced the extreme affluence of his life experiences compared to hers. It alienated him and left her with the irresistible urge to shift uncomfortably in his presence.

He rapped his knuckles on the tabletop before leaning forward with his arms folded. "I'm attending a gala on Reipon. Required attendance, mind you. Why don't you join me as my guest, and I'll introduce you to a few people of interest regarding your inquiry?"

Sagan mirrored him and leaned forward in a power move to close the distance this time. "What are the terms?"

"A dress. A dance. And potentially . . . a kiss."

"To make it convincing?"

He shrugged one shoulder and widened his smirk into a smile. "Maybe for fun, too."

Sagan Seamswalked out of the booth and headed for the stairs. Clearly, she could Seamswalk out, but she wanted Razor to stop her. To reconsider his terms.

"I wouldn't ask you to betray him," the Pain Curator called after her. "My sense of humor isn't for everyone. I apologize."

She turned, folded her arms over her chest, and raised a brow. Her honor demanded more groveling.

With the grace to look ashamed, he shook his head and spread his hands out in a shrug. "What can I say? I've apologized more to you than anyone in the last two million years. You challenge me, and I'm unaccustomed to it. If I reduce the terms to a dress and a dance, can we return to our discussion?"

"I select the dress. And your hands don't roam during the dance."

"I accept." Razor walked over to her with hands and legs loose, looking harmless. "Wear whatever you like, but we arrive by car. No Seamswalking to reduce unwanted attention. In six days, arrive at the Emporium after Gait nightfall. The location on Reipon shares the same day and night cycle."

Sagan lost the aggressive posture and nodded. Changing the subject, she commented, "I don't see Matt here. Didn't see him at the Emporium either."

"I've promoted him to backstage work. I eagerly await the day you're primed to see it." Razor searched her eyes with the orange and green halves dancing in his. "Won't be long now."

"Razor, what *are* your motivations for taking me to this gala?"

He gave a rich chuckle. "Well, to be candid, I can't wait to see the look on their faces when you arrive on my arm." Gingerly, touching the swelling, he continued, "I wonder how they'll punish me afterward."

Sagan quit listening. A projection behind him stole her attention. Security footage of an Iona. And Rayne ripping bodies apart inside it.

"How?"

Razor turned to the scene right as the King of Earth and Cinder slammed two bodies together in a graphic wash of blood and bone.

Sagan cupped a hand to her mouth and turned away. Deep breaths. In through the nose and out the mouth.

"It's security footage. I don't have anyone's pain. I use it to advertise the experiences. I thought you'd consider it a fair compromise as to the other footage." His voice went remote, as if unsure which tone to use. He made no move to touch her and respected her space.

But something needled Sagan. These attempts on her boundaries weighed on her old anxiety habits. Necessary tests to see where the other stood. Diplomacy and all that. But...

"Korac gave me that footage, and I gave it to someone—" Andrew "—for safekeeping. How did you get it?"

"Sagan."

Oh, she really didn't want to turn around. His voice sounded sincere and cold at the same time. It was fucking bizarre and sent a chill down her spine.

She Seamswalked behind him. "How?"

Razor held up his hands in surrender. "An engineer provided it. CCTV footage is easy to retrieve. I'll try another avenue of advertisement."

From one second to the next, the Pain Curator deflated and sagged in his tall bones. He looked exhausted and concussed. Pinching the bridge of his nose, he gave an incredulous laugh. "Nothing ever goes as I expect with you, Seamswalker. Please, pass on my regards to our good General. I'm retiring for the evening."

This was the first time *Razor* walked away from *Sagan.*

And Elden, did it bother her.

{Gait}

Korac stepped from Infernus block's lift bay. The imprint seal required Executive Warden blood. Unable to travel between blocks, he contemplated asking for Sagan's help in his investigation.

He glanced over to his cell, expecting her to manifest from his thoughts. Did he want to see her? Always. But he also wanted to keep things civil between him and Pehton. She was due to arrive any minute to investigate Inanis, and a visit from his favorite Progeny might incur the Executive Warden's wrath.

Revisiting that topic threatened to choke the sanity from Korac, as he wandered the block. Then the business with the floor below. Finally, Sagan's preoccupation with Razor. He meant it when he said he'd support wherever her work took her. He understood dicey situations came with a General's territory. But her heart was so big and so fragile.

Like with his blockmate. Sagan reached out to Remorse without hesitation. Extended her friendship to him.

Korac stopped in front of the man's cell. The other prisoner slept curled on his side with his back to the hall. The swirling energy of the nacre shield distorted the image, rendering the man unidentifiable from this angle. Always asleep when the Icarus wandered. Intentional? Korac suspected—

Air released from the lift bay. Gait's Executive Warden stepped out, sketchbook underarm. She looked a little dejected at his idle freedom.

Korac held up his hands to placate her. "I'll go right back in." He waved to the imprint. "If you'll unlock it."

The exhausted-looking Lyrik glared at him as she stomped in her boots to the nacre shield. Appearing casually interested, he watched the advanced technology scan not only her DNA but her fingerprints and...

Hormone levels? Interesting.

"Get. In."

He threw Pehton a smirk as he walked nonchalantly inside. Without glancing back, Korac knew she checked out his ass in these jeans. That's why he wore them. Skintight and properly disarming. The Icarus pitied her honestly. The neglect in her sex life affected her scent, but the sadistic motherfucker in him couldn't resist distracting her this way.

Korac practically heard Pehton shiver behind him before she regained full composure and commanded, "No more walks. You say you're here on your own honor?"

He turned and nodded.

"Then stop risking my job for your amusement. I've done nothing to you—"

"The First Wave Progeny disagree."

Pehton actually stamped her foot and squared up with him in the cell. It was adorable. "Elden, dammit! I followed my orders." After she pointed a finger in his face, her voice tightened with anger, "And don't you *dare* tell me you kept your hands clean under another's command. I've seen the footage of what you're willing to stomach projected in every one of Razor's establishments."

Korac kept his face and voice neutral, "I serve Cinder. Even under my new King, who offered forgiveness in return for my stay in a cell that cannot hold me. And so I serve Cinder by wasting here. How will you make up for your sins, Executive Warden?"

The Lyrik dropped her hand, threw the sketchbook on his bed, and turned her back on him. Frustrated, she growled. The nature of her race made it a melodic sound. Beautiful. Like a whistle more than a throat crunching noise.

"I hate *that woman.*"

Korac recoiled at her confession. Any details about her rumored relationship with Celindria intrigued him, but he refused to pry because he valued privacy. However, if she volunteered the information herself...He remained silent and waited for her to continue.

Pehton sniffed with her back to him, and he settled on his cot when the scent of salt hit him. Apparently, their relationship was more involved than he imagined.

"She promised to help me find the children. To topple Razor's empire and retrieve the memories to solve Inanis. I was just another casualty in her wake. She truly is a monster." She wiped the tears and faced him. "Did you see her smug face at the Tribunal? Of course, you did. How could you miss it? I don't wish ill on those Progeny. But I *know* her. No one could stop her from taking them."

"Can you get to them?" Neutral face. Neutral voice. But inside, Korac embraced possibly another comrade fallen to Celindria's lies.

With red eyes haunted, Pehton shook her head. "No one can touch her now. Unless they were already in Enki. I heard she never leaves the lab." She grimaced until another emotion flickered in her gaze. "There is one way."

"I'm on the edge of my seat, Executive Warden."

She coughed, but he heard the giggle she hid beneath. Even as she disguised it, her shoulders loosened a little, and the tears dried. "The Sovereign Ambassador. She holds residence there. I can arrange an investigation with her. Will that better satisfy your part to solve Inanis?"

"Well, that depends."

Incredulous, Pehton searched his face. "On what?"

"Can you get me in a Divine Booth? In my memory, I can't see the men's faces." He held out a hand about bed-height. "Too short an angle. But I understand Razor can provide us with the technology to step outside ourselves and look around."

Pehton's eyes widened cutely the more he went on. Her mouth even gaped.

Couldn't hurt to add some more items to the already tall order. "And another thing."

"Dear, Elden. What?"

"We need to interview Karter and Para. They're among the few survivors I know from Umbra's Thailea campaign."

Pehton folded her arms and grinned. "Oh, I certainly don't mind seeing them again."

Korac crooked a questioning brow with a smirk.

"Celindria may have used and abused my heart, but my libido still fucking works."

FOURTEEN

LOSE PRECIOUS LITTLE SLEEP OVER BROKEN PROMISES

{EARTH}

WAS THIS THE BREAK THEY NEEDED?

Three hours ago, Pablo left Lynn asleep in his bed. It took two hours of meticulous attention to every one of her details. Then another thirty minutes of lying in bed, watching her breathing relax. Those thick lashes closed on her dark cheeks. Her black locs contrasted beautifully against his white pillow case. She hogged both sides of the bed per usual. But he loved every second.

Afterward, he headed for the lab. As he hurried down the suspension stairs, Silence bumped into him.

No, literally.

The striking Icarean female nudged him, clutched his arm as she apologized in her deep voice, before carrying on with her jaunt.

With a sample of Pablo's blood.

He almost didn't feel it. Bumped, grabbed, and pricked within seconds. All under the guise of a considerate act.

Now, Pablo followed her everywhere in the building via the extensive security system. Was this the break they needed? Should he inform the others? What were her motivations?

Throughout the evening, Silence visited the atrium with its open glass view of the ocean below. The conservatory and its collection of rainforest medicinal plants. And the lunchroom where she ate two pieces of bread and a slice of meat, all separate from each other. By 2:00AM, she wandered down toward the labs.

Go time.

Calling for backup, Pablo kept his eyes on the screen to ensure he never lost her. Within seconds of the call, Kyle rolled in with Lucas. Both men looked exhausted. Caring for Andrew in such a sad state drained the Shadow crew. If left alone for more than five minutes, the fractured Progeny fell into a rabbit hole of probable realities. Friendly faces served as the only anchor. Otherwise, they kept him sedated as these two did before leaving him alone.

"What's she doing?" Kyle rushed over to the monitors.

"She's in the detainees' hall off Med Lab 2. Strolling."

Lucas watched over their shoulders. "Does she seem interested in our Imminent prisoner?"

Kyle frowned at the Icarus and the implications.

Pablo shook his head and pointed to her on the screen.

Silence, hands in pockets, casually glanced into each of the detainees' cells. Asleep during the day, they kept their active hours at night. Would she release them? Start a rebellion and destroy the ecology? Why—

She stopped in front of Twenty-One's cell. He sat back against his bunk set into the far wall. Intrigued by her, the Icarus stared from the floor. Silence fed the capsule of blood into the seal and stepped inside. The heavy Icarean male scented the air and gazed up at her.

Kyle whispered as if concerned she could hear him, "What do you think she wants?"

"Only one way to find out." Lucas nodded at the monitor.

All three men in the security office watched transfixed as the female warrior crossed the small cell. When she stood over him, they all held their breaths.

Twenty-One reached for her. Silence slipped out of the suspenders, dropped her pants, and straddled him in one fluid motion. He groaned loud enough for the mic to pick up. When she threw her head back, Kyle looked away.

Lucas looked to the ceiling and explained, as if offering excuses for her, "Valkyrie are known for ferocious appetites. Including sex. If not well fed, they tend to lose themselves and behave savagely."

As if she heard him, Silence let out an animalistic cry. They all turned back. The male Icarus stood now with her clinging to his front. As they moved, he opened his wings, forming a cradle behind her. The female lay back against the feathers. Hands fixed to her hips, he controlled their movements. She locked her ankles around the back of his neck. They both seemed plenty satisfied with this position, judging by the chorus heading to its obvious crescendo.

"If you ever wondered what proper Icarean copulation looks like..." Lucas cleared his throat and indicated the scene.

From a scientific standpoint, it *was* fascinating—

"Turn it off. It's her private business," Kyle ordered as he turned to leave the room.

Pablo stopped him. "She stole my blood for this purpose. And Twenty-One is a special patient. We need to consider ulterior—"

Oh. Oh, Elden, no!

The doctor bolted out of the room and ran straight for the labs. The others followed, calling after him.

The virus.

Pablo never rushed faster to Med Lab 2. He burst into the residents' hall and banged on Twenty-One's glass cell. "Stop! Silence, no!" He rushed to open the seal.

By the time he entered, Silence clutched Twenty-One, who surrounded them with his wings. Through the pinions, she peered at Pablo. Her gray eyes told him he was too late.

Completely. Sated.

The Icarean male looked spent and perplexed. Fair point, considering it was the first sex he'd experienced in almost three years. With their wordless exchange, they potentially transferred the most important product of Pablo's research.

Lucas rushed in behind him and took in the state of things. "Darling, we need to ask you a few questions. Is now a bad time?"

Silence focused beyond them to Kyle standing in the doorway. Awkward tension stretched between them. The Progeny looked away first. After a rough second, she met Lucas' molten gold eyes.

"There is less time than you think."

{Cinder}

Para ended the last of Bones' resilience with a turn and a grind of her hips. With a loud groan from him and a soft cry from her, he finished.

The Valkyrie snickered with wicked satisfaction as she separated them. "I'm getting better with your tells, soldier. Soon, I'll play you like a familiar instrument."

"I look forward to the journey." Bones let his head fall back on the palette and smiled lazily at the mango scent filling the chamber. He enjoyed watching her dress afterward, like she worried about them getting caught fucking.

The first buckle under her breasts and the following three harness straps around her midriff and shoulders. All leather. All toting blades. The little denim shorts just looked cute on her toned ass.

Oh, what's that? He was ready to go again?

Para chuckled. "Down boy. I think our King tires of our games." She fluffed her short blue hair and stretched.

Bones smiled while returning his tactical pants to their upright and zipped position. Happy. Happier than ever he could remember in his life. Good friends—almost a family at this point. A mission; a purpose. And regular sex with the smallest of the legendary Valkyrie.

No, he wasn't in love with Para. Nor she with him. But these guard shifts got awfully lonely and boring. He appreciated her familiar Icarean company. Sex with no commitment because they already shared an important connection as Icari. They served Elden's prerogative.

Para sat in the rough red soil and set her elbows on her knees. With her face in her hands, the Valkyrie stared across the lake at their King. Her black eyes mirrored the water. Standard operating procedure.

Bones left her alone and headed for the kitchen. A sandwich sounded good—

"What do you think a Tritan nicknamed 'the Chef' must be like?"

"Clearly he'll be tall, dark, and handsome. It'll make sharing in our duties even more interesting." Bones smirked to himself as Para giggled into the dirt. He piled on the roast beef and some extra mayo. "Maybe he's a fantastic cook?"

"Maybe. Or maybe he's a skilled killer."

He turned with the plate in hand and headed over to her perch. With her back to him, she watched Rayne as if taking the duty literally. So when he produced a plate with her favorite sandwich and chips, Para gave a small cry of pleasure.

Worth it.

Bones laid out on the dirt beside her, empty-handed. "I love to stargaze on Earth." He imagined the little diamond chips on the black rock ceiling. The breeze from the vent fed them more ashen air. No stars up there.

"Did I ever tell you about the first time I met Rayne?"

He arched a brow at her and nudged her playfully with his boot. "No."

Para pushed her hair behind her ears and cleared her throat. "We piloted the colossal crawler—Chris calls it the Mobilizer 5000—across the continent. We walked it right up to Iona-29's roundabout. A girl stood there. Unflinching. Strong. Mighty, really. Especially given her height deficit.

"She glowed with a proper shine. Karter told me that Xelan had a hand in raising her. So I instantly trusted her as our leader. But as I climbed out of that beast and took a look at her, I thought, 'This young thing? This is our General?'"

Bones nodded along. He thought the same thing. How was that little girl supposed to kill Nox?

"Then I looked in her eyes." Para shook her head to emphasize her comprehension. "I'd die for her. For her brother. Then it extended to Chris. And the Progeny. And you. And Pablo and Lynn—An entire family. I'd die to protect the Shadow..."

Para's voice softened until the words stopped. Her eyes shaded with foreboding.

Bones sat up and placed a comforting hand on her back. "What is it?"

She swallowed hard and tried to speak twice before getting the words out. "I've felt this way only one other time in my life. I begged Umbra not to accept the campaign against the Ancients on Thailea. He threatened to cut out Karter's tongue and cauterize it with gold if I shared my concerns with anyone."

He cursed and spat. Fucking bastard King.

Para shook her head as if that weren't enough. "I appreciate your support, but you're missing the key point. A part of us didn't survive that battle, and I fear many of us won't survive the upcoming one either."

"You believe the situation is more dire?" He looked off at the Martyr Complex.

"For some. Maybe for me. Our part will become more clear, but make no mistake, I'll die to save this family." Para turned her gaze to him. The black of her eyes shone like a star with determination. Hard as a diamond.

"She won't let it come to that." He nodded over at the island in the lake.

The Complex glowed with a white light, emitting warmth across the water. Bones and Para bathed in it. In the surety of it. The same warmth and surety he saw the first time he looked into Rayne's eyes.

No more deaths allowed in this family.

Bones leaned into Para and whispered, "Maybe we should find some place more private to fuck."

{GAIT}

"Peh Peh, you're doing wonderfully with the Icarean General." Razor leaned against the Divine Booth, waiting for her to emerge.

Pehton learned nothing more from this journey into her memory than any other visit. The children crossed Mercy Row with her. The light of Inanis emitted from the prison and expanded over the planet. It washed them away in a blinding white emptiness. Erased them. When the light faded, only the surrounding adults remained. All of them poured tears from their burning eyes. And then from their broken hearts.

Where did the children go?

Razor's rich melodic voice cut through her thoughts, "I hate watching you do this to yourself." He reached out and brushed a tear from her cheek.

Pehton jerked back on instinct. Too soon after the immersive experience. Her heart was too raw.

Shit.

He froze into a statue with ice hardening his brown eyes.

Rejecting the bastard did her no favors. The Lyrik shifted gears and pouted her lips. She leaned against the doorway, appearing smaller and more vulnerable, she offered, "I wish there was some way to change your mind."

Razor rested his elbow high on the booth and leaned forward. He raised an unconvinced, yet curious brow.

"Never say never." Pehton referred, of course, to their earlier exchange when he assured her he'd *never* want sex from her. Fat chance. But humiliating herself should boost his ego back to its normal over-inflation.

The Pain Curator shook his head and walked away. Over his shoulder, he called, "Keep up your half of the bargain, Peh Peh."

At the use of his pet name for her, the Executive Warden of Gait sagged with relief. Forgiven. Wow. And to think, she normally resented the familiarity.

"I'll be back tomorrow."

Razor waved his dismissal as he walked toward the kitchens.

Reduced to groveling. Pehton almost spat.

To wash the foul taste from her mouth, she took the lift down to Infernus block. Korac's company breathed fresh air into her life, stagnant with filth and vice. The only drawback—

Ahh, he sat innocently in his cell this time. Another relief.

"Executive Warden." He nodded to her from where he laid on the bed, reading.

Many things could certainly be said for the General, but her favorite among them was the respect he paid to titles. Better than Razor ever managed.

"Something on your mind?" Korac sounded more curious than concerned.

"I'm not sure how we get you there, but we'll need to wait until Razor's out of the Emporium. Unfortunately, he doesn't maintain a consistent schedule, so no one can learn his habits. Do you think Sagan can find a window for us?"

Pehton sat on the floor with her back leaning against the wall opposite his cell. She crossed her ankles to keep him from looking up her armor's short skirt. Her head thudded against the cold metal behind her.

Korac stood to his agreeable height. She honestly meant to thank Sagan for the wardrobe. Pehton much preferred objectifying him when he dressed for the ogling. Red leather pants. Black muscle shirt, well filled out. Yup. Delectable to look at.

The Lyrik must have released a sigh she meant to keep to herself because the Icarus' lips twitched ever so slightly into a knowing smirk.

The devil looked good, and she no longer cared if he knew.

"Karter is guarding the King Regent. And Para is guarding the King proper. We're missing a lot of action back on the Two Worlds, you and I." He rested his arms on the wall above his nacre-deterring barrier and leaned against them. "They're not readily available. But I have a Plan B. Are you familiar with Kyle's abilities?"

She arched a brow. "Story Taker? We can see our memories, so how can he help?"

"He might combine them and allow us to see each other's. We'll gain more pieces to the puzzle." He crooked his neck to the left. Then to the right.

Pehton almost felt the relief in her own shoulders when Korac's neck popped loud enough to reach her in the hall. His suggestion bothered her. What if they learned her secret? Could she trust them?

"I'll go first," Korac offered as if he sensed her reticence.

She almost smiled. Elden, dammit! She didn't want to like him so much. Any of them, really. "I'll consider it." After another moment, she asked softly, "What do you think caused Inanis and why?"

He straightened and paced calmly in front of the barrier as he considered her question. Reasonably, he confessed, "It feels . . . familiar to me."

Pehton perked up to that and sat forward. Afraid to break his flow, she kept quiet.

"I don't believe it's atmospheric or some light phenomenon. In each instance in which I experienced it, I sensed a heartbeat at its center."

She recoiled. Inanis was a person?

He stopped pacing and continued with his reflection, "Alive. Like someone letting out their breath. Or flexing a muscle. And I want to say that I recognize it. But that's not the right word. I *know* it. Like they were with me at the time . . ."

Pehton tried the idea on for size. Inanis. A person. A person able to bleed and die. Oh, she liked this idea the more she thought on it. Strangling the person who took everything from her—

"Who's in the cell beneath us, Executive Warden?"

Peering back up, Korac watched her reaction through the barrier like a hawk. He searched and scanned for any response that might give the secret away.

The Lyrik shook her head. "I can't tell you. Confidentiality and all that." She stood and stretched. Time to go. "Thanks for the insight and the information on your friend. I'll let Kyle take a story or two from me to stop Inanis."

"I find the Progeny trustworthy. Mostly," Korac added for extra assurance.

"I'll return, General." Pehton mock-saluted him before the lift carried her to the bottom level. Stepping the few feet into the darkness, the sound of her boots on the metal echoed.

She recalled the description Tumu gave her of the prisoner. *"So deadly, he isn't allowed space. So clever, he isn't permitted interaction. So evil, he isn't granted light."*

Into the shimmering light of a nacre-deterring field that blanketed the floor... into the cold... into the nothing... Pehton whispered, "Who *are* you?"

No one answered.

{Earth}

Silence, fed and sated, sat atop the black table in the little room. Cold white tile floor. White walls. Black ceiling. Great air conditioning. The three men in the room—one human, one Progeny, and one Icarus—swallowed the deficit of space. Their dispositions and spicy scents quickly warmed the room.

The human, Dr Suarez, tapped his shoe and pinched the bridge of his pleasantly brown nose. His kind voice sounded hoarse, as if he recently lost it while shouting, "Why... of all the residents... did you choose Twenty-One?"

Censure. Misplaced.

Before she left the prisoner's cell, Silence retrieved the pants the golden-eyed Icarus lent her and braided the suspender straps along her midriff. They preferred her less exposed. With her legs folded beneath her, Silence centered herself on the tabletop.

Said generous Icarus with beautifully gilded eyes searched her own as he crossed the room. Steady with his hands free. He knew how to treat a lethal threat when he saw one. "My dear—"

Silence liked his familiar way of speaking to her.

"—We're only concerned about your wellbeing. Your health. Some residents here are ill. This is a hospital, after all."

His words rang with partial truths. The deception bored her. Silence needed no lies. No hiding. She stared into his molten gaze and answered, "I liked the size of him."

He recoiled at her brazen honesty. Though she figured from the fit of his pants that the sandy-blond Icarus was perfectly familiar with that quality in a male.

A smile fueled by her audacious pride spread across her lips until she glimpsed the Progeny male behind him. Kyle watched her with a sorrow hidden in the green depths of his gaze.

Each of these men interrupted her feeding. At the time, the Icarus' cell filled with the scent of their mating. Citrus and lilies. But when Story Taker entered, another scent followed. Sharp cedar.

She liked it. Wanted to smell it on her skin. But the look on his face now...

The strong Icarean female reflected on her brief encounter with the massive Icarus named Twenty-One. So lonely. So lost. Why should she explain herself? How could she confess that she saw in the male a kindred isolation from the ways they both knew? It was more fun to punish them for interrupting.

And yet...

"I want to speak with Kyle. Alone, please. Now."

He started at his name on her lips, but Story Taker recovered quickly. To Dr. Suarez he muttered, "Let me talk to her alone. I'll see if she remembers any other motives."

The generous, golden-eyed Icarus followed the human out with one look over his shoulder at her. Such a strange expression. Measuring and calculated.

Familiar... It looked familiar. She almost recognized—

He shut the door behind him and the memory she tried to grasp.

"I want you to know that we're not angry with you," Kyle started.

"Dr. Suarez feels anger."

"Okay. So, not all of us are angry with you." He took a step closer. "Silence, he's not actually mad. You accidentally—or at least I think accidentally—placed him in a tight spot. Do you understand?" Another step closer.

She nodded once, curtly. "It upset him that I stole his blood and fed on one of his prisoners. One of my people."

Frustrated, Kyle shook his head and raked a hand through his hair. "Twenty-One and the others are well cared for. Their prisoners of the war you read about. And they *volunteered* to stay with Dr. Suarez. They like the man."

Silence let his words in. The feeling behind them. The stress in his shoulders. This mattered to him. "You worry what they think of me." Not a question.

He stared at her a minute before answering softly, "Yes. I do." Taking a step closer, he searched her face. They met at eye level with her on the table. "Because if they decide you're dangerous, they may not let you back outside. But if they think of you as I do—"

"How do you think of me?" She blinked at him. The men here mattered to the people outside. Important authority figures. They could help with her memory. If only she controlled her appetites better.

"I think you need to feed. A woman with your needs, unmet as long as they were, could only resort to instinct. You *are* dangerous, Silence. But I don't think you're a danger to us."

She smiled.

Kyle reached his hands out to either side of her face. He raised a question with his open, honest expression. "But will you let me check to make sure? For their sake?"

Silenced assented with a single nod.

He touched her, closed his eyes, and concentrated. She could tell by the wrinkle between his eyes.

A road opened to her. A path lined in moving images. Her memories. Kyle's hand took hers and led her down the path. To several hours ago when she bumped into Pablo.

Silence drowned in her desire. Rational thought barely registered. Feed. Her body needed to feed. So neglected. Starved.

Icarean. Male. One heavy enough to pin her to a wall and fuck her into oblivion. Hours. Days. She wanted so much.

The bright, fresh floral scent of lilies permeated the room. It distracted her even now.

She couldn't recall the atrium. The conservatory. She barely remembered the cafeteria. Fog surrounded these memories. Hazing the images.

Silence recalled seeing the male she sought on the way to the Imminent prisoner's interview room. That image was more clear. Dense fog blanketed the memory of her coating the seal in Dr. Suarez's blood. She'd almost forgotten it.

She did not forget what happened next. Twenty-One, as they called him, satisfied her. Unsurprisingly, Kyle skipped the details. He fast-forwarded to the end and recoiled...

The memory blacked out after the men rushed into the cell. Just emptiness.

Story Taker released Silence and stepped back. His face drawn tight in a confused frown. Deep green eyes wide with shock. "Silence," he breathed.

She cocked her head to the side. "Yes?"

"Do you remember what you said? What you said when I came into the cell?"

Silence frowned. The men came into the cell and... she left with them. That's it. "I said nothing." As his furrow deepened, she pressed, "Did I not?"

"There is less time than you think."

Silence and Kyle whirled on the third person unexpectedly in the room. A frail woman with black skin and purple

Atramentous eyes stood there clutching the unconscious Imminent prisoner.

Kyle stared at her with his mouth and eyes gaping open. Shocked, he whispered, "T.A.O."

The small woman peered between them before adding, "She was right. And now there is none left."

Then she vanished like the pretty blond Progeny girl Silence met at the fortress. Only with less pleasantness in her wake.

FIFTEEN

INFINITY DOESN'T BELONG TO ONE CONTENDER

{GAIT}

MATT RIPPED THE HOOD FROM HIS HEAD. The coarse black material stifled him. Suffocated, he shed the black bodysuit that shrouded nearly every identifiable trait of him aside from his height and the chain around his neck. The badly lit, all-black locker room was left empty to protect their anonymity between shifts. The bench supported his heavy muscles as they weighed down his skeleton. Sweat dripped from his face and splashed on the floor. The cool water from a standard issued bottle soothed him. The scalding water from the shower revitalized him.

But nothing would get him clean.

Bleeding knuckles, freshly raw with his misdeeds, accused him. The echoes of screams in his sullied memory judged him. And the evidence of his hedonism—hard, as always—condemned him.

Lucy wouldn't like this place.

With her name on his lips, Matt finished his self-gratification on a growl. Angry for enjoying the inhumanity so much. Without her...

This was all wrong.

The all-black hall to the all-black stairs up to the all-black catwalk took him to the all-black door. With one good shove, the redheaded man left Hell behind and squinted into the whiskey lights. The Emporium, with all its vices, glared like a beacon from Heaven.

Matt wanted to go back down. Immediately. But…

"She'll be here any second." Razor waved him across the kitchens to the addition. All the spaces were left hollowed and vacant until the doors opened.

Apparently, Sagan asked after Matt at her last encounter with the Pain Curator. Always attempting to ease her, the crafty alien made sure this time she'd see him. Smart move.

"I got it." Matt rushed to help Razor carry experience supplies for tonight's refresh. They paused near one of the advanced booths. Curious, Matt asked, "Hey, boss?"

Razor turned from his task with the same congenial smile he always wore when Matt called him that. "Yes?"

"How do the ports work?"

The Pain Curator pushed a dark blue hand through his light blue hair and whistled, impressed. "If downstairs can't satisfy you, I can't imagine the ports will stand up to the task."

Matt ignored whether he found satisfaction in the basement. Instead, he pressed, "I'm curious about the extra immersion you advertise. And I should know in case a customer asks me." That should convince him.

Dark gray eyes scrutinized the redheaded human. After a heartbeat, Razor shrugged and explained, "Ports pump all the chemicals from an experience into the nacre's interface via an implant. Give or take an enhancement or two." He pointed to his own sternum. "Here. The client can port in and enjoy the moment even more emphatically than the donor."

Matt frowned and threw in another boundary tester, "But you don't have one."

"No. I don't." The Pain Curator finished loading an experience capsule into the booth and indicated for them to move along to the next one. He knelt at each panel to load a fresh kaleidoscope of experiences. Concentrating on his task, he continued, "Contrary to what some may think, I'm not that interested in sampling the product. I'm more interested in my clients and how they respond. The more interesting the response, the higher the priority."

"Full service customer support?" Matt offered with a false grin.

Razor chuckled while shaking his head in amusement. "Something like that."

"Where do I rank?"

They both turned to find Sagan with her hands on her hips. She wore a man's white silk shirt belted at her waist, and the sleeves rolled to her elbows. It swallowed her short frame, skirting the top of her black thigh-high boots. Short blond hair messed. Heavy eye makeup smudged. Tan skin glowed. Honestly, the JBF look worked for her.

The alien beside Matt stared at the Seamswalker. Almost gaped. A tension rippled across him, rolling over the considerable muscles throughout his body. Razor shifted and transformed for Sagan.

His voice calm, his tone even, he answered with a truthfulness that the redhead found disturbing given what occurred over the last five seconds, "You're my favorite."

Matt fucking believed him, and now he worried for Sagan.

After one more second, the excitement melted from the alien and the professionalism returned. He calmly stood from the panel and straightened the carbon fiber suit. Prepared for his next performance.

Judging by Sagan's narrowed gaze, it'd better be Oscar worthy.

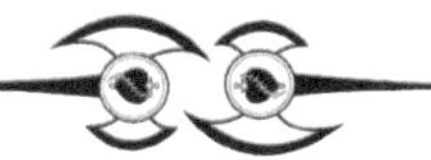

{Gait}

Sagan glanced at Matt, who peered between her and Razor. Both wore a carbon fiber jumpsuit. Both recently brushed their red hair. Presentable. Though Matt's freckles swayed for easier trust. It also helped his eyes were a solid dark brown and not a freaky two-toned orange and green.

Something weird passed between the trio. It reminded her of Korac's words from not even five minutes ago, *"He knows how to lure you in before you realize he's caught you. Beware the other flies in his web. They'll watch him eat you if it spares them his voracity."*

Razor smiled bright white teeth against his tanned skin and stepped toward her.

Sagan frowned and took a step back, almost opening a conduit to escape. She clutched the pendant on her chain. It unnerved her that she thought so much of the pain experiences while with Korac. No matter how much he gave her, she still wondered what experience Razor cultivated for her next. She wrote it off as curiosity. But it gnawed at her like hunger.

And that's why she stayed.

The Pain Curator retreated and carried himself loosely, appearing harmless. His eyes swept over her again. Never appraising. More assessing.

What would she look like wrapped in his silk?

He spun his web carefully with a gesture toward Matt. "We're preparing for the evening, but you can begin now if you like."

The younger redhead gave a wave.

She nodded to him and turned back to her "guide." Her next question concerned her, but it couldn't hurt to ask, right? "In exchange for tonight's sample, I want to bring Korac to the Emporium."

Her words rang in the empty warehouse. Echoed off the decorative copper and tin ceiling tiles. Bounced along the metal and glass walls. The Emporium passed judgment on her.

The swanky space translated her request to "Bring a convicted galactic war criminal into this establishment to suit the whims of one Earth girl."

Matt stared at the back of Razor's red head as if he found the man's stiffness alarming.

Said stiff alien darted out his tan hand between them. Empty nail beds and all. "Deal."

Sagan took his hand and shook it. Instantly, she relaxed. No matter what he planned for her tonight, at least she helped Korac and Pehton.

Razor let a small smile slip at her relief before he turned and led her to the booth. He sounded eager as he directed, "Tonight's event is special, and you unknowingly dressed for the occasion. How delightful."

After the reminder, she snuggled a bit into the collar and breathed deep of Korac's scent. Snow and pine. Home to her now.

"I'll head back now, boss. Unless you need me," Matt asked as he backed toward the kitchens.

Razor shared a certain smile with his employee. "Enjoy yourself."

After Matt disappeared, Sagan asked, "What's the behind-the-scenes work like?"

The depth of the alien's chuckle startled her. "Don't worry, Seamswalker. He's fine. And while I appreciate the innocence in your curiosity, you're not quite at the level to prepare you for it just yet."

She cocked her head to the side. "What level is that?"

"Desperate for it."

His words burned her. Too close to the yearning she already felt for these experiences. Sagan wanted to understand her desires at their core. And Razor offered her that insight in a way too unique to ignore. But enlightening enough and infrequent enough to crave.

With a knowing smile, he raised a chair from a panel beneath the floor. He fell into it as he announced, "I'm sitting in on this one."

Sagan recoiled. "No. Why?!"

He laughed, full and happy. Genuine. Razor's strange eyes even glistened as he finished and said, "I need to measure your reactions to prepare the next one. I have a few ideas, but I want to cater it properly. Also... You'll want someone here to catch you. The floors are hard." He tapped the parquet wood with his heavy boot.

At her frown and continued hesitation, he assured, "I'm a professional. While it's true that you *are* my favorite client, it's not for any sexually nefarious reasons. I'm simply charmed by your Earthiness. Pun intended."

Okay, so she smiled a little at that. "All right."

Razor stood once more and retrieved the goggles from the console. "Here. Let me help."

She met his eyes as he installed the gear over her head. The green swirled to the top of his iris. Orange to the bottom. Close enough to kiss, he appeared truly unaffected by their proximity. The only indication came when he returned her gaze for a heartbeat or two. "Beautiful," he said, as if stating a fact. Then he sat back down.

How confusing.

The experience started in a place devoid of light. Complete darkness. No. Not exactly. Something sat over her head. A hood. Black, hot, and coarse. It made it hard to breathe.

This wasn't Sagan.

"Hold your arms above you and take the grips." The distorted voice came from behind her. Nothing identifiable about it.

The memory holder raised their hands, and Sagan copied. Only a small part of her wondered what Razor thought as he watched before she cried out with the memory holder.

Scalding water. Hot to the point of boiling. It poured down her shoulders and back. Blistered her skin. Immediately, the cool air kissed the torture. Even with the sting, it still made it better.

But that couldn't be all. Her chest heaved while she almost hyperventilated in the waiting. Waiting for more.

Blind. The genderless tormentor moved silently. When would it come? It had to come.

Sagan shrieked when it finally poured down her front. Breasts, abs, between her legs. The heat steamed her eyes. The grips crumpled like foil in her fingers.

The cool air once again rewarded her for staying conscious. Ice applied to her skin, soothed her. She wept in gratitude.

"You were good this time, 324," the distorted voice assured. "We can try the pokers again tomorrow. And if you behave, you'll earn another break."

324?

The experience faded. The memory with it.

When the next experience loaded, she fell blissfully into the familiarity of it. Her memory this time. The dream where Korac confessed his preference for their kind of sex.

"I have wronged you," he said. When she opened her mouth to protest, he stopped her with a finger to her lips. "I let this go on too long."

In this experience, Sagan sat astride Korac. He returned to coaxing out her pleasure as he went on with the confession. She remembered feeling relieved. She wasn't alone.

For so long, she wondered if there was something wrong with her. When he pinned her to the bed, was it one-sided? The way he refused to let her orgasm for four years. Was he cruel or was it a mutually shared intensity? His control over her. The promise of pain. The kind of sex he asked of her. The love he wanted from her.

By the time he finished confessing and chained her to the wall, she was well on her way to another orgasm. So when he produced the knife, she cried out in acquiescence. She trusted him.

So young. So fortunate Korac proved a man worthy of her trust.

The experience melted away. They always came in threes. Maybe she should tell Razor she'd prefer finishing on a familiar note—

Someone locked their legs around her on the floor and strung something around her neck. Strangled her in a hold of inter-threaded limbs and... she was pretty confident they choked her with a belt.

She coughed and squeezed air in and out. The effects of hypoxia kicked in quickly, alarming her. Blood rushed to her face, and tears poured from her eyes. She scratched every bit of exposed gray skin. Coughed. Choked. Died.

"Say 'banana,' and I'll release you."

That voice.

Outside the experience, Sagan collapsed. Powerful arms caught her and swept the goggles from her face. She coughed and choked in his embrace. She hoped he thought the crying was from the strangulation and not from hearing—

Whose voice again? It slipped from her memory already.

But warmth... a loving warmth stayed with her. Unfortunately, the enduring kindness left her clinging to Razor on the floor. Don't let go. Hold on to it.

No way he'd mistake those sobs wrenched from her heart for remnants of the experience. As the memory poured down the drain and left her empty, Sagan wept onto the Pain Curator's offered shoulder to cry on. Enveloped in his arms, the warm vanilla scent surrounded her.

He even rocked her. Whispered soothing words to her. "Shh... I won't let go. I've got you now. You're all right."

It was kinda nice.

But oh dear Elden, this was a dangerous and precarious position she got herself into. How in the Two Worlds could she get out now? When he squeezed just right, her heart cracked in two.

In Razor's arms, Sagan whispered against her enemy's chest, "Please don't let go."

{EARTH}

John stared at the object on the table. So did Kyle, Pablo, Lynn, and Silence. Tameka and Lucas went to check in on Andrew. Caedes took Pax to the conservatory. Tumu guided Abresson through the labs.

The door opened with a soft hiss, and Smith walked in. "Whoa. It's tense in here."

Kyle groaned in frustration before he gestured at the object. "We don't even know if it belongs to that Imminent soldier."

Lynn offered, "We can test it though. If it has the same spotty memory bank—"

"—We can work on the decryption," Pablo finished, beaming at his brilliant wife.

John was happy for them. "It sounds like a good plan."

Silence knelt until her eyes leveled with the nacre on the table. She asked in a voice filled with curiosity and a hint of skepticism, "Why go through the trouble of taking the soldier if she intended to leave this?"

The room went quiet to her namesake. It was a good question. John thought about the tiny woman he once saw from a distance. T.A.O. once Seamswalked Tameka back to the Volcano Day battle so the powerhouse could drain an entire army. Then later he heard of the ancient Progeny's capture and felt sad for her. They tried day in and day out to find Celindria's lab and rescue the First Wave Progeny. The founding experiments of the hybrid race deserved better.

John assured while tugging on his pendant, "She wants to help us. We don't know her circumstances or her motives necessarily, but we know that woman is a hero. Not a villain."

Kyle nodded encouragingly. "That's right. Let the nacre do the talking." He turned to the power couple in the room. "Can you two get to work on it for me? After you finish, we'll see if I can get into it without a brain attached." He tapped on his temple to emphasize his point.

"We won't let you down, Story Taker." Lynn snatched the amber pearl from the table.

Kyle winced at the name to which Pablo mouthed, "Sorry."

Only Tameka liked her name. And John would tell no one that she picked it herself.

The door opened, and the devil he thought of walked into the room. The redheaded Progeny searched their faces before asking, "How are things in here? Did we decide?"

John noticed Silence stood and peered over Tameka's shoulder. Was she searching for Lucas? That seemed odd. But what didn't seem odd after today?

Smith edged for the door and muttered to John, "Getting a bit crowded in here. Let's head for the cafeteria and grab some food."

With his head reeling from recent events, John didn't argue. After retrieving two trays of food, they sat together and chowed down. The cafeteria sported the same interior decorating attributed to the Iona facilities. Light gray slate tiles, charcoal gray walls, and a black drop ceiling. It smelled of roasted rosemary chicken and garlic mashed potatoes.

Of which Smith shoveled a large forkful into his mouth. He swallowed hard before asking, "So, how are things with you? Are you returning to Enki soon?"

John slurped some juice and sighed in satisfaction. Cranberry. So tart. "Yea. I'm gonna miss the food here more than anything. Tritans don't really eat, and it shows."

The other man laughed, full and rich. "Of course." He shook his head, exasperated. "Man…it just keeps coming, doesn't it?"

Yea, it did. What the hell were they supposed to do with this flaming pile of—

"How are you? Are you returning to the arsenal soon?" John wished more pleasant topics came to mind, but alas.

"Where Lynn goes, I go."

The younger man frowned. Odd way to phrase it.

Smith changed the subject, "You gonna open a school on Earth and on Enki? An exchange program?"

That was a great idea. "Maybe. I like the sound of it. Kinda hard to do with—"

"We'll get John's school started as soon as we get back."

They whirled to find Caedes getting a tray with Pax. Tameka entered the cafeteria at the same time.

"Hot damn. All four of my favorite Enkians in one room." Smith smiled and waved at the toddler.

The kiddo ducked his eyes and darted behind Caedes' legs. The Icarean "uncle" chuckled and nudged him out. "You don't need to be shy, kiddo. He won't hurt you."

Tameka glared at the weapons expert for the cursing around the minor.

Smith sheepishly mouthed an apology. He hopped up and held out his hand for Pax to shake.

After a pause, the young boy accepted it. "Hello, Mr. Smith."

John frowned. Odd. Were they introduced before—

"You've shown me the cafeteria four times now, Tumu." Abresson sounded irritated and inconvenienced. Both Tritans entered on their unofficial tour of the grounds.

"Yea, but this time there are other people available for me to foist you onto." Tumu folded his arms and leaned back against the nearest wall. "He's all yours, peeps. I've earned a break, and the King Regent is still waiting to hear from me." The taller Tritan kept his eyes on the shorter one as Abresson wandered further into the cafeteria.

The short, dark blue, almost indigo, alien considered the company. Tameka hugged Pax and glared at Abresson with barely veiled distrust. Caedes looked poised to attack. Always.

Smith raised his hand. "Me and John can keep you entertained, Eminent."

Fuck off, Smith. Keeping up an act for Abresson drained the life out of John. The stress of the last twenty-fours tightened the amputation site of his leg even with a nacre. After ten minutes with Abresson, John might not walk tomorrow.

"How pleasant of you, Smith. Now, can anyone put together a decent plate for me or will I require a poison checker?"

"Mommy, can we eat in our room?" Pax whispered at Tameka's knees. Eagerly, he beseeched her from their height difference.

Caedes chuckled and headed to the door with both their trays. "Let's go."

Tameka grinned gratefully at him before turning a frozen mask to Abresson. "Good night, Eminent."

"I leave with them tomorrow." The indigo Tritan's voice went flat. No smug satisfaction. No anger. The absence of negativity made John's ears pop.

Tumu went to follow the family out of the cafeteria. Over his shoulder, he called, "That embargo won't last forever."

With his back to John and Smith, Abresson bristled by clenching and unclenching his fists. When he turned, he reapplied the smug superiority like a disguise. "Food?"

Smith made him a plate, careful to eat a forkful from each item. This pleased Abresson immensely. John rolled his eyes and lost the desire to finish his food.

After all that, Abresson sat at the table and talked without touching his plate. "I'm glad I came to Earth when I did. It's incredibly beneficial to see how your people respond to a crisis, Educator."

John rubbed his nub where it sheathed into the prosthetic. It hurt. Much more than usual—

"Smith, do you have a knife?" A pain needled John's skull as he reached for the two-inch the Weapons Engineer offered. Without preamble, the younger man cut the back of his hand. Shallow, in case...

One heartbeat passed. Two.

The room held a breath. Even Abresson sat stone still. Soon, their eyes widened, and their mouths gaped. The wound didn't heal.

"Oh, what next? Will Imminent steal my leg gear, too? Fucking. Assholes."

{EARTH}

"Reipon."

Taken aback, Chris's brows shot to his fantastic hairline.

Jack caught their surprised expressions and nodded. He asked over the comms, "Are you sure, Tumu?"

Ross held her breath and squeezed Karter's hand.

"Yup. The vendor transferred her via conduit from Earth to Reipon. I promise I knew nothing about this secret economy or I would've stopped it. I *have* stopped it." The Officer of the Third sounded sincere and a little ashamed.

Chris liked Tumu and wished the Tritan were worthy enough of the trust they kept having to place in him.

A sob broke from the teenage girl, and Karter pulled her in for a hug. "We've got a heading, Ross. We'll find her."

Jack's face fell as he watched the girl lose herself in the Valkyrie's comfort. Chris hurt for all of them.

"Your majesty, there are still some complications you need to be aware of before we send out a search party."

The other shoe had to drop. Jack nodded as he ordered, "Go ahead."

Tumu explained the current events like he grew tired of delivering bad news, "There's an embargo preventing Progeny from entering Enki. That includes you and Ross."

The girl croaked, "How can we get there, then? Sagan?"

They practically heard the Tritan nod in agreement. "I was just about to suggest that. However, there are other dangers. That nacre disabler that hit you earlier this week? Jack, it's getting around. We've got ancient Seamswalkers stealing our prisoners and one intentions reader completely out of commission."

They let the information sink in during his pause.

"If I might recommend...lie low for a while. I'll send in an agent or two to feel around. It's possible she went to Reipon for auction—"

"Auction?!" Ross cried out. Her face contorted in pain as she searched the room for someone to tell her she heard that wrong.

Chris cleared his throat and asked, "Officer Tumu. What sort of auction?"

As if it took him a second to consider how to answer, the Tritan fell silent. Eventually, he said, "There are laws in the Vast Collective that protect her until she's eighteen years old. The textile mills on Lukemore most likely employed her. The silk trade there always requires more labor. Don't worry. I'll send out some people to investigate. By the time they find something, the embargo will be lifted."

Jack squared his shoulders and started sternly, "Tumu—"

"I promise. It *will* be lifted." He meant it. The entire room relaxed at the certainty in his voice. "Wait some time before employing Sagan's means of travel. I don't like the situation here on the surface."

The King Regent of Earth wet his lips with a glance at Ross before he asked, "How's my sister? Have you checked on Rayne?"

The Tritan chuckled. "Don't you worry about your sister. She's the safest person in the entire Vast Collective. On my word. Over and Out."

Jack smiled across the device at Ross. "We have a lead."

The young woman looked a little shocky, but then Karter smiled down at her. Chris grinned, too. Infected by the love in the room—because that's what it was—Ross glowed. Her lips spread into a fantastic smile she must have kept hidden under all that practical, too-afraid-to-hope.

The device came to life. "Jack? King of Cinder? Kiddo that lost his tooth trying to peek at me changing clothes in his sister's room?"

Oh, hell! Jack's face flushed like a tomato. Chris doubled over and laughed until his eyes water.

"Tameka, thanks for calling. We needed that," Karter answered.

Ross popped a brow at the mortified teenage boy who stared hard at the floor like it was the most important surface in the stronghold.

"I have Pax. We're coming to see his daddy's—" A slight hitch in Tameka's breath clogged her voice. "We'll visit the stronghold in a few days. Hopefully, we'll have a better idea about the embargo by then, too."

"Uh. Thanks, Tameka." Jack still kept his hazel eyes on the floor.

"Aw. I'm sorry. Ross, don't you worry. He got over me by ninth grade."

Jack bolted out of the room. Ross, bewildered, stared after him.

"Haha!" Chris choked on his laughter. Until he saw the look Karter gave him.

That statuesque Valkyrie folded her corded arms in a stance that said, "We won't be fucking tonight if you don't make it up to Jack."

Shit.

Chris nodded and left the room to the sound of Karter giving Fury a lesson in sensitivity. The woman apologized furiously. She didn't consider for one second Ross was actually in the room.

"Jack?" Chris called up the glass stairwell.

The kid popped his head out of an archway. "I'm in the study, you traitor."

Chris rushed up there, still fucked up over the stair mechanics. "I'm sorry. Tameka is very sorry. We're all sorry. You know we're all seeking a little light in all this dark. Jokes are comforting."

Jack waved him away as he plopped on the couch. "It's not that." He looked at the fire a second before adding, "I talked to Ross. She's aware I like her, but she needs to find her sister. And I respect that. Damn, do I understand. So… I'm giving her some space." When he turned and locked his serious gaze on Chris, it sent the older man recoiling. "I'm trying to respect that. I'd like for you to do the same."

Caught. "Okay. Yea. Of course. You're both good kids. Karter and I just want you happy."

"Happy doesn't mean together like that, necessarily."

Wow. Chris was watching Jack grow up before his very eyes. "You're turning out all right, did you know that?" He ruffled the young man's light brown hair.

"Yea. Yea." Jack straightened it and peered toward the entryway.

Karter and Ross joined them. "Hey," the Valkyrie called.

Ross went to the shelves and pulled down one of Xelan's diaries. "I wonder if there's any information on Reipon auctions or Lukemore textile mills?"

"That's a great idea." Jack hopped up and snatched a volume for himself. It was the perfect change of subject. Until the teenager frowned at the page he opened. "Karter, you're in this one."

"Oh, yea?" She smiled at the celebrity mention. With a skip in her step, she hopped over to him and glanced at the page. The color drained from her dark gray complexion.

Chris walked over with a frown. He didn't like his girl upset. "What is it?"

"... And she refused to discuss her pregnancy with me. I care for her so much. Her lack of trust in me hurt. I endeavor to try again tomorrow..."

Jack met Chris' eyes over the book. Then they both turned and looked at her. She'd hung her head and looked away.

In...shame?

No. Chris reached out to her. To take her hand and tell her, "It was okay."

But Karter snatched back. First time for everything.

Ross watched the entire transaction. Her face tightened in concern. Gently, she reached out, "Karter. I think I speak for everyone when I say this is a safe place. For all of us. You don't have to share anything you don't want to. Just know that we're all here for you."

Chris couldn't have said it better, himself. He smiled cautiously. "Ditto."

The Valkyrie smiled softly with a sniffle. Her voice hoarse with emotion, she said, "Right. It's not something I'm ready to share. Not yet."

Jack blurted out, "Who's ready to play Twister?"

Slowly, they turned to him.

Chris also blurted, "I call Ross' team!

After three heartbeats and a quick shuffle around the stronghold, they found themselves in a tangle of limbs and giggles.

"Okay, Jack. Right hand . . . blue."

"Fuck."

Sometimes things got too serious with the whole end of the world business. Sometimes friends just needed to play a game and ridicule each other. They needed to hug upside-down and cross-legged. It made the losses easier to bear. And the ones to come easier to face. Keep moving forward.

Together.

SIXTEEN

PRAY FOR PEACE; PITY THE WAR TRODDEN

{GAIT}

KORAC RAN FASTER THAN NORMAL EYESIGHT. So that meant the treading floor struggled to keep up or provide any sort of challenge for him. Platinum weights from Pil strapped to his ankles and wrists slowed him down enough to equalize the machine for recreation. When he wasn't recreating with a certain hot blond General, he spent his time this way or reading.

To an outsider, his prison sentence sounded relaxing. But memories resurfaced in his nightmares. The toxic smell of this place unearthed events he loathed to relive. Helping Pehton helped Sagan. Helped Rayne. It also caused some trouble for his old world.

That, he didn't mind one bit—

"You always smirk while working out?" Pehton called from the other side of the nacre-deterring barrier.

Korac barely heard her through the ear inserts from L. Caprent. Sagan even loaded them with music for him. He smirked a little wider. A mixtape from his lover.

"Elden, who knew one joke would make you smile so much?" The Lyrik teased, but he knew his ease unnerved her.

"Executive Warden." Korac turned to face her with sweat glistening on his shirtless body. Loose drawstring pants hung off his hips and covered the rest. Lucky for her.

Pehton's eyes darted away. She cleared her throat before speaking, "Are you listening to music on contraband?"

Korac chuckled as he unstrapped the weights and headed for the shower panel. He turned and raised an eyebrow at her.

Pehton gave him her back with a huff.

He slipped out of the pants and rinsed away the sweat. "Listening to Earth music. Guy named Marilyn Manson. *Personal Jesus.* The song reminds me of Rayne." The water stopped, and he patted down with an Egyptian cotton towel.

"Why's that?" Pehton, ever the professional, kept her back to him.

"No particular reason. You can look now." He dressed in purple jeans faded to the color of Sagan's eyes. A thin white tee stretched over his shoulders.

The Lyrik faced him again with less humor than he expected. Honestly, her red eyes, like garnets, looked heavy. Tired. Her lips, normally a black like Earth's darkest calla lilies, paled to tombstone gray.

Dammit. Korac liked her. Was he becoming a people person? He scowled and tossed the ear inserts on the bed. The Icarus glared at them with his hands on his hips, contemplative. How could this happen?

"You ready?" Pehton obviously thought better than to ask about his sudden foul mood.

He raked a hand through his growing hair and grunted his assent.

"Good. Cause we're here." Sagan stepped through with Kyle, who instantly glared at Korac.

The last time they saw one another, Korac shot Kyle twice with nacre tranquilizers. The Icarus stifled the urge to bait the Progeny and stuck out his hand. Roughly, he offered, "Thank you for your help."

Kyle sighed in exhaustion and gripped the offered hand firmly. They stopped after one shake. Sagan's eyes widened a little. Discretely, Korac winked at her. Diplomacy was an important trait of a planetary General.

"Pehton, it's nice to see you." Story Taker nodded to the Lyriki warden.

"I wasn't expecting this for our next encounter, Progeny." She opened the barrier and stepped into the cell. "But as Korac said, I'm glad that you're here. In exchange, I can return the favor on Earth sometime."

Hands on hips, Kyle blew out an exasperated breath. "Yea. Well. I might take you up on that. At the rate shit's going down, I'd say for you to expect my call tomorrow."

Korac's brows shot up, and he glanced at Sagan in concern. "Is it that bad?" Was she sparing him?

The Seamswalker walked right up to him and searched his gaze. Sure. Confident. "The second I think we need you, I'll be here." Her cheeks flushed cutely. "Want you, well..." Climbing onto her tiptoes, she still didn't reach his lips without his help for an inappropriately timed kiss.

Kyle gagged behind her. Pehton folded her arms and rolled her eyes.

"After," Korac whispered, noting the sparkle in her eyes. Sadness flashed before she looked away, hiding it from him. Ahh...She went through Razor's second experience. They'd talk after.

Pehton sat on the cot. Kyle directed for Korac to follow. Then he announced in a way that stripped away all confidence from his audience, "I've never triangulated the same day for two people before now. So, this might suck. Ready?"

Korac rolled his eyes. "I hope you're prepared for life as a turnip, Pehton—"

Kyle touched them both, and the cell disappeared into a black space. In the fog, the Progeny stood between the Lyrik and the Icarus.

"This is a change from the intention-reader, Story Taker." Korac indicated the flashing screens of memories down either side of a long corridor. His along the left. Pehton's along the right.

Kyle ignored him and directed, "Take us there."

Pehton accessed her memory so often that Inanis was the first screen on her side. She stared into it. Lost.

Korac frowned and searched his side. Fog shrouded several of his memories into complete darkness.

The Progeny hissed. "I've seen that in only two other heads." Eyes wide with concern, he confessed, "Korac, I think someone tampered with your memory."

The Icarus shook his head, solemnly. He laughed with a bitter edge. "No. No, that—" Korac pointed to the darkened scene. "—I created for myself. Some memories require burying, Story Taker."

Every time the General called Kyle by that name, the Progeny's left eye twitched. So Korac continued to do so.

"They're gone."

They both turned to find Pehton staring in horror at her memory. She looked back at them. "They're gone! The children are gone! I can't see them. Where did they go?!"

Kyle ran to her and took her hand. They disappeared from the corridor. Korac searched for them. Confused at first. But slowly, he scanned the image Pehton was shouting at. They were inside.

Mercy Row. Right in front of the prison, not even a quarter mile from Korac's location on the same day. Pehton reached out both hands and crossed the street like she held something. Or someone. Invisible. Gone. Right there. A man in a white suit and hat crossed toward the prison and stepped around one of the invisible children. The Lyrik instructed the child to pardon itself. An audio gap cut from the memory. An entire second of silence removed to hide the child's voice.

Well, that was disturbing.

Korac trekked down the hall until he found his own memory. Tiny, he walked in a line to the prison yard. Two kids behind him and two kids in front. Men flanked them. Wait...

The General narrowed his gaze as he scrutinized the image. One man wore the same clothes as the one from Pehton's memory. Korac kept his head down so he only recognized the pants. But the suit was white with black stitching. An unusual color in a dirty city.

"We can't find them," Kyle called out to Korac down the hall. The young man assured Pehton, "We're working on decrypting nacre memories. Once we've made some progress..."

Salt. Korac sniffed Pehton's tears. He no longer doubted what he suspected was true. But later. Wait and confirm when they were alone.

He looked back at his own memory. This part he didn't understand. The Icarus hardly remembered. A small hand squeezed his own. Warm. Affectionate. Never. Not in that hellhole.

The white light came. Afterward, Korac lay in the snow. The sun glared at him until a man stepped between him and the star. Silhouetted. Unrecognizable. Aside from those pants.

In a deep voice the General hated so much and never heard again, the man promised, "Now they will never find you."

"Whoa."

The Icarus startled at Kyle's intrusion.

Mercifully, the Progeny let it go. Maybe Kyle wasn't so bad after all. "You sure you don't recognize that guy?"

Korac shook his head. "I saw him in Pehton's memory. But not his face."

Pehton seethed. Her gliders flared. "But at least now we have a connection. And we can use it in the Divine Booths."

"You said you can see the kids in Razor's capsule?" Both Kyle and Korac turned to her.

She swallowed once before answering in a voice thick with emotion, "Yes."

Kyle released them back into the glare of Korac's cell. Sagan, worried, was a sight for sore eyes. He opened his arms to her, and she reached for him instantly. Even climbed into his lap where he cradled her.

"We'll start meeting once a week. Do some memory therapy. Retrieve all your memories of the children and see if they were all tampered with." Kyle paced the room as he prescribed a treatment. "If everything is compromised, then Razor possibly contaminated what they look like. So you wouldn't recognize them. He wants you to think they look like the kids in the capsule. Or..." He frowned so hard his lip curled.

"Or what?" Sagan growled in frustration.

"Sorry. Or it's possible the contamination took place after you copied your memory to him. You know... so he'd be the only source for your retrieval." Kyle's voice hardened with disgust the more he divulged.

Korac looked forward to his next encounter with the Pain Curator. Many, many impulsive aggravations came to mind.

"Thanks for your help," Pehton reaffirmed. But this time she looked hollowed out, like someone scooped all the hope from the Lyrik.

Shit, was Korac about to comfort her—

"We'll do everything we can, Pehton." Sagan. Of course, his beautiful, sweet, compassionate girl. Gingerly, she left Korac's embrace and touched the other woman's shoulder.

The Executive Warden blinked at the blond girl. A strange emotion passed through her red eyes. Guilt. After another second, she cleared her throat, "Why don't you two get some time together?"

They exchanged a surprised look. Korac smirked as a blush crept onto Sagan's freckled cheeks. Permission to indulge in watermelon. Nice.

Kyle gave a big, "Ahem."

After he left, of course. Korac saluted to Pehton as she headed for the lift. "Thanks, Executive Warden."

She nodded to him before disappearing. The loss in her eyes would haunt his dreams. By the time he turned around, Sagan disappeared Kyle back to Earth.

"That was fast." He grinned at her until he caught the weariness in her posture and the sadness in her eyes. Gently, he pressed, "Tell me."

"Razor agreed to let you in."

Korac recoiled. Surprising turn of events, but he worried... "What did he take from you in exchange?"

Sagan held her chin high, even with the growing shimmer in her eyes. "I went through with the second experience." A tremor arrested the woman he loved and stole away all that courage.

He held out his arms to her, and Sagan gripped him tightly. She never sobbed. Only little shakes to let him know how much her heart broke.

"I don't even know why I'm crying. I can't even remember—I feel like I'm cheating on you or something."

Korac placed his hands on either side of her face. She kept her eyes down. He brushed his thumb over her cheek. "Sagan, look at me. You're not betraying us by doing this. I know some part of you must feel that way. But I trust you."

She finally looked up at him. And the fear in her eyes tightened his chest.

He kissed her lips and continued, "The moment you felt uncomfortable or strained, you came to me. That's trust. That's us. I won't punish you for that or the course of your mission. Do you trust me with Pehton?"

Gravely, she nodded. Sagan's eyes danced with the confidence of it. "Completely."

"To me, it's the same." Korac kissed the top of her head. "No matter what happens, I will not let you go."

"I promise to never go where you can't find me."

{EARTH}

Kyle stopped Sagan before she left the Medical Ecology. "Hey, I wanted you to know that Korac's repressing some serious shit. His memory is a wasteland of trauma the size of Enki. Feel me?"

For the first time in a long time, Sagan wrapped her arms around him and squeezed. Her voice came out tight as she said, "Thanks. I'll keep that in mind." She pulled away and spared him a sweet smile before departing back to Gait.

He got it. The way things unfolded here, he expected to find all the couples pairing off for a little stress relief—

"Kyle?"

He turned to find Silence waiting at the top of the suspensed stairs. It took a force of nature not to flashback to the memory of her in Twenty-One's arms. Satisfied. Beautiful. Not his.

Why did that hurt so much? Kyle barely knew the Icarean female and with all the trouble she caused…Ah, fuck it. He trusted her already. Dense fog shrouded her memory-scape, leaving her so lost and alone. Yet he wanted to help her find herself. Even if some of that journey included sex with men of her species.

The woman approached Kyle as he contemplated her trustworthiness. Or his inherent trust in her, rather. It was the day after the last basket of surprises. She changed into new clothes. Gone were Lucas' sharp white slacks. Today, she wore one of his longer t-shirts. Kyle didn't even know Lucas owned a t-shirt. It covered enough of her, but just barely.

Silence glided on long legs left exposed in their grace.

Losing his self-control, Story Taker barked out a laugh.

She stopped and frowned at him. Head tilted questioningly to the side.

"Sorry, sorry. It's just…you're so comfortable in your own skin that it makes the rest of us uncomfortable because we aren't equipped for it." He shook his head and chuckled. "I'm too immature for your level of confidence, Silence. You're calling me out on it every time you change your clothes."

She peered down at the shirt and looked up with…Oh Elden help him. The gorgeous woman pouted. "This is the most comfortable garment I found in his wardrobe."

After a little flustered pause, she added, "It's a *very* big wardrobe."

"You look beautiful."

That wiped the frown from her face.

"I—"

They both went to their knees. Against their will. Open to the floor below, Kyle checked around the banister. Techs knelt on the slate tiles. Cries and shouts carried throughout the facility. But one very loud bellow carried from the patient rooms.

Andrew.

"Don't sedate him!" Kyle called out before groaning as his face hit the floor. "Andrew! Andrew, it's Kyle! I want to try something new. Let me help." The sound of his own voice echoed through the rafters and their beams. Softly, to himself, he repeated, "I want to help you."

Just. You.

What the fuck? Andrew's voice came from inside of Kyle's head. Whatever, he stopped straining against an invisible barrier of his will. Released, he scrambled by Silence and called to her as he took the stairs, "I'll be back. Try to relax."

She watched him go, bewildered. A little excited, even. Her curiosity never satisfied.

Later. Worry about her later. He ran into Andrew's room with its door wide open. Lucas lay unconscious on the floor. With a raised brow, Kyle regarded his best friend, "You do that?"

"In six hundred and seventy-two thousand, nine hundred and ninety-two probabilities, Lucas betrayed us during the war." Andrew turned to face Kyle. He looked starved. Not just of food. Affection and warmth. Elden, he looked close to the edge. "You betrayed us in twice as many."

Kyle winced and looked away.

"But you were honest about it with me. I felt it in your intentions. You and Tameka. Sagan. You're real to me. I can feel Rayne, too."

Story Taker's brows shot up in surprise.

"She's always the same. Sometimes she's in a relationship with one of the Progeny, but…Always the same Rayne." He blinked and stopped, staring into the abyss. "Help me."

Crossing the room in two strides, Kyle made to reach for Andrew. "You sure?"

"Yes. Please."

Kyle touched the other Progeny and walked into his memory. His nose bled immediately. His head pounded as if someone banged it between two cinder blocks. Could he throw up in a memory-scape?

Swirling static. Corrupted data. Like Celindria.

Andrew flashed in a strange panorama of spinning fan blades. The blades swiped away one memory and replaced it with another. But that wasn't exactly right. It was the same memory with different Andrews. Different colors in the background. Different people wearing different things.

Andrew stood in the same room over and over again, but never the same life.

"Messed up, isn't it?"

His brother's voice from behind startled Kyle. "Jeez, get a bell or something."

"Sorry. I can't explain this to anyone. Lucas says he understands, but…I really think I needed someone to see it." Andrew swept his arm to indicate the ever-shifting moment.

Kyle swallowed hard and wet his lips before he confessed, "I don't know how to fix this."

"You're being here helps. But…" Andrew brushed at Kyle's top lip, coming away with blood. "I don't know how much longer we can stay."

"Andrew, I don't know how to say this…"

"You think I'm dying. I feel it in your intentions." Conscience pointed to the screen as the scenery changed.

The dark of night lit by roaring fire as acres of Vittle crop burned. As the fan blades spun, the events of the scenes morphed and multiplied.

Jumped in. Thrown in. Fell in. Pushed in.

"I can't solve it. But . . . I think we're in one of the Probabilities where I was pushed. They intended for me to die from it. I think."

"I'm afraid to ask how many pushed you in?" Kyle wished he had a fucking blunt.

"Only twelve."

Holy shit. "We can solve it then. We can do it together. We'll find that motherfucker and make them pay for this." Kyle stared at the scene and felt even more sure as certain details rendered. "There's a hand on your back in all of them. But the hand is never the same." White. Gray. Brown. Ring. No ring. Nail polish. Nothing. How fucked was that?

Andrew fell quiet, prompting Kyle to turn toward him. "I need to orient myself to these Probabilities. I'm limited to my experience and perspective. But I can still hear... their minds." He stared at the display and set his jaw. "I won't die."

"Then you need to eat something. Drink something. You can't keep laying in that bed—"

"Will you help me? They tried to kill me with this. I want to stop them with it." His soft blue eyes burned with determination.

"Yea. I think I know how. But you have to trust me. Implicitly."

Andrew cocked a brow and looked at the images beyond.

Kyle took a step into the messy kaleidoscope and held out his hand to his brother. "I'll highlight the memories you lived so far that I can corroborate. I'm hoping it will anchor you to this Probability. It may take hours, and I suspect we'll have to refresh it often...maybe forever. Are you ready for this?"

Without hesitating, Conscience took Story Taker's hand, and together they went down the rabbit hole.

{Earth}

"No one touch them," Pablo warned as he checked Andrew and Kyle's vitals.

Tameka and Lucas held the gathering crowd aloft. "It's okay. We'll take care of them." She took the Icarus' gray hand into her tawny one and squeezed.

Dr. Suarez appreciated her bedside manner. He also appreciated the space as he and Lynn looked over the two Progeny locked in some kind of messed up mind-meld.

Lynn whispered, "How are they doing?"

"Their vitals are fine."

Green eyes stared unblinkingly into blue ones. Kyle stood over Andrew as if locked in place. Pablo murmured, "If anything, I wish we could get them in a relaxed position. Depending on how long this venture will take, they could cramp or something..."

Lynn snickered a bit with her eyes ducked away.

Tameka pushed the onlookers back into the hall and closed Lucas in with them. She rushed over to the bed. "Please tell me they're all right."

"Medically, they're fine." Pablo gestured to them. "Nacres seem to work and everything."

"Kyle is guiding Andrew," Lucas announced.

They turned to the exhausted Icarus.

Lynn wondered aloud, "Have you seen anything like this before?"

He shook his head gracefully. "No. But there's no other cause for this." He stared into Andrew's eyes and smiled sadly. "I hope they're successful."

Pablo headed for the sink to wash up. "At first, I thought we had another disabled nacre on our hands. I'm sure Tumu will eventually take offense to all these donations. But..."

Tameka slumped against the wall and sank to the floor. She blew out a heavy sigh. "What a fucking mess."

Lynn caught Pablo's eyes in the mirror. She nodded her head in their direction and raised a questioning brow. "Now?" she mouthed.

Pablo beamed at her and nodded.

"We came upstairs from the lab to tell you..." Lynn smiled as Lucas and Tameka focused on them. "We decrypted the Imminent nacre."

Both the Icarus and the Progeny's eyes widened.

Pablo elaborated, "It took a combination of the research we put into both of our projects. We disabled the memory drive and reconstructed the material using the shields in the virus. Once Kyle is ready, we can check the memory bank."

"That's wonderful news." Some of the age disappeared from the Icarus' face. "You're geniuses!" He hugged Lynn.

Pablo tapped him on the shoulder with one eyebrow raised. "Ahem..."

The Icarus started, but immediately released the married woman in confusion. "Sorry, I—" And laughed heartily when Pablo threw himself into Lucas' arms. Lynn piled on. Then Tameka hopped in.

They breathed deep of their family's warmth and sighed in relief. One small break. The most important thing to remember about the Shadow was their ability to exploit a chink in their enemy's armor. They needed this break to win.

A knock sounded from the door.

They separated, and Tameka answered. Silence stood outside, looking a little lost in the flowy t-shirt. She spied Kyle beyond them.

Awkwardly, she made to turn away. "I'll be in the library—"

"You can stay," Tameka offered with a hand on her arm. "You and Lucas can watch over them...? If that's okay with you?" She looked back at the Icarus.

He smiled warmly. "I welcome the company."

"Great." Tameka let Silence in and lingered in the doorway. "I have to go see John and Caedes off. I guess Abresson, too. Tumu promised to stay until we resolve who or what is disabling our nacres. I... Elden, this will sound weird, but I wish Pax weren't here with all this mess."

"It's perfectly understandable," Lynn responded fiercely. "Protect that little boy above all else and don't worry about us."

A sadness filled Tameka's eyes, and it broke Pablo's heart. "That's not what *he* would want. Anyway, I'll see you later." She left them for the lobby.

"Lynn, I'm heading over to check on John before he leaves."

His wife hugged him and murmured against his ear, "I won't take my eyes off her." She kissed his cheek and saw him out.

He loved her so much for recognizing and understanding his suspicions of Silence without words.

In the lobby, John, Caedes, and Abresson waited for Sagan to Seamswalk them out. Tumu and Tameka came to say goodbye.

Climbing the stairs, Pablo overheard Abresson boast, "Fortunately, for you a Gargantuan Tritan was nearby."

John grimaced. "No offense, Tumu, but your blood tastes pretty gross."

The Tritan laughed with a pat on John's back. "Imagine what everything else tastes like."

The crowd paused and looked at him with various expressions of confusion and bewilderment. Maybe a little disgust.

"Your faces!" The tall blue alien snorted.

The rest of the group joined in the humor. Pablo shook his head, smiling as he approached. Caedes grumped and folded his arms.

This enormous family.

Except for Abresson. He stared upside Tumu's head. "Would anyone here know the taste of those fluids?"

The cutting up cut off abruptly.

Something passed between the two Tritans. Serious. Terrifying.

The depth of Tumu's voice resonated so hard in Pablo's chest that his heart bounced. "No."

Abresson relaxed. "Good."

Weird tension. Pablo sliced through it by walking between the group to John. "Let's look at you before you're discharged."

"Yes, Educator. What a scare you had." Abresson turned his back on them and headed for the glass walls. "Fantastic location, Dr. Suarez, if I've never mentioned it before."

"Thank you," Pablo answered automatically as he palpated John's throat and warmed the stethoscope.

Tumu asked across the lobby, "How are you with cosmetic surgery, doctor? Like scar removal..."

The tension came back. Abresson turned inch by inch and glared at the taller Tritan.

Yes. Everyone noticed the scars on Abresson's deep blue skin. No one dared comment on it. Was Tumu looking for a fight?

The offended Tritan bristled and growled, "How. Dare—"

"Uncle Caeda! Don't go, uncle Caeda."

The gruff Icarus knelt with his arms out to sweep the boy from the floor. Tameka, distracted as everyone with the drama, kissed her son's red curls.

"Sorry, I tried to keep him back." Smith looked properly abashed. "He's slippery."

Pax gripped Caedes tightly. Near tears, he pleaded, "Don't go."

Across the room, a silence fell as everyone caught their breath. The toddler's separation anxiety squeezed Pablo's heart.

"Auntie Ray said stay with us..."

Okay, that changed the atmosphere a bit.

"Did she now?"Abresson's cold tone frosted the glass behind him. Literally. It iced up.

Sagan Seamswalked into the middle of it and took in the scene. After a tense heartbeat or two, she folded her arms and asked, "So...what'd I miss this time?"

{Gait}

During his rounds between the Emporium and the Complex Lounge, Matt let his thoughts drift. To Lucy. And now to Sagan. He didn't care for the state she left the booth after her last experience. Razor's arm around her shoulder, chafing her bicep in a comforting gesture. The powerful woman looked small and vulnerable in his arms. It bothered Matt.

But until she asked directly for his help, he trusted her undercover skills. He learned that much from Lucy. Smiling, he remembered his reaction to her coup on the first CON—

"What has you in such a good mood tonight?" Razor found Matt loading an auction prize into some Lamia's antigrav caravan. He prodded, "Is downstairs keeping you satisfied?"

No. "Yes." Matt loaded the nacre glass statue while sweeping the vicinity for additional listeners.

The older man chuckled. "Just you and me." With hands in the pockets of his tuxedo pants, Razor strolled into the street. He leaned on the antigrav car and watched Matt work. "It's Icarean, you know?"

At first, Matt thought he meant the statue. His biceps bunched, and he grunted as he nestled the bulky thing in with the rest of the lucky prince's winnings. "Sorry, boss. What?"

"Your nacre."

Fuck. He can tell? "Well, it likely wouldn't be an Earth one considering we don't have any yet—"

"You ripped it out of an Icarus. That's no small feat." Razor sounded genuinely impressed. He surveyed Matt more openly before adding, "One with Korac's blood, I assume. It explains your strength and stamina. You're putting the other downstairs employees to shame." The man's stoic expression blossomed into a genuine grin. "I'm thinking of promoting you."

Matt raked a hand through his short auburn hair before locking eyes with the devil. "Sure, boss. What'd you have in mind?"

The alien stepped away from the car and waved for Matt to follow him back inside. The night waned into the morning hours. With the auction over, the swankier guests spent the last dregs of the evening seeking desperate company. Halfway across the floor, Matt got twitchy amid the crowd. A hum alerted him to the strangest gun before he even saw the shooter.

"Razor, down!" Matt collided into his boss, bringing them both to the floor.

The bullet went into the nearest man, who buzzed and cooked under a blanket of electricity that covered his entire body. Shivered and shook until he kissed the parquet hardwood.

Matt stared down into Razor's gray eyes. They swirled and the young man swore he saw storm clouds. There. A strike of lightning in the iris. What the fuck—

"Let me up." Steel. His voice rang like cold metal. Stiff muscles soon followed. Was this what Razor looked like when angry?

The crowd seized the shooter and his weird gun. Smooth metal. Matte. A handgun. Loaded with only one golden-cased bullet, the assassin gambled on a hail Mary shot and lost.

Razor straightened and rolled up his sleeves. Loosened his bow tie. "How many does that make this month, my honored guests?"

The crowd shouted in a chorus, "Six." A tension rippled across them like the gathering of a tidal wave that rose and opened its massive jaws.

"Matt, this is good for you to learn. I am not well liked by most outside this Emporium."

Some people chuckled and laughed. Some nervously. Some while practically licking their lips. None of them liked him. They liked what he did for them.

"But we like assassins here. Don't we?"

Uhm. Somebody moaned in ecstasy. The anticipation even infected Matt with a craving for next. What would come next???

Two Mon3 drones lowered the would-be killer to his knees. He glared up at Razor, but not exactly unflinchingly. "You won't get anything—"

The boss treated the guy's head like a football during kickoff for the Superbowl. Red blood sprayed in an arc. Matt narrowed his gaze. Human. How'd this guy even get here?

Most of the spray coated the faces of a triangular man from Yun and a Luk jellyfish guy. They looked at each other and instantly locked mouths.

Razor chuckled at the crowd as they watched, envious. "Don't worry. There's plenty more to go around. Matt?"

"Yes?"

"You're doing great in your promotion so far. But now we'll test your stomach. Get a knife—"

Matt produced a six-inch combat knife from a pocket in his cargo pants.

The crowd laughed in menacing approval. Someone behind him purred. The Pain Curator beamed at him. "Perfect. I want to know who sent him, why, and where he got the gun. Use any means necessary as long as it's painful. Then remove his nacre completely intact for me. We'll see if you're worthy of the top shelf."

The auburn-haired twenty-year-old tortured plenty of Cult of Night freaks. Tormenting pedophilic bastards kept his conscience clear. He stared down at the barely conscious human on the floor. The man peered up and locked brown eyes with his own. Grimacing, he begged for a quick death.

Matt sank to his knees, looked the man in the eyes, and shook his head. He shoved the knife under the guy's ribs. Tears streamed down the assassin's face as he clenched so hard he chipped a tooth. The redhead withdrew the knife and sluiced blood at the audience.

Razor grinned wickedly behind Matt, and the crowd cooed their approval.

"You heard the boss. Who, why, and where?" Matt held the knife to the back of the guy's ear. In the meantime, he ground his own teeth from the stress. And he was pretty sure that couple from earlier just…yup. They finished.

The man hung his head, groaning and spitting blood. "I don't remember where."

Matt punched him in the jaw, rather than take his ear.

The hit-man grunted and drooled blood from biting his lip.

Beneath him. This was beneath Matt. Lucy wouldn't like it. The sooner this guy gave up the information, the sooner he could end it.

"Don't tell me you don't remember. You were carrying it." Matt punched him again. "Surely, you remember retrieving it from the source." When he punched him this time, the guy's orbital bone exploded and sprayed blood onto another lucky member of the audience.

Sure enough, they sighed and giggled with excitement.

Fucking weirdos.

Matt put the knife to the guy's ear. "Who?"

The captured human sagged further to his knees and vomited in answer.

"What's wrong with your nacre? Can't it keep up?"

He made to punch him again, but Razor grabbed his wrist. Touching him right now was a mistake. He whirled on his boss and wondered if he let the inside slip onto the outside.

If so, Razor didn't mind it. He calmly assured, "It's possible he doesn't remember." The alien reached a hand out to him. "We may employ other measures."

Matt took it and followed Razor to the booths. The drones dragged the captive behind them. The crowd followed while many of them made conversation along the way.

"Very gifted protege," a Lyrik commented.

"Yes, he could attend the gala next week."

The rich Lamian prince agreed, "We haven't seen anyone this promising since Xelan."

It took an act of god to keep Matt from reacting to the last one. That was worth sharing with Sagan during her next visit.

Only three fit in the booth. The Lamian prince grinned expectantly at Razor until the boss shut him down. "Matt's in here with me. He's earned it." They shut the door while the others sulked away.

"We'll download his memory and check for anything unusual. Put that set of goggles on." He put on a set for himself.

With the memory loaded, Matt expected to see the guy's life flashing before his eyes as he bled out. Instead, they saw nothing. Blackness.

Wait.

A figure appeared in a haze. It kept glitching like a faulty connection. Female. Rich black skin. Black dreads and braids fell to her waist. White ribbons and beads adorned them. White clothes that suited her fit figure with its delicate curves. But her eyes were what shocked Matt into removing his headset.

They were a bright blue. Like Rayne's.

Razor stared at the dying man. Hunger burned in his steely gaze. Not for the prisoner. No, he wanted to hunt premium game. But unfortunately for the guy, he was here, and she was not.

"Celindria."

Faster than Matt could see. Faster than anyone other than Sagan. Razor clutched the man and carried him outside the booth. The people waited eagerly, almost as if they shared in his hunger.

"He's all yours."

Fascinating. He threw the man to the crowd of well-to-do motherfuckers coming here night after night to find a thrill in their immortal lives. Apparently, ripping an assassin apart while he screamed for death worked for them.

"Don't forget to retrieve his nacre, Matt. And congratulations on your promotion. You did exactly as I expected." Razor made to leave for the mezzanine.

Matt called after him, and he stopped on the spiral staircase. The younger man needed some clarification. "Boss, what do you mean?"

"I saw the assassin casing the place, and I thought it was a perfect opportunity to test your loyalty. You passed admirably. Aren't you pleased?"

No. "Yes."

Razor beamed. "Unless you're downstairs easing your troubles, you're with me wherever I go. Got it? You work security from now on."

The man's screams died into wet gurgles behind Matt. Squelches drowned even those sounds out.

Matt reached for his chain and considered his position. How deep would the Shadow approve for undercover work? Was this already too far? Without Lucy around, how much did he care—

"Matt? Do you take issue with anything that transpired tonight?" The blue-haired, blue-skinned alien leaned on the banister, looking bored.

"No, boss."

He smiled that special one reserved for the title from Matt.

"Good. Sagan's big day is tomorrow, and I need you on board. Goodnight to the one human truly unlike any I've met so far." Razor waved as he ascended the stairs and disappeared on the second floor.

Matt turned, prepared to dive into an orgy of blood-soaked aliens to retrieve that human assassin's nacre.

And he never missed Lucy more.

SEVENTEEN

ENDING IN ME

{???}

NOX EXPERIENCED EVERY MOMENT OF RAYNE'S EXISTENCE IN DEPTHS HE NEVER IMAGINED POSSIBLE. Sensory. Thought. Emotion. All of it.

Yes, he cried. Rayne wept often in her brief life. And often because of his cruelty. Case in point, the image currently stilled on the screen. Nox's hand crushed over her mouth in the observatory after their dance. While he grieved this moment in his own reflections, living it as her...

Rayne's regret for trusting him destroyed her. And now him. He wanted her to see a monster, and he was quite thorough in his work.

Nox almost asked her to shut it off. The combination of her broken heart and his shame crippled him. But he needed to see this. He asked to know why he was wrong.

Elden, was he ever *right*?

Only a moment later, Rayne paused it and offered, "We should stop and recover for a while." She set aside the considerable length of rope she fashioned whenever her hands were free.

Even with the interruptions, Nox caught up on Rayne's life in only a few days. The brevity of it compared to his existence sorrowed him. For so much of it involved his torment of her.

"I need time to process this," he heard himself request. The mixed association of the experience overwhelmed him.

Rayne walked over to the image of herself trapped between him and the bookshelf. The tears. The loss.

"I may not be six million, but looking at her... I feel ancient in comparison."

She sounded so lost. *Was*. Was so lost. He felt it through their connection. He looked away and focused on anything else.

"The Progeny wonder when you'll leave the Martyr Complex. Are you planning to assist them?" Nox stood slowly, conscious of keeping himself loosened and his hands somewhat distanced. Unarmed. Nonthreatening. This made her the most comfortable.

Rayne turned around to face him. Her skin glowed like moonlight in this space. Commanding, strong, she assured, "It's not time yet. Someone is testing us. Strategically, they aim to weaken our weapons and medical research. It's smart. But the facilities and backing are better prepared than Imminent expected."

"Astute."

Her gaze fell to the floor, and she chewed on her lip. After another moment, she muttered, "I worry about T.A.O. and Silence. About Jack." The woman locked inside her own head looked to the ceiling and closed her eyes as if she basked in sunlight. "All I can do is worry."

Rayne pulsed a blue the same color as her eyes. The same color as his blood. She dressed in flowy tunics lately. The jeweled tones complemented her pale skin and black hair. The carefree comfort of her clothing contrasted with her usual combat gear.

Gear she wore always in preparation to fight Nox.

"I never imagined... Pax. I wonder if I should tell Tameka about grandy Primary?" Rayne looked at him across the space and hugged herself. "You knew?"

Nox nodded. He recalled the exact instant he learned of the Progeny's pregnancy. During the battle at the caldera, he momentarily captured his brother's woman. Smelled the maternity in her scent. And immediately discarded her, unharmed.

"You didn't tell me."

"Not a scenario enters my mind that would explain why she didn't confess it to you before you entered the Complex." He spread out his hands. "Sincerely, I didn't know."

Rayne concentrated momentarily, as if sensing the truth in his words. Satisfied, she asked, "What do you advise?" She swept up her hair and tied it back from her face.

He glanced away and considered her question. "She should know. But I'm not sure to what end. I doubt even Enki knows. Just those closest to that Primary. I understand he seeded many children without Enki's knowledge."

Rayne walked around the space until she stood in front of him. With her hair back, her cheekbones looked more prominent and drew attention to her nose. Her frown crinkled it as she asked, "But why? Why keep it a secret?"

"If Elden's Prerogative was to act in betterment of the Icarean race, then the Tritan's mission is to reproduce within their species. They're dying. And they created us to observe their unmaking. To create outside of that, as the Primary has done, is to break that prerogative."

Her eyes widened at that. "Primary Rem used almost those exact words when we met him."

Absorbing this information, Rayne paced away. When she brought her thumbnail to her lips, a pang hit Nox in the heart. Startled, she looked up at him. Conscious now of her adopting Xelan's habit—the recognition of it—her pain almost doubled Nox over.

He winced and rubbed his temples. She rubbed her chest, almost gasping.

Grief hurt. His time with Rayne convinced Nox that he never experienced true loss until now. He hated it. For him and for her. He tried to imagine his life up to this point with emotions this potent. No. He'd perish already. Not because of the weapon. To feel as Rayne felt meant suicide for Nox.

The rejection of his parents. The divide with his brother. Celindria's betrayal. And the death of his unborn child. Just...no.

"You're capable of so much more than I imagined. And you're so much more than ever I could hope to be..." The words choked him.

Rayne stood only steps from him. Caution narrowed her gaze. Curiosity brightened her eyes.

Nox wanted nothing more than to convey a significance to her without in any way obligating her in return. He didn't want or deserve her forgiveness. But to let her know...

Regret. Remorse.

She gasped in a shaky breath and stared at him in disbelief with wide eyes.

He fought not to wince at her shock.

"No." Gravely, Rayne shook her head. "Not yet. We'll have that discussion. But you've yet to earn it. Not until we've been through everything together. Every. Last. Moment."

Nox hated the gravity in her voice, but he understood. And she was right. "Agreed. Is it time then?"

"No. I'm not ready. Are you?"

He looked away, ashamed of his fear. "Not as such." After a long moment, he cleared his throat and tried for more appropriate conversation, "Why do you want Caedes here?"

"I'm unsure, but Tameka has to feed, right?"

Nox nodded, understanding now.

"Right. So if Caedes leaves with the embargo active, she has no one to feed from. And I can't..." She sat down on the couch near Nox, rope in hand. She looked up at him and continued, "I can't shake this feeling. Have you ever felt this way? Like you're on a familiar course?"

Her eyes sparkled electric blue up at him. She was so tiny from this angle. It dizzied him. He sat down on the other end of the couch. Better. "Yes. The Valkyrie. Almost every event with them seemed not necessarily predictable so much as if it already occurred. I could see those moments from far away, but they also felt inevitable."

"Right." She drew closer, scanning his gaze. Eager in her quest for his knowledge. "Do you think the Probabilities are like that with everyone or…" Her words trailed off in a spiral of curious assumptions.

"I'm afraid, your majesty, that I wouldn't know. You're the first person I've shared this eerie perception with."

She blushed at his use of her title.

Nox stood abruptly and took a few steps away. Rayne's proximity affected him, disembodied or not. And any reaction to her felt inappropriate given their circumstances. To think, only two years ago, he couldn't care less about appropriate.

Now? Inside her conscience?

Rayne shared his thoughts and emotions with him. *Everything* with him. After watching her survive so much with a grace and strength he could never hope to match…

Nox loved Rayne more than ever.

Through living most of her life with her, he recognized the impossibility of it. The incorrectness of it. He always knew he was never quite right, of course. But he had thought he grasped the basics of caring for another.

He was wrong. Elden, was he wrong. Leave her the story of his life and disappear without ever facing her. That was the plan. The only one that made sense at the time.

Nox turned to find Rayne looking up at him, expectant. As always, she surprised him. She waited for him to answer.

"I believe the more events coalesce around us, the stronger the perception."

She stood as he spoke, still looking up at him from chest-height. Fearless. Without reason to fear. Rayne found peace.

Well, more or less. A pretty blush crept on her cheeks as she quipped, "Let's hope this perception doesn't include anymore of my friends coalescing in the pit."

Nox laughed abruptly, recalling her face as the soldier and the Valkyrie went at it.

"Again?!" she cried.

He tried to hide his amusement, aware of the strained gulf between them on the subject.

But since she bridged the chasm first…"The moment you showed me the installation of cozy couches and palettes, I knew. And I knew it would be two Icari."

"Why's that?" She tilted her head to the side and folded her arms. Her long ponytail swayed with her movements.

Nox waved dismissively. "Humans waste time. I'm surprised it took two years for my people to take advantage of the quiet venue."

At the generalization of her kind, Rayne's eyes hardened into ice. "Maybe humans are more respectful of the space."

No, no fierce warrior. He wouldn't tolerate that kind of talk. "Do you think for one second Para and Bones feel anything less than the utmost respect for you?"

Love for her people melted that icy stare. She shifted uncomfortably before letting her arms fall to her side.

Nox continued to defend them, "They simply didn't know, Rayne. And the moment you let them know, they stole away to somewhere more private for your modesty. Because I assure you they don't have any."

"Why not?" With curiosity in her voice, she idly snatched up the rope and continued manifesting it. As if her hands sought it out when otherwise unoccupied.

"Why don't they have the modesty of humans?" He phrased the question to better understand what she wanted for an answer.

At her nod, he contemplated the least insulting way to explain it. Funny that. He spent most of his time since death carefully considering his words for her. Well, everything about his time with her. Not only his words.

"Religion repressed your people. Icari couldn't afford repression. They lived in semi-public dwellings with mandatory demonstrations of consummation. It was necessary. Repopulate. Thrive. I can't speak for the entire Vast Collective, of course. But humans are the most repressed beings I've encountered thus far."

Leveling with his gaze, Rayne's voice softened as if she feared her next question, "Does that include you?"

What did she want from him? He survived by suppressing his urges for millions of years. Denied himself. But..."I am no longer the man you read about in that Verse. I haven't been for thousands of years."

"No. *That* man was incapable of what you did to me."

Nox clenched his jaw shut.

"*He* was a man worth knowing." Rope in hand, she turned her back on him and took a few steps away.

Nox chuffed bitterly. If only. Meeting Rayne before the invasion plans. Before the madness.

Once upon a time...

"Why the rope?" He couldn't contain his curiosity any longer.

As she spoke, Rayne kept her eyes on the knots. "Rope can make a bridge, a net, or a noose. Where you see a way to strangle someone, I see a way to connect."

"To what end?" The ongoing mystery of her would forever puzzle him.

"A rope is what you make of it. With more knots it can be something with purpose." Rayne tossed him the end. "Replicate the knots. I could use your help. It takes a lot out of me to work on this construct. I'm afraid I won't finish in time."

Ignoring the foreboding in her words, Nox grazed his fingers along the smooth material. The filaments. They were—

"Glass? Rayne, is this—"

"It's made of me. From my nacre," she offered this explanation as if it weren't completely impossible.

Nox refrained from gaping and sat with his end. He admitted, "I trust your instincts."

After another quiet moment, he stared down the rope at her. She concentrated until a little furrow creased her brow. Nacre glass formed at her fingertips, drawn from her chest and woven immediately into the rope.

"Rayne, use my nacre." He raised a hand to stifle her argument. "Don't waste yours."

They both turned and gazed across the mindscape. After a stretch, the tiled floor transitioned into sand. The sand into surf. The surf into an ocean.

And on the horizon, clouds gathered across that ocean. The storm so vast and broad it never ended. It spanned the waters with bolts of lightning. From here, in the screening room, they heard the thunder in the distance. Salty water misted on the occasional breeze, stronger now than two years ago.

With her voice hushed in awe, Rayne asked, "Will I finish in time?"

"Yes." Nox knew for certain. Because he knew what she'd yet to understand.

Rayne was the storm.

EIGHTEEN

OBLIGATE MY KINDNESS AND I'LL OBLIGATE YOUR END

{EARTH}

TAMEKA SQUEEZED PAX'S TINY HAND AS HE FIDGETED NERVOUSLY AGAINST HER LEG. Proof that Nox didn't lie about at least one thing in his Verse. Her son took after his father in toddler shyness.

Caedes knelt and assured the small child. "Auntie Sagan will take us on a trip. No pain. No tears." He put his fist to his chest, and Tameka's heart squeezed as Pax copied him.

"Ready to go?" Sagan took Tameka's free hand.

"'Eady." Pax nodded sternly after an encouraging pat from Caedes.

With the toddler wrapped around her leg, Tameka stepped through the Seam and into the stronghold. The place meant for her and Xelan to build their life together after the war. Elden, it smelled of him. And flowers, water, life. It smelled of life.

"We're here," Sagan called into the kitchen. As if the food waited for her to arrive.

"Mommy, look!" Pax detached from her and darted into the koi pond.

"Baby. Why?" She laughed softly as one fish nipped his finger before swimming under the planks.

"Don't worry, Pax. I'll teach you to fish." Karter strode in with Chris behind her. "We're up in the study. Searching for Bethany clues." She and Tameka exchanged a brief hug. The redhead came to the Valkyrie's shoulders.

"I'd love to help."

Karter chuckled. "Oh, I think Jack is avoiding you."

Tameka winced and squeezed out, "I really had no idea—"

Sagan cursed from the kitchen. She Seamswalked beside the two women and leaned on them both. "I need to get you guys some proper food. I'm starving, and I promise you there's better stuff out there than bologna."

Chris scoffed from the entryway, "That's what the barbecue chips are for." The dark knight always impressed Tameka with his immaculate grooming. Especially given the inconsistency of their living situation.

Sagan bowed to him. "I fall to your flawless logic."

Caedes returned from the waterfalls with Pax sitting on his shoulders. Her son rudely gripped his bald head like a lifeline.

He bounced and squeezed his knees. "Go faster, Uncle Caeda!"

Tameka pointed to the floor. "You'll want down for this part, honey."

Pax squirmed as Caedes set him on the hardwood. He took his momma's hand, and the group migrated into the chasm.

"Wow..." Her son looked up and then down. "Where it go?"

She kissed the top of his red curls. "Go on, sweetie. It's a special space your daddy made."

As far as Tameka was concerned, Xelan walked up beside her son, accepted his hand, and they took that first step together. Glass appeared under Pax's untied shoe. He cried out in delight. The wonder in the sound broke her heart and expanded it all at once.

A warm hand touched her shoulder. Sagan beamed at her. Tears sparkled in her violet eyes. Tameka squeezed her hand in place. This support system kept her chin up.

She frowned a little. Bony. Sagan's hand was bony. Her face a little thin. Tameka opened her mouth to say something when Pax cried out, "I found it!"

Found what?

She rushed to his side with others lingering nearby. Some strolled casually into the study. Pax pointed to a strange translucent page preserved in glass plates. Lines. Grids. Some kind of architecture and blueprints.

"Sagan, do you recognize this?"

The Seamswalker checked it out and frowned. "I can't make it out. Pax, why did you show us this?"

He turned his face into Tameka's thigh and flushed in his brown skin. Those adorable freckles highlighted from the redness.

Caedes humphed and leaned into Sagan, whispering to her.

Her eyes widened and filled with warmth and kindness. Gently, she exclaimed. "Oh..." To Caedes, she added, "I'll go see what the others are doing then."

Pax watched her leave from his mother's side, and she figured it out. She mouthed to Caedes, "Crush?"

The Icarus nodded, solemnly.

After another second, Pax led them by the hand to follow the Seamswalker into the study where Sagan approached Karter. "...So you don't mind?"

Jack and Ross called out greetings to the new arrivals from the chess table.

Karter sat on the arm of a chair and folded her arms. "Para and I would be glad to help. What does Pehton need?"

Sagan stood in front of her and glanced awkwardly around the room before muttering, "It's about Thailea. About Inanis."

Tameka didn't eavesdrop. She went to the other side of the room and found the most recent entry into Xelan's expansive journal collection.

Pax opened it and pretended to read.

Softly, she told him, "It's your father's writing. He wrote that for us."

Her vision swam, and she clutched the shelf for support. Chris rushed to her side. "Are you all right?"

No. Tameka caught Caedes' concerned frown from across the room. She kept putting it off, but... "Do you mind watching Pax for a bit?" she muttered to Batman.

"Sure. We'll entertain the kiddo."

Ross waved Pax over to the chessboard. "Hey, do you know how to play?"

Tameka hoped the girl brought her A-game. Eminent Wiw couldn't best her son at chess. Caedes followed her out of the study without a word. Down to the third floor. Fourth door. She took in the pictures Xelan framed of her and her friends all around the room. The room he decorated with her in mind.

"He thought of everything." Caedes glanced around the space without putting his eyes on her.

Tameka understood. She sat on the bed and whispered, "We don't have to do this."

"I made a promise." Caedes sat on the bed beside her. Calm. Resolute. No more words. He bared his forearm. The veins in his wrist faced upward. Faced her.

Faint. Almost weakened, Tameka brought his arm to her lips. He looked away, examining her photographs. Giving her privacy with his blood. Typically an intimate act, Caedes worked to make it as clinical as possible for her benefit.

"Thank you," she whispered.

"As I pledged. You're welcome."

He didn't moan when Tameka bit into him. Although, she stopped herself from doing it. Blood tasted so good with a nacre. She wondered if it ever got awkward with Caedes feeding on John—

A knock sounded from the door, and Tameka jumped two feet off the bed.

"Tameka?" Sagan learning how to knock saved them a lot of trouble since that time she interrupted Lynn and Pablo with the trapeze.

Caedes stepped across the room and leaned against the wall, affording some discretion.

"C'mon in," Tameka called.

"Sorry. I'm heading out." Sagan came over and hugged her weakly.

Tameka quirked a brow at her. "The bad boy toy?"

A shadow cast over the blond girl's eyes before she looked away. Sagan shook her head and cleared her throat. "No. The mission, you know?" She offered a weak smile.

Fuck that. Tameka clutched her sister in her arms and held on tight. "You are more important than some objective. Take care of yourself first. If anything happened to you, I'd drain the Vast Collective." She pulled away and brushed the girl's hair back. "Do you hear me? Be careful."

"Yes, mom." Sagan rolled her eyes and then winced at her own joke. "Sorry." She patted Caedes on the shoulder. "You two get back to whatever it was I interrupted." With a wink, she walked into the Seam.

"Did she look thinner to you?" Caedes asked into the remaining quiet.

Tameka groaned and screamed her frustration into a pillow. Why was everything falling apart? Again.

{GAIT}

It took every ounce of Sagan's self-control not to eat all the stronghold's rations. For one thing, it would be rude. For another, nothing appealed to her. Despite her starvation. Not when she knew a guy with access to delicious and exotic food from all over the Vast Collective. But now it was a matter of asking him without revealing her developing dependency.

Daytime in the Emporium shone sunlight beautifully through the stained glass panels. Varying shades of gold and amber squares mosaic-ed across the wood flooring. Like twilight in a bottle. It took her breath away.

"Hey, Sagan!" Matt called to her from the museum where he unloaded a crate.

She Seamswalked to him and took the heavy cargo in one hand. "Where to?"

He grinned. It looked cute with his ginger freckles. "Right here."

She helped him place it in storage beneath the displays. "New exhibit piece?"

"New conquest."

Sagan whirled to find Razor leaning in the doorway. Did the man not own casual clothes? Black slacks. Black silk button up. Undone vest that matched a missing blazer, no doubt. He let his five o'clock shadow grow in to a fine red stubble against his tan skin. The rugged look suited him.

Matt nodded to his employer.

Razor smiled at his employee. Then the man said the only two words she'd find agreeable in that moment, "It's lunchtime."

Sagan feigned sheepishness. "I guess I'm one more mouth to feed?" She Seamswalked to the other side of the museum. "I can head out and come back at a more convenient time?"

The Pain Curator glanced at Matt before smirking at Sagan. "Nonsense. I look forward to you trying Reipon bore. Barbecued."

Was her stomach as loud as she thought? When Matt cut over to her with a veiled smile, Sagan blushed. Yes. It was that loud. Remaining cool, she held up her chin. "I suppose I could donate my presence to your company."

There it was. Razor's rich chuckle. Like a double-edged sword, it sounded pleasant, but with a cost. With every laugh, did he lose a year off his life? Or did she lose one off hers?

Within seconds, yummy smelling exotic dishes crowded the buffet near the kitchens. She sat on it with her legs dangling off cause fuck manners. Licking the barbecue sauce from her fingers, she admitted the bore tasted excellent. The Luk pickled vegetables, superb. Fish cakes from Pil, delicious. Only after she sated her hunger did Sagan realize Matt disappeared.

Razor shook his head in astonishment. "You are quite impressive, Seamswalker. Your appreciation for food might even count as its own experience—"

"Stop right there." Sagan held up a hand to stave him. "I take my love of food even more seriously than my love of pain. It's quite private—"

A growl from her stomach cut her off. Her blood sugar plummeted despite the meal. Sugar crash, maybe? Too much desert. Not enough protein.

"It's fortunate you dropped by."

Sagan forgot her stomach and looked across the way where Razor leaned in a doorway. Arms folded, he put more effort into his fitness than she first assumed. It garnered a little respect. Easy to let oneself go with a nacre.

Back on topic. She asked, "How's that?"

Razor frowned and pushed away from the wall to approach her. Arms still folded. Safe. "Well, I encountered a hiccup in our plans for the gala. I'm disappointed to say that I'll need to retract my invitation."

She frowned and almost cried out with disappointment. "Why?" Dampening her initial impulse to accuse him of bait and switch.

The Pain Curator stopped in front of her and turned only his head to face her. A little close. The green and orange in his irises spun like pinwheels. Dizzying her. The roughness of his voice complemented the rugged look of him, "I can't fathom a single thing I want more in the Vast Collective than to take you."

Genuine. His words felt genuine. They smothered her anger.

Observing her carefully, he pressed onward, "After the Eminents announced their attendance, off-list guest entry requires a nacre port which you don't have. And I thought it better to assume you couldn't attend than to suggest you accept one."

Beyond, in the addition, Matt entered Sagan's peripheral vision. He froze mid-carry with more crates to the museum. The stillness unnerved her. The redhead and his blond bombshell partner were renowned for never breaking character.

But now, the perfect infiltrator frowned in concern before returning to his task.

Sagan shivered in her Lyriki coat.

Razor silently committed the response to memory.

Proceed with caution. She pushed her hair behind her ears. "What does the implant entail?"

"Incision site here." He traced from the dip of his clavicle, stopping just between his pecs.

Her eyes followed. Before she realized, Sagan peered at Razor's chest through his open shirt. Flicking back to his face, he observed her with no reaction. Only the alien pinwheel eyes.

"No scarring." Razor mercifully carried on as if he didn't catch her ogling him. "The implant creates a port to directly access your nacre during experiences."

Playing with her chain nervously, she wet her lips before asking, "What are the benefits?"

"Your nacre regulates your brain chemistry and hormones. This port temporarily suspends the regulation, allowing for increased endorphins and adrenaline." Razor took two steps back, giving her space. He looked beyond to the kitchens.

A man in a chef's toque waved for him.

"Excuse me." He left, holding up one finger.

Sagan wasted no time Seamswalking to Matt. "Hey."

He opened a crate and set up the next exhibit. Quietly, he returned the greeting, "Hey."

"You never seem surprised to see me?" She folded her arms and cocked her head to the side. "Why is that?"

The redhead laughed, a pleasant, happy sound. No weirdness with Matt. "I suppose I don't care who's around me. As long as you don't snatch me away from my car again."

Rolling her eyes, she nudged him a bit. The gravity of her visit weighed on her, and she suddenly felt tired.

"Are you okay?" He paused with some super heavy nacre glass fountain basin in hand.

"I'm fine. I'm not sure how far I should go for this mission." Remembering who she confided in, she pressed, "Did you or Lucy ever go too far? Did you feel it beforehand? Like a warning . . ."

"No. And I get what you mean by a feeling. But no. We never forgot why it mattered. Forgiveness came later if needed." He stacked the basin onto a stand and kept at his work. After a second, he seized up. "Sagan?"

She gave him her full attention.

"It was never needed." The boy's smile was cute. Lucy was a lucky girl.

"You don't know where she is, do you?"

He winced and looked away. "She'll let me know when it's time."

"I know she will." Sagan squeezed his shoulder before Seamswalking back to the open floor of the Emporium proper. She walked into one of those beams of whiskey light and gave into the moment. Soaked in the rays.

She decided.

As if he read her mind, Razor stepped languidly around the corner. Unassuming. Nonthreatening. No pressure. Because he already knew the answer.

"I accept."

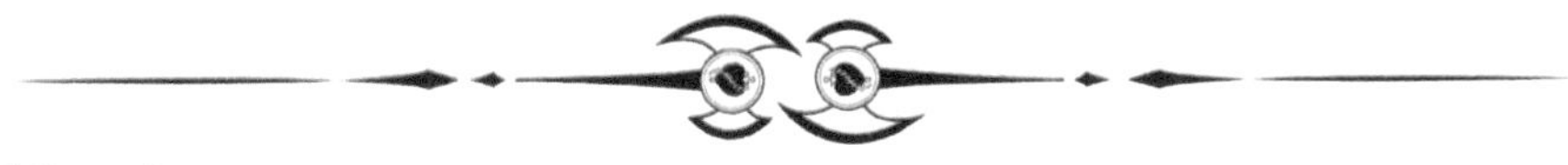

{GAIT}

Pehton needed to see their faces. Even if it wasn't really them. Even if Razor tampered with her memory. She woke night after night terrified at the vacancies. No faces to kiss. No hands to hold.

The Executive Warden stopped on the steps to the Emporium. Clutched her chest and held her breath. Two and a half million years. And she still couldn't let it go. Maybe Korac was right. Maybe they were all dead. Even in that case, she still needed to know.

Because then Pehton would shatter every nacre on Gait to stop Inanis. She looked to the sky, to the satellites that waited. Yes. Every nacre.

Gait's Executive Warden stepped into the Vast Collective's most infamous vice factory and came to a complete stop.

"I accept."

Razor stalked around the short blond Seamswalker like a sable tiger from Earth. Hungry, enticed, and in command.

Pehton didn't know what Sagan just agreed to, but the little Progeny girl couldn't possibly fathom his intentions. Protective, the Lyrik chimed in, "How pleasant to see you here, Seamswalker. Pain Curator."

When she nodded to him, Razor's cognac eyes hardened into glass. He didn't like anyone encroaching on his territory. And the Lyrik knew better than to test him.

Sagan peered between the two. After a second in tense silence, the Seamswalker frowned prettily and offered softly, "I think I'll go find Matt. You two talk or whatever."

"Please, give us five minutes." He smiled at Sagan in a way Pehton never saw until today. Warm. Friendly. Almost kind.

It disgusted the Executive Warden. After the girl poofed away, Pehton fought every impulse to sing for him.

A requiem.

But Elden, dammit. They couldn't afford her throwing down a turf war. Not in the middle of this investigation that relied so heavily on him. She closed her eyes and counted to ten. When she opened them, Razor stood inches from her.

After her initial recoil, his lips spread into a grin. "Peh Peh, I think I like you better feisty." He brushed the back of his knuckles down her flared gliders. "Tell me, how close are you to the Chorus?"

How. Did. He. Know?

His laughter fell around her like broken glass. "Don't underestimate me, dear Pehton. Now, tell me something. Why was Sagan in my Emporium not but days ago wearing Korac's clothes? His *scent*? Asking to allow that contaminant thug into my respectable establishment?" Razor posed the questions and turned his back on her, stepping away. Never ground his teeth. His voice never rose. If anything, it hardened to match his eyes. He hung his head, pinching the bridge of his nose. With his back to her, he reminded, "We had an arrangement."

"I can't stop her movements. I *am* working to distract Korac, but so much of it relies—"

He cut his hand in the air. "She's returning. Remember. You brought this on yourself."

Sagan returned to the warehouse proper before Pehton asked him to clarify. "Are you two good now?" She indicated them both with a wag of her finger.

Pehton shrugged innocently. "We're fine. I didn't cover my balance the last time I was here. Razor was nice enough to lend me a session for free."

Sagan broke into a beautiful smile and directed some of it at the Pain Curator who didn't miss a beat. "That's right. It was a small misunderstanding." He shot a knowing glance at Pehton.

She congratulated herself on assuaging some of his ire without hurting the Seamswalker. To which, she asked, "I have to know about the coat. It's beautiful."

"Yea? Triss and Oleen crafted it for me." The adorable young woman even spun around for her to see.

Razor observed, "Perhaps the wardens could fund raise with such amazing talents. I'm hosting the Prisonborne orphanage benefit this year. Pehton, what do you think?"

Sagan glanced at Razor as if he surprised her.

Pehton almost retched. Yea, he hosted it every year, all right. And sure, the orphanage received all the proceeds.

But the only people invited benefited as much from the mingling of business with pleasure. And in which case, why didn't they raise funds year round—

She spiraled, and she needed to get back on Razor's good side. "I'll check with them back at the prison. It's another great idea, Razor."

He smirked at her, practically digging his dirty claws into the impressionable young woman beside him. Something must have shown on Pehton's face because he tilted his head with an intrigued gleam.

Feisty. He said he liked her feisty. Anything he liked was bad.

Calm. Down.

"Not to be nosy, but I am the planet's Executive Warden. What did I walk in on?"

Sagan blushed and ducked her eyes before answering, "I agreed to a nacre port..."

Agreed, but she sounded unsure still. Pehton met Razor's eyes. The hardness. The cold. This was the Lyrik's punishment. He nodded as if he sensed the realization.

Swallow. Suck it up. Do the job. *What counts.*

"I had one."

Sagan's eyes widened into bright amethyst shards. "You did? Did it hurt? You don't have one anymore?"

Pehton shook her head. "It's completely reversible with no scarring. See?" Her armor retreated enough to expose her chest, including the tops of her breasts to further appease Razor.

His brown eyes shone with approval and appreciation.

"It didn't hurt. I slept for a day after. That's the only discomfort I recall," Pehton elaborated. Razor let her sleep it off in an infirmary reserved for employees. A long, long time ago. "Your human friend who works here should look after you while you recover."

A warning.

Sagan nodded firmly. Resolved. "Okay. I'm not needed anywhere for a few days, so now's the best time. Thanks, Pehton."

No. No, sweetie, never let Razor know you aren't expected somewhere...

Razor led Sagan to the spiral staircase. She stopped and looked back at Pehton. "Could you please let Korac know? I don't want him to worry."

The Pain Curator smiled warmly, giving the illusion of understanding. Silkenly, he assured, "I'm sure the Executive Warden can oblige. Matt?"

The redheaded human with the freaky dark eyes crossed the Emporium. "Boss?"

Razor's smile shifted into something more knowing for the boy, too. Elden, it terrified Pehton to watch him manipulate all these people she came to value.

"Join us. Would you like that, Seamswalker?"

She ducked her eyes. "It helps." When the redhead approached them, the blond girl pulled a long chain overhead and endowed Matt with it.

He tugged on it. "I'll give it back once you're done."

Razor nodded approvingly at the pair. "All settled then? Let's go. Remember, you can change your mind whenever you want. Pehton showed you. We can remove it after the gala if you like. But I think you should try it with at least one experience . . ." His soothing voice trailed off as they disappeared over the mezzanine. The smile in it one of mirth and comfort. Dressed incidentally flattering to his features.

Yes. The Pain Curator spun his web carefully. With even finer silk than he used for the wardens. Because Triss and Oleen weren't at the prison. They were here. Like the others. All of Gait's wardens served their master.

All but Pehton.

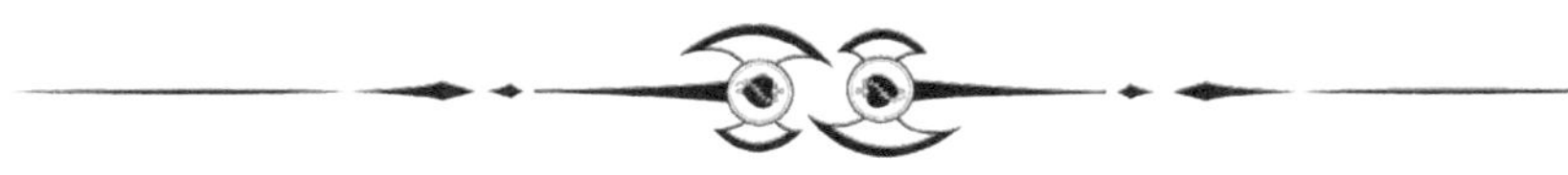

{EARTH}

Memories. In order. Clear. So much more clear.

Andrew and Kyle awoke hours ago. Rested, hydrated, and fed. The door revolved with people—wonderful, well-meaning people—checking in on him. Tameka even requested a call once he felt up to moving around. Soon.

During a rare moment alone, he tried to apologize to Lucas, but the Icarus waved him off with a delicious smile. "You'll make it up to me when you're well."

Yes. He certainly would. Honestly, exhaustion aside, physical comfort sounded beautiful at that moment.

"—It's not responding like we hoped, but we will get it to work," Pablo assured someone in the hall as he stepped into the room. He caught Andrew sitting upright and eating another bowl of oatmeal. "I can't begin to tell you how relieved I am."

The doctor's intentions warmed Andrew with their sincerity. "I think I'm getting you loud and clear."

To the Progeny, Pablo nodded. "Good." To the Icarus, he asked, "Now, tell me the truth. Is he following the doctor's orders to rest and fill up?"

Andrew laughed.

The other two in the room snapped to him at the sound. Both of their intentions read gratitude and relief. It overwhelmed him.

He changed the subject, "What's not working?"

The doctor shook his head sternly. "Talking shop is not resting—Kyle is trying out the nacre's memory bank, but it's not fully responsive despite the decryption program we ran this morning." Pablo put his fists on his hips and frowned at Andrew. "Dude...not cool."

Lucas hid his smirk and chuckled behind a covered cough.

Conscience pushed, "Bring the nacre and Kyle to me. Let me try to help."

The sexy and sometimes quite stubborn Icarus protested, "I don't think that's best right now—"

"I didn't survive this attack to sit here and eat." The harshness in Andrew's voice made him flinch. "Please. I need to contribute."

Under his own intentions, Pablo nodded and left the room.

Lucas stood and came to his bedside. With his intentions bare, he brushed his fingers into Andrew's hair and took his breath away. Kissed him a little more gently than usual. But the younger man understood.

When they separated, Lucas beamed down at him. "Ever the brave knight."

"I think it's your kink." Andrew smirked for him.

"Lucky for you." The Icarus walked away from him to reach into the suitcase. Bent over, teasing him. His ass always looked fantastic in slacks.

Yea. Physical comfort. "You know? I think I'm feeling up to—"

The door opened and an entire cadre of his favorite people piled in. Lynn wheeled over a bedside table with the questionable nacre set on a stainless steel tray. Kyle took up beside Andrew on the far side of the bed.

Smith strolled in, hands in pockets of his coveralls. "You think you can crack it?"

Too little left unknown about the Iona employee. Goosebumps broke out over Andrew's skin. Strained. Uncomfortable. He cleared his throat to regain some calm. "Hopefully." To Kyle, he asked, "Where's Silence?"

He ran a joint-free hand through his hair and blew the air from his cheeks. "I thought you'd prefer essentials only."

"Right. Let's stop putting this off." Andrew stared hard at the little ball of amber colored glass. An entire nano computer functioned inside harboring a man's life. With no interface, it was only a matter of—

Kyle put his hand on Andrew and then grabbed the nacre.

Black. All dark. No light. No sound. They stepped into a place not unlike the memory-scape. Only nothing existed here. The nacre-bearer's last wish to keep it a secret. The last vestiges of his truth remained. Behind one wall.

"We need a password," Andrew called into the darkness.

"Pfft. You got any idea what an Imminent soldier might use other than 'password1'?"

He thwacked the other Progeny upside the head. "No, smartass, but you would. What was the last thing this guy saw? The last thing worth caring about?"

Andrew waited. In the dark. In the nothing. So when Kyle spoke one word into the void, it shocked Conscience to his core.

"Silence."

Lights. Sounds. Ghosts of people walked through them. Over them. Under them. Fast, sped up so fast. Andrew's head spun with the whir of it. The guy's entire life into this memory.

Induction into Imminent. A desperate, Invasion Day survivor. His intentions filled with hope for a future where Earth could survive. Where the Progeny died.

Andrew and Kyle both frowned as images of them and the girls swirled. Monstrous strength. Ferocious power. Greedy. Hateful.

"What the hell propaganda was this guy fed?" Kyle scoffed. Hands on hips, head hung in disgust. "It's like he had no idea what the war—"

Rayne. In front of a star inside of a Dyson's sphere. Blue eyes filled with tears. Alone and afraid. The entire Vast Collective wiped out by her death.

Andrew snarled and pushed through the intentions as they filled his head. "Where is it?" No time to watch this rerun prophetic, garbage. The last few weeks. "Where..."

There was no hope. The Progeny allowed my family to die. My children murdered, buried in rubble. Corpus Christi's earthquakes never got that big. Ever.

If Rayne and the others never went there—Hell, if she'd turned herself into Nox, they'd still be alive.

"Would you like to make them pay?" A woman gripped his shoulder. Beautiful black skin. Her hair in long locs and braids. Eyes the most arresting blue. Her soothing voice eased his suffering. The words empowered him, "We can give you the significance to affect your revenge. Leave everything behind and come with me."

"Who are you?"

She looked into his eyes. "I am the first. And when I am through, I will be the last." Her eyes focused beyond the man and into Andrew's soul. "Conscience, I will be the last."

Fire. Bright and red consumed it all. Everything.

Andrew screamed awake and Kyle with him. The disabler. The virus. The memory drive decryption. Everything... Celindria led them to this. She knew how, where, and when they'd complete her tasks. It was in her intentions.

The two Progeny connected the dots at the same time. Kyle cried out, "Holy shit!" He bolted from the room without another word, presumably to find the comms device.

"Right behind you!" Lynn followed him.

"Check on everyone. Check on them now!" Hands held Andrew down as he tried to get out of bed. "It's Celindria. She—"

Pablo held his wrists aloft. The good doctor tried to reassure him, "It's okay, Andrew. Calm down first. It's been a lot on you recently. Please."

Lucas put some muscle into holding him down. "You've been through too much. Rest. Kyle will call them."

Couldn't they see her?

T.A.O. stood in the room behind the others, watching as he struggled. Andrew's sanity splintered at the sight of her. "It's happening. Do something!"

"You're safest here."

The other two men gawked in shock.

"Stay, T.A.O. We can help you," Lucas offered eventually.

Pablo cried out, "Safe from what?"

"The beginning..."

When she vanished, the air in the room went with her.

NINTEEN

REMEMBER TO COUNT YOUR SINS ALONG WITH YOUR BLESSINGS

{ENKI}

JOHN HATED THAT HE RETURNED TO ENKI ALONE, BUT HE UNDERSTOOD THE MISSION TAMEKA PUT HIM ON. Alone was necessary. While he enjoyed the privacy of the empty bungalow, he preferred hearing Caedes' grumping, Tameka's motherly admonishing, and Pax's cries of delight.

He missed his family.

The walk to the lecture hall reminded him once more that things were not right in the Dyson's Sphere. Every Tritan he passed ducked through the halls. The few he passed anyway. Maybe two of them? In a trek that spanned one colony and three continents. Two seemed awfully light for a dominating species.

Thirteen conduits later, he walked into the open amphitheater surrounded by ocean. Wiw waited in the stands. John expected more of an audience, but welcomed the fairly benign Tritan.

"Eminent, hello." John greeted him by pounding his fist to his own nacre.

The Tritans learned to expect this salute from the Shadow without fully understanding its significance. Wiw smiled warmly from his great height. Thin fingered-hands waved for the human to relax. "Hello, Educator. I am pleased to see you. I missed your lessons."

"I'm honored, sir."

"How was the Sovereign Ambassador when you left her? Not so saddened by the embargo with her son on Earth, was she?" Did the old man just wink?

John was pretty sure he winked. Err on the side of caution, "It's unfortunate that Primary Bol enacted an embargo—"

The Eminent's double-take almost gave John whiplash. The Tritan's black voids doubled in size, genuinely startled. In the course of a second, his face warmed and softened. "You're mistaken, Educator. Primary Rem issued the ban. Not Primary Bol."

What the fuck—

Eminent Lance rushed into the lecture hall. "John! John, come see. It's Earth. It's happening all over Earth."

Heart in his throat, John ran as fast as his prosthetic would tolerate. No. Not again.

Please. Not again.

{Earth}

Lynn and Kyle called everyone they knew outside of the Ecology.

"Find shelter. Be alert. Imminent is planning something big."

"Celindria planted it in that guy's nacre. She meant for us to find it. It's a trigger of some kind."

"Check on Bones and Para. Make sure Rayne is all right."

"Where's Tumu?"

"The Brethren haven't answered."

Smith ran into the comms room. "Come see this. Now."

Lynn and Kyle exchanged a glance, holding their breath. They burst into the lobby and stared out of the surrounding glass.

Oh, no.

The sky. In the sky...

"No..." Kyle rushed outside.

She shouted after him, "Get back here! It's not safe out there."

The ancient Seamswalker's image spread across Earth's Sphere. Deep skin. Solid violet eyes. And so very sad. Her voice quaked with the sorrow of it, "Beware the black fire and all the calamity it brings. Let the sleeper sleep. Elden waits."

The imagery shifted and spanned the horizon. Lynn frequented the beautiful chateau while establishing the Iona facilities. She met Tempest there several times to work on the Arsenal's design.

It exploded into a ball of red fire.

Lynn cried out and gaped.

Next image. The Hoover Dam and the brand new facility beside it. The building sank into the ground as if the Earth opened and swallowed it. All the Dwarves' work on quantum communication washed away into the dirt.

Kyle sank to his knees and cried out to the sky, "Why?! Why would T.A.O. do this?!"

A vacuous roar boomed outside the Ecology. The facility shuddered with it. Was that from the—

"NO!" Lynn howled.

Flames engulfed Kyle through the conduit, always split open between the Ecology and the Arsenal. A fire erupted in the cylinder, spiraling to the entrance at the bottom.

"Kyle! No!"

Familiar, powerful arms encircled Lynn as she shrieked, kicked, and clawed. Her people. All of her people. In danger.

Or worse.

{EARTH}

"Okay. Everybody remain calm but haul your asses to the safest point in the stronghold. Now." Chris didn't like this shit one bit. It raised his hackles and set his teeth on edge.

Karter and Jack burst from the dinner table.

Ross went to clear the plates, but the young King Regent stopped her with a gentle touch. "We'll get it later."

Caedes appeared in the entryway after his impromptu nap. "Did I hear that right?"

After Chris's confirming nod, the Icarus took up a guard post on the redheaded Progeny.

Tameka collected Pax from his spot at the table. He trembled in her arms, and Chris hated it. The young mother soothed, "Don't worry, baby. Daddy built this place to withstand eons. We'll be safe—"

War couldn't prepare them for the thunderous boom and crack of busted rock. Miles and miles under the desert. No one could predict this. Now, no one could save them.

Chris snatched Jack into the nearest archway and crouched over him. In horror, he watched as Karter knocked Ross out of the way and disappeared under the debris. "NO!!!"

"Get down!" Caedes threw himself over Tameka and Pax. They watched terrified as slab after slab of carefully honed rock collapsed on the mighty Icarus.

Worst. Case. Scenario.

The stronghold's entrance, deeper than bedrock, collapsed and caved in.

{GAIT}

Pehton headed down to Infernus block. She wanted to make good on her promise to Sagan. Otherwise, the young woman's entreating eyes threatened to haunt the Lyrik's conscience forever.

Razor's eyes on the Seamswalker certainly would. Lust failed to describe it. Desire, also, not strong enough. Devour. That was it. The Pain Curator wanted to consume the most overpowered Progeny. No offense to Rayne.

It hurt Pehton to watch him lead the sweet girl away. So, delivering the message to Korac hopefully absolved the Executive Warden.

Right?

Fuck.

Exiting the lift, she mentally prepared herself. What would it be tonight? Leather? Denim? Or altogether nude? The Icarus haunted a few of Pehton's dreams, himself—

Korac slept curled on his side, facing her. As she spied him sleeping, he frowned and clenched the sheets. No, even shirtless, there was nothing sensual about how small he looked. Standing, the man towered over her. Asleep... whatever struggle he faced in his nightmares reduced him to a mere mortal like the rest of them.

"Contaminant thug."

Admittedly, Pehton never once heard so much prejudice in Razor's voice until that moment. Something about Sagan smelling of Korac bothered him in particular.

Well, if the Lyrik got any say, she'd ask Sagan to rub all over her suitor before every engagement with Razor from hereon.

Fuck that guy—

"No!" Korac cried out as he bolted upright in his bed. Frantically, he searched the cell as if re-acclimating to his surroundings. He locked eyes with her through the nacre-deterring energy shield.

Pehton took a step back, caught.

As if relieved by her presence, he relaxed and fell back onto the pillow with a sigh. One arm across his eyes. Voice deep with exhaustion despite waking up only seconds ago, "How can I help you, Executive Warden?"

She opened her mouth to ask if he was all right, then thought better of it. "Sagan—"

At the mention, the Icarus sat up abruptly and gave her his full attention. Pale gray eyes grew focused, alert.

Pehton couldn't stop herself. She barked out a laugh. It was so endearing and hilarious at the same time.

He quirked a brow at her disrespect, but brokered no defense. "What about her?"

"She—"

The communicator in the Lyrik's palm vibrated her entire body in a sensation similar to electrocution.

Instant. Terror.

It only activated on that frequency for intergalactic emergencies. Without another word to Korac, Pehton opened the missive. A three-dimensional model of events played in her palm. Events on Earth.

"What the fuck is happening, Executive Warden?" Korac watched the same display as her. He knew.

Pehton shut down. Professional mode meant distancing herself. No adrenaline. No, that's what they wanted. Panic and distress. She wouldn't give them that. Never again.

Another missive followed. With her voice remote, Pehton announced, "I've been summoned to Enki. They're considering the attacks an act of war against the entire Vast Collective given that Earth is a junior applicant."

As if he recognized the shift in her, Korac asked softly, "Pehton, where is Sagan?"

Oh.

Shit.

NINETEEN PLUS

AN EPILOGUE TO RUIN

{???}

Red. Pale green. Orange and green. Gray. Brown.

Carpet. Hardwood. Rock tile. Glass tile.

Black sheets. White sheets. Blue. Red. Green. But never violet. Not until now.

Shifting. Always shifting. The revolving scenery. People. Lives taken. Lives granted. Bodies in motion. But nobody like her.

The Seamswalker slept soundly in silken sheets the color of her eyes. The bed, suited for twelve, swallowed her frame, slighted from all the activity since her first arrival on Gait. The rest of the room painted in black, pitched in darkness.

The man known as Razor observed the beauty who slept in his bed with such fascinating trust and abandon. Spent from her encounter with the surgeon. Triss kindly prepared the girl for him. Their audience—Matt, a delightful enigma by his own rights—monitored the alien's propriety through the cameras and all their many vantages.

Protect her virtue.

Unnecessary. The Pain Curator wanted little to do with her admittedly enticing body. He admired her sharp mind and reveled in her kind heart.

Both desirable.

But the true aim lie in his reflection of her soul. Such a pure entity that around him she cracked. The splintered shards made the most beautiful mess.

The man known as Razor leaned against a steel column supporting the glass floor above his room. Idling in her presence, he soaked in a sigh that escaped her lips. Soft. Feminine. Deep asleep.

Unaware of the destruction she wrought.

He waited to deliver the news. A supportive ally in the war against Imminent. Matt attested to the assassination attempt from Celindria, generously bolstering Sagan's faith in the Pain Curator. But it suited his purpose for her to entertain the adage, "The enemy of my enemy is my friend."

And that vindictive viper, Celindria, could go straight to—

With a shift in the sheets, Sagan slipped out from under them. Toned legs exposed from the hem of his silk shirt. The textile mills on Lukemore dyed it for him to match her eyes. So very long ago.

Let her return to her lover smelling of vanilla and darker things.

The Pain Curator approached the bed with his hands in his pockets to appease her chaperon and prevent Matt's intrusion. He knelt at the bedside and counted the blond lashes closed softly against lightly freckled cheeks. Even with an audience, the temptation to kiss her clenched his fists. Not to know her taste; although he considered it many times. No. He wanted to leave his taste on her.

He couldn't wait to ruin her. The Atheneum would suffer in the reflection of her shattered soul. Broken. Worse than dead.

Never would the man known as Razor allow his carefully constructed empire to fall. Not to the likes of the Atheneum. And not to the likes of the Progeny.

Not even to the Seamswalker.

AUTHOR'S NOTE

Sometimes author correspondance like these Author's Notes feels fake. I'm not giving you fake. I love these characters with all my heart, and I hope you do, too.

But I also hope you're on the edge of your seat terrified that Caedes and Karter might be dead. That Razor might be less than trustworthy when it comes to our innocent Sagan.

And where the fuck is Lucy?

So keep reading for a taste of Pyrite Prison, and remember...

I'm never forgiving in the second books of my trilogies. Just ask Xelan and Rayne.

PYRITE PRISON

STRONGHOLD

{EARTH}

"UNCLE CAEDA! UNCLE CAEDA!"

Tameka Phillips, Sovereign Ambassador of the Two Worlds, opened her green eyes and scanned her surroundings. Smashed hardwood planks cut trails over otherwise aesthetically pleasing waterways. Busted walls painted gray. Overturned plants. Buried waterfalls. The scent of exotic flowers and millennia of old rock dust.

Xelan's underground stronghold.

Slabs of rock collapsed onto the kitchen and dining area. The explosion in the cylindrical entryway, miles under the Egyptian desert, blocked their exit and any rescue attempt.

Her two-year-old son cut through the structural rumbling again, "Uncle Caeda!"

"Pax? Where are you? Be careful!" Trapped in a pocket of rock, Tameka rolled onto her back and pressed palms flat to a chunk of limestone. Push! Her tawny brown biceps bunched and ripped. Ligaments popped. She screamed through the pain and pressed, anyway.

"Mommy!" In his searching for her, that sweet baby jumped right on top of the limestone with enough weight to send it crashing back down on his mother.

Tameka curled on her side surrounded by her waist-length red curls with her arms folded inward like a bug. She suppressed sobs in the dirt as the soft tissue repair system in her nacre—the nano computer in her chest—healed the damage. Before round two. Coughing from the dust and dirt, she answered, "I'm here. Under the rock."

His brown face with darker brown freckled cheeks, like her own, appeared in a small opening. "Mommy, Uncle Caeda gone."

A hot tear slid down her cheek as she relived it all. They sat down to dinner when Chris, resident hero and bodyguard to the King of Earth, got a call from Kyle at the Iona Medical Ecology urging them to find shelter from Imminent attacks.

Rocks exploded from the entrance.

Caedes. Stood over her and her son. Shielded them from the collapsing structure. His deep green, almost black eyes, filled with so much pain as slab after slab of rock fell on him until he disappeared.

Tameka smiled weakly as her son tried to pry his way into the pocket with her. "It's okay, baby. We'll find Caedes. Have you seen the others—"

"Karter?!" Chris shouted through the mess. Some rocks shuffled around and debris stirred, indicating his excavation. Coughing and croaking, he asked, "Are you all right, Jack?"

"Alive. My leg broke in two places, but it's already healing. I've got Ross. She's unconscious, but breathing." The eighteen-year-old King of Earth reported their status from closer to the exit.

Oh, thank Elden. Tameka waited to hear from the Valkyrie.

Chris moved about the space, disheveling bulky rubble and shifting dust. "Karter?" He crawled closer to the dining room table. The last place they saw the tall, muscular Icarean warrior before she pushed Ross out of the way of the collapsing ceiling.

Tameka closed her eyes and hoped the two Icari survived—

Crashing and rumbling erupted from the entrance, and rocks caved further into the cylindrical lift. Slabs chucked into the smashed living room.

"Pax! Get down!" Tameka cried out and reached to her son through the hole. As fresh dust plumes rose and fell, he disappeared. "Pax! PAX!" No. No, she wouldn't watch someone else she loved die. "Answer me!"

"I've got him," Chris called to her from only a few feet away.

"Batman gave me gum." Her son sounded pleased in the man's arms. The codename suited the black veteran's one hundred percent heroic ass.

Shuffling around the rock out of her sight, he assured, "We'll get you out, Fury."

Tameka smiled slightly at her self-chosen codename. "I can almost push it off, but I need help."

"We need Rayne." Jack said it first. And his voice squeezed as if in pain as he said it.

"Is it time?" Chris' question rang through the collapsed cavern.

Tameka gripped the chain around her neck. It just might be—

"Stronghold. Batman. This is Bones. Come in. Over." The comms device, boosted by Tritan alien technology, allowed them to communicate with team members across the world. Bones, another Icarean warrior, currently watched over King Rayne of Earth and Cinder as she slept.

"This is Batman. An explosion took out the entrance to the stronghold. Jack, Ross, Pax, Tameka accounted for. Searching for Karter and Caedes. We need help. Repeat. We need assistance to get the hell out. Report. Over."

Xelan. His hidden home. Damaged and forever compromised.

"How did they find us?" Tameka rasped with emotion clogging her throat. It hurt to think of her lover's heart breaking at the loss of fortitude after thousands of years of secrecy.

"No idea. A spy? Maybe we weren't discrete enough. Although, I can't imagine anything more discrete than Seamswalking," Jack offered reasonable deductions.

"Batman. We're sending help. Try to keep calm and avoid structural weaknesses. We'll fill you in on the other instances once we arrive. Over and Out." Bones disconnected.

"Other instances" hung in the air. What the fuck happened? How were they blindsided so badly? And with all of them in secure locations.

Rubble shifted around. "I'm coming to help you, Tameka. Pax, stay and watch over Jack and Ross for me. Can you do that?"

"Yesss."

Tameka's heart squeezed at the sweetness in his excited voice. "Get me out of here, Batman, so I can hug my son."

"Yes, ma'am." Did he salute? She wished she could see if he saluted. He stuck his face in the small gap. "Are you injured? Palpate for me to check for neck injuries."

She wanted out so badly she almost screamed in frustration at his perfectly reasonable request. After following his instructions, she checked out fine. "No headaches. No nausea."

"Okay. You know what to do. On the count of three. One. Two. Three!"

Nacres imbued their bearers with strength and increased healing. As a Progeny—the hybrid of an Icarus and a human—Tameka inherited a few enhancements, including greater strength and faster healing. Not to mention the unique ability to drain energy from anything with a nacre. Time and place, and this wasn't it.

Again, she pushed and screamed as if drawing her might from her voice. Chris' groans harmonized. Almost there. A little more—

It lifted suddenly with ease.

"Uncle Caeda!"

Caedes stood on the other side, revealed in the settling dust. The tall, bald, gruff Icarus needed a med unit, badly. Blue blood soaked his face and the back of his head. Likely scrapes swelled along his back. After settling the limestone away from Tameka, the warrior wrapped his arms around his ribs and collapsed to his knees. He vomited a wash of blue.

She bolted from the dusty floor to check on him. Chris, the only one in the room with official medical training, immediately checked the Icarus' vitals. While Batman searched for injuries, Caedes stared into Tameka's eyes. Breathing. His primary focus. Inhale. Exhale. Don't die. The effort to keep going written in his eyes.

"Will you make it?" Jack called out from the more structurally sound side of the room.

Chris answered for the Icarus, "We need to get him to the Medical Ecology. The hard tissue repair system will work overtime until then. We'll get you across the room, and then I don't want you to move unnecessarily. You got me?"

Caedes nodded so very slowly.

Chris threw one of the Icarus' arms over his shoulder. Tameka took the other. For a brief moment, her bright green eyes met Caedes' deeper ones. No wasting time. "Thank you—"

A boom and a crash interrupted her. The place vibrated with the shock of it. Another explosion?

The comms device whirred and Bone's voice came on the line, "We're here to get you out."

Chris snarked, "With what? A bulldozer?"

"The crawlers."

www.ingramcontent.com/pod-product-compliance
Lightning Source LLC
Chambersburg PA
CBHW020458310726
48979CB00016B/2707/J
9781735671338